Harvest of Shadows

By

Stella Jorette

Harvest of Shadows © 2024
by Stella Jorette
All rights reserved
EBook ISBN: 9780648725572
Print ISBN: 978-0-6487255-9-6

Jorette, Stella.
Harvest of Shadows
Imagine Imprints
Paperback. First edition

Cover art by 100 Covers
Section art by Stella Jorette
All rights reserved

Table of Contents

TO ALL THE RESILIENT SOULS

who've navigated the trenches of less-than-
ideal workplaces,
this one is for you.

It matters not how strait the gate,
How charged with punishments the scroll,
I am the master of my fate,
I am the captain of my soul.

—WILLIAN ERNEST HENLEY

BY THE AUTHOR

Science fiction, fantasy, and time travel novels and novelettes are available from the author on stellajorette.com/stellas-books. Membership provides access to web serials and short stories.

A Sorry Excuse

Not Worth Heat Stroke

The sun beat down on Agnet Krause's neck like a molten hammer head. Heat shimmered off the roofs of buildings and blasted up from the crazed pavement; if she stood here much longer, the soles of her boots would melt. They'd done their job but couldn't leave until the guard finished with the skinny kid in patchwork pants, probably a runner. He kept giving the guard lip and backing away. Pretty ballsy, resisting arrest in this blistering sun. She moved closer while flipping down her ventilator. The lousy thing blocked air flow but made her seem less relatable and more like serious trouble, a look that came in handy when wrapping up loose ends.

"They come and go masked up and wearing white costumes," the kid said as he pointed to a faded yellow, warehouse-style storefront. "We hear pinging and yowling from inside. It's not natural."

"Get in the van." The guard slapped his baton into his palm for emphasis.

Agnet grabbed the kid by the back of his shirt and lifted him off his feet. All bones, this boy, underfed, or drugs had obliterated his hunger. "See these donkeys? They're baking out here. So am I. Get in or you walk to Central."

He stared at her wide-eyed; his pupils, reduced to tiny dots, careened back and forth like the ants swarming on the scorching sidewalk. "It ain't right, you rounding us up and letting them keep at it. They're more trouble than we've ever been."

"Maybe. Maybe not. You seem trouble enough, both high as a kite and resisting arrest." She half-dragged-half-carried him toward the van. He kicked at her legs, so she hoisted him by his belt and tossed him, bony ass and all, onto his associate's laps.

"Don't pay him no mind," she told the guard. "Reassess after he's sober and fed."

The team gathered round, sweat dribbling down their faces: Alice, Mac, and his two trainees, both wet behind the ears but eager; she hadn't locked on to their names.

Mac mopped his forehead with a filthy-looking rag. "We going to roast in the street or check out the cult?" His usual easy-going demeanor had evaporated during the operation. Not that she blamed him. The drug ring had been low quality quarry, with their homespun equipment and emaciated leader, his pants held up by twine.

The gang had scrambled like a bucket of blind crabs during the bust, more pathetic than dangerous. It'd been overkill, sending a tactical squad to shut down this operation.

She shrugged. "We're under no obligation to check out the druggies' neighbors. Besides, cultists can toggle from spreading peace and love to raging lunacy in seconds."

"Might as well demonstrate surreptitious entry." Mac thumbed his trainees. "Besides, Central would've surveilled that dump pre-mission. They're probably aware and not taking the cult, or whoever, seriously."

"The mission's been bloodless, so I have plenty of supplies. Might as well see if anybody's starving or needs medical attention." Alice wrinkled her nose. "Smells like a-mutation-a minute out here. Nobody should spend time in this wasteland."

She had a point. The slumping buildings, edges softening in the relentless sun, must be off-gassing nasty chemicals. The reek permeated these badlands, a former light industrial zone transformed into melting ruins. A deep step down from "look on my works, ye mighty, and despair," but the poet had gotten the despair part right.

"Does that say 'Soil Probe'?" Mac pointed to the UV-faded lettering above the building's door.

One of the young uniforms snickered.

Agnet studied the sign. "Suppose it does." And the address had been stenciled beside the door: four-twenty-one. But she wasn't thinking about signage. She was calculating risk, not risk to the team or civilians, but personal political risk, a petty consideration that aggravated her beyond reclamation. How many times had she been reprimanded for mission extensions, even legitimate extensions that'd saved lives and property? But Central's new campaign against independent thought and professional judgment kept smacking her down, changing simple decisions into ruminations fraught with despair.

This decision should've been easy, since most cultists were homeless who'd joined up hoping for a square meal, unaware that holy war was on the menu. And sometimes cults snatched kids off the street, brainwashed, or caged them. A peek inside the dilapidated warehouse might be worth a demotion.

"Y'all ready for another reprimand?"

"Inspect, don't inspect; they'll reprimand us either way," said Alice, sounding more cynical than usual.

Mac eyed the building's front wall, as if performing an internal calculation. "Nobody will question a quick look-see."

A donkey brayed and pawed the dust.

"You need us to wait, or are we done here?" called the guard from his perch on the wagon.

"Pull into that patch of shade." Agnet pointed down the road. "We'll be twenty minutes tops." She signaled to Mac. "Let's scope out the front. The rest of you stay put."

Shattered glass and wind-blown trash had piled up against the front door. Regardless, they steered clear of the boarded-over windows. No obvious gun slots, but camouflaged peepholes were easy to miss. She gave the handle a gentle tug and found it bolted shut.

"Notice anything?" she asked, keeping her voice low.

"Somebody retooled this door, and recently. The framing's fresh, and the lock's mechanical but reasonably modern. It'd take me a while to pick." He squinted a moment at the sun.

Messing with the lock wasn't worth heat stroke. "Forget it. Nobody's used this entrance in ages. I should've asked the runner exactly where he saw the cultists enter." The wagon sat in the shade of a sagging storefront several blocks down the road. Too far in this heat. "Let's look for easy access in back."

They rejoined the others. "Building's been secured recently. Could be anybody. Be ready and on the alert."

"And mask-up, everybody," said Alice.

One youngster grimaced. "But it's hot enough to fry an egg."

"Doesn't matter. According to the runner, the cult masks-up before going inside. We need to be prepared in case they deal in biologics."

"Here's where you listen to the medic," Mac told the recruit, his expression stern.

The two boys, looking like a pair of overeager hounds, took point; Agnet slathered her face and neck with a handful of precious canteen water, checked her weapons: Central's cheap-ass plastic gun, her trusty blade, and a short-handled ax—all at the ready, and followed.

A gap in the warehouses, courteously provided by a long-ago fire, gave them access to a derelict service alley. The trainees dutifully inspected bins and dumpsters, finding not one dastardly bad guy.

After they'd pronounced the alley "all safe," the team congregated in the shade of four-twenty-one's loading dock. She wiggled her sleeves, trying to generate a breeze beneath the ultraviolet-resistant but slick material.

Alice took a swig from her canteen, then said, "Hope we're not exposing ourselves to these fumes for nothing."

Mac knelt at a man-door beside the industrial roll-ups, pulled his loupe from his pocket, and inspected the handle. "Lucky day. This lock's a newer model, so low quality, and I have the over-ride." He pulled out a pack of keycards, flipped through, selected a bright green example, held it up, and gave it a quick shake. "This'll do the trick."

Agnet gave him a thumbs up. "Always grateful you sided with the good guys." The man's fascination with burglary tools, both antique and newfangled, often came in handy. They moved into position. Mac delivered a few instructions to his trainees, then waved the card over the reader.

The door clicked open into what had probably been one large cargo bay, but a recently constructed curved wall now divided the room into two sections, an antechamber, in which they now stood, and a rounded chamber accessed via a faded blue door.

"What sort of tomfoolery is this?" asked one junior.

"Lawbreaking tomfoolery. This zone's off limits. Can't miss the postings, lest you're blind," said the other.

Somebody must've salvaged the old and weathered blue door from the adjacent former-residential zone. Agnet laid her hand on the knob, a real old-fashioned doorknob. It was cool to the touch, smooth, and silvery. Didn't look right for painted wood, plastic, or ceramic...

Stars above. It was metal. She gasped.

Alice echoed her.

"Dang," whispered Mac.

"Dang is right," said Agnet. "But no scrapping on mission." She made eye contact with each junior. "Everybody hear me?"

They chanted in unison, "yes, ma'am," then exchanged a wide-eyed stare.

"Take your positions. Let's see what's inside." She rotated the knob, taking care, having heard of rust and squeaks and such-like, but the door, though much heavier than she'd expected, cracked open quietly and with ease. She listened a moment, hearing a faint but constant ticking sound, otherwise...the expectant silence of an unoccupied room. She widened the opening so Mac could assess the terrain from his angle. He gave the all clear, and they stepped inside, Agnet still holding the door which pushed against her, as if on a spring closer. She glanced at its backside, curious about the excess weight. Lo-and-behold, metal sheeting covered the blue-painted wood, metal bars set at intervals ran the length of the door, and the hinges were huge—serious reinforcement. No wonder it was so heavy. She found Mac's eyes, then side-eyed the door. He scanned the fortifications and frowned.

"Position your guys," she said to him. "Then we can look around. Alice, stick with the juniors."

"Hastings, stand here, lean back against the door, and hold it open. It's heavy, so put your weight into the job. Kasparzik, watch the lobby."

The room, unnaturally cool, no warmer than twenty-five degrees in mid-July, was circular and devoid of any furnishings save an object set dead center on a pedestal or standing desk. Cables stretched from the thing to the ceiling. On closer inspection, it was a machine with a miniature hammer continually tapping a rolling strip of tape. A glass bell, reminiscent of those fancy pastry displays in bakery windows, covered the gizmo, and every so often, a bolt of static electricity connected the glass and the spot where the hammer's head struck the tape.

"You think this thing's the cult's god?" Mac asked.

"Celestial telegraph, more like. Direct line to the deity."

"Careful with the sacrilege. See that mini-lightning bolt? It could reach out and zap you."

"Oh. I'm being careful. That door is armored for a reason— don't want to know why. And all this metal—on the door and in this gadget—"

"You're thinking a cult would've picked this place clean, and this ain't no shrine."

"Exactly. I smell hush-hush and heavy funding. I think we've seen enough."

"Me too. Let's scram."

They backed toward the door, then *rattle*, *crash*. One wall rolled open like a cargo door. A vile odor filled the room, and—

Something bellowed, the sound rising to a shriek, rage mixed with pain.

Behind, somebody screamed, then *boom*. The blue door had swung shut. Hastings was gone. Alice and Kasparzik's mouths dropped open.

Clomp.

She turned. Her mouth dropped open, too.

Straight off the Fryer

Agnet pulled her gear from the allocation box, quickly inspected each item, and laid those that required a closer look to one side. The gun, for instance. Its dull, black allotrope shell looked intact, but it'd need a full disassemble and inspection for cracks, scratches, and dents. She didn't need a bill for excessive equipment wear and preferred to keep both her hands, thanks.

The gun brought back memories; that massive thing hurtling towards them, her unloading an entire chamber full of bullets, Mac leaping forward...

She swallowed her distaste and tossed the gun into the box. It might come in handy for hunting night-rats. On a brighter note, all her uniforms were the correct size, but bad news. A bright yellow radiation meter nestled beneath the clothing, boding fun times. Project Management, claiming overwhelm, hadn't released the assignment's location, but now it seemed her destination was another toxic wasteland.

A hard plastic shell encased the meter, as if it were brand new, but nothing was brand new anymore. On closer inspection, scratches marred the display window and the wand's sensor ring. She ripped open the packaging—why did they bother? —flipped the switch and aimed the wand at the peculiarly resilient potted plant that'd graced the prep room's windowsill since the dawn of time.

Tick, Tick, Tchick, tchshshsh. She recoiled. Had someone poisoned the plant? Sure, it was ugly, and people wagered on the date of its demise, but nobody would intentionally kill it. Even if somebody had developed an antipathy to its mottled purple-green foliage, which was understandable, why use radiation when a simple herbicide would do the job? She needed a negative control, maybe the freshly laundered clothing. But the clicking didn't let up, not one jot. So, she tested a pair of coveralls, the door handle, the table leg, and her own shoulder. The meter was contaminated; no other explanation made sense. After a moment of relief—the house plant would survive—an ugly fact remained. Thanks to Property's carelessness, she'd just been exposed to high-energy subatomic particles.

Though time was short, she jogged to a low-ceilinged cluster of below ground domes, a location suited to the double-dealing underworld that was Property, and banged through the door. Passive-aggressive quiet permeated the dimly lit corridor; those skylights could use a wash. A yellowed sign, "Equipment and Requisitions", arrowed left into the belly of the dragon.

"Hello?"

Her call fell flat in the deserted office. At thirteen hundred, somebody should be manning the counter, but maybe they'd extended lunch for a team meeting or afternoon nap—could've posted a sign.

But no. Not Property.

Storage might be expressly off limits, but she'd been irradiated, so screw them all. She slipped around the counter and into a corn-plastic and grease scented warren of crammed wooden shelves labeled with blue-tinted biolume. Property, in its infinite perversity, had filed the radiation meters under "G" instead of "R". Ten minutes lost to some sicko's fetish for archaic nomenclature.

The first unit she plucked from the shelf looked in better shape than the contaminated reject. Its needle flicked when she powered it on, and it detected little until she pointed the wand at her first meter—*tchssssss*—clicks so fast the sound was practically white noise—hot as a johnny cake straight from the fryer. Imagined scenarios skittered through her head—the wand dangling against her thigh or tucked in her breast pocket—the unit stored in her backpack, her using the pack as a pillow. A cold sweat moistened her hands. She wiped them on her trousers and grabbed both meters. This properly functioning model would do nicely, and she'd stash this hot piece of junk in the contaminated locker.

Back out at the counter, she hesitated. She should fill out a requisition form and report the swap. Then she should report Property to the Section Head. But...

Instinct was nibbling at her heel, saying "keep quiet". And every time she ignored it, calling herself an over-thinker, high maintenance, a loose cannon, or even crazy, basically parroting her performance reviews, she'd been burned. Every. Single. Time. Except for once, a few months ago, when she'd followed her instinct into a trap. And now, in her precarious position, she needed to consider politics. What happened when a pariah reports a screw up? The pariah is labeled a complainer, on top of everything else. Yep. Her instinct was correct. Best to keep her mouth shut.

A Box of Chocolate Dipped Turds

Back in the staging area, Agnet tucked the clean meter into her gear. Four more piles had accumulated in her absence, telling her that the rest of the team had been and gone, and she would be late, thanks to Property. She headed to the D-wing briefing room listed on her orders, trying to feel nostalgic. Her early missions had originated in D-wing. And now, twenty years on, thanks to the fallout from July's disaster, she was returning to D-wing to hear about an assignment that smelled like "sidelined". Should've resigned, but she'd been useless, sitting around, staring at the stains on her kitchen table, and waiting for the inquest result.

Click, click, click.

Oh, no. Here came Evangeline Ramirez wearing heels and a tight pink skirt, a miniature pig on stilts who loathed her. She'd never intended to undermine Evangeline's Human Resources empire; she'd just asked questions and made suggestions, trying to be helpful. Still. The woman, a hard-core hierarchy-fixated rule-follower, despised her.

With a patently fake smile affixed to her moon-pie face, Evangeline stopped to speak with somebody standing at HR's door. Her kindergarten-teacher delivery-style drifted into Agnet's ears. As she drew near, Evangeline shifted her position, using conversation and her back to eliminate any potential for inclusion or even polite greeting. Seventh grade all over again. Taking the not-so-subtle hint, she swerved around the pair, but glanced over her shoulder, and met Alice's gaze. The talented medic was probably in the process of being reassigned. Was that pity in Alice's eyes? Good grief. Her situation must be more fragile than she'd assumed. She threw Alice a rueful smile and picked up her pace.

Five people had beat her to D-24a which was fitted out as a classroom, not a meeting room. And they'd started the meeting, further undermining her already fragile sense of authority. She ran a hand through her close-cropped hair to feign presentability and, feeling like a tardy ten-year-old, announced her arrival.

"Hello. Sorry I'm late. I'm Agnet Krause."

A gray suited Central administrator standing in front of the chalkboard, and someone else leaning against the windows, backlit and obscure, raised their hands in greeting. As did three people seated at desks: a bruiser, a bookworm type with outrageous white-blond hair and spectacles, and—wow—a stunner. Tall, dark, and look at those cheekbones! Sharp dresser, too. A winner of the post-bottleneck genetic lottery, who'd never give her a second glance. He was probably too slick for her taste anyhow, but he sure was a joy to view. The bruiser de-wedged himself from his desk, stood, and saluted; she waved him down. He must have been recently discharged and hadn't transitioned to civilian service.

"Chief Krause." The window-leaner approached, a gaunt older gent with a somber countenance and—oh, yeesh—a NeuroCorp insignia on his blazer. "So nice of you to join us. Allow me to introduce myself, Dr. William Rasp."

They exchanged handshakes, his grip chilly and lank. She fought off the urge to wipe her hand on her pants.

The young Central representative jostled towards her. "And I'm Chuck Teaser, Project Management, good to meet you." He pumped her hand as if he expected her to spurt water. "Meet you again, actually. We met once. Just once. But you wouldn't remember me, a junior face in the crowd. Honor to work with you, Chief Krause."

Honor? He must be out of the loop. Even so, nice to be appreciated.

"Pleasure, gentlemen."

More introductions flew, the names vanishing in the pathway between her ear and brain quicker than licorice on sale. The big ex-military guy was security, as expected. The bookworm was—a historian? But worse, the looker was Philip Spool, a perceiver. From what she'd heard, he was smart and composed, and an asset to any team. But perceivers meant strange: strange clients, strange teams, and creepy weird cases that were emotionally scarring and an administrative nightmare. Could this day get any lousier?

Agnet smiled and nodded, playing it cool. "Just the one perceiver?" The weirdos usually came as a pair.

The NeuroCorp rep—best not to know why he was attending this meeting—replied. "The working hypothesis is mass hysteria, so we felt this assignment would be suitable for training. Hence, the second perceiver is a trainee."

A memory of Kasparzik. She batted the image away. "And where is she?"

"She's being collected." Collected—like an exotic bug? Spool's elegant facial muscles did not twitch in response to the news he'd be supervising a trainee. Either he already knew or had excellent self-control.

"And you're a historian?" She grinned in the general direction of four-eyes, though his eyes impossible to meet, wandering as they did behind those thick lenses, like soap bubbles in the breeze. He was plump to boot, not an easy accomplishment on rations—unless you were in management.

His milky cheeks reddened. "Yes, uh. Fitted out with the latest InfoCorp chip set, and at your service."

She glanced at the project manager—crepes on a hot rock. What was his name—Pleaser? She hoped her expression transmitted her questions about the mission's objectives.

He gave her a reassuring grin. "We're air lifting you inland to Ridgelands Penal Colony, a work farm north-west. Not to worry. It's a low-risk, low-security facility. No hardened types incarcerated on the premises. But the prisoners are seeing something strange out in the fields. They're reporting—well—monsters."

Hopefully, she'd misheard. "Did you say monsters?"

Pleaser flushed with obvious embarrassment and ahem-ed. "You heard me right, monsters." He pressed the air in front of his waist away with his hands, as if fending off unspoken objections. "And I appreciate that 'monsters' sounds ludicrous, and probably is ludicrous. But the Warden's worked himself into a state. Quite a state."

"I can imagine. Any details on the—uh—monsters?"

"No details. None provided. A shame, an egregious shame. Always parsimonious with the pigeons and paper, Warden Honing."

"Malingering and sociogenic delusion are much more common than monsters," said the NeuroCorp rep.

"Yes, of course." Pleaser's head bobbed like a clothespin on the line. "So, our level of concern is low or lowish. A brief with all the known and relevant facts will be ready when you ship. You can catch up on board. Departure is tomorrow, 6AM sharp. Early bird catches the worm, and so on."

She lifted her eyebrows.

He pulled a handkerchief from his front pocket and dabbed his upper lip. "Sorry about the rush-rush. It's just that the mission's been marked top priority. The toppest—topmost."

"Top priority?"

"Yes, well. Temperatures are dropping out west. Freak winds from the North Pole, bitter cold, and so on. Never know about the weather these days, does one? You'd think they'd rejoice, given our brutal summer, but the Warden's fretting about the apple harvest. The prisoners are too afraid to leave the compound and refuse to pick the fruit."

She let her incredulity hang in the air for a moment. "Oh, well. If it's apples."

"Exactly! We'll drop by Staging, pick up your gear, and load up. You'll be ready to roll—or fly rather—at dawn," his reply suggesting he'd either missed or ignored her sarcasm.

"Fantastic! First flight for me," said Muscles.

"Mm-me too," said Bespectacled.

Spool shot her a look that may have said, "Why me?"

This mission was shaping up like a box of chocolate dipped turds: no time to test her equipment, no time to get a feel for her team, and no information on the—*can we be entirely serious*—monsters. On the other hand, given the team's makeup—no medic, no sharpshooter, no bomb detecting canine—management wasn't concerned about bodily harm. Maybe internal affairs wanted her out of town for a few days and had dreamed up a minimal-risk excuse. Which was fine, especially if fresh, ripe apples were involved.

NeuroCorp's representative shaped his mouth into a half circle, a smile-equivalent learned from the lizard-folk who must've raised him. "Best of luck, Chief Krause. We're counting on you."

"Thanks." She passed a skeptical eye over her team. Even luck offered by NeuroCorp was better than no luck at all.

Carpets Kicked into a Corner

After a flail with possessions, equipment, and Philip Spool's urgent messages to a friend—laundry in the wash, plants to water, perishables to consume—etcetera, they bunked down at the airfield barracks. Next morning before dawn, Agnet and her team of strangers boarded an airship headed northwest. Hours of awkward conversation loomed in her future, and small talk was not her strong suit. Her strong suit had been making decisions and solving problems. Now...she could at least read the brief. So, she retreated to her seat and drew the surprisingly thin folder from her satchel. First up, a map showing rows of irregular folds, like a carpet kicked into a corner, and a handful of winding rivers. Ridgelands Penal Colony sat in a furrow between two creases. She flipped to the next page.

> Five hundred million years ago, a volcanic island collided with an ancient continent. The primeval cataclysm hurled immense jagged peaks toward the sky. At that time, the continent lay near the equator, so a dense tropical forest flourished, cycle after cycle of lush vegetation blossoming then decaying in damp, oxygen-depleted soil. Thus, a layer of rich organic matter transformed over millennia into vast coal deposits. Subsequently, eons of ice, rain, snow, and wind whittled the mountains down to a series of near parallel ridges running tens of miles in parallel to the coast.
>
> Rivers carved gaps through the oak, hickory, and pine covered crests. Bear, wolf, and owl hunted the forests. Then humans arrived: first hunters and gatherers, then farmers and miners, taking advantage of the rich soil, swollen rivers, and the energy-packed carbon. The population grew steadily until most of the major industries became non-economic and collapsed.

Quite interesting but remote. Shouldn't a brief contain material about—oh, maybe—*the present?* She skimmed, searching for useful information, such as anything relevant to the Warden's distress signal.

Page seventeen explained the radiation meter in her gear; a nuclear meltdown at a power plant down river from the farm had spread radiation over the surrounding territory. A later section described the penal colony, its purpose, and chain of command. But what about recent events: descriptions of the monsters, the timeline, the eyewitness testimony, images, anything? It's not as if monsters—monsters? —are an everyday complaint. Sure, the brief never precisely matched the situation on the ground, but this write up was an insult, almost negligent, InfoCorp doling out intel the way the Home had doled out jam, one teaspoon for every acre of bread. She slapped the case file shut and stared at the sky.

The ship rose above a layer of clouds; the ground and horizon grew hazy and uncertain. At the airfield, she'd kept expecting somebody to cry "gottcha!" and admit this ludicrous mission was a prank. But nobody had twitched a lip. Her joke fantasy evaporated on lift off; Central would never waste precious airtime on a prank.

She tapped her pencil on the armrest. What did she have? Just "investigate the Warden's complaint about monsters." Hopefully, they'd find nothing more than an enormous bear or a prison guard with a talent for costumes. Whatever. Just let this mission be straightforward: no hard calls, no deviations, no interpersonal drama. Because despite it all, she still couldn't imagine her life beyond her career.

Her excuse for avoiding a series of "pleasant chats" had evaporated. And now, the chats were unavoidable, given that the personnel briefs had been *truncated to the point of dereliction of duty.*

An hour later, Agnet slumped back into her seat, her mouth and soul as dry as the insides of a vacuum bag. Chatting at length while obscuring the embarrassing truth that Central had given her no concrete information had felt like an hours long one-sided tango.

Wind rushed along the carriage, and the historian's voice droned on, a different type of wind. Sure, all chip-heads loved their data and wanted to share. But this one... The man's name was...Yoder. Jemin Yoder. Jemin. A strategy to lock in everyone's name before they landed took shape. She burrowed a hand in her bag, pulled out the brief and a pencil, and jotted his name down. Thanks to Yoder—Jemin Yoder, she now knew *even more* about the region's geology. He clearly lacked a boredom-in-others meter.

Granted, she'd never worked with a historian before; maybe they were all like this guy. Every so often, he'd toss his thick blond bangs out of those googly, watery-blue eyes. A bang-trim might be a better solution than the incessant hair flipping.

The conversation with Yoder had highlighted her aversion to chips. She'd scored high on the exams, but her own mind was busy enough. Why add extra head noise? Might've led to extra pay—it'd be nice being able to afford quality clothes like Spool's—but chips meant heavy debt and, not infrequently, mental problems.

Now, Spool, unlike everybody else on this team, had pertinent field experience, a decent reputation, and seemed normal—though with undertones of remote and damaged. She underlined "experienced," clinging to the positive since the negatives were vast. Perceivers died on mission, now and again. Not in the line of fire deaths but dropping to the floor for no apparent reason deaths. A worry, since both her career and her mental health demanded that this mission be death-free.

Yep. Perceivers could be strange. Consider the lady who'd negotiated with that Canuck rebel leader, and the pair who'd helped her team pry out that hawk-nosed traitor: odd balls, all three. The girl perceiver, Orl—no last name and dressed in black—also looked odd, but she'd been asleep when Agnet had dropped by to introduce herself, so too early to judge the size and weight of her peculiarity.

What about Brandt Collins? He seemed a classic type, the soldier recently released from service, working security while adjusting to civilian life. His time on the border hadn't filled him with hate. In fact, he seemed remarkably cheery and open-minded. Not the sharpest tool in the shed, and this mission was his first. But he seemed to be a good egg. Emphasize the good not the green.

The passengers settled into silence; Yoder probably had lulled them all to sleep. But truly, napping might be the best strategy. She tucked away her pad and pencil and closed her eyes.

So fascinating that a part of his brain could survey the chip for useful tidbits and broadcast directly to his mouth, enlightening his seatmate, while this talky portion performed a meta-analysis on the phenomenon that was himself, Jemin Yoder, a valuable professional, dispensing knowledge. A pleasure, these new discoveries, though he could've used more practice time before shipping off. He'd need to log each experience and bounce his data off his superiors on his return.

And the Common Folk thought historians were all chip and no brain. Ha. He'd earned a top-notch chip through hard work and persistence, and the Lord, praise be, had blessed him with natural gifts, abilities to select, curate, and cull information for each audience, distill the essence, pull together bits from disparate sources, and generate novel hypotheses. Information was nothing in the absence of synthesis.

Yes, the chips were unnatural. And true, seduced by knowledge, he'd abandoned the path of the righteous. Sure, he'd pay in this life and in the afterlife. But ruminating about damnation, chip-debt, and the sad demise of his academic dreams would do no good. He could still provide a valuable service.

Observe how he'd enthralled the security officer, this Brandt Collins, who clearly spent most of his time in the gym. The treatise on airships was irrelevant to the mission, but machinery often fascinated physical types, a little boy's enthusiasm for vehicles persisting into adulthood. Of course, enlightening soldiers wasn't the career he'd hoped for. But someday, he'd prove the faithful could function in the modern world. Maybe he'd uncover a valuable clue in historical documents and solve this mystery. Imagine revealing his findings to a packed audience of rapt admirers. Ambition, maybe. But in the service of the Lord on High.

Or...a monster might pluck off his head and toss it into the brush. Monsters! Chief Krause hadn't provided any details, meaning whatever she'd read in the brief was terrifying. *Lord, have mercy upon the soft and uncoordinated house of my soul.* Though realistically, the Lord couldn't change his pudgy body or stop his spectacles from sliding down his nose. Hopefully, the big man seated adjacent could take care of the monsters while he quietly pursued his research.

Oh!

His seatmate had drifted off to sleep. Just as well, using the chip drained him dry. He should be more careful.

Brandt had only said, "Is this ship excellent, or what?" And the ship was excellent. Sleek, silent, and ultra-emissions neutral. Could use a sexy flight attendant serving drinks on a tray, but overall, a high-class ship, down to the silver-gray color.

But "or what" had put him in the crosshairs of a lecture. Sure, the historian's high-tech details would wow smart guys, but not himself, a soldier who could only understand every fourth word. Harvesting hydrogen from bladder warts? At least bladder warts had turned out to be some kind of plant because otherwise—yuck. Tensile strength of bamboo versus allotrope toxicity versus whatever...he couldn't keep up. Good thing chip-headed Jemin talked non-stop and didn't ask questions.

The glossy carbon-black arm rest felt cool and smooth beneath his fingertips, toxic allotrope or not. He shouldn't complain; a lecture was a small price to pay for this ride, an experience way above his pay grade, most likely his one and only flight. The first mission of his new career was off to a great start. The Chief, a fine-looking older lady, impressed him. She had things under control, though the mission parameters seemed loose and confusing. Still, taking on monsters and rescuing helpless civilians, like frogeyes here, would suit him. And best yet, the team included perceivers, that pair across the aisle, fancy-pants urban guy and quirky girl. He'd heard perceivers were different, and that pair sure looked different. Yep. This mission would be incredible. He could feel it in his bones.

The stone-faced teen seated beside Philip Spool had stopped feigning sleep, but she still didn't or wouldn't speak. He'd expected endless yakking, although who was he kidding? His knowledge of teenage girls would fit in a teaspoon. Perhaps stone-walling adults was all the rage with kids these days. Still, he'd had plenty of experience with trainees, and her behavior was decidedly odd for a trainee; trainees answered their supervisor's questions, hoping to impress or befriend them.

The seat's cheap plastic fabric grated against his pants as he leaned forward to tuck her dossier into his satchel. He hadn't come across neurological or psychiatric problems in Orl's psych report, so why didn't she respond? He wasn't usually intrusive, but now was the time to switch tactics. Should be easy; their chips were compatible, or so the dossier said.

He switched on and lobbed a couple polite questions as language-equivalent transmissions. The moment hovered like a frozen pendulum. The transmission should have hit her auditory system almost instantaneously.

By now.

Well by now.

Might as well scream into the abyss. He faded the communications module. Messaging over a distance was a perceiver's trump card, a skill that'd left him and others not-dead many times. NeuroCorp could experiment with chips all they wanted, but they shouldn't...no...they couldn't mess with the communication function. And sure, they could hardly recruit normals, but some basic social skills should be mandatory.

A blast of air buffeted the ship to one side. The aerodynamic equivalent of an egg crate, this ship, toothpicks held together by paper, hoof glue, and packing string. He preferred his feet firmly planted on the ground, so the low vibration of the engine felt reassuring, technology battling gravity and winning. At least for now. Every time he'd flown, he'd broken into a light sweat. Yet Orl, on her maiden voyage, "slept" like a baby.

Please let immaturity explain her silence, because the next option was malfunctioning circuitry, or worse, a malfunctioning brain. If her problem was technical; they were doomed. Because nobody at a remote, rural work farm could help them with a chip glitch.

Work farm. Slivers of memory flitted by: green cloaked hills, peeling the husk from an ear of corn, the smell of late afternoon, summer's golden sun...glitter ringing his vision...the smell of wet rock, screaming that wouldn't stop, a desperate urge to run. Thoughts like space junk wheeled through a vast and empty cosmos, no context, nothing ringing true. *A seizure prodrome. Shut it down.* He groped in his pocket for an ampule of MemStop, crushed the glass and snorted. A rush, then—

His eyes opened to an unfamiliar place, a tube fitted out with seats and little round windows. An odor like menthol clung to the lining of his nose, and something damp lay in his fingers, a MemStop ampule, meaning he'd just narrowly avoided a seizure. The instructions on the ampule read, "Wait patiently for orientation to return. Forcing recognition can re-trigger the adverse event."

"Adverse event" sounded like purest corporate bullshitery, and—ah, yes—speaking of corporate bullshitery, "orientation" was returning: the idiotic mission that even his Chief inspector couldn't explain, his sartorially challenged silent partner, and he was hurtling through the air in a highly flammable, paper cylinder. Plenty of reasons to suffer an "adverse event".

Such an idiotic situation. A person who can't concentrate and can barely work up the enthusiasm to take a piss, much less fight monsters and train bright young things—or dull young things like Orl with her baggy black clothing, perpetual scowl, and silence—should be at home recovering from surgery.

A thread looping from the seat's fabric had found its way between his fingers. He twisted it and tugged, giving into minor vandalism in the service of frustration.

The Man buzzed in her ear, but Orl ignored him. She *could* ignore him. Now that she'd stopped taking the Bad Pills. Triumph. Victory! (No, not Yet). But still she felt Good, a warm Glow, a Rush of excitement.

She could Leave.

That one thought Persisted. All other thoughts had flowed like tea leaves down the drain, the dregs of who she was Before. She wasn't that person anymore, the one who was supposed to Do Something. (What? What'd she been supposed to do?)

No matter. She was Light and Water. She could Spread. Anywhere.

She reached out. The minds of the ship-people, though she could hear a smattering of their thoughts, were still Closed to her. She reached out again, her thoughts forming a filament of pulsing energy. Beyond the ship she touched a small and simple Consciousness which became a glowing Dot, an energy deposit she could flow toward.

Swoop, flap, swoop, flap, the rushing air, the forest below, gravity's pull, the glinting sun. Falling! Orl's stomach lurched.

Confusion and fear swamped her small host, a Bird who dove, expecting a hawk, danger from above, not understanding Orl was the source of sudden alarm. It spiraled, a moment of Panic, wings flailing. A flash of Earth, then sky as they somersaulted. (Small! Be small.) She must be small, a buckwheat Groat, a Grain of sand, hiding from the bird until it righted and flew as if nothing rode in its Mind.

Then wind filled their wings, and they flapped, the journey and Hunger tugging the fabric of their reality. A new sense like a Smoky Cloud hovering before their eyes guided them. "Go now," it insisted, "Leave, fly." Yes, this bird's mind suited her victory, sky-bound, clean and simple, Free and Leaving.

They flew. And now, having flown, she could never return to the Dormitory. They'd drug her, then Know what she could become. Rasp would twist her so she could never leave. The Treatment Room, the sharp smell of antiseptic, the bench sticking to her naked thighs. Her Fear sent the bird diving again, more danger from above. The Hawk... Orl slipped.

Snap.

She was in her seat, the human minds around her chittering, the Cool of the ship's casing. But it'd been time to Return. The bird was traveling far. And she couldn't be a bird forever, though the bird had Accepted Her. People would never understand. Take this man seated next to her; His Aggravation hung in the air like a Foul Smell.

Hovering Above an Open Field

A substantial river, ridges and valleys, the view from Agnet's window suggested they were closing in on the farm. There! A slash of tan and muted greens materialized in the autumn-mottled hills.

"That must be it!" The security guard—Collins—Brandt Collins, thick of neck, and broad of chest, hopped forward, seated himself next to her, and pointed out Agnet's window. "Ridgelands Penal Colony." He said the name of the prison using the reverent tone she'd use for "oyster soup with sourdough bread." At least the mission excited somebody.

The steward, fussy lipped and disapproving, probably as a matter of course—nothing personal—positioned himself at the front of the cabin. "Given the destination's dubious nature, prepare for an *air-landing*."

Brandt applauded. "Wow! Fantastic. I hoped for an air-landing."

Agnet raised an eyebrow at him; he reminded her of a large, friendly dog always ready to chase that ball. She wriggled a finger to bring the steward close and whispered. "Excuse me, but Ridgefield Farms is a low security facility. The prisoners are called 'trainees.' We're talking embezzlers, petty thieves, low-level black marketeers. Why not land?"

The steward's mouth pruned, conveying disapproval and a stubborn streak thick as the walls of a blast bunker. "Regulations forbid ground landings at penal colonies, including *Ridgelands*, so no ground landing. Captain's orders."

She maintained a stoic face while the butterflies swarmed in her gut. Behind her, Yoder whispered, "Pardon me, but what's an air-landing?" Philip Spool, the lead perceiver, chuckled, but she couldn't hear his reply. The man was soft-spoken and a bit...languid. Be interesting to see how a city boy like Spool handled himself on an air ladder. But she wouldn't notice; she'd be busy trying not to die.

Half an hour later, the ship hovered over an open field, the carriage slowly descending, but not low enough. A gallon of adrenaline dumped into her system as the steward opened the embarkation hatch, tossed out a rope ladder, and made an ushering-out gesture.

"A ladder?" Brandt's mouth drooped at the corners.

Was he anxious, now faced with an air-landing's harsh reality? She should explain.

"Our destination is too remote for a tower, lacks a large body of water, and a landing would expose this highly valuable ship to various hazards."

"Like what, trainees charging with pitchforks and torches?" asked Spool, sounding amused.

She ignored him. "So, we'll need to climb from the carriage to the field below."

Brandt shrugged. "I figured no tower, and I'm fit to climb a ladder." Did he just flex? "It's just I hoped we'd be paragliding down. Paragliding's a rush, so the ladder's kind of a letdown."

Yoder eyed Brandt like one would eye a babbling weirdo blocking the sidewalk. But the soldier's face held no psychosis or bravado; he was sincere.

She let him down easy. "Sorry, no paragliding today."

Good thing her security man didn't suffer from vertigo, since she'd take bullets, machetes, or bombs over heights any day. And nothing was worse than a midair disembark, whether by ladder or, for the love of Pete, *paragliding*. The rest of the team, presumably also *non-paragliders*, looked stiff in the face. She'd better go first, just to get it over with and to set an example.

Agnet wiped her moist palms on her pants, knelt at the threshold, and gripped the handholds, smooth wooden brackets set into the cabin's floor near the hatch. A gust of wind ruffled her hair and jostled the carriage, but she refused to die, not today. She stretched a leg out a comfortable distance and placed her foot solidly on a rung. The ladder lurched to one side as she reached out her other leg, as if she was supposed to be a trapeze artist. Once both feet were firmly planted, she stopped shaking and re-solidified.

The next move would be the worst. She released the hand hold, offering herself to the void, and felt for the rope because she couldn't look down. Got it! The shaggy cord felt reassuringly thick and absorbed the sweat on her palm. The next hand was easier. Now, she was fully out of the carriage and staring straight ahead; survival seemed possible. One foot and one hand at a time, and she was down.

When they'd all assembled on terra firma, the steward retracted the rope ladder, threw them a wave, and the carriage floated skyward. The ship silently vanished into the clouds, taking with it the non-existent risk of a prison break. The air crew would return to their comfortable homes, having marooned her in a muddy field beneath a gunmetal sky. The breeze carried a whiff of manure, reminding her she was off her turf, urban crime being her specialty, a specialty that'd kept her busy; lots of people meant lots of violence. Maybe rural people were trouble too but kept a low profile by quietly burying their victims. An easy chore, given all the soil.

The trainee, Orl, young enough to fall victim to an unfortunate fashion subculture, stared west into the lowering sun, an expression of bliss on her face. Hopefully, she was just glad to be on the ground, but might as easily be stoned or stark, raving mad. The girl opened her mouth and sort of...croaked. Philip shot her a woeful expression, then stared into the sky as if willing the ship to return. Jemin, who'd been standing with eyes shut, hands clasped and pressed tight against his chest, probably allowing air-landing terror to subside, flipped open a rag book and began sketching. Brandt stood at attention. Nice that one of the team looked remotely professional.

An emergency, they'd said. Read up on the plane, they'd said while dumping responsibility for this mess in her lap. They knew she'd care, even though nothing but chaos stemmed from her caring about outcomes: mission outcomes, interpersonal outcomes, organizational outcomes, outcomes for herself and the flipping planet. She'd made decisions and suggestions, improved procedures, and asked questions, getting people killed and pissing everybody off because she cared. Caring was the worst. Caring was a mistake. Caring left you vulnerable to disappointment and frustration. Caring made you a target.

She shouldn't care about this ridiculous mission, at best some kind of excuse, window-dressing, or cover up. She wouldn't care. She wouldn't worry about these people and their competency, or lack thereof. They could be anybody: criminals, dissenters, deviants, whatever. She just needed them to survive this mission because she couldn't take any more sadness, bad dreams, looks askance, or hushed whispers.

Five people approached across the field. Orl retracted into her hood and stepped behind Philip, like a kid hiding behind mommy on the first day of grammar school. At least she wasn't croaking.

"Here comes the welcome committee!"

She sighed. Brandt sounded enthusiastic and looked indestructible. Once upon a time, she'd been enthusiastic and indestructible too. But now, she was tired—tired but still professional. She willed confidence, straightened her posture, and prepared for introductions, carefully worded conversation, and the dreaded but inevitable chatting.

The prison staff closed in.

A Reality-Based Person

Warden Bergamot Honing, a man well into a hale and hearty prime, and his officers escorted them to a group of rustic timber buildings. The overall look, a pleasant surprise, suggested logging camp more than prison. He dismissed the officers, giving Agnet an opportunity to forget their names, and gathered the team around a rectangular wooden table in the mess hall. Heavy trusses marched across the ceiling, like the gigantic ribs of some prehistoric beast. But the belly of this leviathan was cozy, thanks to heat-radiators and steaming tea. Agnet fingered the initials gouged into the worn-smooth pine, so many overlapping, they'd formed a cross hatched patch, only a few names and dates legible, a testament to the many who'd sat beneath these beams. The hefty timbers must seem remarkable to some of the team. Such a contrast to the city's ubiquitous coralcrete block.

The Warden's bald dome shone in the lamplight. He'd greeted them, seated them, and now was describing his domain. "She's hard land, hereabouts. Soil's shale and limestone decomposed into heavy clay that drains about as well as a bucket. So, what do we grow? We grow buckwheat. Tough as weeds, buckwheat. But it improves the soil. We rarely have success with winter wheat or corn, on account of the blight. Our honeybees feed off the buckwheat, and apple and raspberry blossoms." He stared over the darkening field, his brow furrowed. "The apples ain't in yet."

"Wouldn't honeybees fly into the containment zone, load up with contaminated pollen, then poison the honey?" asked Philip.

"Slim pickings for bees, past the valley and the woodlot, so they stick to the farm." The Warden gave Philip a quick once over, a sunny grin, and a raised eyebrow. Philip probably attracted appreciative looks regularly, from women, men, even honeybees. Perfumed blossoms, these perceivers, thanks to rumors of special emotional and sexual skills. And Philip's tormented-actor-look added to his appeal.

"Speaking of flying the coop, I notice the perimeter isn't secured."

Welp. Brandt clearly hadn't taken the meaning of "low security".

"No need. We're too remote. And too many hazards between here and the next viable settlement. Out there's your mutant wildlife, your ferals, and radioactive fallout. A trainee skips every so often. But we just feel sorry for them when they do."

"Why run this facility as a rehab? Sure, the trainees provide free labor, but aren't most ill-suited. I'd imagine most would require substantial training to come up to basic standards. Wouldn't AgroCorp manage the land more efficiently?"

Ouf. Yoder's tactless question hung in the air like a fart, but Honing displayed no offense.

"That question comes up now and again. Way back, during the founding of this colony, the owners wouldn't sell to AgroCorp, figuring the enterprise would last about a year under the stewardship of corporate money launderers, buying themselves forty-thousand-dollar pitchforks and such-like. Not that you heard me making critical remarks about our government. The owners followed an ancient religion partial to redemption—this was back before the outbreaks and the uprisings, you see, so their feelings were taken into account. They believed offenders would find purpose working hard out here in the wholesome countryside. One old guy even stayed on and shared his expertise with the first Warden. We're still farming old school style, and we're still about redemption. We offer a way out and up. Our people do pretty well with the chance they've been given. Usually."

The Warden paused, but his reply seemed to have rendered Jemin speechless, his expression amazed or awestruck. What had surprised the historian, the choosing of redemption over efficiency? Be nice to believe the man's heart wasn't that hard.

Honing nodded, marking the question as answered, then continued. "Right now, we're struggling. The heat this summer set us back despite the shields, but now I can't get workers out in the fields. My people keep babbling about spooks. I've never seen one, so I can't vouch for the truth of these...whatever. But we've had a few grisly incidents, and the population is terrified. We got pumpkin to harvest, too, and time is growing short."

Orl's head popped up at the word spooks, and her eyes focused on the Warden. Interesting, as she'd ignored several direct inquiries while they'd walked across the field. Eventually, the prison staff decided Orl was hard of hearing and stopped asking questions. But seemed deaf must not be her problem.

Agnet pulled her notebook and a pencil from her front pocket now that the conversation had moved on topic. Pleaser had called the problem "monsters" not "spooks." Was there a difference? Maybe she'd just skip over the change in terminology, in case someone in Intake had misheard. No need to let the Warden know Central wasn't paying full attention.

"Spooks? We heard you had monsters," said Brandt, talking out of turn, so much for tact.

Honing laughed. "Monsters, spooks, goblins, haints, not much difference in my book. I may have used 'monsters' up front, but later, the community settled on 'spooks.' They decided the things weren't really alive, and spooks seemed a better fit."

"Monsters sounds better to me. Spook means ghost, and ghosts are see-through, no substance to them, at least in fireside stories. I'd rather fight something solid." Brandt swung an imaginary bat.

"I see your point. Guess I'm a monsters man too. Though, I'm a reality-based person. My people are seeing *something*, but I'm having trouble accepting a supernatural explanation."

Brandt's face sobered. "You're probably right. But I'd still take monsters over spooks."

Philip snorted, an ineffective attempt to smother a laugh.

Agnet glared at Brandt then Philip and made a show of flipping open her notebook to a blank page. Then she donned a reassuring smile for the Warden's benefit. "I'm a reality-based person myself. But we're here to help with whatever you got, spooks or monsters, *your* preference. Though, personally, I'd favor zombies for not alive monster-like things. Any who, we'll need everything you've got, your story and the testimony of any witnesses. All the details."

The Warden pulled in his chin, his eyebrows high on his forehead. "You're here to help *us*?"

"Of course. Why else would we be here?"

"I was about to ask. Excuse my surprise. Shock, actually. Been sending out distress calls since July and haven't heard a peep. Sure, we're remote. The wire between here and New Delphi was stolen decades ago, then replaced with filament. But that went down in an ice-storm years back and won't ever be repaired, so I'm reduced to pigeons. Usually the pigeons do us fine, but three pigeons gone, and no reply. Other government teams came through, but they had their own business and looked at me as if I was crazy when I mentioned our problems. We stocked 'em up, and watched 'em head out, hoping they'd give our regards to Central. I finally assumed nobody was taking me seriously. Not that I blame them."

Two unexpected twists, the Warden's astonishment and other teams passing through. "Now I'm surprised. How many teams and when?"

"Two. Spoke with the leaders briefly. Said they was looking into the environment."

"What did they find?"

"No idea. They didn't come back this way. I figured they traveled to a pickup point somewhere downriver."

"Many visitors pass through here?"

"No. We're well off the beaten track. So, we appreciate you coming out. You really here about the sightings?"

"Yeah?"

A huge grin overtook Honing's face. "Well, that's just fine, and I hope you can run them creatures off before the frost. Let me tell you what I've learned." He described four, for lack of a better word, manifestations, child-like figures in various states of decay, but strong and grabby. One casualty to date, a man drowned during an attack near water. The other witnesses survived, frightened but unharmed.

As the Warden wrapped up his story, a tall man in worn coveralls rolled up a bamboo partition, revealing an industrial style kitchen, a row of big vats, tongs and strainers hanging from a rack, and dishes in piles. Looked as if meal prep was commencing. People laid baskets on a long counter. A meal cooked close to the source of naturally farmed food—now that'd be something.

Warden Honing followed Agnet's eyes to the kitchen and a knowing smile flashed across his face. "We'll start in the morning. The lights go out shortly after supper; dark falls early and power generation's slack, given the cold, the cloud cover, and angle of the sun. Besides, people will be too tired to talk business after dinner."

"Sounds good. Our first steps will be interviewing the witnesses and inspecting the premises."

"Alright." Honing laid his hands on the table and pressed himself up from his chair. "Let's set up your quarters. Then, you ever taste apple crumple? Was dreaming of crumple, so myself and the admin team picked a bushel yesterday. You're going to love it."

WE'RE NOT SUPPOSED TO TALK ABOUT GHOSTS

After they'd stashed their gear in their quarters, Honing returned the team to the mess hall and excused himself. "Make yourselves at home. I have to count heads. I'll touch base after supper." A rectangle of late afternoon light silhouetted him at the door; then he was gone.

Jemin popped out of his chair and gandered about, sticking his nose up, down, under the table, all the while jotting notes in his floppy, thick-paged ragbook.

"What are you?" asked Brandt. "The health inspector?"

The historian's wide-set, bulbous eyes glistened blankly. Then he pursed his overly red lips, evoking a peeved catfish. "Do you jest? This place is a treasure trove. I'm collecting observations." He tapped the ragbook with his thick black pencil "A goldmine. Imagine, a colony, cut off for a century. Going its own direction—"

"Except for the steady flow of new inmates." Philip ineffectively hid a smirk behind a curved finger.

Confusion skittered across Jemin's face. "Well. If the staff is permanent, and most of the inmates are lifers, a culture could develop. Did you notice the woodwork? The details are unique. Reminiscent of—"

Orl shot out of her chair, a shock of black hair covering one eye, her pale skin almost iridescent beneath her hood. Agnet waited for a fit or tantrum. Instead, Orl tipped up her chin, pointed one finger at the ceiling, and croaked, looking and sounding like a half-blood crow.

Their faces turned to the shadows beneath the eaves. Agnet's eyes adjusted to the dark—there! A white form loomed above a hefty crossbeam, barrel-shaped, mushroom colored, probably a meter high. Could this be one of the Warden's spooks? Her fingers curled around her sidearm, a flimsy one-shot wonder, courtesy of Central's new gun fetish. At least a bullet wouldn't ricochet off those wooden beams. She briefly mourned the absence of her lovely, repeat-action crossbow which was sitting on a shelf at home, thanks to the disorganized rush to the plane. The creature swiveled its dish-shaped sensory array in her direction.

Jemin inhaled sharply. "An owl!"

"A what?" Brandt asked.

The historian glanced at him, emanating pity tinged with zeal. "An owl is a large predatory bird. This example is probably *Tyto alba*, the barn owl. Once widely distributed, now vanishingly rare. The outlying ecosystem must be healthier than I expected."

Agnet squared her shoulders and slid her hand from the pistol. Embarrassing, being spooked, so to speak, by a mere animal. "Is that over-sized pigeon going to poop on my apple crumple?"

"No. They're carnivores, prey on rodents, and regurgitate the skin and bones, anything indigestible, as a pellet." Now everyone was staring at Jemin, who cleared his throat. "In lieu of pooping, that is. So worst-case scenario would be an owl pellet, much drier than feces at any rate."

Terrific. Apple crumple with a side order of skin and bone.

"Though I suppose owls must also defecate, to some degree."

And a topping of bird poop.

The trainee setting up dinner called out. "Don't let ole Flossie worry you. During the day, she holes up here. Come dusk, we open the doors for dinner, and off she goes to keep down the vermin."

Agnet waved her thanks to the helpful stranger. "Just in case, let's move from under that bird."

They migrated to a table outside of the owl's firing range. Hopefully, everybody was now ready for business. Brother, did she miss Mac and her old get-down-to-it team.

She waved Jemin over. "Do your anthropological research on your own time. Let's focus on the mission. First up. Philip and Orl. What did you pick up from Warden Honing?"

"He's mostly on the level," said Philip. "But I detected lies or omissions during the discussion about the other teams."

"You're saying he knows more about those teams than he's letting on."

"Correct."

Agnet searched for Orl's eyes, but her hood's shadow obscured her face. "Orl, can you confirm?"

No reply. The girl started picking at her cuticles

Philip shook his head. "Sorry. I've been meaning to mention—was hoping she'd straighten out on her own—but something's wrong with her or her chip, or both. Would've been nice if we'd been vetted as a functioning pair *before* they packed us on the airship."

"I saw her perk up when Honing mentioned spooks, so she's not deaf and can follow a conversation. You want to tell us about spooks, Orl?"

The girl glanced at Agnet through her bangs, shook her head, then retracted into her hood until only her chin was visible.

Agnet asked Philip, "They supply you with her dossier?"

He opened his satchel and passed her a thin folder. "Pretty skimpy, but nothing out of the ordinary. Training completed with full marks. Chip should be compatible with mine." He shrugged. "But I can't connect."

Brandt asked, "Don't perceivers normally read each other's thoughts?"

Philip gracefully cringed. "We don't"—air quotes—"'read thoughts'. We message *each other* via chip, and messaging is similar to talking. Right now, I can't reach Orl on her chip because of a...malfunction."

Terrific. Her second perceiver was twice over mute. Perceivers could be daft as bed bugs in a frying pan, but they needed to communicate with their partner.

"That's a shame. I thought you-all were psychic."

Brandt appeared crushed while Philip tried to cover exasperation with ennui.

"No. Not psychic. We pick up emotional detail from subtle physical cues, temperature and color changes, pupil dilation; it's all psychology and a bit of silicon circuitry, nothing more."

Agnet spared Philip further questioning. "Well, Orl. We can allow for neurodivergence or minor psychiatric issues, but I expect all team members to perform their functions. Understand that your keeping quiet could jeopardize our mission as we may need to communicate over a distance."

Silence.

Grrr. In her book, communication over a distance was the main reason to add a pair of perceivers to a team. Despite Spool's claims of enhanced perception, only some perceivers excelled at interviews and negotiations. Most were too bleeping weird. She lobbed silent curses at Human Resources, that tribe of sadists who'd probably cackled while dumping the girl on her team.

Philip murmured, "It's alright. I've worked solo before."

Great. But it took two to relay information. Would've been nice if NeuroCorp had provided another fully adult, functional perceiver.

"Be better for everyone if you can coax the girl out of her shell. So don't throw in the towel, yet. We'll make time for this communication issue and get it straightened out."

Brandt tilted his head and spoke to the darkness beneath Orl's hood. "Do you know anything about spooks, kid?"

Her head moved almost imperceptibly.

Brandt grasped Philip's shoulder. "See? She knows something! Can she write?"

Philip rolled his eyes. "She wouldn't write about spooks because NeuroCorp could *use the document against her.*"

The emphasized end of Philip's statement sounded like a warning, probably meant for Orl. Agnet knew NeuroCorp was malevolent, but petty came as a surprise. "Given the world's rather dire state, why would NeuroCorp have an issue with ghost stories?"

A pained look crossed his face. "NeuroCorp expressly discourages the use of terms like 'ghost' or 'spook' or 'haint' under the theory that 'ghost' bolsters the concept of 'soul'. Proof of souls might foment insurrection on the border."

Brandt asked, "Can ghosts run a still or dry good-time weed?"

"No?"

"Then nobody on the border will give a hoot. Come on, tell us your ghost stories. I love a case of the goose bumps."

Agnet tapped Philip's arm. "You can't dangle 'we're not supposed to talk about ghosts,' when ghosts might be relevant to the mission."

He massaged his forehead with thumb and forefinger. "I've obviously said too much already.

"Spill it."

"Good grief. Why me, why now when I'm exhausted." He heaved an oh-so-weary sigh, but beads of sweat dotted his upper lip, a nervous man hiding behind a blasé front. "You know, missions are usually normal, no monsters or ghosts, and team members communicate like adults." He glared at Orl. "But here we are. So, if I tell you people how perceivers understand 'ghosts' as a concept, keep it quiet. For your own sake, unless you want to be on the wrong side of EBT." Philip glanced around the table, meeting each team member's eyes, likely performing some perceiver-style prattle-risk calculation.

"I, for one, have no difficulty with discretion, especially in service of a greater truth." Jemin's watery eyes floated behind those thick lenses, slightly undermining his genuineness.

"Don't keep many of my own secrets. But I always keep other people's." Brandt lifted a finger to his lips. "Silence is golden."

Agnet leaned into Philip's gaze. "I'd sew my lips shut to hear whatever's so weird it freaks out NeuroCorp. Get on with it."

"Fine. Just please, don't make me regret my candor." He held eye contact with Jemin a bit longer.

The historian flushed. "If you want something to use against me in return, just know that as far as I'm concerned, the Evidence-Based Taskforce impedes the search for truth. So there."

Philip chuckled softly, then patted his face with a handkerchief—undoubtably clean and perfumed. "Well, then. Fair is fair. Here's my take on"—finger quotes—"ghosts". He paused, gave his head a slight shake that seemed to say "can't believe I'm doing this," then continued. "After death, consciousness persists as a high frequency energy signature that usually—um—dissipates. But sometimes, that energy remains in situ, vibrating."

"Where's Insitchew?" A frown of intense concentration creased Brandt's forehead.

"In place, I meant in place, as in where the death occurred or near remains."

"Oh. So, where they died or at a grave?"

Philip nodded, admirably maintaining his poise.

Brandt grinned like a kid. "So just like in the stories. But that'd blow, hanging around your old bones. So why do some get stuck?"

"Confusion, usually. Some consciousnesses don't process death accurately."

Agnet searched Philip's face but found no traces of fun-making; he actually believed this rubbish. "Sounds like a slice of crazy. I've never read a mission report mentioning ghosts. None of my neighbors have complained about them. I've patrolled places that should've been haunted and weren't. So if ghosts are real, why don't they turn up more often?"

"Rarely, the energy signal becomes constrained and drops into a visible frequency. That's when witnesses report ghosts, UFOs, unusual weather phenomena, religious visitations, etcetera. However, only some people in certain circumstances notice them."

"Seeing one would be great, but I kinda doubt I'm the type," said Brandt, looking woeful.

Philip waved a dismissive hand. "Count yourself lucky. Ghosts really aren't that interesting. They're leftovers, stains on the present."

Maybe leftovers and stains to Philip, who'd obviously intellectualized death to...well...death, probably to conform with NeuroCorp standards. But normal people, like the prisoners, would leap to all sorts of fanciful conclusions. Brandt, for instance, was practically glowing with excitement. "You perceivers can see them, can't you? You can see energy, like you see...extra fast or something?"

Philip forced an apathetic expression, but she sensed a host of unpleasant memories swirling beneath his mask. "Matter doesn't really exist as a separate thing. It's just energy slowed down. We all see energy, you too."

Brandt's face went slack as an empty potato sack. "Whoa. That's deep." He thumped the table, which shuddered. "But seeing ghosts! That. Is. So. Excellent."

An oh-so-bored eye roll. "Or it's a non-useful side effect of my chip."

But a side effect that explained why perceivers walked around invisible obstacles and stared at nothing, giving everybody else the willies. Sort of like house cats, and house cats were a bunch of low-key psychos. She was a dog person, but still, no harm in encouraging a rare—thank the freaking stars—skill. "Chip glitch or not, ghost vision might come in handy on this mission."

Philip shrugged. "This situation doesn't sound like ghosts to me."

"Ghosts, monsters, zombies, mass sociogenic delusion, why not keep our options open? Tomorrow, Jemin, *resisting any urge* to go down a pottery-shard lined rabbit hole, scan your chip for pertinent and recent information on this compound, the Warden, the staff, the inmates, and the adjacent lands. Keep an eye out for repairs, major projects, visitors, inspections, prison breaks, new personnel, etc. But don't fry your brain; your implant's fairly new, and we don't need another malfunction. Philip and I will interview the witnesses." Figuring Brandt would treat Orl as a fun new adventure, same as he treated everything else, she assigned the pair to survey the compound and the perimeter. "Stick to the prison grounds. We'll ask the Warden's permission before we explore the fields and surrounds."

"That's Orl and Brandt, the A-team." He gave the expressionless girl a thumbs up. "Maybe we can rustle up some ghosts."

Philip looked aghast.

Agnet cleared her throat. "So tomorrow, first stage, collect information. Tonight, at dinner, play nice. Obviously, don't go on about spooks or monsters. No need to stir the pot. And remember, the 'trainees' are criminals with maladaptive social behaviors who've made poor life choices."

She scanned the team. One of Orl's arms rhythmically twitched, as if keeping time to an imaginary beat. Jemin was sketching a free-standing cupboard pushed up against a nearby wall. Philip, a look of vague despair crinkling his brow, gazed off into the distance while Brandt grinned like a kid in a candy store. Here she sat, with a pack of kooks deployed on a ridiculous mission. A pox on Central and all its minions.

On the other hand, this team would fit in just fine at dinner.

Schnokered and Gossiping

A few hours later, Agnet was enjoying after-dinner drinks with her brawny security agent. After their second round, he asked, "What kind of person knows about owls?"

Raucous singing drowned out Agnet's reply. Maybe breaking out a barrel of the hard stuff to celebrate the "spook-hunters" arrival hadn't been the Warden's brightest idea. Though the booze could improve the man's chances with Philip. They seemed chummy, over there, tête-à-tête. She spotted Jemin's blond mop amongst the chorus of trainees; he'd gone over to interview a few, and "subtly extract" the essence of their culture. Maybe they'd broken into song to display that culture. Or to avoid being interrogated about minutia.

The song dwindled to a mere uproar. "Jemin's a history specialist, anthropology, politics, folklore. You name it. But I don't know why he'd know about birds. Some people have scholarly interests outside their field."

Brandt, who seemed more of a shoot-first-read-a-book-never type, tapped his rather significant chest. "I have interests outside my field, too. But I'm telling you, the guy reminds me of somebody."

"You perceiving behind my back?"

"Heck, no."

Still, Brandt might be onto something. Regular people could read people too. "So, who does Jemin remind you of? Just curious."

"I'm not saying he's trouble or anything, just... It'll come to me. Hey, check out Phil and the Warden." He pointed out the pair with a wave of his glass. "Hope he's packing condoms."

"I'm sure he's prepared for all contingencies." Spool, who hung with both the hip and the cultured crowd, such as existed in 'these trying times', probably hated being called "Phil." But the combination of his reputation and his spotless medical record suggested pockets stuffed with condoms, a suitcase full of condoms, long-term investments in multiple condom factories. By all accounts, the man enjoyed physical contact and wasn't particular about gender. Sure, promiscuity often was a response to trauma. But who wasn't traumatized these days? Plus, good-looking agents often used hanky-panky as a tool of the trade.

Not her style, for a variety of reasons, starting with her utilitarian approach to fashion and grooming, but the strategy didn't faze her, if the agent was circumspect, had a thick enough skin to handle emotional fallout, and limited themselves to consenting partners. Sometimes those rolls in the hay revealed interesting details.

Brandt snorted, sounding disgusted. "Some guys have all the luck. I'm a ladies only guy, and this place is slim pickings. Ninety-five percent of the women here are terrifying."

"Terrifying?" she asked, eyeing Brandt's impressive pectorals and shoulders, muscles that might require special-order shirts. What could terrify this man?

"Yep. The type of woman who slits your throat while you're sleeping. I asked the kitchen 'what're prisoners using to cut up all those vegetables?' Turns out, the kitchen has a fine set of ceramics; better quality than what I used on the border. Kept under lock and key, and an employee does the prep, but still. Don't tell me access to that key can't be had for a price."

"Hadn't really thought about vegetable prep."

"I'm security. It's my job to scan the environment for threats." He formed circles with his fingers and lifted them to his eyes, binocular style.

"Your mother make your shirts?"

He grinned proud as a cat with a lizard's tail dangling from its mouth. Had she hit a vain streak?

"Custom made on my own dime. But my fine attire is wasted on this bunch. The non-terrifying females are too homely or old."

Brandt delivered his too-much-personal-information with a slight slur. He'd better cool it on the booze.

"Now, a girl like Orl—and don't worry. I know she's just a kid, and it's nice the ugly kids have their own style, with the black lips and the eyeliner. But Orl's not ugly, so I don't get it. Sure, perceivers are supposed to be strange—that's just how they roll from what I know—but it's sad to see her hiding behind all that black."

"Don't worry about her. Lots of kids experiment with style. And she's dressing for herself, not for anybody else. She's not here to decorate our world." Hypocritical, since Agnet thought Orl looked affright in those inky rags. A girl's only young once and might as well look pretty while she has the chance, not that she herself had followed that piece of advice. But Orl was a kook. No ifs, ands, or buts. She'd looked so strange after dinner, dancing, and mouthing words... Sending her off to bed had been the right move.

Brandt mopped the condensate from his glass. That move, plus the custom shirts, suggested a fussy side to the big bruiser that could give Philip a run for the money. "Yeah. You're right. She should dress however she likes. And I hope she comes around because we could use her help with the ghosts."

"Philip's pretty sure we don't have ghosts. We have monsters. Or maybe zombies. Make peace with it."

"I can still dream we've got all three. And I'll bet Orl knows ghosts same as a normal kid knows—hey, look. Lover boy scores a point."

Philip and Honing were off to fraternize. Jemin was probably boring witnesses to death. Orl was both mute and asleep, and she and Brandt were schnokered and gossiping. An inauspicious start to the mission, but a distraction from her other...troubles. And now, she felt exhausted, tired enough to slip into sleep without remembering. She said goodnight and hit the sack.

Not Everybody is in Bed

This room was Orl's, for now. Though it was cold and smelled Not Used, it had a Best Ever; she could lock the door from Inside. The Leader had shown her how to flip the lever, shutting Everybody Out. A first-time experience in her world of Locks Outside. A taste of Free, though she wasn't ready. Her mind had needed the pills, more than she'd realized. All this noise, the Singing and the other people's Thoughts, clouded her own thinking. But soon her mind would clear, and she would Leave.

Not Locked Inside and Alone felt good, though a lie had created the Alone. The Leader had said Everyone was going to bed. But Time had passed, and everyone was Not In Bed. No. The garbled Noise of Many People, like wet gravel rolling in a drum, floated up from the mess hall. Local proof of Not Everyone In Bed. Also, the book of Stars and Planets had shown that the Earth spun on its axis and right now, a portion of the globe faced the Sun. Most of these daytime people were Awake.

Double Hence, Not Everybody was In Bed.

She considered the Leader's Lie. Did it anger her? Hard to tell. She wasn't used to Feelings. The Pills had evened out her emotions until they lay flat as this old pillow.

The lie was best considered a Data Point, possibly part of a Pattern, like the patterns of this coverlet, barely visible except in the slanted rectangle of moonlight that shared her bed. Each fabric square she tented with her fingers felt Different, one silky, the next nubbled, the next felty and soft. In combination, the multitude of Small Squares formed the Entire, the coverlet. Like people. Some have a large square of Lie. Some a small.

The Supervisor lied too, a different type of Lie. He'd tucked his feelings into a square and hid them with a Self-lie. He heard the Singing, too. Once their feet touched the stubbled field, the Song flowed through their chips. It'd filled her mind, connecting her to All Things, an overwhelming Belonging. But he resisted the Song, wouldn't acknowledge hearing it, not to himself, not to the others. And why did he lie? Because he was Afraid of the Signal, new and unexpected...or forgotten. The Song must be Rasp's precious signal, the signal she'd been trained to perceive from afar. But "Signal" was the wrong word to describe the Singing. Rasp was looking for a machine; she'd found a Singer.

She opened her mind and waited, but Time passed in a vast absence of Song. Was the Singer unkind, withholding the music to torment her? Maybe the Supervisor's fears were justified; he was Older, after all. Maybe the Singer was Not Good. Hard to believe, considering the beauty of the Song, but Rasp and his henchmen wouldn't hesitate to send her after something Evil. They didn't care if she was Hurt or Killed.

The idea of Hurt worried her more than Killed. She tuned her Blue chip and listened to the building. Nothing beyond the noise of the Living. She left the Bed—justified because everybody was Not In Bed—and stood at the window.

Behind the curtains, Night coated the yard. Cool white moonlight dusted the forest's trees with glitter. Some Dead congregated in a section of the yard, vibrating squiggles from this distance. The Supervisor was correct, ghosts were no trouble. Especially harmless, these ghosts who'd stayed Too Long. Their thoughts were few and on repeat, the usual set: excuses, unfinished business, regrets, blame, yearnings. Nothing new to add to the category of Dead-Thoughts.

Mommy? Where are you?

Orl snapped toward Elsewhere beyond the yard. There! A dead shimmering at the edge of the forest, Separate, and Alone. She opened her other chips to see clearly, even though Open meant risk and danger. But she'd no reason to fear one small, lost ghost. He quickly became Crisp. (She was stronger without the medication another of Rasp's lies Exposed). This forest-dead shone brighter than most of the yard-dead, more Present in the Now. She steeled herself for a dead-conversation; the dead, adrift in time and place, spoke even less Sense than the living.

Where did you last see your Mother?

She helped me zip up my costume. We were supposed to walk around the block and get home before the big kids came out. We weren't supposed to stay out past dark. We didn't. We were good. But...something happened. And now we're late, and my brother's gone.

A wave of confusion followed his story: *"late, alone, gone,"* all common complaints among the dead. Dead usually couldn't answer "when" questions, but no harm in asking.

When did your brother go missing?

Yesterday. One minute we were going home, then he was gone.

Yesterday might mean Yesterday or yesterday five hundred years ago. *Were you walking toward the Door?*

No? I have to get home. Mommy will worry. But I'm lost.

Your Mother went through the Door. She's waiting for you.

Oh?

Maybe your brother's there too. But if I find him here, I'll send him to you. Go on. You're Late.

You're sure?

Yes. And anyway, you can't stay here Alone. Go.

The dead wavered, flipping through Memory: gravel roads, a tidy cottage, a three-wheeled vehicle, a red ball, the all-encompassing presence of Mother, a special night, a treasured costume.

A real childhood with Mother. What would that've been like? Something hot splashed on her fingers. Tears. Had they come from her? She touched her cheek and found Wet. A phrase of the Song joined the boy's memories, and a swell passed through her, tingling and warm, a Good Feeling shared with the boy and the Singer. A kindness. Kindness was rare. He deserved kindness in return. She willed him to focus on his Door which was now well-defined, his personal door, a bedroom door or his house's front door. *You should go. She's waiting for you. She misses you.*

I miss her too. Bye. And if you see my brother, tell him to come soon.

I'll remember. I will.

And in that instant of Receptivity, he crossed and was gone.

Back to being Alone, she swept her perception across the border between yard and trees. Nothing. The Singing quieted down, and a vacuum yawned open in the Song's wake.

Wait.

In the crystal moonlight, trees and fences cast attenuated Shadows, gray on gray. And there, in the ink-black gap between two trees, something cold and Silent regarded her. An Awareness, but curiously Empty and not one of the Dead. Its watching rubbed her raw, paring her down to Less. This something was Unknown and Not Right. She stepped away from the window and hid trembling under her blanket.

WALKING THE PERIMETER

Dawn rose misty and pale. Brant zipped his field jacket and flexed his hands in his pockets as he crossed the yard. A few prisoners—whoops—*trainees* greeted him as he entered the warm and welcoming commissary. He stopped to joke around, even though he felt like a bucket of slops. After toast and two much needed cups of chicory...or something, he joined the team in the admin building's courtyard. But despite the chicory, Brandt's head clanged like he'd been sleeping with a grenade launcher.

Walking the perimeter would shake off the hangover and put distance between him and these offices. He could almost smell the paperwork. Imagine being convicted out here in the countryside, then assigned to admin instead of outdoors work. What a disaster! A body in motion stays in motion, and problems should be real, attacking, and prepared to die. And here was the Chief, bright eyed and bushy tailed; along with her other assets, she must burn through booze like wildfire.

"Ready for patrol, ma'am. Where's Orl?"

"Orl? You here girl? Time for patrol." Chief Krause called out to the girl, but kept her eyes fixed on the forest edge like a fox looking for mice, an Amazon in profile. Kept her hair too short for his tastes, but given her job, he could see the sense of short hair. Short or not, her hair was glossy and thick, and she had nice hips, a narrow waist, and an excellent pair. He wouldn't turn her down, even though she was older. Older could mean eager, and better funded, a private apartment, higher-grade rations—

He glanced away, squelching the fantasy, and met Orl's eyes. She stared straight at him like she could see through to his guts, even though she was using just the one eye. A shock of black hair covered the other—be the stereotype. Funny looking kid. Barring some feral tribes, this girl and Jemin were the whitest people he'd ever seen. Though Jemin was more pink than white. Their families must've picked up mutations along the road.

He whispered to the Chief. "There she is. I'll do my best to draw her out, but don't get your hopes up."

"Come on over, Orl. Patrol with Brandt and look for the things he can't see." The Chief's grin filled him with confidence. "Don't worry. You'll do fine. Just talk to her. If she doesn't reply, figure out a communication strategy. Apply it. If she senses anything, and she tells you, report the information. Simple."

Fair enough. He liked this Chief's style, low-key, no pressure, leaving room for his best judgment. He saluted, kicked himself for forgetting he was a civilian, waved Orl along, and sauntered across the paddock toward the fence.

Though Orl walked behind him, he could feel her, as if she put off a vibe, this witchy-girl with her bone-white skin, snarled hair, and ratty long skirt. Her shawl reminded him of moths, and he'd never liked moths, always clinging to the clothes hanging from the line. He'd unpin a pair of pants and end up with dusty wings flapping in his face. But flail out and kill one of 'em, and there it'd lie, tiny, fluff and dust, him feeling small and stupid for over-reacting. Plus, the other kids and the matron would laugh at his jumping around. Maybe it'd be better if Orl walked in front, so he could keep an eye on her.

Then she slipped past him, as if she'd read his mind, and shot ahead. Who knew she could move so fast? He jogged to catch up. "Don't touch the white tape. It'll stain your hands with glow dye." He warned her, even though she should already know, if she'd read the brief. If she could read.

But she wasn't paying attention. She stood at the fence, her hands lifted chest-height like she was feeling the air. Then she pointed toward two substantial tree trunks curved toward each other, creating an arch about two meters tall, a trailhead, maybe.

"Something interesting down that way?"

Orl flinched, then nodded, keeping her gaze fixed to the dark space between the silver smooth trunks. Lots of cover in that forest. A monster could be hiding behind every tree, if they were slim. "You see a ghost?"

She pointed again, her mouth fixed in a grim line.

"Not a ghost? Something else? Well. Whatever it is, we'll request access and inspect. Suppose we'll need lanterns because it's dark in that forest."

They walked the rest of the perimeter without event. The air finally warmed up, the trees were all sorts of colors, and the grass or hay or whatever had turned a golden brown. This prison farm reminded him of fall school camp. Though he doubted the Warden offered target shooting or archery. Still, this job was pretty cush.

His hands slipped into his pockets, and thoughts of a country stroll with a pretty girl on his arm crossed his mind. He could dream about the Amazon Chief, but as his commander, she was off limits. Way off limits. He'd never open that can of worms. Never. Well, maybe not never. But it'd be easier if he came across a local homestead and met the farmer's daughter. She might show him the haystack.

Something tugged on his sleeve. Ah. Orl. She pointed. He looked. Pointing and looking must be their "communication strategy." The Chief would be proud. But the view wasn't much, just a barn and a small paddock holding a flock of plump and healthy chickens.

"You hungry for roast chicken? I sure am."

She frowned and shook her head.

"You see something I can't?"

She nodded.

"Like ghosts?"

For the first time, she looked directly at him, her pale face earnest. She gave him a bigger nod this time, almost looking like a regular kid.

"Great! Show me where."

She led him to the barndoor and paced off a weedy square. Who'd haunt a shabby chicken pen? If he were a ghost, he'd haunt an old mansion or museum. A place with character. And why no sensation, like a chill or tingle, hairs raising on his arm? No surprise really, him being a reality-based person.

Brandt marked the rectangle's corner with brick scraps, while Orl paced the yard. Occasionally, she'd stop and listen...or something...or kind of gurgle, almost a rhythm to the sound, like bits of song sung through a garden hose. Oddly tuneful, but creepy and outside of his remit. He'd turn this info over to Slick Phil as fast as he could flip an egg. Which was fast.

A Curse on Fever and Fire

After breakfast, Jemin escaped the mess hall's clamor and bolted for his room. How enervating: all those close-packed crude prisoners making unpleasant jokes, and that snide apostate, Philip, insisting "a consciousness persisting as high frequency energy" differed from a soul. Imagine the blighted ideology that could produce such drivel. And the apostate had repeatedly punctuated his blasphemy with air quotes. How he loathed air quotes. Philip's air quotes were especially irritating. They weren't just cutesy or supercilious. No. They meant "this term or phrase, just spoken by Jemin Yoder, is a load of bull dung". So annoying, being incessantly undermined.

Communing with his chip in blessed silence, praise be, would be a relief. Every archive would reveal valuable clues, and he'd present them brilliantly to the team. Envisioning Chief Krause's face suffused with gratitude and awe, he rounded the dormitory's corner and *slam*. He smashed into a person.

Jemin stepped back. So terribly unpleasant, physical contact with strangers. "I beg your pardon."

But the clumsy transgressor just stood there in his shabby prison uniform, the collar frayed, wrists dangling from too short sleeves. Two others, similarly attired, cowered behind the first. With relief, he noted their scrawny necks and sunken cheeks. If they beat him, they wouldn't do much damage. All three boys had that not-fed-enough-protein-growing-up look that accompanied dental problems and a sparse head of hair, the look of those who lived outside the dominant culture: street urchins or the children of pariahs.

They doffed their hats, revealing close cropped fair hair—a flash of recognition. These convicts weren't thieves or thugs. They were kindred. But why would children of God lurk in a Common Folk's prison?

The lead man raised his palm and murmured, "Sorry to inconvenience you, brother." The lilt, cadence, and rounded vowels of the old tongue caressed Jemin's ears. It'd been so long. Not wishing the language to tangle his tongue, he took a moment before replying, keeping his voice low, lest someone overhear.

"No offense taken, jungerman. Greetings to you too."

He gestured toward a path between two buildings. "Turn here with us, sir, if you would. We seek words with you."

Jemin followed, curiosity trumping fear of discovery. He could always claim to be conducting interviews and attribute his facility with an archaic dialect to his chip; frightful how, after all these years among the Common Folk, lies flowed from his tongue like honey.

They led him into a washhouse, empty except for a row of chugging machines, sounding underpowered thanks to the scudding clouds and the chill.

He drew himself into a formal posture, accentuating his seniority. "Greetings. I go by Jemin." Better to hold back his family name; some brethren stewed over strife between clans for centuries.

The boy who'd greeted him held out his hand. "Malakai, good sir." He hardly looked the part of leader, with that thick rope hitching up his pants. Probably was just the most outgoing. Jemin gripped his hand firmly and shook, ignoring the risk of contagion in favor of tradition.

"What led you to this place of the Oppressor?" He waved a hand, vaguely indicating the farm and surrounds.

Malakai grinned. "Not crime, praise be. The Warden, a righteous heathen sent by the Lord, took us in when we left the wood."

"The wood here local?"

"Aye. Hereabouts."

"When did he find you?"

"Just a couple months back."

Merciful Heavens! They'd recently abandoned the settlement he'd meant to study! Jemin waited a beat for further explanation. None provided, he choked out a prompt. "These fine woods are far from their cities. Shame to leave them."

"Yep. Fine woods. Would be amongst them today, but first the disease passed through when we was kids, somebody making a mistake of trading with a stranger. Then the village burned, and only a few survived. We struggled for a time until the dead walkers started stumbling 'round the village at night."

"Dead walkers? You mean the monsters Warden Honing complains of?"

"Yes, sir. Those things. They aren't right."

Of course the monsters weren't right. No monsters were right. Nothing was right. That village had been ripe for study, a private project to make this mission and all his recent choices bearable. And this boy was telling him he'd missed an intellectual peach by a matter of months? A curse on fever, fire, and all forms of devastation.

He glanced about, trying to latch onto anything that'd explain this disaster. Nothing here, just a mop and bucket sitting in a dreary prison wash house. An urge to crush the bucket with his foot and scream in frustration flooded him. Instead, he clenched his hands. The secular majority always expected the faithful to respond with heedless passion, but he'd moved beyond their stereotypes. He was an expert at burying impulses in intellectual rigor. Acting as natural as possible, he slipped his fists into his pockets, but his heart still slammed in his ears.

"So the entire village cleared out?"

The boys exchanged nervous glances. "One stubborn oldster refused to come with us, thinking we'd lost the way, but we ain't. We just couldn't make it, and them ghouls was the last straw. We tried wardings and prayer but finally had to move on. The Lord don't want us killed by ghouls, do he?"

Jemin withstood a wave of nausea, but the youth also looked stricken. He groped for pity, but the boys should've kept to the village and stayed a unique and isolated study population. Now they were nothing but prisoners. And what did Malakai mean by wardings? Had the village strayed from the Word? He bristled at the idea. But harsh judgment would drive these boys away, and he needed information. A kindly elder would offer words of comfort, even if those words were lies or undeserved.

"No. Our merciful Father wouldn't ask you to die in the woods. You did right."

Relief washed over Malakai's face, and talk poured out of his mouth. "The Lord sent you and those governmentals to stop those unholy risings. We thank you and wish you God's speed. We're trapped here by those ghouls, and they's interfering with the harvest. And the way these godless farm, all higgle-piggle, by mid-winter, we'll be without enough to eat, and they won't let us loose to hunt. We sought you out, our brother, because we know something of them undead and wanted to tell you. In case it helps." He gestured at the room: baskets of dirty linen and supply shelves. "But private-like, in case you travel quietly."

"I always travel quietly. I don't need their eye on me." Not to mention Jemin Yoder, historian, had a career which would evaporate were it known he was "feral." And substantial chip-debt, a Common Folk curse these villagers wouldn't understand.

"Warden Honing told us to lay low and avoid the faith-haters." Malakai glanced at his shoes, looking sheepish. "The Lord travels with us, but no sense in getting beaten to death."

Malakai and Jemin sought proof of secrets well-kept in each other's eyes. Secrets weren't a problem. Jemin knew secrets. For years, he'd calculated what to say and what to hold back. Here he stood, doing the same with his own kind. He fished for a believable story to answer the question: what's one of The Fold doing on a governmental team? The best lies contained scattered grains of veracity.

"I'm practiced at holding my tongue. My kin died in the first wave, and the State took me in. Kept myself to myself, and now I work with them when my faith allows, solving problems outside the city, where their know-how peters out. Like these undead disturbing the farm workers."

He paused, leaving the partial truth hanging in the air, like an open window waiting for a pie to be placed on the sill. One boy rubbed the floor with the toe of his boot, his withered arm hanging uselessly from his left sleeve. "Old Cain says the undead came from over the ridge."

"He's got the sight; he do," lisped the third.

The "sight" reminded Jemin of Philip's pagan talk of ghosts and energy vibrations. More evidence the boy's settlement had drifted from the Word. "Who's got the sight? You, young fella, or the oldster back in the village?"

Malakai laughed. "Not Brennan, here. No. Grandfather Cain who hears and sees at a distance, even though he don't see with his eyes too good anymore. When them ghouls first started their waving and dancing, he sniffed the air then laid his ear on the ground and listened. Time passed slow, then he stood and pointed with his cane to the breeding ground of that great evil. So, we traveled right quick in the *opposite* direction, met up with the Warden, and came to this farm."

"Don't blame you," he said, though he absolutely blamed them. "Food isn't bad."

"Yep. The food's right fine. The Lord blessed us when he shepherded us here." Malakai clasped his hands in the way of gratitude. "Warden Honing was walking the track the very day we left the mountain. He concealed us, as Jebodah was concealed from the Magadha kings, and hid our secrets from the other trainees." The lisping boy held a hand over his mouth as he spoke, as if hiding a cleft lip or palate. Jemin bore most of The Fold's usual physical stigmata; the light complexion, short stature, and blue eyes spaced too far apart and hidden behind

45

thick glasses. No surprise this trio had recognized him as one of their own. But the good Lord had spared him a blighting that broadcast "too many generations born of too few mothers." Of course, radiation poisoning might account for these boys' defects.

The fellow with the palsied arm piped up. "He gave us clothes and told us to 'fit in' until we decide what to do."

Decide what to do? Ah. The conversation was meant to be an exchange: information for advice. But young men welcome unsolicited advice as enthusiastically as a chicken traipses through a fox's den. He waited for one of them to ask.

Malakai shuffled his feet and looked askance. "We ain't sure what to do, exactly. Adel here says 'no' to their halfway house. Brennan and I are unsure." He paused; his eyes fixed on Jemin's face.

That look was the asking. But Jemin, having lived an unhappy life betwixt and between, felt uniquely unqualified to give advice. He wasn't a social worker. All he could do was report a version of his own experience; they'd have to decide for themselves.

"You boys brought up in the Word?"

They nodded, appearing earnest.

"Alright then. Best to let the Warden guide you to understanding social workers; I bet he knows a few. Without papers or family, they'll place you in a shelter. Most of the Common Folk have never met one of The Fold, so they won't know you by sight. If you keep your tongues still, the others won't mark you. And plenty of them's touched by contamination, so your deformities won't give you away." Adel flinched; had he used the wrong word? "Even if you give yourself away, don't believe your old Auntie's tales; they won't feed you to the lions, or anything." The kids would mostly pretend they didn't exist until a bully decided it was time for a thrashing. "But start preaching and you'll land in re-education, subject to lessons about their ways. Earnestly taught lessons about science and rational thought, explaining how our beliefs are foolish and dangerous."

The lisper looked close to tears, and rightfully so. This conversation brought back years of faintly cloaked disdain, polite curiosity tinged with amusement or pity, and endless well-meaning questions that left him feeling like a laboratory animal, a frog pickled in holy wine. Those cursed lessons had sparked a search for truth that'd eventually shackled him to InfoCorp. He would've been better off as a bricklayer.

46

Feeling like a fraud—giving comfort never felt natural—he placed a hand on the fellow's shoulder. "You don't want to suffer through lessons, *and*, in re-education, you won't learn enough to survive amongst the Common Folk. Best to stay quiet, take the mainstream classes, and learn a trade. Many of your classmates will be inebriates, disrespectful, or temperamentally unfit for work, giving you an advantage. Keep to yourselves, and you can live quietly amongst them and follow the Word in private; I'm living testament to that fact."

More or less.

A moment passed. Given their faces, his optimistic portrait of their future hadn't gone down well.

Adel tucked his lame arm into his coveralls, as if foreseeing cruel comments and lost opportunities. "Sounds like a lonely road, praying alone, no fellowship or family. Any more of our folk living outside the Commons?"

Only degraded refugees, mired in liquor and drugs, women-folk and kinder terrorized or for sale, false prophets entertaining visitors with all kinds of superstitious rubbish passed off as the Word. He inhaled deeply.

"I've not found a village peopled by the Godly. If you travel far enough, you may. But be careful of those calling themselves The Fold. Hold your judgment while you lay your eye on them. Deeds reveal the truth of people, not words. If you find yourselves amongst the godless, keep quiet, keep your faith, and move on."

The boys looked grim, so he drew the conversation to happier matters like the common room's fireplace, buckwheat groats, and apples. Eventually, they were joking about the prison men's clumsy ways with tools and crops, and the bold and whorish convict women. Every word rang precious, this outpost of the modern world as viewed by the surviving members of a sect that'd lived separate from the mainstream for over five hundred years. And these three youths were the nearest to kin he'd encountered since his sister's death all those years ago. He'd need to interview them later, in depth.

When the patter tapered off, Jemin asked after their village's exact location. That old man was an invaluable source, both for his private studies and for the mission. He'd hike to that village alone if he had to. And he'd better move fast because ailing and possibly demented "Grandfather Cain" had been alone on that mountain for at least a month. Only God's grace could've kept the man alive.

47

"A costume?"

Beatrice Chou's bead hard eyes couldn't stay still as she answered Philip's question. "That's right, a three-cornered hat and an officer-style jacket, all raggedy but looked like it'd been fancy once. Fringes on the shoulders, and everything. The water came up to its waist, so I couldn't tell you about the pants."

Her eyes flitted to Agnet, to the ceiling, to Philip, to the wall.

"What happened next?"

"Lincold ran over; he was brave, but his eyes weren't sharp. He didn't stop, despite my yelling, until he was too close, then he must've noticed how wrong it was, because he backed up a step. But it grabbed hold of his leg. He hollered, tried to wrench free, then clutched his chest, moaned, and toppled into the lake." The woman's close-set features squinched up even tighter, and she heaved a sob. "That thing dragged 'im under. So I ran. I'm not proud of it, but I ran."

Agnet leaned across the cafeteria table and squeezed the woman's callused hand. "We're not here to blame or shame you. It's natural to run from that kind of..." *No, don't use horror, too intense a word.* "...situation."

"You couldn't have done much, given the circumstances. Other than getting yourself killed." Philip filled the prisoner's—trainee's—cup with tea. Hopefully, she could sip past the trauma and not fall to pieces like the last interviewee.

While Bea composed herself, Agnet jotted a few notes about the interviews, a parade of far-fetched tales, body odor, dingy overalls, fear, and attempted manipulation. The visitations had a pattern: people in twos or threes respond to what appears to be an oddly dressed child waving or gesturing. Curious or trying to help, they take a closer look, then recoil in terror, and run like mad. Each encounter happened near the settlement's edge where farm met forest and mostly at dusk, tired people glimpsing something in low light. Unfortunate Lincold was the only fatality.

Bea, a minor black-marketeer serving her time in the compound's machine shop and thankfully the last witness, idly warmed her hands on the cup while gazing at Philip's handsome face. He artfully deflected her interest, so she hit him up for a sick note, instead. He politely obliged, and she left with a wink.

Agnet gathered her papers and tapped the edges straight. "In short, manifestations in a narrow geographic radius, the uh—perpetrators not particularly aggressive, but horrifying, and capable of inducing lasting fear. Do you buy the trainees' story?"

"I didn't pick up dissembling."

"What about Bea's testimony? Was wondering about those darting eyes."

Philip shrugged. "The chest clutching suggests Lincold suffered a heart attack, possibly brought on by the shock of seeing that monster up close. I'd bet he died of a combination of natural and very unnatural causes. Regardless, seems Lincold's death was enough to scuttle the harvest."

"You're sure Bea didn't shove him in?"

"Positive. She was speaking her truth. But 'pulling Lincold under' might be an embellishment. Have a feeling she sprinted off the moment he fell and believes she should've tried to save him."

"I got the same vibe. Welp. The prisoner's stories are consistent though they could be rehearsed."

"What'd be the point of making up stories?"

"To skip out of work, I suppose."

"Makes sense until you consider they survive off of this farm's produce."

She tapped her pencil. "You're right. Who wouldn't harvest those apples if crumple was at stake. So, let's take the prisoners at their word. They're seeing creatures of some sort and barring a growth hormone deficient maniac with a severe skin condition, disintegrating clothes, and diving gear, we've excluded human culprits. Then what are they seeing: animals, spooks, or monsters?"

"Not spooks, if by spooks you mean ghosts. Ghosts rarely engage with solid matter."

"What would the rare instance look like?"

"A marble rolling off a desk, a puff of frigid air. Grabbing and pulling are well beyond a ghost's abilities. Honestly? Ghosts are usually too self-absorbed to notice the living. But don't tell Brandt. I wouldn't want to disappoint him."

They shared a laugh.

Agnet said, "He'll recover because we're back at monsters. And he claims to be a monsters man; ghosts are only a sudden enthusiasm. You have any experience with monsters?"

"Just the human kind."

"Me too. What about this farm? You sense anything out of the ordinary?"

He set his face and put out his feelers, or whatever they did, these perceivers. Must be a nightmare, being exposed to so much weirdness. Five minutes ticked by. Agnet sipped what the facility passed off as tea, boiled bark and sticks, most likely. Every assignment came with its own version of tea and/or coffee. The variety was staggering, and, having tasted neither beverage in its original form, she was game to try them all. The farm's tea wasn't bad.

Philip returned to local reality with a sharp shake of his head. "I'm picking up a buzzing or humming sensation with an undercurrent that makes me feel...observed. Started when we landed, but I can't pinpoint the source. Should be around the farm, since my range isn't enormous; I'm more a face-to-face asset. But the sensation seems familiar, sort of déjà vu. He paused and drummed his fingers, as if considering options. "But déjà vu is a known lacuna side effect."

"Lacuna?"

He looked startled. "Yes? Wasn't the procedure mentioned in my file?"

"No! How recent?"

"Not entirely sure—sometime between mid-summer and early fall."

She stared at him, realized her jaw had dropped, and snapped it shut. "What the slobbering pup are you doing here?"

Philip sighed, his expression settling into persecuted-employee mode, a look she knew well. "I don't know. Me being on mission is idiotic, but I couldn't turn down the assignment. Bills for the lacuna started rolling in, and the mission was,"—finger quotes—"urgent. The apple harvest, after all. And I was the only adequately qualified perceiver available, blah, blah, blah. Sounded like purest bull dung to me, but here I am."

"Am I hearing right? NeuroCorp bills you for lacuna surgery? Isn't it a cure for mission induced trauma, as in work-related injury?"

He fumbled with his tea, opened, then shut his mouth, as if grappling for a response. Had it never occurred to him that NeuroCorp should cover a blipping lacuna?

No wonder he seemed vague and depressed, flung out on mission right after surgery. Snakes alive, Human Resources must be losing their collective minds.

She toyed with the idea of commiserating—her current psychological slag heap was as high as his—but leaders didn't over-share, especially with unfamiliar associates. "You should be home recuperating, so don't strain yourself or hide symptoms, no matter how steep your bills are. Alright?"

He pressed his lips together, probably trying to control their trembling, then said, "Don't worry. I'll be fine. I'm carrying medication that should squelch any serious sequelae. And I'm hoping the humming comes from Orl. It might be related to that funny dancing or mumbling she does. That'd mean her chip is live and repairable." He inspected the tabletop, not meeting her eye.

"What else about Orl? Don't hold back on me."

His grimace suggested an unpleasant taste had spread across his tongue. "I've been mulling it over since she squawked at that owl. NeuroCorp recruits perceivers from State Home Services, selecting certain types: kids with high emotional IQ, introverts, intuitive types, weird kids, 'different' kids, outsiders. But according to unofficial news passing through the perceiver community—so please don't quote me—they've homed in on kids with communication difficulties, abnormal affects, cognitive processing dysfunction, aberrant theories of mind, in short kids well past 'different,' kids with real problems for whom the other option is institutionalization."

"So Orl doesn't talk because she's autistic or something?"

"Well, maybe, but they might've stripped her vocal cords."

His words zapped her spine straight, as if they carried an electrical charge. "Excuse me?"

"Apparently, NeuroCorp mutes these kids to force communication through experimental chips. After hearing Orl squawk twice, first time was just after we landed, I realized she might not be capable of speech." He dropped that bomb and kept talking, visibly struggling to maintain a conversational tone while she struggled to pay attention because fury threatened to blow off her scalp. "Anyway, brutal training and social isolation would leave a person pretty odd."

"I'll say." Her cheeks burned like toast over a high flame. She'd had a private laugh each time Orl had croaked. How immature and insensitive can a person be?

Philip squirmed in his seat, looking miserable as he worked to regain his urbane mask. "Yeah, I know, barbaric. And people say her cohort is a crap shoot. Some can't function but some display amazing talent. So, I have no idea how she'll perform."

"So now NeuroCorp mutilates at-risk kids? Do they also bill them for the privilege?"

His chin dipped, conceding reluctantly.

"And if Orl can't function, because she's mental—mentally different—how will she pay off her chip?"

He gazed off, his eyes flat and blank. "We probably don't want to know."

Suddenly far too warm, she ripped off her jacket. NeuroCorp had always given her the creeps, and her instincts had been dead on. Serve them right if a rogue perceiver stomped in there and blew those sick bastards to dust. "I think we owe her a chance."

"Why?" He'd recovered his feigned indifference, but Agnet saw through to his fear. How would NeuroCorp treat *him* if he couldn't pay off *his* chip?

"Because that's what we do. Because she's one of the team. Because we need to preserve our humanity. At least that's how I see it." And to stick it to NeuroCorp, which could dissolve in a heap of stinking ostrich poop, as far as she was concerned.

For a long moment, Philip didn't respond. He just sat, arms folded, absently tapping a rhythm on his bicep with one finger. Then he looked her straight in the eye. "Don't take on NeuroCorp; they're completely amoral. Cross them once, and they'll annihilate you."

His intensity took her aback, but he was right to calm her down. She could easily cross a line and end up battling NeuroCorp, the government's most feared corporate body. And that battle would've had nothing to do with monsters, apples, or her career. Hadn't she thought "let's take a quick look for captives" before they'd bumbled into that cult's shrine? Helping the weak, holding out a hand to the marginal, trying to do good: those impulses were her sticky trap, and brother was she ever tired of being a fly, an impulsive fly prone to righteous indignation. But she didn't want to end up a spider, either.

"Relax. I'm only helping one girl. But honestly, I'd hoped her troubles were teenage drama."

Philip's face softened. "Can't exclude a component of teen drama."

"Can you deal with teen drama? Because it's not my area of expertise."

He lifted an eyebrow. Apparently, teens weren't his strong suit either.

"Welp. NeuroCorp must know she has problems, and their rep didn't sound worried about this mission. Believe he suspected mass hysteria or something similar. Let's hope hysteria is what we've got. If so, we should have time to straighten her out and save the apples. Just continue to draw her out, include her in trivial tasks, and converse with her even if she doesn't respond. Are you game?"

He cracked a portrait-worthy smile. "Absolutely."

A Confidential Source

While Agnet and Philip jotted their interview summaries, the kitchen crew started their shift. Pots and pans clattered, and a blender whirred. The sounds of a busy kitchen always soothed her. Unless she was cooking.

The rest of the team dribbled in and seated themselves around the table. At her request, Jemin led the report. He blushed like a sixteen-year-old handed a rose then stammered. "A confidential source—um—informed me about—um—a witness."

An amazed look flashed across Philip's face. "Confidential source? Are you under the impression you're something other than a government agent? What? A doctor? A lawyer?"

The pink on Jemin's cheeks brightened to red. "No, but—"

"A source! Great. Who?" Brandt slapped Jemin's shoulder, a friendly gesture, but the historian's glasses dropped into his lap. He reset the spectacles on his nose while Brandt apologized. Boy, those lenses were thick; he must have spent his entire childhood in a subterranean room, nose in book.

"An elderly man living in the woods—"

"A feral? I know my ferals. Worked the border down South." Brandt's eyes glowed with enthusiasm. Every one of his days must be a grand adventure. "May have to take that testimony with a grain of salt. "Some ferals are full of moonshine, depend—" He bit off the sentence, side-eyed Jemin, and grinned. "No offense."

Jemin pursed his lips. "If you know your ferals, then you realize the term covers many groups, each group with a specific name, depending on ethnicity, location, or culture. And each individual "feral" varies, depending on life history and temperament. Hence, we won't be able to gauge the witness's value until we interview him." Having finished lecturing Brandt, he turned to Agnet. "The village is also of historic significance. You must understand, the last recorded contact was about seventy years ago."

"Or maybe he thinks he's a journalist." Philip lobbed the comment to her gently, as if tossing a peach.

She rested her chin on the heel of her hand. Worst team ever without a doubt, clueless, traumatized, defective... "Jemin. Great lead, really. Thanks tons. But reveal your source. We're a team here."

The historian leaned forward, twisting a pencil in his finger, and whispered, "I...I can't. Really. To the point, I debated mentioning the witness at all. Just know that the source means no harm and has done no wrong."

"Twenty questions?" asked Brandt. "Are we talking, inmate?"

Philip snorted.

Worst team ever.

"No. The source isn't a pris—trainee, exactly, but a person under the Warden's protection. Even so, the source's position is precarious; I don't wish to compromise anybody's safety or privacy. Oh, and the source arrived this summer, perhaps explaining the wobble Philip noted in the Warden's testimony, his lie about 'no other people passing through.' He was probably protecting the source's privacy. It's delicate. Trust me. And divulging the source's exact identity wouldn't add anything."

Agnet pinched her forehead. "Well, no. *It would add something*, but I'll let this go for now, so we can concentrate on the witness."

"We should talk to that guy pronto."

Thanks, Brandt brilliant. "So may I ask, 'witness to what'?"

"The witness has pinpointed the source. Uh. I don't mean my source, but where the monsters come from. Originate. The monsters. I mean, the witness knows where the monsters originate."

A brief silence fell. Philip's expression bespoke skeptical. Orl hid beneath her hood, possibly napping. Jemin, all jitters, dabbed his forehead with his sleeve.

Brandt blurted. "We definitely have to talk to this guy."

Thanks again, Brandt. "Agreed. You say he's in the woods? Where exactly?"

"Yes, the woods." Jemin opened his rag book to a hand-drawn map. "In a settlement down a trail and halfway up the ridge."

Brandt signaled to Orl. "Maybe this trail is the alley you showed me."

Orl's hood bobbed assent.

He added to the team, "South-west of the compound, trees arch over a shadowy trail. Oo-we, it's spooky, but she says there's something interesting that way."

"A shadowy trail?"

"Yes, ma'am."

A spooky, shadowy trail? Good grief. She fished the regional map from her bag and compared it to Jemin's sketch. "A village? There? How the heck is anybody living there?"

Jemin drew in his chin, as if affronted or perplexed. "Probably hunting, collecting nuts and seeds, growing vegetables, and dairy, probably goats."

"No! I mean the contamination." She searched the map for a bow-shaped curve of river and tapped the location with her finger. "The Riverbend ruins are here, in the valley right below your village. Apparently, the perfect site for a nuclear plant, until it blew."

He flushed again. "I wasn't aware. You told me to search but stay recent, so I focused on the last fifty years."

"I'm not angry. I'm stunned. Who could survive that level of exposure?"

"Marginalized people are used to living on marginal land," the historian said, looking prim.

Philip leaned back and crossed his arms. "And why should we non-marginal people hike through an exclusion zone, putting ourselves at risk, on the word of your dubious source?"

Jemin spluttered. "That village has been thoroughly documented! I double-checked. It's there. It's always been there, witness or not. Isolated sure, but real as the nose on your face."

Philip narrowed his eyes. "You're quite interested in isolated cultures. So perhaps you invented the 'secret source' to justify a visit."

The ragbook in Jemin's hands jumped back and forth like a rabbit stuffed in a pillowcase.

Brandt leaned in, ending Jemin and Philip's deadlocked staring contest. "Won't know 'till we suit up and go look. Shouldn't be a big deal."

"I agree. That village is only a day hike away." To change the subject, Agnet asked the flustered little historian, "Did your search turn up anything interesting?"

He opened his top collar button and flipped the pages of his ragbook. "I looked for likely scenarios, such as a cold-blooded organization trying to run the farmers off the land for the usual unimaginative motives: profit and power. I found talk of AgroCorp co-opting the farm, improving efficiency, trialing a topsoil removal process, permanently doming the valley as a precaution, all their plans sounding impractical and unpopular, no surprise considering what happened down South with domed agriculture. But don't quote me." He shot Philip a snarky look. "I also found feasibility reports for extracting mineral resources from these mountains using robotic assets left over from the asteroid debacle. EarthCorp's desperate to make use of those robots somehow, but that talk was some years back. The project must have quietly failed."

Brandt asked, "How about real estate? Any dirty development deals in the offing?"

Worst. Team. Ever. Except for that eye roll, well done Philip, excellent performance, ten out of ten. "Look around, Brandt. Isolated, minimal local industry, no attractions, *and surrounded by an exclusion zone.* Who would live here?"

"And the farm's a media darling. Any number of fluff pieces discuss the bracing effects of the countryside on a person's character. In short, I doubt we're looking at a corporate scheme to take the farm." Jemin folded up his notes and blushed again. The man changed color quicker than a boiling shrimp. Why? Was he hiding anything else?

"Alright. Let's investigate Jemin's lead. Pack for a day in a contaminated zone with potential undesirables, alive and undead. But before we leave, Orl and Philip, you two need to sync up."

Philip's neck apple bobbled. Orl stared at her lap.

"Don't worry, my friend. I'm sure she likes you." Brandt leaned his head so he could peer into Orl's hood. "You like him, don't you Orl?" She hunched and pulled down the hood.

Philip radiated embarrassment. Good. Let him squirm. His mortification might spur him into action. And she needed two functioning perceivers or their options in the field were limited. Splitting up, for example, would be impossible.

"What's your plan?" she asked him.

He coughed into his fist, then spent a long moment dabbing his lips, an obvious stall.

"Excuse me, sir." Brandt saluted, caught the reflex, and acted like he'd been raising his hand. "You and Orl could interrogate the ghosts she found."

Agnet's eyebrows crept up her forehead.

Philip shot her a despairing look. "Well. Ghosts aren't usually knowledgeable or helpful, but we could clear them off."

"What for?" asked Brandt. "They got here first."

"True." Philip shrugged. "But, on the rare occasion a ghost becomes bothersome or just out of pity, we help them along on their...journey. Better for them, better for everyone, if they move on."

"Good beans! I'm sure the Warden will be thrilled," said Agnet.

Philip's eyes widened. "No. Don't tell him or anybody else. Please."

Brant slapped Philip on the back, a bit too hard, given Philip's gasp. "Orl knows exactly where the ghosts are; I'll bet she's an expert at ghosts. And who knows? Maybe one will give us a clue about those monsters. Can I watch you run them off?"

Philip tightened the corners of his mouth. She couldn't tell if he was grimacing or trying not to laugh. "Um. No. Really. Would be better, just Orl and me, so we can...focus. Sorry. And no record, no mention, here or back at Central, now or ever. Seriously, NeuroCorp doesn't condone...uh...ghost hunting."

One by one, Agnet locked eyes with each team member. "Orl and Philip need to integrate, and these ghosts provide them opportunity to practice. NeuroCorp may disapprove, but sometimes you've got to step out of bounds for the good of the team. Anybody got a problem?"

Nobody said a word.

"We agreed?"

A round of "yeses" and a head bob from Orl.

The Door Ahead Your Only Friend

The night had fallen clear and cold. A gibbous moon cast shadows across the old graveyard, a nondescript rectangle of dirt. Philip placed the lantern on a fence post. "The dead will stand out better if we aim the light away."

Silence.

Her communication issues had their pluses; usually, partner mind-noise drove him up a tree; he much preferred to work solo, doing what he knew: simple work, interviews, hostage negotiation, conflict resolution, sifting dialog for emotional undercurrents, lies, motivations, and weaknesses. But here he was—out in the cold, battling post-lacuna doldrums and an eerie watched feeling, while chasing ghosts with a recalcitrant teen.

And right now, Gervais, the worst last-minute apartment sitter imaginable, was warm, feet up on his upholstered furniture, probably running the laundry of a dozen lovers, billing them while charging the expense to his laundry card. By mission's end, Philip would be bankrupt, thanks to laundry fees and detergent expenses, and all the house plants would be dead.

Orl stood staring at him, looking fey if not crazy, a dirty mop wrapped in a bulky winter coat. She folded her arms, as if impatient.

So, he hiked up the frequency on his chip and set it to auto-focus. Fuzzy gray smears gradually resolved into dimly glowing semi-transparent figures, the lay of the graves made obvious by the positions of the grave-clingers. Pathetic, those that tethered themselves to their own remains. Why not lurk some place with emotional resonance: a home, a park bench, or even a workplace? Why spend centuries tethered to one's own moldering corpse? Fortunately, grave clingers often asked the same question, once shown their true situation. If everything went to plan, he and Orl would bond over ghost hunting and guarding NeuroCorp's dirty little secret.

Why wait?

Admittedly, he was stalling. He'd been avoiding ghosts as part of his strategy to live until forty. And the Door's pull had been strong last time he'd popped a ghost. When had that been? Maybe five years ago. He was much weaker now, practically hanging by a thread. Could he withstand the temptation to erase thirty-two years of crap with one step? Small wonder NeuroCorp discouraged interacting with ghosts; losing a chip was expensive.

Then stand Back.

The girl's youth and stubbornness would defend her; look at her, tapping her fingers on her forearm like he was wasting her time. He could stand back, sprint and tackle her if she ran for the Door. He wouldn't jump through while saving someone else. Would he?

It's COLD!

He stamped his feet to kick start some circulation. Sure was cold. Might as well get busy. He surveyed the graveyard's blurry ghosts, all long-term leaseholders. One ancient relic wasn't much more than a translucent energy smear. The one more recent arrival, crisp and bright, paced by the barn. Best to start with the blurred crew.

"So, tune your chip's visuals up-frequency until the remnants come into focus."

He stood by Orl and pointed out a few examples. She donned a pitying expression and nodded. Good thing she knew everything already, being eighteen. But at least she'd responded to him, after a fashion.

"Why, why, why?" chanted an indistinct specter trudging a small circle around its grave, hands clutching a translucent halo of white hair.

"Go ahead. Communicate with that one like you'd communicate with me. If you were communicating. Here, I'll show you." She rolled her eyes, so adolescent. Philip ignored her and shot his reply directly at the ghost.

Why not?

Not a good Question.

True. He'd learned not to ask questions of ghosts. But it'd been the best he could do while cold, irritable, and being disrespected by a twerp he was trying to help.

Orl tugged on his sleeve and shook her head—as if communicating! Not verbal communication, but a sleeve tug was better than an eye roll. Had she heard his snarky question to the ghost and disapproved?

"If you have a better approach, don't let me stop you."

She stalked off and got right down to business. His chip picked up every transmission, as if their communication problem had been a frequency mismatch. Would've been nice if Orl's dossier had mentioned the correct setting, but how could he miss something so simple? He must truly be a mess.

The girl moved from ghost to ghost like a pro. Her messages: the answer, your beloved, the truth, whatever, is through that Door, were to the point, but not unkind. Doors materialized and blinked out so quickly he didn't feel the pull. The heavily degraded ghost even vanished spontaneously, possibly following the example of its fellows. Not bad work. Maybe her cohort snuck off during recess to the local bomb shelters and popped ghosts for kicks and giggles.

Only two remained. That rotund spook by the fence was probably a hedonist clinger, at worst evil-lite, most likely just irritating. But Orl, coming straight from a NeuroCorp training facility, would know little of earthly pleasures, and shooing this one through the Door might present a challenge. Time to mentor.

He ambled over and pointed out the oldster. "Eyeballing that guy, I'd guess he's attached to pleasures of the flesh: food, drink, and carnal desires, so he's clinging to his body. Body-clingers can be tenacious because they crave what's here on Earth. So, passing through won't solve their problem. But his era may help you out. The waistcoat, breeches, and stockings date Tweedle-dum to the 1700s when the dominant religion promised an earth-like paradise after death. Since body-clingers are all about paradise, promising paradise is an option."

She slashed the air with her hand, and *BAM*, an explosion of needles, prickled his skin and set his teeth on edge. Her transmission, *NO LIES*, arrived like a tsunami. Great to receive a direct communication, but if she delivered every thought like a lightning strike, chatting with Orl wouldn't hold much appeal. So irresponsible, over-chipping a kid that age.

A repeat, *no lies* came at lower voltage.

He messaged back. *Thanks for dialing it down. That first 'no lies' singed my arm hair.* He waited for a laugh, but she continued to stare, the one eye glowering out from behind her ratty hair, the female adolescent incarnation of Odin. Just needed the raven on her shoulder. He soldiered on. *I'm glad your transmissions are coming through. What fixed the problem?*

I found you.

Well...good. Whatever "found" meant. *So you don't like lies. Neither do I, most of the time. But I'd talk out of both sides of my mouth, nose, and ears to blink out a body-clinger. And paradise is your best bet because body-clingers of his era often fear reprisal for sin in an anti-paradise. But go ahead, try a 'no lies' strategy and see what happens.*

She approached the remnant, now tapping virtual leaf into his pipe. He "lit up", took a deep inhale, then blew nothing out into the chill night air. With a flourish of his pipe, he proclaimed to the desolate yard.

Is it not natural for a prosperous man to indulge? Are not the fruits of our labors a bulwark against arduous toil? Do not these pleasures distract us from sin's siren song?

Yep. A body-clinger, the glutton variety, fear of reprisal subspecies. The vain were easier. One clear-eyed peek at their rotting remains, and *poof*, off they'd go.

The ghost rattled on. *Fine wine, a velvet chair, a waft of French perfume, these things distinguish us from lowly beasts.*

Ugh. To pop this pompous ass, he'd spout lies like a fly spews a brood of hungry larvae: forty virgins, harp slinging angels, bosomy Valkyries serving pitchers of mead—anything to shut the specter up. Nothing rankled him more than the past's self-satisfied, self-important gentry: access to imports, holding slaves, owning property. Hard to listen to their complaints after living on yeast cake for a month.

But the unworthy, Injured and Alone seek to find themselves Outside. They are Lost.

Well, true... Honestly, his mind must be wandering, one lateral thought after the other, this last hitting too close to the bone. But who didn't prowl around for distraction? No harm, if one avoids the extremes...

He should've sucked on a MindEase before heading out.

Fortunately, Orl launched into a superb distraction. *Nothing fancy here,* she told Old Fatty. *Just a square of dirt in a prison yard.* Her arms spread wide, indicating the mundane surroundings the ghost had been ignoring for hundreds of years.

The specter tucked his chin, as if affronted. *Do you take me for a fool, Mistress? This fecund orchard is no prison yard. Nay, I stand in the blossom bedecked bosom of nature's bounty.*

And he was correct, in his way. Ghosts, trapped in their own dream, missed or misinterpreted most new stimuli.

You're standing in a Graveyard in the moonlight.

You sully my orchard with the appellation "graveyard"? He took an indignant puff off his semi-translucent pipe.

Orl shrugged. *No smoke. Cold air. Hollow chest.*

He pressed a hand to his chest. *Come now. Do not hoax me, here in the company of fine friends.*

A dog yipped from the barn, probably reacting to the loudmouthed specter. Dogs never took to ghosts. And in life, this man would never have taken to a deeply pigmented, non-binary unbeliever like Philip Spool.

Hmm.

If he could recall the era-appropriate slurs, he could weaponize the ghost's prejudice. But he drew a blank. It'd been one memory slip after the other, lately. His chip and the lacunae must be slowly eroding his cortex.

Wait a moment.

Black.

The archaic term for dark skin was "black", and as one of the few who wasn't post-bottle-neck blah, he might pass as "black". Time to stir up discord.

Friends? You mean a dog, a witch, and a black man?

Sure, Orl wasn't exactly a witch, and maybe his own skin wasn't quite "black", but the specter took the bait. His face froze in a mask of horror, the expression confirming that Squire Tubby was not a member of his era's tolerant minority. He drew himself straight, then—wow—stretched to about three meters tall, becoming in the process haggard and gaunt, and wavered back and forth like a blighted reed.

"This move would terrify a civilian," said Philip, in case Orl was spooked. "But it's ghost-fear, a bewildered specter attempting to survey its surroundings. See his 'eyes' flicking from side to side? He's trying to take in information from his real-world surroundings. I hope he sees enough to penetrate his defenses."

Orl raised a pitying eyebrow, the pity clearly aimed at Philip's brief tutorial.

A Negro? The ghost wailed.

Ah, yes. The word was "Negro". But seemed "black" had hit the mark. Interesting that a pigment phobia would trump "witch". Philip would've bet on "witch".

Orl lifted her arms over her head, her hands drooping down, as if she were casting a spell.

Attend the painful truth,
All is dust and crumbled soot,
Your time on earth is at an end,
The Door ahead your only friend.

Her message blew like a chill wind and whipped the specter's pipe from his fingers. Brilliant! But how'd she do that? He'd never been able to affect a single hair on a ghost's head. Every touch or shove—the shove a cringe-worthy memory—had traversed empty air. Still, he loved the witch act. Very creative, shoring up "witch" and thereby "negro" with a "spell".

And—*pop*. Effective!

Fat-ghost abandoned this mortal coil with a sudden steep drop in barometric pressure. Philip cleared his ears. That'd been diverting, so much so that he wouldn't mention Orl's bit of theater came close to a lie.

I didn't like him. Orl glared up through her lashes. *And I'm not a witch.* The air crackled around her, somewhat negating her assertion.

He stepped away lest she zap him. "Well done, anyway. As you saw, ghosts often aren't the best people. So, I don't think you should worry about lying to—"

I don't like lies. She furrowed her brow. Yeesh. This girl was intense. Thankfully, she dropped the witch-arms.

"Alright. No lies. Don't be grumpy because you're doing great. Look. Just one left to free."

He pointed to Mr. Pacing-By-The-Barn whose outfit—an ill-fitting prison jumpsuit, a headscarf, and canvas shoes—confirmed a recent demise. Funny that Berg hadn't mentioned this death. As they moved closer, the ghost's muttering became distinct.

Going to kill the bastard. Squeeze his neck `til his eyes pop out. Then I'm gonna dig out those eyes and shove `em down his throat.

Ah, cheesits. A revenger. "Revenge is a powerful motivator, a kind of justice gone savage. But it tends to boomerang and smack people in the head, leaving behind ghostly roadkill. Same as the other outward focused emotions: anger, hate, lust, greed, and envy. Hot emotion raises the possibility of "hard evil" and real danger. Remember, a remnant this strong and fresh has options, including possession. So keep up your guard."

Seeming to agree, the dog inside the barn bayed and growled. Philip pulled Orl out of the ghost's range. She thanked him with a glare.

"First step, let's see if he's still sane."

He's sane.

"You can't be sure."

I hear him.

A long day, and she was telling him riddles. Philip tried to meet her eyes, but they shot left like marbles. Funny how kids toggle from arrogance to insecurity in a heartbeat. "You hear him? So what do you hear?"

Orl waved toward the prisoner. *It's all there at once if you listen. He wanted to back out. But they wouldn't let him.*

"Back out of what?"

Going somewhere to be in an experiment.

"As a test subject?"

Yes.

Odds were high, Orl could relate to the ghost's predicament. "You think our ghost deserves his revenge?"

Yes.

"We could offer to avenge him in exchange for exiting."

We can't lie.

"We won't lie, but let's be clear. We avenge him within the bounds of the law. No shoving eyes down anybody's throats, don't go avenging on your own, run any vengeance plan by me first, and until we have more information, keep this encounter to yourself. Murder begets murder. Alright?"

Orl nodded.

Had he just made a mute girl promise to keep a secret? He must be exhausted.

"Good. Then let's have a chat with Mr. Prison Ghost."

An hour later, warm, and sipping on a glass of brandy to smooth out the edges, Philip slid his rook down the board and waited for Berg to realize the game would be over in four moves. Two moves later, the Warden got the message.

"Oh. You beat me again." He tipped over his king, then swallowed a mouthful of whiskey. "You're much better than me at this game. Sorry I can't offer a challenge."

Philip leaned back in his chair. "No. You're good, and a lively match is always a pleasure." Especially since it'd been a weird couple of days, between Orl and that haunting presence, a presence he now knew wasn't his partner. She had an entirely different feel—more like electric eel crossed with pinecone. "You're playing better than last night."

"Benefit of taking on a stronger player, and tonight the alcohol's less strong. Must remember to stay away from that 'shine." Berg raised his glass and held Philip's eye a little longer than necessary. The man was flirting, a tempting proposition. But Brandt's oh-so-subtle "nudge, nudge, wink, wink", conveyed that the team assumed he was sleeping with the Warden. And sure, sex was a great distraction, his favorite hangover-free coping strategy, but how dare they typecast him. And why should he indulge their fantasies? Besides, he'd perform under par, thanks to post-lacuna malaise. As Gervais had so kindly pointed out, over and over.

No. This meeting was all business. Instinct told him Berg was a decent guy, but Philip needed answers to a few sticky questions he'd need to pose carefully.

Berg must've sensed hesitation because he straightened up and began resetting the chess board. Philip pulled a lip balm from his pocket and semi-discretely applied the ointment. It didn't hurt to keep Berg interested, but also the chill in the yard had dried him out. The temperature had dropped inside, too. Must be nighttime power conservation which translated to icy toes in bed, another reason to keep his bunking options open. He laid the lip balm on the table to serve as a reminder of sorts. "Heard tell of a small cemetery on the property? It's out that way." Philip indicated the general direction with a wave. "A chicken run between a barn and a paddock. The earliest burials predate the 1700s, so the grave markers must've disintegrated long ago."

Berg's eyebrows shot up in genuine surprise. "I know the yard you mean. Had no clue it was a graveyard. How'd you find it?"

"Our historian came across a mention in his archive." He'd need to remember to bring Jemin in on this lie. Hopefully, Jemin didn't have a problem with convenient lies in the service of a greater truth.

"Hmm. That's a surprise. The founder's records don't mention a graveyard. Suspect it's an old family plot. This land was in private hands for centuries, a large prosperous farm, then several smaller, not so prosperous farms. Wouldn't surprise me if several generations are buried on site. Later, when the region was more populous, they buried folks just over the river in a worship-house plot." He frowned. "That cemetery the home of our monster?"

Philip chuckled to divert serious consideration of the supernatural. The Warden's monsters—seen in daylight by normal people, no special senses or chips required—must have some rational explanation. "We inspected and nothing's disturbed. Seems folks are laying quiet in those graves."

Berg looked thoughtful for a moment. "Wonder if it's disrespectful, running chickens over folks at rest."

"No. People who are gone have no claim on the land. Life goes on."

"Well, maybe. 'Cept I have to twist some folk's arms to pen the chickens at dusk. When it's your turn, it's your turn. But a few complain that yard gives 'em the gooseflesh. I thought they were lazy, but maybe I was wrong. I'd appreciate your team keeping those burials quiet. Wouldn't want to lend credence to superstition."

A few of Berg's chicken-minders must have low-level perception; amazing, given the odds. "What happens these days, if somebody dies at the farm?"

"Any death is official business, so we notify the regional coroner and transport the remains to New Delphi. Their office documents cause so nobody's left wondering what happened. The family, if we can find one, can't ever afford transport fees, which are astronomical, given the refrigeration. So, the remains are utilized in the reforestation effort around Delphi. They're trying to counteract borer damage by planting resistant tree species. Our folk end up as plant food, is what I'm saying. Like you said, 'Life goes on.'"

Berg drew the circle of life sign in the air. "Course, we couldn't find Lincold's remains, which caused me a pile of paperwork. Come spring, he'll be feeding the tad—"

The candle guttered out, leaving "tadpoles" hanging in the air. Just as well. Any more talk of mortuary practices would make his interest seem excessive. And the verbal and sub-verbal information he'd gathered confirmed the Warden's ignorance of the barnyard's recent grave.

"Hang on. I'll find some matches" Berg stood and started patting down the top of a bureau while Philip's eyes adjusted. Strong moonlight through the window cast a wavering rectangle on the rough wooden floor. Shadow cloaked the room's corners, and indistinct shapes silently loomed blue and black against the walls. He knew the dark masses were furnishings covered with clothing and mysterious objects in states of partial repair, farming implements or some sort of hobby; Berg was not a tidy man. So why was he unsettled?

He shifted to limit his view to Berg's search. Turning off his perceiving would be such a pleasure, but his mind, restless and relentless, kept sending out feelers.

Nothing. Nothing is out there.

Tap. Tap.

"Somebody knocking?" muttered Berg. "Must be one of your crew, 'cause none of my people are bold enough to disturb me after dinner. Where's those dog-gone matches?"

Philip felt outside the door, then probed the hall, finding nothing either alive or dead. Nobody was knocking at the door. The hair rose on his arm.

Tap. Tap. Scritch.

Not the door, but—

A hiss, a flare, a hint of sulfur, and Berg lit the candle. "Got to reseal that cuss-blighted window again. First the candle blows out. Now the room's cold as the icehouse."

Tap. Tap. Scritch.

Berg hopped toward the door, covering an impressive distance in one move. "And that noise ain't coming from the door! That's coming from the floor!"

"Yep." Philip could sense it now, something stone cold, powdery, and highly disordered. Dust and mold. Something terribly...not alive but in motion. He shoved his chair from the table and joined Berg near the door.

"Dang, it's freezing all the sudden. Hope we ain't lost the apples in this snap. Please tell me we're hearing rats."

"Nope. Not rats." Philip outlined the shape's hazy edge. It recoiled momentarily, then *thunk*. The floor shook, and with a screech of nails, a short board popped up, leaving a two-centimeter gap. In the dim yellow candlelight, four long fingers grasped the floor. Adrenaline shot through Philip's belly like lightning.

Berg grabbed the back of Philip's jacket and yanked him to the door. "Don't be fooled. That ain't no kid."

"Too big for a kid, and busting through floorboards pretty much excludes—"

"Don't matter. I'm not big on dead things that move. Let's get out of here."

CRACK. An overly long arm burst through the floor, and they bolted into the hall. Berg locked his door, his face grim in the emergency exit tape's dim blue light. "Never thought I'd be locking something inside my room."

"A locked door won't matter, since it can access the crawlspace."

"I know. But locking the door gives me a little comfort." Berg frowned. "Steaming piles of poop! We can't have monsters creeping around, sneaking up on sleeping people. What're we going to do?"

What *were* they going to do?

Orl pushed between the two of them and pressed her ear against the door. He tuned his chip to the slightly higher frequency that optimized her signal. It picked up an energy field spreading from the places her fingertips met the wood and generated a visual representation for his benefit, a radiant field of blues and gold.

Philip turned to Berg. "Maybe wake everybody and gather them in the mess hall while Orl and I investigate the—um—phenomenon."

Berg eyed the bedraggled girl leaning against the door and raised an eyebrow. "Alright but be careful. Those things aren't only disgusting, they're lethal. Don't get surrounded. Run at the first sign of trouble. Second sign gonna be too late." Then he was off rapping on doors.

Philip tried to link into Orl, but Agnet and Brandt interrupted him.

"What do you have?" asked Agnet.

"Mass without consciousness, so not a ghost. I'm presuming a...um...monster." Such a stupid term. "Orl's investigating, but I can't contact her; the—uh—monster must be swamping her band width."

Agnet frowned, as if thinking Orl was throwing up walls. But she was wrong; he'd update her later about their successful cemetery visit and the recent murder. This wasn't the time.

Consciousnesses suddenly crowded the hall, the tumult interfering with his perception. Staff passed by, shepherded by Berg, and Jemin popped out of a door. He gave off a vibe that said, "interested in an academic, low empathy manner but not interested enough to risk my neck." At the stairs, he stumbled, his glasses slid off his nose, then rattled downwards. He crawled after them, clutching the rail like a sailor in a hurricane. Just as well the all-brain-no-body historian hadn't stayed to "help". Now the others needed to clear out, so he could focus.

"We'll need some space to work. Give us a few interference-free minutes to analyze this thing."

Agnet and Brandt exchanged a concerned look.

"It's just the one?" she asked.

"I think so. Move away and let me check." He shooed them to the stairway, opened his chip wide, and scanned Berg's room. The dark thing barely registered beyond a pervasive chill. It moved slowly, almost randomly, as if it'd lost its focus or goal. Two people radiating fear and excitement trotted past, breaking his contact.

"Just the one," he told Agnet.

"Alright," she called from the stairs. "We'll wait here."

"Too close. Go down a flight. I'll need about ten minutes. If we get into trouble, we'll run."

Unease flitted across her face. "Ten minutes, starting now. Then we're back with...what should we bring?"

"Hard to say. All I know is that it's cold and life-less but successfully interacts with matter."

"Might burn," said Brandt.

"So might the building," said Agnet.

"Then we make it colder. Freeze it solid and break it up," said Brandt.

"All right. Collect ice, an ax, a broom or rake, and a big bag," he said, desperate to get rid of them.

He'd been half-joking, but they both hurried downstairs, action types on the move.

The jabbering and high emotion settled like dust once the hall was empty. Orl still leaned against the rustic door, silent as a stilled heart, thick black eyelashes feathering her cheeks. Hopefully she'd learned something, since he had no freaking idea what to make of this monster.

"You picking up anything?" he asked.

She didn't answer, hopefully communing with the entity and not malfunctioning or ignoring him. The door felt cool against his ear. Inside, the creature slowly lumbered across the floorboards.

Hello?

No answer. Ghosts were usually chatty, dying to tell you their tale, so to speak. This thing felt...desolate and never-alive. He shivered; they must not bother heating the hall. He glanced down. Orl's unruly dark hair snaked over her shoulders.

"So Orl. What are we dealing with here?"

No response. Crikes, this girl was tedious. He knelt and peered directly into her face, close enough to be offensive. But how blue her lips appeared in the emergency strip's meager light. Or... Or maybe her lips actually were blue! Had her skin always been that pale?

"Orl?"

He touched her hand and recoiled; her skin was glacial.

"Orl! Are you alright?"

Her shoulders remained rigid when he shifted her away from the door, and her eyes stayed closed.

"Orl?"

He hugged her tight. Maybe some of his body warmth would penetrate, but she just stood like a fence post.

He gave her a shake. "Wake up, Orl."

Blood of a contagious whore. A valuable new-edition perceiver was about to die on his watch. What to do?

The hall seemed too quiet now. He laid her down, dashed into the room across from Berg's, snatched a blanket off the bed, and wrapped it around her. A tub of warm water or a hot shower might help. Best to chuck Orl into a bath fully clothed. NeuroCorp would toss him out on his ear if she straight up died, regardless, but misconduct accusations would cancel his severance pay. She didn't look heavy; he'd pick her up and...where was the bathroom?

Did Berg shut off the hot water at night? His thoughts fragmented and ricocheted like hysterical shrapnel.

Think.

The hall is cool but not frigid like Berg's door. The monster must be radiating cold. Therefore, that creature must be freezing Orl. He probed around for a link between the girl and the creature; perhaps it was an energy parasite. But he couldn't detect a connection. Could he be more useless? Maybe thoughts would shake her loose: *fires, stoves, blood, mittens, his old red parka*, everything that evoked warmth. Her lashes fluttered, and she gasped.

"Orl?" Her eyes were wide with fear...or something.

"What happened?"

Thud.

Berg's door shuddered in its frame. Philip's heart lodged in his throat. He wasn't a physical guy. He was a mental guy; his weapons were communication, observation, and analysis. He'd observed enough to know he couldn't communicate with this empty creature. Time to run elsewhere and analyze.

"Let's get you out of here." He bundled Orl to the head of the stairs, nearly colliding with Brandt who was toting a heavy-looking composite canister.

"See what I got from the medic? Liquid nitrogen ought to slow it down, then we can hack it to pieces." He hoisted the canister as if it was light as a package of lentils and shook it in Philip's face.

"Ah. I'm not so sure. It's already ice cold. It nearly froze Orl."

Bam.

The door bulged outward with the impact.

Brandt glanced up the hall as if the raging monster was a minor inconvenience. "She better now?"

Philip glanced at the girl. Her cheeks had minimally pinked up. She pointed at Brandt's canister. Then looked up at him, a question on her face.

"You think it'll freeze?" he asked.

She shrugged. Great, thanks. Thanks for the insight. But at least she'd come around. He seated her on the landing, expecting her to collapse, but she rose, grasped the banister, and sidled down a step.

"Buzz downstairs to the common space. They've lit a fire in the fireplace. You can warm up," said Brandt. "Go on. You

71

looking so blue is making me nervous. I'd carry you down, but me and Phil have a monster to clobber."

Oh, freaking terrific. He didn't want to be a hero, especially not a hero named "Phil," for pity's sake.

Pounding echoed down the hall.

Agnet bounded up the stairs, paused for a moment to speak to Orl, who'd scooted down three additional treads, then continued toward them. "Here you go." She thrust a hammer into his hands.

A hammer? Its head gleamed in the low light. But despite the weapon, he would die because he wasn't a hammer wielding guy. The dratted thing was heavy, and he was a talker, not a doer. Should be obvious.

"Maybe I should assist Orl downstairs."

Agnet shook her head. "Spool, you open the door. Brandt hit it with the nitrogen. Frosty freeze. Then I'll hack off its head."

"It might fight headless. It's not—"

But Agnet was already at the door, Brandt right behind her. They fell into ambush poses on the knob side, Brandt brandishing the sprayer, Agnet wielding her ax. Philip reluctantly positioned himself near the hinges and grasped the knob.

Thump.

Narrow gaps momentarily appeared between the door's boards.

"Philip. Open the door, now. Be quick—it might lose its balance."

A horrible but comforting realization dawned. "Sorry, but it's locked! Berg has the key."

Brandt sputtered an elaborate string of highly creative curses.

Crea-craa-crrsh!

A splintery seam split the door like a gaping wound. Agnet and Brandt drew back but held their positions instead of dashing to the stairs. Forced to stay put by their thick-skulled bravery, Philip hoisted his hammer.

A pair of thick thumbs wrapped around the wood. The door pouched outward and snapped in two, same as a rye biscuit. A gust of frigid, moldy air, redolent of wet sock tucked behind the washer gasket, struck his face. And there it stood, about seven feet tall, vaguely anthropomorphic, brown-green, and dripping.

Gadgets stuck out of it—tools and a rusty wheel out of that shoulder, metal studs from the thigh, and fix-it doodads all over its chest. He'd noticed that wheel an hour ago, hanging on the wall, Berg's idea of decor. The monster had *accreted* Berg's odds and ends and—grown.

"What the—I thought these monsters were kid-sized!" cried Brandt.

"It looked big coming out of the floor, but not this big."

It stepped a spindly curved leg forward, the foot tapping the hall's floor, a nightmarish blind man's cane. The leg ended with a small hoof... No! That was a chair leg! It'd swallowed Berg's furniture! No wonder it'd expanded.

"The leg! It's wood."

The monster gurgled and roared, sounding and smelling like a sewer drain's belch. Brandt hurled the nitrogen canister, which plunged into the monster's chest and sank out of view. Without missing a beat, Agnet knelt and swung her ax. The leg splintered, she rolled clear, and the thing toppled into the opposite wall with a hideous *splot*.

Green muck oozed down the paneling and puddled on the floor. Bits of metal clinked and clanked as they tumbled free. A chair with a broken leg toppled sideways out of the disintegrating mass. Layers of slop spilled away, gradually revealing a man-sized core. It rose unsteadily. Agnet hefted the slime covered canister, but before she could pull the trigger, the thing's head and arms sloughed off. The head rolled toward Philip, shedding hair, tissue, and teeth, and stopped about half a meter from his feet. The jaw, still attached by rotted sinew, clacked weakly. Reflexively, Philip kicked the repulsive object to the wall, dislodging the jawbone which lay still.

"Welp. That was revolting," said Agnet.

As if trying to outdo revolting, the monster's torso crumbled like a piece of moldy fruit. Its legs teetered, then fell—first one, then the other—and lay twitching. Philip whacked it with his hammer, desperate for it to be still. Brandt and Agnet also hacked and spritzed anything twitching, and a few minutes later the trio stood awkwardly, weapons dangling from their hands, the surrounding floor cluttered with Berg's flotsam, piles of dirt and moss, bones, scraps of door, chess pieces, a broken chair—

And—oh, gross—a small unraveling cardboard tube—his lip balm.

Into The Woods

The Warden is Cross

Cutlery clinked and clattered, a dismal reminder that Agnet could be plowing into the scrambled egg she'd lovingly heaped on her plate. But she'd foolishly abandoned her meal to fetch a glass of milk, and Warden Honing had waylaid her, agitation and woe contorting his face. Breakfast was breakfast, but she could be patient. The Warden was rightfully upset. Nobody appreciates unexpected visitors, especially a decomposing, radioactive furniture-eater. Not convivial, that sort of company.

"Everything about last night was wrong. My people reported small, kid-sized monsters at the edge of the property, not huge horror shows inside the compound. Why the change? Why now?" His eyes shifted toward the table where her team sat enjoying breakfast. She could practically hear his wheels grinding: *a day after those people arrive, a moldering behemoth attacks my room.*

"Could be just random; you know, a coincidence," she said, stupidly responding to her own head noise and sounding both defensive and evasive to her own ears.

He glowered at the team. "I've been warden long enough to have lost faith in coincidences."

Good gravy. He might actually believe they were responsible. "Me too, about coincidences, but you don't think we lured that thing inside?"

Honing studied his shoes. "No. Not on purpose. You're a strange bunch, but not strange enough to invite something that repulsive inside."

She eyed the team. Jemin shoveled oats dotted with dried berries into his mouth. Philip, his face slack with exhaustion, sipped tea. Brandt, cheery and enthused, was part way through what must be peak-experience-toast. Orl seemed subdued, probably still recovering from the attack. Tired, hungry, and quirky perhaps, but not flat out strange.

And there sat her plate, patiently waiting.

Her stomach growled. Luckily, she'd slid the egg onto a slice of toast, so it might still be warm.

"Maybe somebody generated an inadvertent homing signal, perhaps one of us or maybe one of your people."

He frowned like a thunderstorm, and she winced internally. That last comment was just her mouth running on post-monster exhaustion, nightmare-induced sleep deprivation, and hunger. She shrugged to soften her words and tried again.

"Who knows what rules monsters follow? We're still investigating, and, right now, we don't know much more about these creatures than you. We need to keep an open mind. So ask your staff what they were doing last night and whether they noticed anything unusual. If we discover some circumstance that draws monsters in, we could turn it to our advantage."

Honing's face darkened. "And do what? Invite another blob of goo inside, let it wreck property and smear the walls with radioactive filth?"

"Mildly radioactive, and I don't propose rolling out the welcome mat. I'd rather dispatch the next monster out in the yard."

The Warden's expression broke into little sheep clouds; the storm was passing. "Well. I'll talk to my staff, and if you figure out why that thing defiled my room, let me know, so I can be sure it won't happen again." He eyed the team, then sighed. "Excuse my bad mood. It's just my belongings are befouled, and fat chance Central will send a clean-up crew to a site this remote. None of it had much value, but I was used to it, that's all." A sheepish look crossed his face. "But I'm glad none of you got hurt, and I appreciate you destroying the thing."

"Thanks. And thanks again to your medic *and* for use of the showers." Someday, she might feel clean again.

He plodded off, appearing placated, at least for now. She hurried to the table, took her seat, and gulped her milk—fresh milk from the compound's small herd. No wonder the inmates treated those animals like gods.

"Good job last night, team." She gave Brandt a nod, and he grinned, a kid on prize day. "Any thoughts about that monster? What was it? Why was it so large, compared to the others? Why did it come by for a visit, etcetera?"

Orl dropped her eyes, but Orl always dropped her eyes, and in Agnet's imagination, Evangeline, queen of Human Resource's labyrinthine treachery, cackled.

Brandt, holding food in one cheek, rodent-style, said, "Who knows? But good news—that monster was a mess. Sure, it was bulky and strong, but when it lost balance and fell, it collapsed like a turd in the rain."

"Yes, poorly constructed." Jemin vigorously bobbed his head, as if he'd seen the monster disintegrate in person.

Agnet sliced into her egg on toast. Instead of pale yellow, the yolk ran deep yellow-orange, marigolds in the sunshine. Glorious. "Do we think it's intelligent?"

Philip glanced up from his plate. Dark rings hung under his eyes, making him look mysterious and even handsomer, whereas, after last night, she undoubtedly looked like a sixty-year-old recovering from the flu.

"Since we couldn't detect a mind, we can't be certain *any* of its actions were intentional," he said. "For all we know, it wandered under Honing's floorboards by accident and inadvertently harmed Orl."

"Did you sense it coming?"

"No. Took me completely by surprise. I didn't have a bead on it until it was beneath my feet.

Orl's head drooped closer to her lap. She appeared fragile, as if a nudge would tip her into a catatonic stupor. If Chief Agnet Krause had a lick of sense, she'd bench the girl right now. But she wouldn't; she'd sully her career yet again by giving somebody a chance. Because she was that kind of stupid. When would she learn to do her own time?

"You and Orl talking yet?"

Philip jumped in his seat. "Oh. Yes. Planned to tell you." He leaned in and continued in a low voice. "Turns out her chip works fine; it's just set to a non-standard frequency. I figured it out while we cleared out that old cemetery, so thanks for the suggestion, Brandt."

"Fantastic!" Brandt grinned like a jumbo slice of apple.

"That's a relief. How'd the—er—clearing go?"

"Really well, with a glitch." Philip tilted closer. "We uncovered a recent death, a murder." His voice had dropped to a whisper. "The victim was a prisoner backing out of a test-subject-deal. The project managers wouldn't provide details, and he suspected the experiment was a one-way ticket."

"When?"

"Not exactly certain, but the man's clothes and conversational style imply recent. I obliquely asked Berg—the Warden—about the cemetery and deaths on site. His answers read like he doesn't know the fellow died."

"Ghosts wear clothes?" whispered Brandt.

Philip chuckled. "Sort of. They project an image that reflects their last earthly appearance."

"Which agency ran the experiment?" asked Agnet.

"The ghost didn't know; they weren't wearing insignia."

"Did you get the prisoner's name?"

"He didn't offer one and wouldn't respond when we inquired. Probably run-of-the-mill ghost-denial: having a name means being someone, and being somebody raises uncomfortable questions, such as, 'why am I endlessly pacing a track in front of this old barn?'"

Agnet turned to Jemin. "Murder's definitely not legal. What about experimenting on prisoners?"

Jemin flushed as if she'd caught him with his hands in his pants. "I'll have to look it up."

"Do so when you have a chance. Be interesting to know if standards have sunk that low." Orl's history crossed her mind, and she swallowed. Must be her day for foot-in-mouth syndrome. "So Orl, how'd the monster hurt you?"

The girl wrapped herself in her arms and shook.

"Cold," replied Philip, taking up the role of translator. "It emanated cold. I felt it too, through the door. But she tried to find its...essence? I suppose that's the word. Anyway, she dove in too deep, and it nearly froze her core."

"Why'd it swallow the Warden's furniture?" asked Brandt.

Orl picked up her fork and opened her mouth wide.

Honestly, they'd been reduced to charades. NeuroCorp, those sickos, needed a kick in the head; mental skills weren't everything, especially in the field. People needed to converse.

"We don't know. It might've been hungry. It might've just been absorbing anything it touched."

In short, they hadn't learned much. She speared a sauteed tomato. "Welp. The piggy thing left behind a social as well as a physical mess, and the Warden's a bit cross. Make that extremely cross. In fact, Honing almost burst a blood vessel over the state of his room, and I'm pretty sure he believes the monster broke in because of us."

Philip tutted and folded his arms. "Completely unfair. It just as easily could've been after Honing himself."

"True. But I suspect some inmates share his concerns, given the dark looks I got in the breakfast line. So keep conversation with the farm residents entirely reality-based and rational. No speculating about the monsters, no mention of ghosts, and please, use big science words—like 'matter-based without a conscious' or whatever Philip said last night." She glanced at Brandt. "Or use short tactical words." She caught Jemin's eye. "Don't reference mythology or any other historic weirdness. If we trigger their fear, they might boot us to protect themselves, and waiting for a ride home in radioactive woods holds no appeal." She dragged a potato wedge through the remains of the magnificent tomato. "Besides, I hoped for more days of this chow."

"Last night was an incursion, meaning the source is outside." Thanks for the vocabulary lesson, Dr. Yoder. He continued. "I'd like to remind everybody that the witness is also outside. So if you're not *exhausted*, we should head out."

Silence fell like a turkey to the ax of Jemin's "exhausted". He'd spoken the word with such a patronizing tone, as if they'd purposely tired themselves out demolishing the monster. She must've heard incorrectly; nobody was that obtuse. Then Philip gave her a side-long glance that said, "can you believe he's that obtuse?".

Jemin twisted his hands, looking anguished. Had he noticed everybody's stunned disbelief at his faux pas, or was he worried they'd delay the visit to his precious witness? "But if you all are too tired, I certainly understand."

Philip quirked one side of his mouth. "Well, battling that huge and hideous creature *face to face* certainly was exhausting."

Jemin ignored the dig. "Still, I am eager to interview that witness. Maybe we could split up. You guys could rest here—"

Agnet rapped her knuckles on the table. "No. We don't know what we're up against, so we won't split up. Not yet. We stick together and investigate as a team."

Brandt clapped Philip's shoulder. "We're ready for a hike, aren't we Phil? And while we're gone, Warden Honing will probably forgive and forget." Philip rolled his eyes. Bull-in-a-glass-house style, Brandt plowed forward. "We got our maps and the path Orl pointed out yesterday. I say let's move."

Orl nodded.

"Yes, absolutely. Let's go." Jemin shone with enthusiasm. Not a warrior, but at least an ardent explorer.

Philip raised an eyebrow. "So, we set off into the exclusion zone following a map hand-drawn by a *secret* source, confront an unknown witness, and grill him about something we don't understand?"

"Sounds good to me," said Brandt.

A trainee scowled as he passed by their table. On Agnet's plate, fluffy bits of egg nestled against golden brown toast. Looked perfect, but maybe a disgruntled cook had added extra "ingredients" to her meal. Only progress on the case would smooth relations.

"Me too. Eat up, and let's roll."

Broken Brick, Rust, and Brambles

Back in her cozy room after breakfast, Agnet prepared for a day trip into the exclusion zone. The hooded suit hung loosely over her clothes. Its specially grown fabric supposedly allowed heat and sweat to dissipate while preventing contamination, but it reminded her of a cookbag she'd once used to boil oats. She snapped down the visor and was immediately reminded of fish tanks. Was she peering in or peering out? Either way, fish tanks relaxed her, but nothing about radiation was relaxing, not after that shit-show in the Carolinas. She clipped the detection badge to her collar. Hopefully, they wouldn't be out long enough for a significant exposure.

The suit added weight, inspiring her to keep her load light. She packed the map, binoculars, a flashlight, blood-sugar-drop emergency snacks, and the radiation meter—a functional meter, no thanks to Property—but left space for the all-important lunch. She affixed her water bag onto the sip-tube, slipped on her holster, and hoisted her backpack. A chipped rectangular mirror glued to the door caught her reflection, a look combining astronaut and donut chef.

"Trainees," gathered into clusters of five to ten, stared as the team crossed the compound. *We're risking our health for you; don't mock us*, she thought as excess fabric swished between her thighs. Sure, she looked and sounded absurd, but better absurd than contaminated.

Orl led them through a creaking gate, across a meadow of browning grass dotted with the fluffy white tufts of goldenrod gone to seed, to a gap in the wood's margin.

Two impressive trees, still holding rich red foliage, formed an arch, between which a path ran ruler-straight into the thick and tangled forest, a feature that explained the faint linear break on her map. Orl craned her neck, as if searching for squirrels between the trees.

"Didn't Brandt say you saw something here?"

Philip relayed Orl's story; she'd witnessed a foreboding, non-ghost presence observing her from the trail.

"Was it our visitor?"

Philip swiveled his mask toward Orl. "Possibly, though she's not sure."

"Good to know. Now that you've synched up, could you report details such as foreboding presences when they occur?"

The perceivers exchanged a look.

"Of course, but, um—" Philip sounded exasperated through his speaker. "You'd claimed everybody was in bed. And she didn't want to interrupt people's sleep."

Warmth washed up her neck. "Oh. Next time, feel free to wake me up."

Ouch. That'd been the night she'd hustled Orl off to bed, concerned the girl would freak out the prison community with her mouthing and writhing. Was Orl calling out her fib? She should ask Orl a few more questions but more conversation would feel awkward. And conversing with Orl through Philip added a speed bump or distortion that threw her off kilter. Orl's singular condition required some finesse; she'd need to upskill.

Brandt pointed down the trail. "It's too straight to be natural and too narrow to be an abandoned road."

Jemin pulled out a tape measure and checked the path's width, then scraped the dirt away in several places with the heel of his boot.

They weren't yet in the exclusion zone, but Agnet couldn't resist saying, "Careful."

"Am being careful."

"I know, but dust is our primary concern."

"I'm aware. Ah. This is an old railroad. See?" He tapped a rust-colored line in the ground with the toe of his boot. "Great carriages ran along these rails, an archaic and inflexible form of transport, dependent on fossil fuels and metals."

"Who'd leave that much metal lying around?" asked Brandt.

"It's of no value, least not anymore."

Brandt regarded Jemin for a moment. "So, it went bad during Powder Fall?"

"No. These rails probably oxidized centuries earlier. Oxidation is a natural process whereby oxygen and water react with metal, in this case iron—"

First year chemistry revised. The lecture moved on to steel and other alloys. Brandt's lips moved, as if he wanted to interject, but Jemin was on a roll. Time to shut him down.

"Corroded or not, the railroad makes a nice trail."

She stepped beneath the trees, and her foot snagged. A lurch forward, a moment of free fall, then the ground slapped hard into her hands and knees.

Jemin squatted beside her. "You alright? Sorry. I should have explained. Slabs run between the rails. They're called—"

"Tripping hazards." Dirt smudged her gloves and pants. No rips or perforations; the suit was well enough made, but she shuddered at the idea contaminated soil lay millimeters from her skin. Scenes from the Wake County mission flitted by—all those people, stubborn, desperate, and not listening to sense, living too close to a leaking source, animal and human grotesques stalking the countryside. But the team should be safe, this close to the farm. No need to whip out the monitor and underscore her anxiety.

Instead, she adjusted the weight of her backpack, implying an imbalance had caused her graceless clown maneuver, then stood, ignoring Jemin's attempts to assist. She rotated her wrists. They'd borne the brunt of the fall and would ache later. "Good thing that happened outside the exclusion zone. Please, everyone, be more careful than me."

A spate of nervous laughter followed her comment, and they proceeded below a varied autumnal canopy; bare trees, thinning trees, trees loaded with yellow, orange, and shuddering, red leaves. Tangles of vines, thick brush, and deep piled leaf litter covered the forest floor. Leaves lay thick on the trail, but vegetation hadn't taken over, so the trail must've been cleared relatively recently. But why?

They marched along, Orl gawking as if overawed by the rampant flora. A leaf floated past Philip, and he swatted at it, as if leaves bit, testimony to a life lived under a dome. She had wilderness hours under her belt, as did Brandt, but even so, this forest possessed an unsurpassed primordial grandeur.

Meanwhile, Jemin yakked factoids. "The reserve is exceedingly remote. Together, the exclusion and buffer zones encompass four thousand kilometers of woodland, and only a few abandoned cabins and homesteads dot the adjacent lands."

No reason to live out here, unless you'd gone feral or crazy, and animals didn't read signs and had probably been multiplying like...animals. Bears, big cats, wild dogs, or maybe even wolves. She eyed a dark recess underneath a fallen tree.

A sound nearly jumped her out of her skin. Boy-o-boy, just Brandt asking, "What's that noise?"

"Hold up." Agnet raised her hand, stopping the others, because, embarrassingly, she couldn't hear over their boots crunching on the leaves. So inconvenient, the tinnitus that'd followed last year's flu, a "permanent infirmity" per the weasel-faced specialist, as if forty-two was old enough for permanent infirmity.

Crreak-up, tick, creaak, creak-up, tick.

"Wind in branches?" offered Philip.

"You feel wind?" Brandt raised his arm, impromptu-weathervane style.

Philip's lips twisted into a look of wry annoyance. "No, given the containment suit."

"Shh!"

The noise came from up ahead. In a few steps, brilliant light flooded her vision. When her eyes adjusted, she took in a clearing, hazy morning sunlight beaming through the sparse canopy. A hazard-yellow sign at the path's edge read "Danger. Exclusion Zone." The global symbol for radioactive-as-a-plutonium-cured-ham-hock hung below the verbiage, and the surrounding grove underscored the sign's message.

Dead trees leaned at crazy angles or lay on the ground. Bark peeled from skeletal gray trunks, and curled rust-colored needles clung to wizened branches. Brittle twigs snapped beneath her feet, so she stood still and let the ticking sound, now more a cacophonous rattle, monopolize her ears.

After giving the sound its moment to shine, she said, "A hundred monkeys rolling hazelnuts on a tin roof couldn't make this much noise."

"Sounds like this thicket is its own oversized radiation meter," said Philip.

Speaking of which, she spun the backpack off her shoulder and rooted around for her own meter, kicking herself for not packing it in the front pouch.

"No. Not radiation. See those dots?" Jemin pointed to the treetops.

Up high, specks zipped from tree to tree, insects, but the buggers must be good-sized, if visible from this distance.

"Those are late season borer beetles, only active where the sun's directly hitting the trunks. See here, under the bark—" He pulled off a section, revealing tangled grooves and scattered holes about the diameter of a pencil drilled into the trees smooth gray wood. "The larvae live in these galleries and gnaw away. They can transform trees into matchsticks in a single season. And if this region burns—radioactive dust will spread for miles."

"Amazing beetles can make so much noise." Philip wrinkled his nose.

"Not the beetles. The clicking sound is their grubs, millions of grubs, their chitinous teeth grinding through heart wood and riddling the trees with tunnels. See the sawdust ringing the base of that tree? It's evidence of their handiwork."

"That's—kinda gross," said Brandt.

"The infestation's a result of the climate emergency and international trade. If Powder had continued to drop temperatures, beetle damage might've slowed down." Jemin sounded almost apologetic.

The team hushed, listened, and looked. Sawdust formed piles at tree bases, and goobers of sap marred the trunks. Terrible place to stand in a windstorm. She wanded the grove for radiation, but despite the devastation, the meter detected not one click above background.

"No fall-out detected, so this mess must be entirely beetle-led. Let's get moving."

Patches of viable forest alternated with blight as they proceeded down the trail, Jemin chittering about host species, microclimates, and failed beetle eradication schemes. But despite mankind's epic negligence, the sickened ecosystem harbored life in abundance. Flocks of birds deserted their perches en masse to continue their journey south. A pair of stocky, long-haired, rodent-like creatures grazed high in the canopy, porcupines, according to Brandt. A herd of small equids, striped beige and brown, drank at the edge of a creek, their funny blonde goatees dripping water as they solemnly observed the passing humans.

A few minutes later, they bunched up on the path. Philip had spoken, but she hadn't caught his comment, though she did catch the silence and the grim expressions on everybody's faces.

Orl stood rigidly facing away from the team, pointing like a corpse dog.

Agnet raised a hand to her ear. "Sorry, missed what you said."

Philip politely restated his remarks. "Orl's sensing remnants that a-way. Says a town lay across the river. I can't confirm from this distance, but I don't doubt her. Heck of a range on this youngster."

Brandt playfully punched Philip on the shoulder. "Got to scope out the ghost town, comrade-in-arms, right?" He turned to Agnet. "Shouldn't we Chief? Our ace perceiving duo could debrief the dead guys. See what they know. Bet we'd collect terrific intel. And any monsters over there, me, you, and ol' Phil here can hashish 'em with our trusty axes."

A sigh whistled through Philip's speaker, angst expressed as a breeze through a lonely windmill.

"Suppose we could, if it were remotely relevant to our mission."

Jemin said, "That town is part of the exclusion zone, so it's been abandoned for centuries."

"Well, then. Since the long dead ignore the real world, we wouldn't learn anything relevant to our case." Relief was writ across Philip's face.

The corners of Brandt's lips drooped. "If they're not paying attention, then what're they doing?"

"Replaying vignettes from their lives, the material they can't relinquish."

"Oh! Talk about boring. In that case, when my number's up, I want to flat out die."

"Rest assured, if anything untoward happens on this mission, Orl and I guarantee you a complete death."

Philip's face betrayed no humor, and Brandt seemed unphased. "I've got full confidence in the psychic dream team."

Philip's next expression deserved patent protection.

"Welp. Let's leave the mass grave for some other team, but I'm sure they'll have...good times." She ushered further down the track and strolled abreast of Brandt. "This your first encounter with perceivers?"

"Yes, ma'am. Was working federal security and extraction, then KP until the cutlery accident. But don't get me wrong; it's interesting, what you guys do."

Had he said KP?

Someday, she'd ask him for the complete story, but not this moment, not in front of the others. Besides, the track now paralleled whooshing and gurgling water, impeding her ability to converse. She consulted her map and identified the waterway as the Pocahauchta River.

"Snow melt feeds these waters, so it's probably seasonal," said Jemin.

"I don't recommend drinking, radiation or no." Agnet took a reflexive sip from her tube. "Pleasant spot, though. Let's break for a meal."

Orl slipped off her backpack and crouched. Probably exhausted, this untrained, indoor-type kid. But she didn't rummage through her bag looking for tucker, a hairbrush, or lip balm like a normal girl. She sat there staring toward the ridge, at least using the correct sitting technique, buttocks hovering an inch off the dirt. What was she staring at? The hair stood up on Agnet's arm. She nudged Philip and indicated Orl with a toss of her helmet.

"Over there," he said, glancing over his left shoulder, "remnants are echoing in a considerable structure, or rather the ruins of a structure. It extends back aways, right up to the mountain."

Jemin's helmet started bobbing. "This area has an industrial history, specifically coal and steel processing." He addressed Brandt, who seemed to be his favorite pupil. "Processing as in removing impurities from ore, not, you know, manufacturing tools or wire." He turned to Agnet. "Yesterday, I accessed a folio of black and white images: a cluster of rudimentary clapboard buildings, disheveled men in caps and baggy work pants, a line of towering smokestacks billowing fumes. The complex was somewhere in this general area." He stammered. "But I focused on recent history, so I don't know all the details."

A pig's eye you don't. Good thing he wasn't obtuse enough to share the chemical details, business models, and environmental impact of the refinery.

"Any ghosts?" asked Brandt.

Philip shrugged. "You'd expect a few work accidents. Accidents are sudden, so people occasionally miss the dying part, and their befuddled consciousness wanders about, trying to figure out what happened."

Good gravy. Some folks feared perceivers, but she'd always felt sorry for them, ethereal types so often mired in other people's pain and confusion. Now she knew they detected the dead's troubles, too.

Orl glanced at her, some complicated emotion lurking behind her eyes, then looked aside. Like many kids, she rarely made direct eye contact, and this instance seemed like a response. But to what? Her mouth suddenly felt dry, so she sipped on her drinking tube, hoping the moment of oral satisfaction would blot out the feeling the girl had seen behind her eyes. But she was being silly. Perceivers didn't read thoughts—or so Philip had said, confirming Central's stance on the issue. A reassuring party line, since many thoughts were embarrassing. She arranged a confident and decisive expression and addressed Orl.

"Any foreboding presences or otherwise worrisome critters that way?"

The girl shook her head.

"Then we should inspect the grounds, but after lunch."

She monitored a slab of rock at the river's edge, finding nothing. So, they spread out, lifted their visors, and ate in comfort. The farm-provided lunch included a fresh apple, crisp and sweet. An act of bravery on somebody's part, probably the Warden's.

Brandt held his apple between thumb and middle finger and gazed at it respectfully. "See here, all shiny and firm? It's perfect. Inspires me to beat back those monsters."

This guy had his priorities straight.

After lunch, they headed toward the ridge and inspected a crumbling brick cube about ten meters square.

"Base of a smokestack." Jemin spoke quickly, aping a trivia night contestant answering the hardest question.

"Must've been tall." Brandt gaped as he stared upward.

"Very tall. Somewhere between one hundred and one hundred and twenty meters. In that era, refineries released poisonous emissions directly into the atmosphere, part of the lead up to the climate emergency. Smokestacks needed to be tall enough to release fumes above the local inversion layer so toxic smoke wouldn't settle at ground level."

Jemin sounded as if he were reading directly off his chip, and supposedly, chip-reading gobbled neurotransmitters and ATP by the bucketful. He didn't look exhausted, babbling enthusiastically about atmospheric mercury levels. So, either Mr. Encyclopedia had read up earlier and possessed remarkable recall, or he was reading at this moment and was remarkably resilient. At some point in history, maybe when this factory belched smog into the sky, everybody had carried little gadgets containing all the world's information. They'd quietly read from small screens, no lecturing chip-head required. Wouldn't that've been convenient?

Just then, Orl pointed at Jemin, and Philip said, "Watch your chip time. Imagine you're just beginning a relationship. You need to ease in. Otherwise, things can go sour."

The historian shot Philip a sullen look, so Agnet said, "Good work, perceivers. We're a team and need to look out for each other."

They picked through broken brick and brambles, passed through a dilapidated brick arch, and passed a row of enormous, heavily corroded canisters.

Agnet took a wild guess. "Silos?"

Jemin peeled a sheet of rust from the canister revealing crumbling brick. "My readings of yesterday," he glared at Philip, "would suggest blast furnace. As I thought, this place is an old metal works."

"What era?" she asked.

"Early to mid-twentieth century." Another spiel on metallurgy crested Jemin's teeth, surged between his lips, then flowed over her head as she surveyed the grounds. Trees had busted through and lifted surviving sections of roof. Substantial curved pieces of crumbling rust suggested the remains of large pipes and girders. Orl and Philip jointly skirted something invisible. Best not to ask. At a pause in the lecture, she remarked, "Sad, all this wasted material."

Brandt toed through a pile of scraps. "If we find anything valuable, is it one-for-all or everyman-for-himself?"

"One-for-all. And the finder treats, bags, and carries the goods, so keep it small and don't let the finding distract you."

Ahead, the ridge jutted steeply up from the valley floor. And wasn't that strange? A huge double door was set into the mountainside. Solid and dull gray, but unlike everything in the steelworks, it wasn't oxidized. "Suppose that's the mine?"

"Huh?" Jemin left off tinkering with something on the ground and glanced up. "Well! No! The mine that fed this plant would've been open pit style and could've been at a distance, given the proximity of the rail line. Those doors are modern."

Brandt, Philip, and Orl already stood at the threshold, gazing upward, probably taking in the scale.

When they drew close, Brandt said, "Size reminds me of an airplane hangar I saw once on the Georgia coast near Waycross."

Jemin shook his head. "Hanger doors require a hydraulic lift—"

"Lighten up. I'm just talking about the size. Lift or not, these doors were expensive." He stroked the surface. "Feels like the butt of my service rifle, high-quality, reinforced fibercarb. What a beaut."

"Check out the man door," said Philip.

The builders had cut a smaller door into the left mega-door. Agnet touched a panel, slightly rough and cool, but not cold. She tried the door handle. Locked, naturally. "So, we follow a reasonably well-maintained trail to centuries old ruins and find a gigantic modern door. What gives? Is Honing using this space for storage?"

Philip shrugged.

"Can you sense inside?" she asked him.

The perceivers shared a hive mind moment, then Philip said, "No. The rock, the doors, their thickness or material, blocks us."

"Should I blow the doors? The big one may be high quality, but I've got her beat." Brandt shifted his pack forward and unzipped it. "Or I could use a light explosive to blast through the littler door. Might be tidier."

Philip almost yelped, "Explosives?"

And yeah, explosives? But Brandt had patrolled the border, and the range of weaponry ex-border guards packed had always amazed her, including those hand-crafted incendiary devices that berserker redhead had hurled with a slingshot.

Still.

She opened her mouth to ask, "what do you mean by 'explosive'?"

But Jemin, his face apoplectic through his shield, cried, "Oh, no. No. No explosives. This could be a storage facility for records, maybe even a clean space holding computer equipment. Who knows what knowledge lies inside?"

"Or a storage facility for toxic chemicals, biohazards, barrels of radioactive waste." Philip was speaking a bit too quickly.

Jemin's helmet bobbled, a peach on a heavily laden branch in a high wind. "A definite possibility. Nuclear power plants dotted the river, all phased out during a waste-storage crisis, and a series of accidents worldwide, including the accident at Riverbend. Just down river..." Jemin paused, tugging absently on the fingers of his gloves, looking frightened and dazed, as if pondering how he'd materialized inside his helmet.

"More than enough reasons to put away the explosives. So please."

Brandt studied the beige cylinder in his hands, his expression mournful or confused. "Thought this was my chance to lite her up, but I see your point. Don't want the place going off in our faces like a pigeon full of popcorn." He tucked his gear back into his pack.

A pigeon full of popcorn? What'd he gotten up to, during his stint in KP? "I presume that device is chemically stable." A stupid question, but the answer might put the others at ease.

"Stable as a judge, ma'am. Until she's detonated."

"That's comforting, in its way. Explosives standard issue on the border?"

"Not unless you're working demo, blasting illegal encampments and hep-hep labs, etcetera. I worked demo. Thought that's why they brought me on board this mission."

Agnet asked, "Who gave you that impression?"

"The old NeuroCorp skeezer." Orl interrupted with a snort and a wheezing sound, possibly her version of laughter. Brandt winked at the girl.

"He gave me specific instructions: 'if you come across an old mine find the control room and destroy it'. He said keep it quiet, but I figured he meant 'don't tell your friends'. Surprised he didn't mention it to you, Chief."

"Didn't say a word." She asked the rest, "Any of you told anything about a mine, control room, or explosives?"

Jemin shook his head. After a brief mind meld with Orl, Philip said, "No."

This mission got stranger by the minute.

"Welp. I say NeuroCorp's private side-mission will have to wait for another team. And they'd better provide that team with the particulars, like the contents of the blast target. Brandt, you can tell them I said so, if they pester you."

Whatever lay behind those doors smelled like trouble. Awful trouble. Agnet peeked at the sun, suspended thirty degrees off the ridgeline, and blazing in a brilliant blue sky. She shivered. Somehow, the looming mountain had absorbed the day's warmth.

"Let's file these doors under 'collect more information' and carry on."

The team stood on a rocky outcropping about thirty meters above the valley, admiring the view. Forest stretched before them, variegated autumnal hues laced with tentacles of rusty red beetle-damage, an arc of river glistening silver in the distance.

A light sweat coated Agnet's skin, despite the containment suit's recycling fan. Jemin stood behind her, huffing and puffing. The trudge up the hill must've nearly killed him.

"Are those towers near the river another old steel works?" The breeze rattling past Brandt's microphone rendered his baritone tinny and intermittent.

"No. That's Riverbend, the defunct nuclear power plant responsible for this stifling gear." Jemin plucked at his containment suit.

"What caused the accident?" asked Brandt.

"Don't know."

"Thought our smart man knew it all."

"Nuclear power is Officially Forgotten tech, so not included in my chip's dataset, naturally. But whatever happened was so bad, this area won't be habitable for twenty-five thousand years."

By that time, might be nobody left to move in.

"Fabulous view, but..." Philip tilted his mask toward the sky. "Just past noon by the sun's angle. I'm thinking we conduct our business pronto and head back."

"Agreed. Nobody wants to camp overnight." Except maybe Brandt, who might welcome a chance to fight another monster. "The feral encampment should be close."

"I believe this group refers to themselves as The Fold," said Jemin, sounding schoolteacher prim.

"Didn't know anybody took arcane subdivisions of rural kooks to heart," said Philip, then he and Orl moved in the same direction, as if somebody was calling them. "This way," Philip gestured, and a trail winding through yellowed bracken suddenly became obvious.

"Speaking of kooks," muttered Jemin.

"You perceivers are better than a tracking dog." Brandt must've registered Philip's icy stare, because he added, "I mean, much better, since you can talk, and everything." His eyes flashed to Orl, and he grimaced. "Mostly."

Agnet hid her smile by checking the radiation level at the trailhead. A straight shot to those ruined towers, and yet, she couldn't detect a thing over background. Weird. She glanced at Jemin; he looked surprised too.

"You're sure the meter works?"

"Yeah. I'm double sure, no thanks to Property. Could you check into the fallout pattern, later, when we're back at the farm and rested?"

"Definitely."

They meandered single file, Philip at the lead, only the murmuring breeze audible over their footsteps. Mature forest gave way to a grove of saplings, their slender, pale trunks creaking in the wind. Spangled light fell through golden foliage, and silvery flowers dangled from the branches. Odd that the trees flowered this time of year.

No.

Those weren't flowers. Those were thumb-sized, white-clad figurines. A sudden breeze tossed the trees, and leaves fluttered from the branches. The figurines whirled and danced. A chill crept up her spine, though there was nothing supernatural about dolls, not at all. Incredibly creepy, maybe, but not supernatural. Still, her gut didn't agree; it felt heavy and cold, as if she'd eaten a bowl of dread.

She swallowed her nerves. "Well, now. Someone's hung dolls from the branches. Could be religious or an—uh—art installation."

The otherworldly figures continued their macabre dance. She steeled herself and took a closer but not too close look. Glittering jet-black eyes stared from beneath halos of snowy hair. "Leave," the thing seemed to say. But on closer inspection, the hair was milkweed silk, something mundane that she'd played with as a kid.

"Handcrafted using local materials, that's all," she said, trying to shoehorn unease into something trivial. Both for her own benefit and for Orl's. The girl's eyes showed too much white. "Look, milkweed seeds for eyes, and the head's a hazelnut."

"Reminds me of a woodsy first grade art project." Brandt tapped a doll and watched it swing. "Had a case of the heebie jeebies for a moment. With all that fluttering, I thought these were moths."

Moths? They had creepy ghost dolls, and he was worried about moths?

Philip wrinkled his nose. "I've seen my share of primitive tribal woo-woo, but nothing this visually powerful."

"Pagan iconography is meant to strike a primal chord..." Jemin stuttered, then cleared his throat. "Fascinating, but not primitive. Nothing existing in the present can be considered primitive. Everything derives from antecedents."

Brandt studied the doll in his hand, turning it over and side to side. "Well. This ain't a Martian rover, now, is it?" He held it up for Jemin's viewing pleasure. "You understand these ferals. Why'd they make these dolls?"

Jemin shook his head. "Not sure they did. *The Fold* descends from worshipers of Hanging Man, so they'd consider these effigies idolatrous."

Brandt signaled "stop" with his hands. "Hold on, professor. Too many words above my pay grade."

Philip side-eyed Jemin, looking unimpressed. "Cultures change. Maybe the locals ditched hanging man for a new god."

A flick of Brandt's wrist set the doll twirling. "But these are hanging—or dangling at least—so they fit with the hanging man theme."

Jemin shifted from side to side. "No, this...installation doesn't mesh *at all* with the ancient teachings. I need to record these objects. Won't take over five minutes."

He wandered about, slashing notes and sketches into his pad, working like a machine with an occasional glance at Philip's scowl.

Philip whispered, "I'd like to remind you the sun sets early this time of year, and religious studies aren't on the agenda. This historian should be museum staff, not part of an investigative team."

"Not dying to camp out, are you."

He pressed his lips, signaling disapproval. "I prefer brief encounters with nature, a quick stroll from a comfortable inn, for instance."

His attention abruptly shifted to Orl, and he followed her to the clearing's edge. They stared at the ground, their helmets moving back and forth in sync.

Now what?

Something strange, no doubt. But if she joined them, she'd at least be clear of these dolls' beady black eyes. She strolled toward the perceivers, keeping her pace casual.

Orl pointed down as Agnet approached. In the leaf litter, something pale and random twitched—a pile of fine bones. The remains of a mouse, judging by size.

"If those are bones, then what's moving? Something underneath? Larvae? Grubs?"

"See what I mean about nature," said Philip. "One disgusting life cycle after the other."

On cue, a brown clump rolled from under a leaf. She'd guess slug, but slugs didn't roll. Stars alive. Milkweed, moths, and now this muck. The goober wrapped around two tiny bones, and the mess twitched, the reflex of an awkward joint. All right. ..welp...didn't know self-assembly was an option. Philip's take on nature started to make sense.

More goo coated a third bone, which then fused to the first two. The ugly mess spasmed and flexed, a limb, but all wrong. Her craw spasmed, so she gulped then averted her eyes. Something was coming into being, a repugnant but very private moment. Philip gasped and took a step away.

"I'm looking at a miniature baby monster; aren't I?"

Philip, a shade green behind his visor, nodded. "Must be."

She hazarded a quick glance. A little bone waggled. "Look. It's waving hello."

"I'm glad you find humor in this...abomination." He wiped his gloves on his suit, a meaningless reflex, cleanliness in the face of revulsion. "I may be sick."

"I may join you; my blood pressure's taken a dive. But at least I can't smell anything through this shield. You perceiving anything?"

"No. It's organic matter with no animus."

"Animus or not, glad I'm suited up, in case that thing's microbial. Speaking of contamination—" She wrestled the counter out of her pack and aimed it at the mini-monster in situ.

Click. Click. Click. Unenthusiastic, but definitively above background.

To be confident, she tested the surrounds: a downed branch, a rock, a sapling, finding the occasional random click. "Yucky bone-creature is mildly above background."

Brandt, who'd come over to join the party, offered to squish the thing. But Agnet didn't see the point of smearing his boot sole with contaminated goop. She waved Jemin over to document the phenomenon.

"Could be a slime mold. Mold is a misnomer, mind you. The slime molds aren't fungi; they're protozoa, amoebas that congregate and form a motile slug-like creature which produces a fruiting body."

"One disgusting life cycle after the other. Excuse me." Philip stepped behind a tree. Orl gurgled a laugh.

Another brown lump rolled to the pile of bones. Jemin's eyes bugged while his mouth formed a little "O". A picture book character, the astronaut frog, flitted through her mind as he cried, "Oh, my! Slime molds don't—"

She cut him off at the pass. "Why don't you sketch it? Then we should move on. Time's passing."

Philip returned, his walk less wobbly.

"Feel better?" asked Brandt.

"Yes, thank you. There's a habitation up ahead." He indicated the continuation of the trail with a wave of his hand. "Right on the path. Doesn't seem this feral pack worked hard to stay hidden."

Brandt shrugged. "Why hide in the middle of nowhere?"

"This isn't nowhere, it's their homeland," said Jemin, channeling his inner school marm. "If we encounter anybody up ahead, can we please be respectful? We'll be visitors on their turf."

"Then why're you holding that could-be-religious figurine? You gonna take it?" asked Brandt, sounding more curious than accusatory.

"Of course. So the witness can explain it, assuming he's still alive."

Philip folded his arms, a combination of boredom, annoyance, and mischief written on his face. "What if removing dolls is considered bad juju?"

Jemin suddenly hurled the macabre little effigy, his throw violent but entirely ineffectual; the lightweight thing fluttered to the ground. He shoved his notebook into his bag and slung it over his shoulder. "FINE. So we don't collect an example of the *unique and entirely anomalous artifacts.*" His voice sounded like a school kid about to kick the dust.

She'd be happy to abandon the freaky "artifact" to the squirrels, having read plenty of tales about knife wielding dolls coming to life, chasing people around, death by a thousand cuts. And these dolls were hanging right above reanimating mobile goop... Goodness. Her imagination was running wild; she really needed to stop reading those trashy serials.

"What about that?" Without looking down, Philip pointed at the roiling mass of bones and mud. "Should we collect that?"

Honestly, this pair.

"No," she said in her firm-boss-lady voice. "Radioactive, self-assembling gunk calls for a biohazard crew, not an empty lunch container." She wanded the doll; it was clean, then handed it to Jemin. "Take this to the village and make your inquiries, but don't bring it back to the farm; it might be...germy. Understood?"

He took it, shooting Philip a triumphant look. Philip ignored him and said, "This place gives me the shivers. And that's me, a perceiver talking. Let's get out of here."

"Onwards. But first, may I remind everybody that respect takes time and needs to be earned, and respect may lie beyond our reach. But we all can manage polite, can't we?" She looked each team member in the eye, and each nodded agreement.

WITNESS TO RUINATION

Jemin struggled to match Philip's brisk pace, despite the cumbersome containment suit, the backpack hanging like a lead weight, and his heavy-as-cinder-blocks boots. With so much to learn, how could he waste time at the gym? And Central, with all the last-minute rush-rush, had overlooked his obvious need for mission-specific physical training. So, if he died of a heart attack, it wouldn't be his fault. And hopefully, his death would egregiously inconvenience Philip, the heathen reprobate.

Past a pile of lichen-covered boulders, the trail narrowed, allowing one foot at a time, and once again, the forest loomed dark overhead. Brush snagged Jemin's elbow, the brown remains of bracken whipped his calves, and sticks rolled underfoot. Then, as if stepping into daybreak, they burst into another clearing.

Silence lay heavy over the ruins of the small settlement, a silence that held no waiting, less a pause after a long exhale than an eternal and absolute settling of the chest. Lord above, how he'd wanted to speak to his people. Well, not exactly his people; they waited for him in heaven. But these people, though a breakaway sect, at least still followed the one true God.

Sure, the Fold might not matter anymore, being nearly extinct thanks to epidemics and attrition. But at least he could've sublimated his family's anguish into knowledge, something pure, almost holy.

Brandt toed a basket's rotted remains. "What do you suppose happened here?"

"Those buildings went up in a fire." Philip pointed left.

Jemin followed his finger. Nothing much, chestnut-colored sprays of dock seed, and—oh—there, the charred corner of a building and the stump of a chimney. Either Philip possessed superior eyesight or—if one believed those tales about perceivers—he could see into the past, smell the smoke, feel the fire's heat, and hear the screams. A chip function as blasphemous as that bewitched grove.

They picked through the ruins, finding naught but weeds and charred wood. A few years back, children probably scampered between neatly kept log houses. His throat knotted. Standing witness to ruination was harder than he'd expected. So, he turned to practicalities. How would he document this settlement? A midden heap excavation, that's where he'd start. But he wouldn't have the time.

"What about those huts?" asked Brandt.

What huts? He couldn't see huts, but everybody had better eyesight than Jemin Yoder who Heaven thwarted at every turn. He tagged behind Brandt and—ah—a line of pathetic hovels strung out toward the right. All unburned, but most had collapsed.

"The flat ones look like giant cookies." Even in the darkest moments, Chief Krause's mind lived in her stomach. She waved the radiation meter's wand over a former threshold: not a click.

He poked his head inside a reasonably intact hut. Poles about the thickness of his wrist supported woven bark and twigs and a plaster of mud, human habitation at its most basic. At least a circle of light shone through the smoke hole.

"Hey! Mister." Brandt hunkered in front of a second intact hut, extending his hand. "I know we look kind of scary in these crazy suits, but we're just people. Nobody's going to hurt you."

Jemin rushed to Brandt's side as a gnarled figure crawled through the hut's low door, a person so aged that gender was anyone's guess. But this must be Grandfather Cain, the only survivor. The boys had spoken the truth, and the Lord had preserved the ancient man. Praise be!

He sat at the entrance and tilted his walnut shell of a face to the sun, an incomplete halo of fine white hair aglow in the light, his countenance similar to that of those accursed figurines. But something was off—the eyes—his irises were clouded or covered by a milky film. Ah, yes. As the boy's had mentioned, the old man was well and truly blind.

Chief Krause squatted, then duck-walked back a few paces, probably repelled by the strong odor of rancid urine emanating from the hut. "Hello. I'm Agnet Krause."

"And I am what's left of Canaan Oberdost." His voice creaked like a rusty gate.

The Chief asked, "Can we help? Do you need anything? Food, water?"

A toothless smile spread across the wizened face. "You outlanders. My brethren would've just served the food."

Jemin whipped his pack from his shoulders and pawed through to the snack he'd reserved for the return trip. He should have offered food! Life amongst these unbelievers had corrupted him. And how annoying the Elder's easy command of English when he could've impressed the team with his fluent grasp of the Old Tongue, acquired, they would've assumed, through years of careful study. After a quick thought about the mechanics of eating without teeth, he tore a page from his notebook, rolled it into a cone, then crumbled the muffin inside. He guided Meister Canaan's hand, helped the bony fingers curl around the paper, and explained. "A sort of cake crumbled into a paper cone."

Pinches of muffin passed from cone to wizened mouth. When he'd finished eating, Jemin poured water into a binocular lens cap, pressed it into the Elder's hand, then sat back, trying to be patient while the others offered their food. This man looked between eighty and ninety. Even if younger and gravely blighted by inbreeding or contamination, he'd lived long enough to have witnessed plenty.

After a final cap-full of water, he wiped his lips on his ragged sleeve. "I thank ye for the meal."

Agnet gave Philip a nod, irritating but not unexpected her ceding the interview to Mr. Sensitive, debauched deviant though he may be. But it was just as well. His foreknowledge of this village and Grandfather Cain might've slipped out, if he'd been doing the talking.

"Why are you here alone?" asked Philip, taking the blunt approach.

Meister Canaan's face grew sharp. "You're sure I'm alone, then?"

"I know you're alone." Philip's tone was matter of fact but kindly.

He shrugged a bony shoulder. "Ah, young man. I sense you have the sight upon you, too. Well. Suppose none of it matters anymore. So I'll tell ye." He shifted in his dirty rags, his hazy eyes fixed on his knees. "We were already few, thanks to sickness. Then fire came in the black of night, and the village burned to the ground. Did our best to save our kin: drenched bedding, hay, and blankets in the creek, but most of our folks had already died in their beds. Fire took more than our kindred. We also lost most of our livestock, the garden seed, and oodles of know-how."

"Condolences for your losses, but thanks for your hard work containing the fire. Would've been bad for everyone here-abouts, if it'd spread."

"We were thinking of our own, truth be told. But I acknowledge your generous words." He bobbed his head in Philip's general direction and continued. "After, wasn't many left: myself, a few women-folk, a handful of kinder. The women died, two of the wasting, and one tumbled into the well. Not helpful, her contaminating our water on the way to her heavenly reward. Not long after, the kinder started babbling about goblins. I figured they'd lost all hope and were losing their minds to boot. Short time after, they abandoned our home. Tried to get me to come along, those boys, but I'd have slown them down. So here I sit. Now you tell me. What brings you city folk to my unlikely doorstep?"

"We've come on behalf of the farm down yonder. They've been having problems with strange creatures, your boys' goblins maybe. Creatures slung together from bone and mud. You—" Philip hesitated, probably swallowing back the term "seen." "—ever hear of such a thing?"

The Elder's face crinkled as if he'd bitten into a sour memory. "No. I didn't know what to make of the boy's unrighteous talk. Figured they'd strayed from the law with no guidance, the lot of them. They even set up a protection and asked me to bless their wardings."

Jemin asked, "You mean the figures hanging from trees down the ridge? Like this one?"

He handed Meister Canaan the doll he'd collected. After fingering it and turning it round in his gnarled hand, his lip curled in disgust, and he tossed it into the long grass choking a path between huts.

"Ashamed to say."

Jemin ignored Philip's narrow-eyed stare and continued. "So, such wardings aren't part of your faith?"

He shook his hands beside his head, as if fending off Jemin's question. "No! I accused those boys of sacrilege, but they claimed to know better than me. Was Hettie got them started; she dabbled in witchcraft, Brother Enod looking the other way because she was his sister. But her dabbling brought the fire down on us, a cleansing; I do believe. And while I could feel Malakai's shame and could've shamed him worse, I was at their mercy, needful as I was of assistance. So I spoke the prayers, the Ologand and the Berkish. Long prayers to the true God, full of power and purity. I'm not proud, but I did." He bowed his head. "But those wardings didn't stop them from leaving."

"Perhaps they've protected you," said Philip.

"Nah. I'm too dried up to catch a ghoul's attention. Though lately, I hear the singing something fierce."

Philip twitched. "Singing?"

The old man stretched a gnarled finger toward Orl who stood a few paces away, facing north-west, her back to the team and the Elder. Not a lick of manners in the girl.

"From that-a-way. Can you hear it? It's singing now."

"I...I think so. Though I wouldn't exactly call it singing. More a signal? What's making it?"

"No idea. But I can tell you it's nothing of forests, creeks, or caves. In fact, I assumed it was a fancy spying device you folk dropped on us from above."

"From above?"

"Happened years ago, when I was in my prime. The night blazed bright as noonday, and a ball of fire streaked across the sky. The next day, the singing started. That's right. That was when. Mmm."

Philip and Jemin exchanged a look. Jemin asked, "Did any of your kin or friends hear the singing?"

"No. Only me. Though many witnessed the lights that night. Brother Theo thought the end times were upon us. And he was correct, after a fashion. But nothing terrible happened right away. We got on with our lives and forgot. If I mentioned the singing, people smiled, knowing I'd been touched by angels at birth and afflicted with the sight."

"About this "sight" you mention. Is it related to your religion?"

The Elder's chuckle sounded like a shaken bag of dried crickets. "No, sir. It's inborn. You should know, you and your friend over yonder." He waved a hand at Orl.

Orl nodded without turning from the so-called singing's source. Philip licked his lips, presumably stunned that a chip-free feral could possess some of his precious skills.

Chief Krause asked, "Anybody else been out this way? Any other outlanders?" A real world/physical evidence type question, typical of her type.

He cocked a filmy eye in her direction. "Been a social whirl, lately. First, I heard voices on the trail, maybe ten folks. Didn't recognize their voices and couldn't understand much of what they said, them using too many special words from outside, and speaking of things we don't allow. Always in a rush, you outlanders; they didn't stop to visit. Next, a man driven crazy by hard times staggered by, weeping and ranting. I prayed for his soul. Then a kindly sort, who asked after my comfort, same as you folks. Offered to move me elsewhere. But I wasn't ready to leave."

"Are you ready now? We could make you comfortable."

"One ancient grandfather ain't worth no trouble, here, at the end of days. My family is already gone, and soon, yours will go too. Lightening or ground fire will spark a tree, and your people's poison will rain from the sky. Just as before."

Sad that the coming of the end times was the only justice his folk would know.

The Chief caught Philip's eye and pointed to the sun where it dipped toward the horizon. They couldn't possibly be willing to leave the old gent alone in the wilderness. A nervous sweat prickled his armpits. His eyes darted, seeking an idea, any other option to abandoning this precious primary source. "Okay, quick construction of a litter for Meister Canaan. Two long poles. Who has a sheet of fabric? Anybody pack a blanket or towels?"

But the Elder waved a heavily veined hand. "No. Best you be home before dark, or them goblins will find ye. I don't want to go. So get. But do me one last favor?"

"What's that?" asked the Chief.

"Before you leave, would one of you kindly kill me?"

101

Canaan's request hung like a lobbed grenade, and in the interstitial moment before the explosion, Agnet tried to wrap her mind around this new complication. People were usually clawing for more time on the planet, so someone asking to die was a novel experience. But he was asking the wrong people. Medics dealt with the dying, and Central, in its infinite wisdom, had failed to provide them with a medic.

"Would be a kindness," the old man added.

She needed to stall. "That's a big request, sir. Give us a private moment to consider."

"You seem to be a nice lady, and I'm sorry to vex you. I'd do the job myself, if my God allowed it. But he's provided for me by guiding you here. He chose my visitors wisely, goblin hunters, no doubt carrying weaponry. And killing me won't stain your souls, since you ain't believers."

Canaan folded his hands and bent his head. Praying, Agnet supposed. The team exchanged glances and moved out of earshot, toward the settlement's edge, where saplings exuberantly strove to reclaim the clearing for the forest.

Jemin, blinking scared-rabbit-style behind his face shield, grabbed her elbow. "You can't be considering—"

"Why not?" asked Brandt. "The man's out here alone, starving. And starving's a painful way to go. Instead of his stomach twisting like a neck in a noose for weeks, after one clean shot, he'd be gone, back with his family on their special afterlife planet, or whatever."

Jemin shot Brandt a withering look. "We should ignore his wishes, take him to the farm, feed him, and make him comfortable. That'd be the *right* thing to do. If he still wants to die, he can die legally, under medical supervision."

"Sure but, he's already refused your invite. Can't force him, can we?" said Philip. "He's out here lawfully, since code cedes uninhabitable land to ferals. Sort of slow suicide, anyway, living out here. They know the risks."

"So you're eager to speed up the process by putting a bullet through his brain?" Jemin clenched his gloved hands.

Philip drew back his chin, looking both appalled and prissy. "Absolutely not! I abhor physical violence. But also, murder is risky for perceivers; it leaves us open to...psychological problems."

Brandt interjected. "Whoa, bro. It's obvious you're no killer, but we aren't talking murder. We're talking about a mercy kill. Big difference. I've been on the border and've seen plenty of times when death is the best outcome. So I'm happy to oblige. Look at the guy, a pile of rags topped by a prune. Like he said, it'd be a kindness."

Pile of rags topped by a prune? For the love of Pete. She set her jaw, refusing to laugh, no matter how hard Brandt had struck her perverse funny bone, as this wasn't a moment for levity. The situation was dire, and everyone else looked so sincere. She regained full control.

"It's only a mercy killing if performed by medical personnel. Law's clear on that point. So if we help Mr. Canaan along, it falls in a dead zone—no pun intended—between homicide and suicide. Then we'd be sitting ducks, because if Central saw an advantage in calling our actions homicide, they'd be called homicide." And more than a few people would be glad to pin a murder on her.

Jemin stared at Brandt, horror writ large on his face. But he took a step toward the considerably less muscular Philip. "So then, you'd abandon him? Leave him to starve?"

Philip took a step toward Jemin. "I say allow him to choose, which differs from abandoning him. But tell me, how does forcing him to come with us differ from kidnapping?"

"You just don't want him slowing us down."

"You just want to feed off his life story."

Now they stood visor to visor. It'd be interesting to watch two low testosterone types, one who "abhorred violence," duke it out in containment suits. But they didn't have the time.

"Stand down, guys. Everybody has a valid point. Yes, that ancient man shouldn't starve alone in the forest, but we can't drag him down the mountain, and shooting him leaves us open to charges. Give me a minute to think."

She folded her arms and turned to face into the breeze racing along the ridgeline. The trees swayed, the rustling of their branches a chorus of mumbles and whispers.

Choose.

High time to make a call. And whatever call she made; she was screwed because, if headquarters wanted her out, it wouldn't matter what she did. Once you're marginal, anything you said or did was the wrong choice. And this situation practically screamed for a wrong choice. No wonder she had the jitters.

The brave Choose. And you are Brave.

Brave she was, alright, or maybe foolhardy, but the choices here, in the remains of a decaying village in the middle of nowhere, were lousy. How could she do right by the elderly man and protect her team from discord? Think fast—they needed to get a move on.

Let the Old Man choose. He is also Brave.

Not a bad idea. But how would he do the deed without violating his religion? They could rig a gun to shoot him, but Property would badger her to the grave if she "lost" a weapon.

Pills.

What about drugs? One of these fragile chip heads probably carried high-powered medication and could spare enough to euthanize one skinny octogenarian. They could mix it with food and set up a random serving of the big sleep.

Agnet held up a hand. "Philip and Jemin, I appreciate both your views. And thanks Brandt, for—um—volunteering, but we're not all on the same page. And, given our differences, any definitive action might leave bad feelings which could interfere with the mission. Now, because of his philosophy, Mr. Canaan can't act on his own. So here's a compromise. We set up an 'accident' and let chance pull the trigger, so to speak. Can anybody contribute, and no judgment, a suicide kit or any...uh...substance that's lethal in high dose?"

She'd bet on Philip. He must be tanked up post-lacuna with anti-seizure drugs, antidepressants, or antianxiety meds. And Jemin, fresh from implantation, must have chip-rejection pills.

But curiously, the person who raised their hand was Orl.

THE GUY KNOWS WEIRD STUFF

After setting Canaan up with food, water, and an exit strategy, they hurried down the slope, nobody enthusiastic about spending a night in the woods. Agnet allowed the team a break when they'd reached the valley floor. While they rummaged through their packs, she squatted on the pebbles beside the stream, balanced the radiation meter on her thighs, and collected another water sample—crystal clear without sediment. She'd monitored this area earlier, but to confirm, she wanded the tube, picking up just the odd click. Nothing above background. Nothing.

So what was the use of this stinking suit?

104

"Folks, you're welcome to fold your helmets, since it's all clear to the farm." She flipped back her face shield, unclipped the helmet, collapsed the clunky thing, and luxuriated in a lungful of fresh air. The others followed suit, and they gathered together, ready to make tracks.

Jemin wiped his sweaty slapped-red cheeks and muttered, "Could've made that call up top the ridge." He shifted his pack front ways and rooted around.

Philip curled his lip. "We're in a hurry."

"Hang on," said Jemin as he pulled a—a drum? Yes, a drum. A small barrel-shaped drum, brown with a white skin.

"Hold this, would you?" he asked Brandt.

Brandt hoisted Jemin's pack like it was a feather pillow. "We planning a circle? 'Cause I normally do my male bonding over automatic weapons."

"Ha. Ha. Hilarious." Jemin slung a strap over his shoulder, allowing the drum to hang in front of his chest. "Alright. Now please hold the pack so I can slide my arms in and latch the closure."

Brandt obliged. Once on the railway path, Jemin started drumming and chanting. The team exchanged perplexed glances. She ought to ask what the flip he was doing, but the answer would be long and condescending, and she was tired.

Brandt called out. "Hey Jemin, the ferals into drumming?"

Jemin paused his thumping, his expression a prickle rash of irritation. "Like I've told you, over and over, 'feral' is a very nonspecific term and inaccurate, if you consider that many fringe-dwellers live in stable societies."

"Sure. Sure. I know. You've got faith-based who want to stay faith-based. You've got your political dissidents. You've got crazies and back to natures. I'm not meaning to offend anybody; it's just that—"

An odd expression flittered across Brandt's face, and he didn't finish his thought, so Agnet intervened. "Jemin. 'Feral' is a catchall term almost everybody uses for out-dwellers. Give it a rest."

"Well, you all should consider the general history of catchalls." He glowered at Philip. "Some of you more than others. But answering Brandt's question, different groups reacted in different ways to marginalization. Some identified with ancient indigenous populations and amalgamated their culture with traditions originating from those tribes. Or popular culture variations on those traditions, hard to say at this point. Drumming is a big part of those cultures. This drum might attract people from that background."

Brandt responded with his usual enthusiasm. "You mean Indians? Indians would be fantastic."

Jemin pinched the bridge of his nose.

Philip said, "I read most indigenes died in the bottleneck plagues. Whether HLA antigen profiles or health care inequity were to blame is quite the controversy. I can't recall the details." He frowned, as if forcing up a memory. "Something about a coverup?"

The historian smirked. "My, my. You vaguely know your history."

Philip shot her a pained look. Sarcasm and Jemin weren't a good match; he couldn't keep it light. And seemed they'd confused Brandt, evidenced by his knitted eyebrows. She'd try to clarify. "Jemin's drumming to let drum-beating locals know we're interested in a parlay. If they respond, hopefully with words and not arrows, we'll talk."

Jemin nodded. "If anybody else is out here, we should speak to them, seeing as we've *permanently lost* our best witness."

Fortunately, everybody knew better than to reply.

Jemin trotted several paces ahead, which must've taken effort, given the exhaustion implied by those ruddy cheeks. The rest fell in behind and walked at a brisk pace, much aided by Jemin's skill on the drum. Orl followed behind them, skipping and twirling, starring in a private show.

Brandt caught Philip's eye and jabbed his thumb backwards. "She grooving to that 'singing'?"

"I think so. But incredibly, she's not my biggest concern." Philip leaned close. "Usually, Jemin seems like a typical InfoChip carrier, a group not known for compassion or tact."

"I've noticed how you've taken to him."

He rolled his eyes. Sarcasm wasn't her strong suit, either. "Like I was saying, most are more bonded to their chip than their team or reality. But he was genuinely stricken when we discussed euthanizing that old feral gent. Initially, I figured he was grieving the loss of a data set, but then I realized the upset went deeper."

Brandt whispered in her other ear. "And the guy knows a lot of weird stuff."

"He has a brand new InfoCorp chip, so of course he knows stuff," she replied, sounding curt in her own ears.

But she didn't wish to follow a rabbit down the gossip hole, even though she could relate to Brandt's comment. Jemin knew more than just history. He knew about the country, animals and livestock—info most city dwellers never came across. And he sure liked to share, unlike most folks in her orbit who kept to themselves; no need to stick a target on your tail. Early in her career she'd ignored that nugget of wisdom and had paid a price. But she was still a cards-on-the-table type, and keeping her tongue was still a struggle.

Philip continued. "I'm not troubled by the knowledge. It's other things. Him characterizing the ferals as 'marginalized,' for instance. The party line is they resisted modernity to the point of plague, insurrection, and terrorism. The government gave them a choice: participate, meaning go with the flow, or leave. So they left. That version of the story is taught in school and would be on Jemin's chip."

Brandt added. "Army told us the ferals were tolerated far past common sense, and ideas to the contrary were treason."

"You think we got ourselves a traitor?" she asked.

"Possibly," said Philip.

"No," said Brandt.

The drumbeat stopped, drawing her gaze forward. Ahead, an outlandishly attired individual blocked the path, and Jemin had come to a halt. She held up a hand. "Leave this for now, because speaking of ferals, yonder, is a fine example."

A Noteworthy Stranger

Inside the song, leaves drifted down, adding fresh color to the forest floor. Hidden creatures scuttled, rustled, and flapped, their Sounds blending with the melody. Now the Squirrel took notice of the music, pulling its body taut, tail twitching. And in the Oak's heartwood, a Worm gnawed to the beat, while an indigo blue and black message of slow Death spread from the oak through the invisible threads networking the porous soil. In counterpoint, scattered seeds sprouted between decaying roots, rejoicing in the chorus. It was glorious, a Song connecting Life, Death, and all Beings.

Those muffling Pills would've ruined the Song, and now the pills were Gone, thanks to the Old Man. The team thought she'd given the pills to Help. But Rasp would perceive the truth and accuse her.

107

OUCH. She'd bonked against something warm that gave, silvery containment suit fabric smelling of plastic and dust—someone's back. She gathered her balance and rubbed the sore spot on her nose.

Please pay more attention. Philip masked his displeasure with a false smile, another form of Lie. She rooted amongst the litter lying on his mind's floor, the most prominent thoughts a dislike of the Woodland, the leaves clinging to his boots, rocks sabotaging his footing, the buzzing Insect (Ha!) that flew onto his arm and gripped his sleeve with bristled claws. Discomfort scrabbled in the background: sweat, hunger, and ache. The Song spun his concerns into an orange thread of annoyance. A memory would soothe him. Here was one: him fitting a drawer with bamboo boxes to corral clutter into tidy packages. But did he deserve her help? No, he did Not. She'd added to his irritation, but not on purpose.

You Stopped with no warning.

Everyone stopped. There's someone ahead blocking the path.

He was correct. She should pay attention to People, but without the Pills, their constant chatter Bothered Her. Easier to block their minds Out with the much more interesting Song. Sometimes, like now, the People intruded through the Physical World, and she had to choose a response, each choice a trial. What now, for instance? Philip still held her gaze. Would a smile be appropriate? She curved her lips, but Philip had hoped for an apology and detected errors in the smile's Style and Timing. He frowned and turned to The Stranger. She needed to practice smiling more often.

Granted, The Stranger was noteworthy. Skeleton-white paint caked his face, except round his eyes, which were outlined in black. Rough fabric swathed his body. Black boots similar to the type Beggars fashioned from Scrap and Husk encased his feet. He held a long cane in one hand. Its base rested in the Dust. Its tip was Sharp. She tested his thoughts and found that like her, this rough sleeper coated in Paint, tried to repel Others with his odd clothing.

Jemin, hoping to impress, raised his hands, palms held flat toward the man and spoke in a Language similar to English but harsher with guttural vowels and too many consonants, his language, a Private Joy.

The Stranger grimaced—no—smiled, waves of hilarity rippling from him. Jemin—all of them bright and earnest in their bulky suits—amused the man.

But disappointment flooded Jemin, who wanted so badly to Perform in his special Language.

"Suppose we ought to converse in English," said The Stranger.

Brandt chuckled, caught up in the man's amusement, no disrespect of Jemin intended. The Big Man was just open in the way of the Child and lacked an Other Self.

"English suits me." The Leader stepped forward, marking herself as Alpha and speaking as her Other Self, the one with no Doubts or Fears. "Agnet Krause, Chief Investigator with Central Intelligence." She raised her gloved hand in greeting and paused, waiting for a Reply. He stayed silent but mocked them in his mind. The Leader continued. "Our team is investigating unusual activity at the work-farm yonder." She waved down the path. "Have you had any trouble with—" She glanced at Philip, seeking suggestions for the best Noun.

Philip shrugged. "Loosely, one might call them zombies or ghouls."

Zombies. The Leader had used this word to express "'dead things that moved." Philip understood the emptiness of these Creatures. So, Zombies might mean *Mud Puppets,* her private term for the things.

"Or mud puppets." Philip glanced around, probably wondering where "mud puppets" originated. Ha! So funny when her Words slid into their heads.

The Stranger grunted. "I see them as the shadows fall and find their leavings."

"Leavings?"

"Mud and rust, moss and bone." He rubbed his fingers as if sifting through Decay.

"They spontaneously collapse?"

"Must do. Though I've never seen it happen."

She scanned him for Lies. No. He spoke his truth, but he hadn't revealed Everything. His mind roiled with blood and bone, mouths gaping and rotten, a whiff of sewage, a scream. She pushed away his madness and fear, lest it devour her, extracted his Name, and inserted, "tell them," into his stream of consciousness.

Wouldn't tell governmental snitches anything. Let them demons eat 'em like they eat everything.

I know! Even Furniture and Lip Balm.

"Yep. File cabinets, stones, anything in their path." The Stranger skimmed the Team, struggling to figure out who'd Spoken. Her last comment must've sounded like a second Person in his head; she needed to be more careful.

The team exchanged confused glances, then the Leader asked, "Have you seen anyone else out here?"

He pointed the direction they'd come from. "Yonder, an old man squats in his own filth. You could ask him."

"We spoke with him," said Jemin. "You from a different settlement?"

Sure, Jemin, butt right in, thought The Leader and Philip, almost simultaneously. Both low-key disliked Jemin, as did The Stranger. Most people disliked Jemin. But most people had Bad Taste and disliked her, too.

The Stranger named Clayton Treadway threw back his head and guffawed. "No. I ain't no feral, and this paint's not tribal markings. I'm just a hermit protecting myself from the x-rays as best I can. Don't have a fancy white space suit, do I?"

Jemin opened his mouth, but The Leader shut it with a glare. "As I was saying. We're seeking information on those monsters and offer refuge. These woods aren't safe right now. Anything you've seen—"

"I don't have more to offer and don't need nobody's help." His Lies felt as thick and sticky as reheated oats. "Prefer my own company, these days, since I've thrown in the towel on other people." *Especially you freaks.* Philip's image was contrasted with that of a fellow seated at a desk. *And I recognize you from somewhere, pretty boy.* Jemin appeared, then a series of visages, each pale with bulging eyes, and white, yellow, or red hair, all from the village just over the border from his father's home. *And dough face, you look like one of them religious ferals to me. I don't need your nonsense—made less sense than the readings Granny took offa knuckle bones.*

The Leader felt his hostility and fumbled for a new Question. "You know anything about the old iron works? The door into the mountain looks modern, and we were wondering if—"

A frown curdled his face. "That's a dangerous place," he shouted, his voice raw. "You stay clear. Contamination, unsteady walls, and plenty rusted metal to give you a blood infection."

The man's emotions hit the Leader like a storm surge, and she understood that something much worse than blood infections waited under that mountain.

Interesting these Untrained People who heard noise from Others. Maybe Rasp could've Left Her Alone to grow without the endless training. Regardless, she'd need to be careful inside the Leader's mind, or she'd Notice her.

The Leader replied. "Well, um. I'm sure you're welcome at the farm. If you're threatened, drop by for a good meal—"

He chortled. Farm buildings and faces floated through his Mind. *Decade of my life lost to that dump.* "Not safe for anybody out here, you included Lady. And I need to stick to my plan, or I'll be in trouble when the cold comes. Speaking of which—" He skipped off the path and was Gone.

They stood in silence for a moment, watching Brandt charge through brambles and search behind trees. What should she do with Clayton Treadway's name, his unsaid Words and memories, revelations that would interest the Leader?

If she were a Good Team Member, she would tell. But she was Not Good. And these clues, plucked from the man's mind, must stay Secret. If they knew she could slip into their minds, they would dislike her More. They might ask Questions, even questions about Pills, the pills that made her Less. And same as Jemin, she wanted to be More.

ORPHANS ALL THE WAY DOWN

The trees were downright soporific, standing so quiet, branches hanging heavy like an unpaid bill. She'd conk out if her calves didn't ache from the walking, and this suit—the thick textile swooshing like a lullaby. But a bright dot of light appeared in the distance and grew larger with each step. That dot was the trailhead, the exit from this dismal forest and the next step toward dinner. The promise of dinner would keep her lively.

Philip said, "Pathetic that returning to a prison work farm fills me with joy."

"Me too. Can't wait for dinner."

"I'm dying for a shower. I'll scrub away every memory of this excursion: the leaves, the twitching bones, that old man's smell."

"Interesting you equate leaves with twitching slime and a dying eighty-year-old."

"Leaves cling, and I'm an urban person. The recreation quad near my building is sufficient nature for me. And speaking of nature, it's calling. I might jog ahead."

Agnet raised an eyebrow. "You could step behind a tree."

"But the leaves." Philip trotted off.

A few minutes later, she stepped out into a sliver of buttery, late-afternoon sunshine, and nearly tripped over a pair of inmates crouching in the grass. A burly man with thick, black curls and a slight, balding man with spectacles stood and whipped off their hats.

Head of curls said, "Afternoon, ma'am. Warden Honing told us to watch for you and escort you to your campsite."

Campsite?

They exchange names, but the men's appellations shot out of her brain like a blown geyser. She would sign up for the memory training class again when she returned home. And remember to go, this time. She glanced around for Philip.

"He's using the facilities." The black-haired inmate pointed to an enormous boulder surrounded by yellowing joe pye weed.

"What's this about a campsite?"

They exchanged nervous glances. The talker said, "A security precaution, nothing personal. The warden will explain."

Agnet already knew the explanation. She waited for the others to gather in the meadow. Brandt arrived with Orl's pack slung over his own. Orl exited the woods and stared around the field, wonderment all over her face, as if she'd portaled to another galaxy. Jemin dragged behind her, looking as if he could've used help with his pack as well. They grimly acknowledged the "campsite" news. Philip returned from "the facilities", looking relieved.

"Leaves?" she asked.

"Problem was grass this time. It tickles, and in truth, I could've used a leaf."

The Warden's men had pitched five tents near an isolated stand of trees about two-hundred meters from the forest edge.

"Gee, thanks," said Agnet.

Curly said, "These trees shelter the cows. They love standing in the shade and rubbing against the bark."

"Man's saying expect cow pies," Brandt said to Orl.

112

"Won't be that bad," said the skinny bald guy. "The cows haven't grazed this paddock since spring."

"Excellent," said Agnet, "Luxury accommodations."

After changing and surrendering her suit for decontamination, she crawled into her tent, stretched out on the thin pad, and propped her head on her tightly rolled sleeping bag. Wind rippled past the tent. She ought to catch a nap but worries rotated in her mind, rattling like a tattered pinwheel.

Brandt seemed ready to detonate explosives as if they were popcorn, possibly explaining his transfer to KP. Jemin reminded her of an overbred albino goldfish and brimmed with obsession, though she doubted he was a traitor, an iconoclast maybe, but not a traitor. Orl acted like a psychiatric patient and might be poised for withdrawal, even though she'd promised her pills were unnecessary, a precaution foisted on her by overprotective worrywarts. And Philip, recovering from brain surgery, was at least depressed and couldn't resist goading Jemin. Then consider herself, dispensing Orl's happy pills to some random feral, and those funny scattered thoughts she'd had in the village. Maybe the "singing" had messed with her mind. And what about the singer?

A pox on that weirdness, but at least she wasn't thinking about Mac. Until just now.

A rustle at the tent flap interrupted her downward spiral.

"Hello?" Philip's voice, hesitant but smooth as always.

"Yes?"

"Can I come in?"

Agnet tucked herself into a seated position. "I suppose you can fit."

Philip crawled in and sat cross-legged on the sleeping pad. Light leeching through the jungle camo fabric stained his skin a deep green, transforming the man into a leaf-hating woodland sprite. How paradoxical.

"Welcome to my suite."

"Thanks. I see they gave you the luxury model with a window tie." He flicked a fabric strip sewn into the canvas above the mesh window.

"As befitting my status."

He mock-saluted her. "Warden Honing walked over with the food service, and I asked, 'Why the tents?' He told me the prisoners decided last night's monster was after us and figured they'll be safer if we camped out here."

113

"I kind of guessed."

"Berg—I mean, the Warden—apologized profusely and registered as sincerely embarrassed. But he needs to keep the peace. Unfortunate, since I'm not much of a camper and could use a solid night's sleep. So, in a bid for a room with a proper bed, I reminded him we risked life and limb to destroy last night's creature and that the permanent damage amounted to one broken chair. He thanked me, reassured me he can build a new chair in a week, and said he regretted the interruption of our chess game. But the prisoners nearly rioted today."

Chess game? Interesting euphemism. "Ah, then. I understand. And feel better about sleeping on the cold ground, a thin sheet of canvas between me and the monsters."

He shot her a wry grin. "Thankfully, the farm's still feeding us."

His comment, a blatant attempt to improve her mood, made her chuckle. "Good thing, since I'm starving. But I'm usually starving." Then she flashed on the elderly feral's bony wrists. Pity he hadn't wanted to join them.

Philip sighed—her face must've exposed her dark thoughts. "Brandt's gone all enthusiastic; he made a fire. Food's warm and being served up. Want to join in?"

"Sure." She'd take her rightful place amongst the worst team ever and warm up. "Let's be careful not to set the woods ablaze."

"Wouldn't surprise me if we did. Fire's built like a fu—" Philip flushed.

"Funeral pyre?"

"Um." He brushed an invisible leaf off his shoe.

"It's alright and morbidly appropriate, given the day's events. So, tell me, what's in the pills Orl gave the old man?"

"No clue. She's being cagey about it."

"I'd appreciate a warning if she withdraws or otherwise goes haywire."

"I'll keep you apprised."

"So, what's the 'singing'? Is it the same as the déjà vu buzzing sound you were hearing?"

Philip idly toyed with the sleeping mat's product tag. "Am 'hearing'. Yeah. Canaan was talking about the same thing; he must have had nascent perceiver talent, but lucky for him, NeuroCorp doesn't recruit ferals. Orl and I compared notes on the way down the ridge. We both noticed the signal or singing on arrival. Like the old man, she describes it as singing."

"Does she sort of—er—groove to that singing?"

He winced. "Yes. I told her to knock it off, or she'd end up in a looney bin. But she doesn't care. Says the song joins her to The Everything—her words."

"Great gravy."

"Yep. She's an oddball, even from my perspective." He met her eyes, his expression somber. "Regardless, something's up in the hills."

"You think this—um—presence is dangerous?"

He went back to spiraling the tag between his fingers, a shock of messy curls hanging over his forehead. "No. Maybe. I don't know. I tried to ignore it, out of ennui at first, then out of fear. I worried the feeling was internally generated: lacunae damage, a chip syndrome, or an organic psychosis. Best thing about today was learning I'm not the only person picking up that signal. Anyway, I've been a wreck and not very nice, especially to Jemin. He gets on my nerves and with the noise in my head and those hills shooting straight up from the valley like walls, the sun sinking into them so early, and the shadows falling so dark... They give me the creeps or claustrophobia or déjà vu or something. But no excuses because my better self could handle Jemin with tact. My apologies. I'll try harder."

Damaged, everybody was so damaged. But she needed Philip. He might be a mess, but he was smart, a team player, and he alone could communicate with Orl. Still, she couldn't let him know how much she needed him, or he might stick around to do the "right thing".

"Like I said, you should be home recuperating and the minute you need out, just let me know. Don't assume for one minute that your responsibility to the team trumps your responsibility to your health. Because if you drop out in the field, you'll endanger the team."

Philip smiled. "I appreciate your effort on my behalf, but people always forget I see right through them."

Oh, brother. Perceivers were such a pain, like traveling with a drug sniffing dog when you're the drug. "I meant what I said, even though you're essentially mission critical. If you need to quit, just quit. I'll back you. But first, was the old fellow right about the singer's location?"

"Yes. The signal intensified in the village, maybe from the proximity or the lack of obstructions. Then Canaan's pointing somehow focused it for me. No doubt, it originates on that ridge's western slope."

"Can you and/or Orl lead us to the source?"

"Yes. But, come on. Let's crawl out of here, join the others, eat, and find out what they did to deserve this assignment."

"Kind of obvious, in the cases of Orl and Jemin. Uncooperative and secretive don't translate into prime assignments. Brandt did something, although he may not have noticed, since he seems to believe KP duty is a natural follow-up to a stint in border security and extraction."

Philip flipped back the canvas flap. "Probably best to leave it lie, then."

"Agreed."

They sat in a cluster, wind to their backs, and dined out of baskets. The campfire's flames reached for the sky, which deepened to a rich purpled-blue. The moon rose, orange and magnificent, its pitted face softened by a hazy band clinging to the horizon.

Brandt gestured to the moon with his fork. "Reminds me of a beach ball. Our Home won a seaside trip 'cause we scored highest on a standardized test. Not that I contributed to the win. But everyone was invited, and they drove us to a nice spot."

"An actual beach?" asked Philip.

"Must've been trucked in sand. But it was clean."

"Which district?" asked Jemin.

"Northeastern."

"I was South. We're about the same age, so you must've beaten us. I don't remember any special trips, even though I aced most of the exams."

"Figured you did, smart man."

Hmm. Jemin and Brandt grew up in the Homes too. Interesting. *On purpose.* Though, the odds were high, considering the epidemics. Logs crackled and snapped. A plume of embers spiraled skyward. She'd been placed in West as a baby, thanks to the Schism. Though the Schism was probably ancient history to this crew. She must be a decade older than these folks—*all orphans*—a glance at Orl, two decades. Perceivers were gleaned from the Homes, since nobody volunteered their kids for extreme training, unless the family was starving, or the kid was unwanted for some reason. Either way, both Orl and Philip would be some form of orphan.

Kind of unusual, an orphan leading a team of orphans.

Heavily flawed problem-orphans.

On purpose. Disposable.

Disposable? There was an unpleasant thought. Disposable meant their lives held no value. But who genuinely values anybody? Your mother, maybe, if you're lucky, your kids, and other family who love you or rely on you economically. Single, childless, an orphan: nobody depended on her. Though she was a talented investigator, others would take her place if she disappeared tomorrow. Heck, they'd be grateful for the promotion.

Agnet cleared her throat. "So just curious. Anybody married or have kids?"

Philip's fork clattered onto his plate. He'd picked up her drift.

"No sense in marriage if you're stationed on the border." Brandt fixed a white blob to the pointy end of a stick. "Pretty nice of them sending marshmallows. Store-bought are softer, but this'll do me fine." He thrust the stick into the flames. The dessert flared and vanished in a puff of smoke. His face fell as he inspected the black glossy tar which coated the stick's tip.

Jemin pinched his dessert, bit, and smiled. "Tasty. Apparently, meringue is more flammable than marshmallow."

"Here, have half of mine." Agnet said to Brandt, as she snapped her meringue in half. "No reason not to share, since—"

"Since none of us will be missed," Philip said quietly, light from the fire reflecting in his wide eyes.

"Well. I was going to say, 'since we're close to the bakery'."

Philip whispered, "As I mentioned, most people forget I see right through them."

Caught like a fish on a line. She sighed.

Lies are Bad.

Since when? Smooth-it-over lies were a crucial component of her social toolbox, though probably a habit to avoid during this mission. Perceivers were lie-bloodhounds, and being caught in a lie, even a white lie, wasn't much fun.

"Wonder what we orphans got ourselves into," said Jemin.

Agnet shrugged. "Not sure. But I assume something dangerous and tangled with power or money."

"Yep." Brandt must've caught up. Maybe his obliviousness wasn't so oblivious. "That grandpa talking about corporate types out in the forest didn't sound good neither."

"The suits bother you? I'm more bothered by the gooey child-monsters," said Philip.

"Nah. Those things are weak," said Brandt. "Think about it. Us three took a big one out with no injury. Realistically, a gator, something normal, would've been more of a challenge. Way more. Sure, a monster dragged a guy into a pond, but not everybody's standing by a pond. Not everybody has a faulty ticker. So, I don't get why the inmates are all riled up. With all the shovels and pitch forks lying around, a crowd of criminal types should do just fine against one of those monsters."

Agnet inspected her meringue. Could the genius who baked this delicacy toss a monster into his oven? Doubtful, but you never knew. He or she could be a beefy street-brawling lunatic. "I take your point. But most people are average people, Brandt. Just regular. And monsters scare regular people."

"You think we've been set up?" Jemin looked highly aggrieved. Poor guy had had a lousy day.

"Possibly. But by who and why? Makes me feel curious and sort of ornery." And truth be told, she cared about this goofy dysfunctional team, about the farm, and about the apples. Cripes, she even cared about that ancient fellow they'd left up the mountain. Sure, caring didn't make a difference, career-wise, and she wouldn't succeed in the hierarchy's eyes, even if she saved the entire freaking world. But screw it tight as a weevil dug into a corn kernel; she'd save the world anyway, just to spite them.

"Of course, my curiosity might get someone killed. So, if any of you want to sit this one out, I won't blame or report you. That said, is anybody game to chase down an eerie presence? I'd estimate a two to three-day hike with a night or two in the woods, depending on the level of radiation because, if it gets too hot, we call it quits."

Philip, Mr. Outdoors man, looked grim.

"I'm in. Anything for that cookie-half." Brandt grinned and held out his hand.

Agnet passed the meringue-half over, glad he was willing. Brandt was her best defense against monsters. Still, no tracking the signal without perceivers, so she turned in their direction. Orl nodded. Philip shrugged. Tepid, but she'd interpret that shrug as a "yes".

The historian, on the other hand, would be dead weight. "How about you, Jemin? Are you up for more adventure after today's disappointments? Or would you rather stay at the farm and interview more prisoners and staff?"

He shoved his glasses up his nose. "Today didn't discourage me. I'm a professional. I know field work is erratic. Sometimes you win, sometimes your colleagues assist the suicide of a key informant."

Philip grimaced. "We're all sad about Mr. Canaan, really. But I believe the Chief made the right decision, given the situation."

Brandt delivered one of his friendly shoulder punches; now Jemin grimaced. "Sure be nice if the geezer was sitting here, eating a good meal, and telling his stories. Well, after a bath maybe. But it didn't happen that way. That's just the breaks."

Jemin sighed. "No. It didn't happen that way. But I'm curious, and in pursuit of the truth, I'll gladly venture over the ridge."

A line appeared between Philip's eyebrows; he must've been hoping Jemin would stay put. But why not believe Jemin could rise to the occasion?

"All right. Here's the plan. We follow our only lead, this presence on the other side of the ridge. If that lead is a bust, I'll call in, tell Central we hit a brick wall, and request a lift out. Brandt and I will train the farmers to demolish monsters on their own while we wait for our ride. Seriously doubt the locals will miss us when we go."

Agnet bit into her meringue half. It was crisp and sweet, with a slightly chewy center. The work farm wouldn't be an awful place to land, despite the zombies. Almost worth committing a crime, and that crime could be minor since the place was low security. Maybe back home, she'd take up shoplifting.

"I have a few questions for the Warden," said Philip. "Plus, I'll need a shower."

"Perfect. I was just going to ask you to interview Honing. I'll give you a list of questions to merge with your own. So, we'll take one more day here. I'll write up a report, just as an interim. I don't think we know enough to justify a pigeon. You ask your questions. Everybody rest, clean up, and eat as much as you can hold while seeming polite, then let's go meet ourselves a presence."

The Silent Spinning Stars

The Stars silently spun above, the Moon glowed pale and calm, and The Song wove the camp flames into a tapestry. Immense and beautiful, this night, despite the Minds chattering, their noise Incessant, even when the talking slowed. Consciousness wasted on nonsense. *That suit stank like a gym locker by the end of the day.* So much Emotion: despair, yearning, and the Tired of Older People. Perhaps the pills had served a purpose: shielding her from other minds.

Her thought about the Pills touched Philip, and he responded. *I should ask Orl about those pills.* He removed himself from the Group, and sat beside her, his location inconsequential but proximity was a Habit for him during conversation. As long as he didn't Touch her, Philip could ask all the Questions he wished. She would Choose what to reveal.

Are you ready for a hike over the ridge?

Yes.

Any idea what we'll find?

No.

Sounds as if the man knows his pancakes.

Curiosity battled Unease. The song called her, but what if the Singer was a trap? She enjoyed Pancakes as much as the Leader. She wanted Chances to eat more pancakes and didn't wish to be Destroyed, now that she was free.

What if we run into zombies? Brandt thinks they're weak, but I was really worried about you last night. You were as cold as ice.

A shudder traveled through her at the memory of the Cold. She hugged her blanket close and savored the Fire.

A precious link to the past, and they allowed him to die, even encouraged him.

She'd probed that monster too Close, trying to detect a Mind. She'd let it crawl through the Tunnel she'd created; it'd been attracted to her Life. A Mistake she wouldn't make again. How to explain to Philip while avoiding questions?

She can toast my marshmallow any day.

Ah, yes. Brandt. He was an Example.

Brandt is safe. He has no Openings; he is Solid and One Thing.

She picked up a rock to demonstrate. The rock was smooth and cool, solid, unknowing, unafraid. She handed it to Philip. But we are not all Solid. You and I, the Leader: we are at risk.

Philip stared at the rock, picking through her words for meaning, arriving somewhere close. *I get why you and I are at risk, but why Agnet?*

She is Open in the way of the Solid.

Rambling like a street corner lunatic, this girl. Philip cast about for an appropriate Noun, settling on Empathy with a Question Mark. She assimilated Empathy with a Question Mark, envisioning the thin line of light that outlined a door opened just a crack.

What were those pills, Orl?

Finally, his question.

You wouldn't Understand.

But he would understand; she'd Lied. Not a minor social lie to "smooth things over", a Significant Lie to suit her own Purposes. The worst sort of lie. But if Philip knew why she took the Pills, he would be Scared. They wouldn't take her to the Singer. No. They'd contact Rasp, and she'd be forced to escape and locate the Singer on her own. She usually preferred Alone, but now...

All right, but if you feel poorly, please let me know. We're here to help. You're not on your own.

She didn't reply because she didn't know how to not be On Her Own. Philip sighed, annoyed at her but also Concerned. Not concerned she wouldn't be of Use. No. He was worried about her Actual Self.

Unusual. Almost nobody worried about her Actual Self.

He was complicated, this Philip, heavily layered like an old chimney covered in years of soot. His core felt Lost and Alone. People didn't Understand him either and were often unkind or afraid. So, in some ways, they were the same.

Philip mulled over her Deficiencies. She almost desired to reassure him, but what could she say? The Truth would frighten him, and she didn't wish to lie again. With discretion and care, she drew his attention to the campfire. He excused himself and rejoined the Others, his mind already structuring future chats with the Leader and the Warden. She felt a surprising Pang of Absence when he left.

Had she grown comfortable among these Unafraid but Annoyed people? She preferred annoyed to Afraid. Everybody at NeuroCorp feared her, even Rasp. And she hated them for their fear. A vicious cycle that fear and hate, the attempts to Control, her becoming extra-dangerous in retaliation, and corroding her Actual Self.

She watched a flock of embers scatter into the ink-dark sky. Things could not stay the Same. Things could not stay Hidden. Eventually, one of these people around the fire would Notice and become Afraid. She should stop thinking with them and leave them to their own mistakes. Her ideas probably wouldn't help them, anyway. Because they were disposable; she recognized the signs. And the disposable people always disappeared.

Orl drifted from Philip's mind and touched the Forest's edge. She'd keep watch tonight, and if a monster visited, she would wake Brandt first. Brandt had killed the Monster with gusto, like a big woolly Dog shredding a Toy; he'd almost found it funny. Unafraid, strong, and safe and he found her Actual Self fantastic with an exclamation point. He would protect her from the Cold.

Alone and not alone, thanks to the Song and the other Minds, Orl sank back into the stars and waited.

Kept Quiet, Gone Feral or Dead

A hazy line of yellow heralded the dawn. How Philip disliked this far too early in between state, too late for sleep, too early for everything else. But he was wide awake, thanks to the chill and several stones beneath his sleeping pad. A gray strip of something had landed on his tent during the night, detritus from some tree, no doubt; he plucked it off. No. It wasn't vegetation. It was rotted cloth, an oval set within an oval. What on earth?

Brandt trotted over, looking far too enthusiastic for the hour. "That's one of the monster's ears. Looks like a bunny ear to me."

"Oh." His fingers were touching monster leavings. How deeply unfortunate.

"Orl heard them and woke me. Lucky for us, because the Chief, who was on watch, didn't hear a sound." Brandt swung his fist into the flat of his other hand. "We clobbered them. It went down too fast to wake you. Sorry you missed the action."

"Oh! Uh, no. Sounds like you did a bang-up job. And I don't mind missing out, but I'm always glad to help, if needs be." Hopefully, he sounded convincing.

"Wasn't much of a challenge, given their small size. I even felt kind of stupid when it was over. Like smacking a spider then noticing how tiny it is when it curls up dead." The big man's face fell; nice to learn he didn't take killing lightly.

"Better an easy job than a hard one. And disposing of those things early before they expand might be smart. Glad you didn't get hurt. Is everybody else all right?"

"All good." Brandt grinned like sunshine through the rain. He seemed to be a person who'd slip through a keyhole to restore a positive outlook. "Who knows what monsters we'll find in the forest? Maybe huge ones, full of trees and elk."

"Giant blobs walking on tree limbs and waving antlers would certainly be a challenge."

"Yeah!" said Brandt, as if giant monsters would be fun.

"We'd better be ready."

He saluted then trotted off, probably hunting for a tree monster-worthy weapon.

Philip tucked his hands into his armpits and jogged in place, trying to drum up some heat. Several trainees were trotting breakfast across the field, but no sign of Berg. He'd have to chase the Warden down and make pleasant conversation after spending the night in a tent, sleeping bag zipped to his nose.

A trainee approached wearing a narrow-eyed stare. Philip hid the bunny ear behind his rear and attempted a pleasant smile. He had a hunch the prisoner's suspicions were correct; the zombies were most likely attracted to them, Orl in particular—she radiated energy like a small hostile sun. Best to toss this bunny ear into the fire and not mention last night's attack. No need to spook the inmates further.

Jemin stepped close. "Good thing Brandt's not around to jaw about bashing monsters."

"Man does enjoy a story," said Philip, noting the zipper indent on the historian's cheek.

"I was wondering—would you mind if I accompany you on your fact-finding mission? I'd like to ask Warden Honing a few questions as well, and since he's taken a shine to you—"

"He is quite the chess enthusiast."

Jemin turned pink, the same color Gervais had dyed that yappy poodle. "Yes, well. Chess. I see. Anyway, I need a few minutes with the Warden. And if you could—you know—scrutinize his responses."

No. Jemin didn't want his help. Jemin was just afraid to approach Berg alone. And if Jemin came along, he'd probably stick his foot in his mouth and ruin the interview. He scanned for an excuse while Jemin waited, a combination of hopeful and obstinate.

"Orl and I have some other matters to attend to. Let me check in with her."

He bought time pretending to message Orl, but the kid was deep in stage four sleep, no doubt recovering from last night's drama. While he stalled, the trainees departed, and Agnet began rifling through a basket of food.

Jemin glanced at him. "Come on. We better hurry or she'll eat everything. Afterwards, we can find the Warden."

During breakfast, Jemin ran his idea of a joint interview past Agnet, who approved. Then privately, she reminded Philip of his desire to strengthen his "better self" and a few minutes later, he and Jemin were crossing the stubbled field toward the prison compound. Philip ran his hand over his chin, rehashing his dislike of stubble while Jemin huffed and puffed beside him. Not an evil person, Philip reminded himself, just overly focused on his own interests and socially inept. Remarkably socially inept.

"It'd probably be best if I did most of the talking."

"Of course, you're the expert interviewer," said Jemin, a pinched tone to his voice.

They found Berg in a machine shop and waited for an opportune moment to interrupt. Jemin described the function of various tools, then launched into a harangue about dust-rich air and spontaneous combustion. A worker, radiating anxiety, glanced over his shoulder. The man's workmate glowered at Jemin. "Hear that whooshing noise? That's an industrial vacuum. No risk of dust fires at Ridgelands. Now piss off. Your yakking is slowing us down."

Philip apologized to the man, linked his arm around Jemin's, and walked him several steps toward the door. He whispered, "Lower your voice and be careful what you say. People are already frightened. They don't need to hear about nasty ways to die."

"I'm just sharing information."

"Most people don't want information; they want reassurance. And they remember you by how you make them feel, not by what you know."

"Don't be absurd. Everybody—"

"Trust me. Everybody doesn't. Last night, I slept on the ground because the prisoners fear us. Did you enjoy sleeping on the ground?"

"No?"

"Neither did I. So how 'bout we avoid fear-inducing subjects, like spontaneous combustion, and other forms of accidental death."

Jemin shot him a baffled look, wandered toward some equipment, and began jotting notes. The guy's skull was as thick as the Southern Barricade. He leaned against the wall, mindful of the rough wood planks' ability to pull threads. The smell of pine sap suffused the air. He tuned into Berg's conversation—a long conversation about the extension of a fence, repair of a shed, a retaining wall...

Brother, was he bored. He wasn't a tool user, never had been. Always had to call a fix-it type when knobs came loose, or switches failed. Tradespeople either didn't show up or were exorbitantly expensive. Be nice to have mechanical expertise in-house. Berg beamed in his direction, as if he'd picked up on Philip's vibe, perhaps another regular person with low-level perceiving abilities; he wouldn't have pegged the prison warden as the type, but one never knew.

Ouch.

He pulled his hand off the wall and sucked a splinter from the fleshy pad of his index finger.

Berg strolled over. "Sorry 'bout the camping last night. Just couldn't think of another way to settle my people down."

"Don't worry about it. We'll clear out the zombies, then you and I can have a rematch." Philip couldn't resist tilting his head and smiling in a manner that reeled them in every single time. The Warden smiled in return—score one for Philip Spool, master of flirtation. He raised his perceiving level and hunted for an energy signature—there, a nimbus spinning like cotton candy around Berg's head. "But speaking of those zombies, I have a few questions, follow-ups to yesterday's excursion. Does the prison maintain any facilities in the woods?"

Berg startled. "Facilities in the woods? No, nothing out there. What would be the point?"

"We wondered why that trail's being maintained and by whom."

"Carson noticed that cleanup this summer," said someone with a shrill voice that came from behind the Warden. "Said alls a'sudden he could see straight down the trail, as though somebody'd cleared it." Berg turned, revealing the speaker, a carrot-top, who looked up from his sawdust-covered worktable, a self-satisfied smile on his face, as if he'd solved world hunger.

The Warden frowned and placed his hands on his hips. The inmate ducked his chin and stuttered, "He only stood at the trailhead, looking. He didn't walk off property. I guess he might've been wrong." He gave Philip an apologetic glance. "Th'only folks out that way are your ferals. And they're not known for tidying up, especially so close to the farm."

A twitch of Berg's lips sent the prisoner scampering to a far corner. He ushered Philip toward the door, away from any other curious ears. "Perkins can't keep his trap shut, and Carson's usually full of shit, but he's right. 'Round mid-summer, guards reported the path had been spruced-up."

"Around the time your zombie problem started?"

"Yeah. Now that you mention." He sighed. "Two things never linked up in my head, even though, as I've said, I don't believe in coincidences." Berg's field rippled slightly, a light disturbance, consistent with regretting an unintentional omission. A reaction to intentional-omission-revealed was usually more intense.

"You aware of activity at an old ironworks on the trail, maybe mining, a waste depo, or a research project?"

A thousand tiny muscles played around Berg's lips and eyes. His aurora pulsed and warped—in this context, only truth-evasion could explain such a high deflection. At least, he didn't lie easily or with pleasure.

"That heap of rubble and rusted scrap? I'm surprised you ventured in. What made you believe someone's working there?"

"A pair of heavy-duty, modern doors. They piqued our curiosity but were locked."

Berg was silent for a moment, stalling. The spun sugar glow writhed while he stroked his jawline. He also sported light stubble, but it looked good on him. A shame to think this appealing guy might be up to his elbows in an evil scheme.

"Decades ago, EarthCorp tinkered around at that site, but that was before my time. I figured they'd run a salvage operation. What else could it have been? But I'm unaware of anything more recent."

A blatant lie.

His expression went stern. "Whatever it is, somebody worked hard to keep it private. A sign, in my long and not always pleasant experience, to not look to close. So I'm the opposite of curious. I'm anti-curious, and whatever it is, I'm glad it's downstream of the farm."

"Did you, staff, or trainees look for monsters in that direction?"

"Heck, no. Prisoners aren't allowed off property, and the staff sticks to the compound, given the ferals, the contamination, and now the monsters. If there's been a rare few that's wandered down that way, they've kept quiet, gone feral, or they're dead. Me personally, I've suited up and explored the path and ironworks, but not in a long while. I'm too busy for nature walks."

Jemin, hovering at the edge of the conversation clutching his rag book, said, "So you *didn't* visit an old man in the village up-slope from the ironworks?"

Philip cringed. Tactless, questioning Berg's truthfulness, but when Berg frowned and answered "no" in a gruff tone, the man's magnetic field warped like a palm tree in a hurricane.

Jemin, despite his obvious rabbit-eyed terror, asked, "Any inmates friendly with the local sects?"

"The what?"

"The ferals." Philip clarified.

"Not that I know. Most of the trainees hate 'em because of a bunch of tall tales. In reality, the ferals are poor. Real poor. And often diseased. Because of the health issue, I encourage the community to steer clear and don't try to stamp out their stupid scare stories." Berg shifted from foot to foot, looking over their heads, acting out a desire to flee.

Jemin peered up from his notes. "Can you elaborate on those stories?"

"Uh, snatching babies. Leading the lost astray. Cannibalism. They're supposed to be magical, talking to beasts, flying, cavorting with the underworld. The usual."

"Fascinating. Can you refer me to one of the storytellers?"

Berg frowned. "How's you gabbing about fairytales gonna help us run off these monsters? Leave my people alone; they're jittery enough already."

Philip tapped Jemin's ankle with the toe of his boot to bring him on-topic. His eyes blinked behind his glasses, as if surprised not everyone shared his arcane interests. His neck

127

flushed red, but he blundered forward like a police pig snouting for drugs, "Any new arrivals over the summer?"

"Oh, sure. A few new trainees, as usual, and those couple government teams, like I told you."

The energy around the warden wavered again. That same fluctuation. And that eye movement, a mere flicker, but telling. Philip launched a trial balloon. "Anybody other than inmates?"

"Who the hell else would...oh, you mean staff? No. We haven't added new staff."

Berg thrust his hands into the pockets of his overalls, holding fast to his story and concealing the truth. Time to obliquely broach the subject of the vengeful ghost. "Tomorrow, we head out for two to three-days, investigating the woods. Anybody we should look for? Anybody recently gone missing?"

"We're down seven since this monster business started. One dead, pulled into the pond, as I explained. Six...took off. Good luck to them."

Jemin's eyes went googly. "You mean escaped!"

"Yeah, escaped." Berg was merely following Jemin's carelessly provided lead, as evidenced by the sizable energy deflection underscoring the warden's lie. But the curve of his lip indicated sorrow lay beneath the lie, not the more common fear or sense of triumph. Berg wasn't happy with either his cover up, the "escape", or both.

"Could you provide descriptions of the escapees, a list of names in case we come across them out in the forest?"

"Sure. But don't be afraid or get overzealous. None of them are violent offenders. Just let them know they'd be welcome back anytime, no judgment."

"Any idea why they left?"

"Rumor was the monsters spooked them, and they set off for New Delphi. No protective suits. No counters. No papers. Just took off."

No doubt Berg started that rumor himself.

"Bad choice, Delphi. Bet they didn't like what they found, if they made it," said Jemin.

Berg's face clouded. "I gathered. No produce orders out of Delphi for four months. You got news from there?"

"22N23, kappa variant. Public Health blames a mutant of last year's strain passed through an avian intermediary." Jemin shot Philip a self-satisfied look. Even if the information was tragic, the guy loved doling it out.

Berg crossed his arms and stared out the shop's double door, his face stamped with the tired of a powerful person who's carried the load for too many others far too long. "Some days feels as if this planet don't want us no more; can't say I really blame her. Look, I got to get back to work. You two talk to Roselle in the office, that the small building next to the mess hall. She'll give you the files on those men. I hope you find them. They'd be better off here, zombies or no." He slapped a straw hat on his head and stalked through the door into the yard's bright daylight.

Philip motioned for Jemin to follow him outside. They walked by a group of trainees fixing some kind of farming implement, then another group rubbing rust from tools with rectangular gray stones. Once they were out of earshot, he said, "Warden Honing lied about walking that path and about new arrivals. But you knew that."

Jemin's eyes flicked every which way but toward Philip's.

"Out with it." Philip casually inspected his nails, feigning indifference.

"Fine. My sources entered the farm this summer. Honing encountered them on the trail and invited them in. He's given them safe harbor."

"We're talking about the feral boys who abandoned the village?"

"Well... Yes." Jemin's expression conveyed a stuttering defiance. "The convicts don't take kindly to ferals, so those boys' situation is precarious, and they asked me to keep their secret."

"You think Berg visited the old man and invited him to shelter?"

Jemin nodded. "Yep. Can't imagine anybody else offering shelter out here. The man we met on the path was homeless and mentally ill. He couldn't've helped Mr. Canaan, even if he'd wanted to."

"I understand why you kept quiet about those kids. And I sort of understand why Berg would hide them; he probably isn't sure how we'd treat ferals."

"He put two and two together. Federal policy is harsh, and we're a government team. The boys called the Warden 'a righteous heathen', and, if I take their meaning correctly, I agree. His lying to protect them doesn't bother me."

"Me neither, even though I'm not crazy about mystical beliefs systems. To hate-based for my liking. They used to string people like me up by the ankles. Imagine gradually suffocating as your intestines crush down on your lungs. Hard to understand why brutal murders would please an all-loving god, but anyway. This situation is just sad: that decimated village, that ancient man dying alone, those few survivors hiding out at a prison. They didn't ask to be born out here, isolated, and brought up to believe in fairy tales, any more than I asked to be acquired by NeuroCorp. I wouldn't report them."

Jemin gave him a complicated look. He clearly had something else to say but merely nodded.

"One more detail," said Philip. "Berg also lied about the six individuals who absconded."

"Didn't know about those guys. And I didn't notice him lying. But it's not my job to nose inside other people's heads." Implying "I don't care" and "that's your job." He slapped his notebook shut and slid it into his jacket's oversized pocket. End of conversation, apparently. Jemin had reverted to his usual pissy self.

"You going to talk to those fer—those villagers?"

"No. I'm going to research the nuclear accident, the fallout, the ironworks, the surrounding townships, covering about three-hundred years. I'll be useless when I'm done, buzzed-up but too tired to move. The chip really burns through acetylcholine."

"Sure, but when will you tell them about Canaan?"

Jemin glowered. "I don't know. What would I say? They consider suicide a mortal sin. And how would I dodge the legal and ethical implications of our actions without lying?"

"So lie or omit the details. Just let them know he passed. For closure, you know?"

The historian squirmed. Philip waited, sensing a struggle to express emotion or divulge a confidence.

Pink splotched Jemin's cheeks, and he blurted, "They'll grieve, and other people's grief confuses me. Sure, I feel terrible about the old man's death, but those boys will feel terrible in a different way I won't quite grasp."

Jemin's admission, intense and raw, came as a complete surprise.

"It's been worse since the implant, as if the chip dampens primitive midbrain impulses," Jemin quietly added, almost to himself. "I'll have to investigate that theory...later."

Transforming anxiety into a research project, a common defense for intellectuals. "It's good you've noticed the change. It's not uncommon for people with data-chips to feel distanced from emotion. Some don't mind, having always been cerebral types. Others dislike the effect, but don't worry there are methods to preserve social and emotional fluency. Keep track of your reaction, especially this early on. Engraftoxenophobia is a real issue."

And chip-heads turned into robots all the time.

Jemin straightened up and firmed what passed for his chin. "I am self-aware enough to realize emotions were never my strong suit." His tone was snippy. "But don't worry about me. Unlike perceivers, we usually don't commit suicide, and so far, I haven't felt the urge to take a bottle opener to my skull."

Verbal distancing accomplished, the quirky little man added physical distance by marching off toward camp. Philip headed to the office and chatted up the adorable Roselle. She supplied him with the information on the escapes and favored him with smiles, fluttering long eyelashes, and displays of significant cleavage. On the long chilly walk across the barren field, Philip Spool speculated about those missing prisoners, Berg's personal integrity, and Jemin's personality, such as it was, eroding with each use of his chip.

DOWN THE TRAIL

Agnet checked her pack's side pocket. There it was—her flattened face shield neatly tucked away. Nice they wouldn't have to be use containment suits for a stretch, and if the meter kept reading at background, they'd hike the entire trip unencumbered. Still, she couldn't work up enthusiasm. Her knee ached because of a thin bedroll and the cold ground. And the weather matched her mood. Murky gray clouds hung dank and cold, like wet socks dripping on the line. Everybody else looked excited, or, in Philip's case, attentive. But she'd dreamed about that last mission—the sketchy intel, that grotesque genetic experiment tossing Mac like a used tissue, his blood splashed across the wall like a flung bucket of paint. Mac was gone, so no sense dwelling on the past, but it'd kill her if anything bad happened to this crew.

Good grief.

This team's floundering peculiarity must've triggered her protective instinct, an instinct that could lead to poor decisions. She'd need to watch herself.

She scanned the meadow for Jemin. Where could he be? They'd nothing more to learn here, and Warden Honing wanted them gone, thanks to the blabbing of the breakfast crew who'd spotted a small, partly disintegrated pirate's hat, a parting gift from last night's trio of monsters, little things waving from the forest's edge like horrifically mutated wood sprites. Even Brandt couldn't pump up enough juice to flatten them.

Good thing shooing them off the property included an excellent breakfast and generous supplies for the trek, including a nightmare inspired rifle, an old-school bolt action model with a beautiful wooden gunstock, all metal working parts retrofitted with carbon fiber or flourocarb resins.

Brandt lumbered over. The damp grass had soaked his pants to his knees, but he didn't seem bothered. "That dang hat must've blown off in the wind."

"Or the monster knocked it off, waving and jumping as they did."

"They're trying to lure us into the forest."

"Not much of a lure, something that ugly."

"Still meant the source of this bad is in the forest, and I'm ready to wade through leaves, no matter how slippery, into the heart of the darkness." He folded his arms over his chest, accentuating his biceps.

Wouldn't it be nice if slippery leaves were her biggest concern? "Glad you're eager. Let's hope the heart of darkness is interesting and challenging but nonlethal."

"Something I could take out mano a mano would be nice or maybe Orl will waste some spooky weirdness with her superpowers."

He grinned at the kid who mono-eyed back at him through her bangs. Orl's outfit resembled a basket of used shoeshine rags; the containment suit had been a fashion upgrade. And how exactly could she see properly from under that hair? "Hey Orl, no depth perception with just one eye, and you'll need every advantage to defend yourself from the zombies. Why not tie back your hair?"

She slunk behind Philip, who grinned and said, "She says you're not the boss of her."

"Actually, I am the boss of her. Tie back your hair, Orl."

Brandt hiked a thumb at her. "See there, Phil my man. That's confidence. Confidence isn't just an inborn thing; it can be learned."

Philip shot Agnet a kill-me-now look, hoisted his pack, and set off across the meadow toward the path, Orl trailing behind him, vaguely resembling a pet emu. Here came Jemin, just starting across the corn stubble and dressed in a containment suit; he must've slept through the pre-trek meeting's containment-suit-pack-vs-wear discussion. Agnet waved him to the trailhead, then she and Brandt followed Philip.

Their intrepid historian had the decency to jog the final few meters, leaving him blotchy and breathing hard while he scrutinized the team's faces. "Yes, I'm late, but no reason for looking at me, same as vermin."

Philip narrowed his eyes. "I could list some reasons."

"And where're your suits?" Predictable he'd counter with an attack instead of an apology, and his voice reminded her of her perpetually disapproving neighbor, what's-her-name.

Agnet resisted drumming her fingers on her arm. "At the meeting, we agreed, 'no containment suit until required'. Hiking in a suit wears a body down, and we're carrying extra weight for this longer expedition." She refrained from adding that some of their party wasn't particularly fit. "So strip the suit off and pack it."

"Seems imprudent. Back at Central, I *proactively* downloaded a sixty-year-old survey maps and studied them yesterday and this morning." He twitched a lip at Philip. "One set displays the fallout in minute detail. Radiation should blanket the region except for this valley and the area around New Delphi."

"But I haven't detected any radiation beyond a few clicks off monster remains. Like I said at the meeting, I'll monitor as we go, and if it gets hot, we'll suit up. So go on; strip down to your day clothes and pack your suit."

Jemin gripped his suit's fabric like a baby clings to a lovie-blanket. "And you're *absolutely* sure your meter's functional?"

Endless debate. As she lived and breathed, the man should've been a lawyer. "Yes. I swapped it, last minute, like everything else about this mission. My first unit was hot as if someone'd shoved the head of the wand into contaminated river sludge. Wouldn't have known, but I flipped it on in the prep room. It rattled like a tree of cicadas when I wanded the potted plant."

"Holy bag of buffalo stones!" cried Brandt.

"Radioactivity could've explained that plant's unlikely survival," said Philip.

"True, but the table leg and my clothes set the meter off too. The notion of a big ole sarcoma growing on my thigh after carrying the thing around left me sorely aggrieved."

Brandt wrinkled his nose. "Hope Property was ashamed. What was their sorry excuse?"

Philip flicked a dismissive hand. "Property's a bunch of passive-aggressive clotheads incapable of shame."

"Agreed but, I didn't have the pleasure of their shamelessness. The entire staff was MIA when I helped myself to a new meter. Just checked for a recent calibration certificate, tested it on the contaminated unit, then slapped a hazard sticker on that piece of junk and shelved it. Didn't even turn in paperwork."

Jemin's eye bugged. "You didn't file paperwork?"

"No. I. Did. Not."

That settled the matter. Jemin, possibly inspired by a chief unruly enough to forgo paperwork, promptly struggled out of his suit, rolled it up, and shoved it into his pack. Philip's eyes bored into the little historian, prompting Agnet to throw her elbow into his flank. Honestly, these two.

"What took you so long, anyway?" Brandt asked as he showed Jemin how to fold the shield.

"Here, I'll do it." Jemin snatched the shield, crammed it into his pack, and gave the ties a forceful yank. "Took considerable courage, considering the *awkward circumstances*, but I spoke to those village boys, my—um—sources, as you've probably surmised. They were right sorry to hear of Elder Canaan's 'passing'." Jemin made outsized finger quotes while glaring at Philip. "But I confirmed that Warden Honing did try to coax him to the farm. He let the boys know he tried. The Warden seems to be a good man, despite the information he's withholding. Though the boys said unbelievers can be inconsistent, goodly then vile depending on the wind's direction." He shot Philip a loaded expression, then skirted Brandt who looked to be gearing up for a companionable shoulder punch.

They started down the trail. Today, the foliage seemed more brown than gold. It dripped condensation and coated the paths, each step treacherous in her clunky boots on the matted leaves. Brandt's slippery leaf concerns now seemed prescient.

"Learn anything about the factory?" she asked Jemin, sounding sharp in her own ears, though she'd already have this information if he hadn't snored through the meeting.

Jemin startled and coughed, as if he'd been caught pondering secrets.

"Yes...a metalworks, as I thought, but steel *and* zinc..."

He continued to jaw—Agnet didn't focus on the details. The story was the same no matter the setting, one disaster leading to another, raw greed, poisoned land, a sickened population, and here we are, clinging by our nails to the edge of extinction.

Brandt leaned over and whispered, "Least we'll be armed when the end times come," as if he'd read her mind.

The going was slow, despite their early start. Orl and Jemin struggled beneath their packs, and the day's somber cast didn't help their spirits. Shy of midday, as they drew near the abandoned steel yard, Philip stopped and stared off into the forest. He made a wriggling motion with his hand as if miming a snake.

"See there? Anyone think that's a path? If it is, it's headed in the correct direction."

"Could be. Could be a woodsy death trap," said Jemin.

Agnet peered into the forest. "Could be a fluke, random spacing between the trees mimicking a path." She pulled the topographical map and a pair of reading glasses from her pouch. The glasses had become non-optional this year. Time was creeping up on her. She unfolded the map, and Philip peered over her shoulder.

"We're here." He pointed. "Destination's here-ish." He moved his finger to a spot on the Western side of the ridge.

"That's other-side-of-the-hill from the metal works."

"Exactly. So if this potential trail runs up the slope, over the ridge, and down, we're there."

"No trail markings on the map. Few features between here and there."

Brandt tapped a meandering blue line. "This creek we can follow downhill, worse comes to worst. And see these clearing or bare areas, here and here? I wouldn't mind camping in a clearing. Less dripping from the leaves."

Leaves again. But both she and Philip agreed with Brandt; camping in a clearing would be preferable. The trees were too many and too close.

Brandt stepped off the track and wandered between the trunks. He knelt and brushed the leaves aside in one spot, stood, and inspected a second, then a third spot. "A layer of hard dirt below the leaves instead of loam. This is a trail, alright, but it could be a deer trail. Still, I wouldn't count 'er out, since deer may have business over the ridge, and if the trail peters out, we've got compasses and a map. Forest isn't that dense, but if it thickens up, I can bushwhack with my knife."

"Sounds good. Let's hike in. We move at the pace of the slowest. Stick close. I'll take the lead and monitor every twenty paces. Philip, bring up the rear and mark our trail, in case following the stream's not an option, because of dense foliage or what have you. Stay hydrated but watch your intake until we've tested that stream."

They filed off the track and into the woods.

A Rustle in the Leaves

Agnet paused to monitor a rock and a clump of grass just beside the trail. Hearing no clicks she caught up with Brandt, not a difficult feat, considering the team was moving at a snail's pace. But this patch of forest provided plenty of eye candy: carpets of orange leaves, yellowing ferns, rocks splotched with blues and greens, a rare treat for a city girl.

Brandt said, "Down South, the forest was choked up with palmetto thickets. Had to hack through with a machete. Humid muck passed for air, and those cypress swamps were creepy: branches hanging overhead, moss dripping down, black water full of them slick knees."

"Knees?"

"Wooden lumps the trees use to breathe in the water. They look like the humps of a sea serpent."

"Glad to hear it. I was imagining something else."

Brandt chuckled. "But this forest suits me: fine colors, no biting insects, a man can wear a jacket without sweating. Sure, today's rainy, but I can do wet if it honestly declares itself."

The forest smelled good, too, sort of...woodsy.

"And look at the trees—dignified with serious age on them. The trunk on that one is seven-men-wide. Sure makes a mockery of those spindly Southern pines."

"Not really a fair comparison since these trees have been left to grow for centuries. Radiation poisoning puts a damper on logging. But speaking of down South, did you mention KP?"

He side-eyed her. "Yep. I can flip pancakes like an ace and serve up a couple hundred soldiers without breaking a sweat."

Hopefully, he'd spontaneously explain the demotion if she gave him a moment.

Something's ahead.

She stopped cold. Could she hear something just ahead?

"Halt."

Her penetrating whisper stopped the team dead in its tracks, giving her a moment of silence. Maybe, listening closely, she could hear a faint rustling in the leaves uphill. Or maybe she was just spooking herself.

"You hear anything?" she asked Brandt.

"No."

Danger.

"Me neither, but I've got this feeling—" She hand signaled "stay put" then stealth-walked a few meters ahead, paused, and listened. For a moment, all she could hear was the murmur of wind on leaves and the creaking of branches. Then—

Bruk. Rustle. A louder, *Brup, brup.*

Animal sounds, deep throated with a slight echo as if coming from the chest of a substantial beast. Sweat prickled in her armpits. She'd known an animal encounter was possible in a vast, underpopulated wilderness, but faced with the reality... She wasn't ready. She was still fighting Mac's last battle in her nightmares and memories. But she had to be ready. At least this time, she wouldn't be taken by surprise. And the animal better freaking be healthy, normal, and ready to scram.

She made eye contact with Brandt and signaled "come". He moved carefully toward her, doing his best to step softly despite his size and weight.

When he was abreast, she whispered, "I reckon it's about ten meters west, ten degrees north." He listened for a moment then nodded in agreement. Then they hiked back to the team. All gathered close.

"A critter is foraging up there. Large, by the sound. It'll be unaccustomed to humans so potentially dangerous, so Brandt and I will get close and take a look."

Agnet gazed upward. The tree canopy rhythmically swayed, waving downslope. She pulled a marker from her pocket, and spritzed dye into the breeze. It also drifted downslope.

"Not especially accurate, given turbulence," said Brandt.

"I know, but the drift matches the bend of the treetops, so I'll go with the belief we're down wind. You a good shot?"

"Yep. But I'm not partial to killing animals for no reason."

"Most often, an animal wants no part of humans, and just hurries along, so I'm hoping for no drama, but if its diseased, mutant, or aggressive, let's put it down?"

"Sure thing, Chief."

She slid the rifle out of its sling and handed it to him.

He looked it over, raised an eyebrow, and swaggered in place. "Thanks, ma'am, you're all safe, now that the sheriff is in town."

"I know it's vintage but it's better than nothing."

She pointed to a medium-sized tree covered in ruby-red leaves. "Orl and Jemin, climb up that tree and keep quiet. Philip, park yourself behind that trunk and stay ready."

One of Phil's lower eyelids spasmed, but he nodded; he'd have their back. He was a good man when the chips were down.

Jemin had already started up the tree, but Orl still stood close, wringing her hands, her lips writhing as if she was fighting back tears.

Brandt bent at the knees and found the kid's eyes. "It'll be fine, hon. Just lay low. Most animals just run away." She frowned, shook her head, and squeezed his arm. He gently patted her hand. "It'll be all right. We'll be careful. You be careful, too."

Agnet asked Philip, "She sensing anything?"

His face went blank, then he frowned. "She's worried you're walking into danger. Be very careful."

The team stepped aside and let them pass. Agnet unholstered her side arm. "Let's go in easy and a get a look." Brandt unsnapped the stay on his scabbard, and fell in.

Philip crouched against the tree's trunk, plumbing the depths of his uselessness. He couldn't perceive animals; their brains were too simple, so he hadn't noticed its presence upslope. All he'd heard was the rustling leaves; Agnet must have a bat's ears. And, please, in the name of mercy, may nothing come snarling down that hill, because he wasn't an aggressive gunslinger like Brandt.

No. If death came for him today, he'd go out flailing. A weapon in hand might buy him ten extra seconds. He searched his pack's front pocket, finding a bamboo cutlery set and, more to the point, his bone knife. Its cutting edge was razor sharp, no surprise, as he'd never used it. To him, the blade was more a totem or good luck charm, not that he believed in luck. Angelo believed self-defense significantly augmented luck, hence the gift. *Well, Angelo. I may be testing your theory in a few minutes.* But hopefully, in a few days, he'd thank Angelo for the knife one more time, then he'd transform this horrible episode into a clever tale and entertain a dinner party's worth of friends.

Jemin, who'd showed impressive fear-inspired agility, straddled a sizable branch about half-way up a maple. Orl perched on a limb a few branches down. Periodically, her face contorted as if she was deep in concentration, in terror, or suffering discomfort from a stomach ache or female problem. Maybe best not to know. Anyway, how could he help if she wouldn't communicate?

Time passed in a slow drip. A centipede navigated the bark's crevices. A squirrel launched into a long streak of squeals and chirrs. A sudden shaft of sunlight escaped the clouds.

A splintering ache throbbed in the bones of his jaw, cheeks and sinuses. He clutched his face, trying to pull off the hurt. Get it off—

Somebody wailed, and as quickly as it'd started, the pain stopped. He jumped to his feet and sighted his team members. Jemin, his eyes wide, waved and pointed at Orl, who'd flopped forward and slid sideways. Philip ran for their tree, as Jemin clambered like a pudgy monkey to the branch above Orl. He reached down and grabbed the back of her dress.

Up the trail and a bit to the right, a massive wall of stripy animal flank moved through the brambles. *Rup, rup, rup*. Bigger, much bigger than a cow, the thing busily rooted around in something rust colored. The stink of slaughter filled his nose.

Agnet moved left phantom-style, positioned herself at the base of a tree, grasped a low-hanging limb, caught Brandt's eye, then pointed to a nearby easy-to-climb tree. He gave her a thumbs up and hunkered down by the trunk to wait for her signal. She shifted the gun, letting it meld into her grip. It felt so flimsy, a plastic child's toy of a weapon. Dropping a sizable animal wasn't child's play. Central should've allocated them a rifle or two, given the odds they'd be searching the forest.

"Ahhhhhhh!"

Her flesh jumped at the shriek—it'd come from downslope. One of the team must be down—as in Jemin falling from the tree. Hopefully, nobody was badly injured, and Philip could manage the problem.

The animal lifted its head, and her stomach dropped.

It was hideous and wrong, just like the cult's mutant temple guardian. Fangs sprouted randomly from its massive gore covered snout, most curving forward like the blades of a nightmare blender. Beady eyes brimmed with violence and hate. Her limbs felt like jelly, and her guts seized. The cool dry air, the tapping of the machine's little hammer, that horrible smell, Mac's scream as he flew through the air, that obscene *crunch* as he hit the wall...

Suddenly, the woods came alive, kicking her back to the present. Trees tossed back and forth. Leaves fluttered and twirled. She was here, now, and better focus because the breeze was coming from the wrong direction. The brute trundled forward, tested the air with a *snorp*, and kicked up a plume of dirt. She prepared a shot, but where was her gun? A quick scan of the ground, and there the gun lay, dropped when she'd gone limp. At least she hadn't pooped herself. She slowly bent at the knees, gaze fixed on their adversary, hand extended to recover the weapon. The hog's ears lifted and swiveled. Its nostrils twitched... Then a scream of savage rage tore from its jaws.

Flight or fight coursed through Agnet's veins; her heart pounded; her hands shook. It charged, moving like a cannonball. Brandt fired—a direct hit between its eyes. She could see the bloody hole, for cripes sake, but it kept coming.

Another full cartridge, *pop pop,* into its chest, but her bullets must be as powerful as bee stings.

Almost upon her, it loosed an ear-splitting bellow. She grabbed a branch, hauled herself up the tree, and reloaded.

Crack. Boom.

The tree shuddered from the blow. The monster hog thrashed in the low-hanging branches, tearing with its saber-toothed muzzle. Brandt fired again. It roared and charged his tree. She emptied half a clip into its rear. The animal's flank flinched, like it was shaking off fleas. But Brandt took advantage of the distraction, drew his cudgel from his pack, and wedged it into the hog's horns. It retreated, tossing its horns, and bellowing furiously. The cudgel had slid and might be blocking the thing's vision. But it charged, anyway. One massive flank slammed into her tree with a *boom.*

She emptied the clip into its shoulders and skull, its hide so close that she could watch the bullets hit and... Purple blood welled around silvery discs, the butt ends of her bullets. Two clips-worth of fluorocarbon were sitting in the hog's hide like bramble thorns. Purest bullshit. But the head wound from Brandt's first shot was deep. This beast should be dead.

It circled back, preparing for another assault on the tree. But the monster-boar's charge petered out after a few steps. It came to a standstill just outside the tree's canopy and stood, one ear cocked as if listening. A deep grunt rumbled from its throat. Then it turned, roared, and barreled down the hill.

Brandt dropped from the tree and raced to her. "Thought I lost you for a minute. Are you alright?"

"Yeah. I had a bad reaction; I'll explain later. But did you see that? My bullets lodged in its hide, but your shot should've dropped it."

"Don't know what's under that thing's skin, but it's tough. Would make a nice bullet-proof vest."

"Let's go get ourselves a vest."

She dropped from the tree, and they jogged down the hill.

A series of pops sounded from ahead. No, please, don't be gunshots. More pops—definitely gunshots. Philip climbed to Orl, who lay pale and limp on a thick branch, the back of her dress tented by Jemin's grasp. He brushed her hair aside and checked her eyes—nothing but white sclera under her lids. Veins ran blue on her neck; he felt for a pulse with trembling fingers and found a gentle thumping beneath his fingertips. She'd only fainted. She'd be fine. Sure, she would. More gunfire—at least Agnet and/or Brandt were alive.

Orl's eyes snapped open and stared into his. *We need a Door.*

What? Why?

For the Beast. I hear him. He's in pain, and the Pain has driven him insane. He needs to die.

I think I felt it. Did you feel it too?

Yes. I shared it with you.

Thanks. Thanks, tons. By beast, are you talking about whatever Brandt and Agnet are shooting at?

Yes, a large animal with Problems.

We can't drum up a Door without a human death—don't think anybody would volunteer. And what would we do, politely ask the problematic animal to jump through? If it's dangerous—the professionals will need to straight-up kill it, like normal people.

She grimaced and shook her head, side to side, a look of pity and forbearance on her face. And how did she tap into its pain? Using her impressive range and an ability to read animals, that's how. Implications swirled in Philip's mind, but the sound of gunshot rang from upslope.

Orl pushed herself into a seated position and pivoted toward Jemin's hand, which still clutched her dress. Confusion spread across her face.

He reddened and released his grip. "When you passed out, you started to fall, so I caught you."

Oh. She glanced at Jemin and ducked her head.

"You're welcome," he whispered. Orl tossed her black mop of hair from her face and knotted it behind her neck. *Do you have a rope?*

Good grief, he didn't have a freaking rope. He asked Jemin, "Did you, by any chance, pack a rope?"

Jemin's lips pressed into a prim line. "Of course I brought a rope. Rope was number four on the trekking equipment list. Mine's top-rated steel-equivalent, dragline-silk cables braided around an aramid core."

Orl gave Jemin a thumbs up.

Moments later, they were on the forest floor, Orl glancing over her shoulder and signaling urgency with her hands while Philip and Jemin secured glistening gray cord about a meter off the ground between several sturdy tree trunks.

Philip rubbed his hands on his pants, removing the rope's slick feel.

"What are we doing here, Orl?"

I'll call him. He'll run to me, too angry to see the Rope. Then fall. Then die completely.

Philip turned to Jemin. "She means to lure a savage creature our way, thinks it'll trip over the rope and die. I have serious doubts, but I've never killed anything other than a few insects. Have you?"

Another round of gunshot rattled through the woods. Jemin blanched. "Mice infested the cabinet under my sink once. I used traps."

Orl gurgled, a sound that might've been laughter. *I'll kill him and the pain will Stop. You both climb the tree.*

"And where will you be?"

There. She pointed beyond the rope to a bracken-topped boulder.

Philip said to Jemin. "Climb high as you can and sit tight."

Jemin clutched his elbow. "And what're you going to do?"

"Not much, probably. You just...be a witness, alright?" He shook off Jemin's hand, then said to Orl, "Let's go."

She stared at him a moment, nodded, ducked under the rope, and dashed off. Philip raced to catch up, gave her a lift, then pulled himself up the boulder and into the ferns. He caught his balance and drew his knife. Orl looked at it, and her mouth stretched with silent laughter. A trumpet sounded in the distance, then drums...no...thunder...no...hoof beats. Orl spread her arms. Something huge slammed through the trees, its enormous snout ringed by sword-like tusks. A rhino? For pity's sake, weren't rhinos extinct?

Time slowed. Thoughts churned. Would he shit himself in his last moments? Would Orl experience his agony when that monstrosity skewered him? After he died, how long would

Gervais manage to squat at his apartment and whore-out the laundry facilities?

The rhino-creature plowed into the rope; momentum threw its rear high into the air. With a horrific *crack,* it crashed snout first into the dirt, then flopped to one side.

Orl bobbed her head, as if satisfied with a job well done. *He's All Dead, now, and through his Door.*

Poor kid had it all wrong.

Didn't NeuroCorp explain Doors to you?

No.

Doors are specific to humans, a mass delusion that infected perceivers over the last century, just a handy visual generated by the human brain for a chip-perception we can't grasp. Animals don't have chips or worry about existential matters, so they don't have Doors. Don't know what you've heard, but just know; breaking away from dogma can land you in trouble.

She smirked. So irritating.

I'm just letting you know.

She shrugged.

How did you know the rope would work?

I saw it.

As one does. *Someday, you'll have to explain "heard" and "saw" to me, because I think your definition of those words is idiosyncratic. Maybe we should sit here until we're sure that thing is dead, while you explain yourself. Maybe you can tell me how you perceived that animal's pain from a distance. I'm assuming it doesn't have a chip.*

Orl rolled her eyes and slid down the rock, and Philip, annoyed she'd coopted one of his signature expressions, followed.

Philip's recap of Her-Plan-Which-Had-Worked impressed both the Leader and Brandt. Several of the team Touched her to show Appreciation, which she did Not Appreciate, but they meant no harm. The Leader wrapped Orl in her arms and squeezed, also meaning well, but causing an Emotion similar to Caught-At-Mischief. Usually, she regretted the Being Caught. Here, she regretted the Mischief even though her mischief, Tricking Others into action and being Nosy, had gone undetected.

First, aware the Boar was Angry and in Pain, but being more curious than smart, she'd sent two Mostly Good people into danger: Brandt who thought she was '"excellent" though he disliked her clothes, and the Leader who wanted to protect her, an impulse that arose from a sense of Justice not from pity. Nobody before thought she was worthy of Justice.

But she hadn't Protected them in return. No. She'd Endangered them.

What else could she have done? She couldn't let the team walk past the Angry Boar unawares. She couldn't reveal her Mind Visits. Especially since slipping into minds wasn't always smooth sailing. Case in Point: probing the Boar's pain had Angered him and triggered his attack. Plus, his pain had almost caused her to fall from a Tree. Orl rubbed her jaw at the memory of groaning aches in her jaw, skull, and neck.

Then, she'd angered the boar again, on Purpose. All right, she'd been trying to save the Leader and Brandt, but she'd imperiled Jemin and Philip, Philip who'd been Scared but had stood with her on the ferny rock so she wouldn't be Alone. Yes, she'd wanted to help the Boar be truly dead and free of pain. And yes, she'd wanted to rescue Brandt and Agnet. And yes, her plan had succeeded. But she'd failed else-wise and might not be a Good Person.

The Team gathered around the Great Boar, whose fall had forced his Tusks through his neck and forehead. Once, he'd been proud and strong, the ruler of a substantial territory. Now, he stank and lay twisted, a sick caricature, and thoroughly Dead. Besides, she had *seen* the Boar's Door, a tunnel through the brush. He'd galloped through as his True Self, two sets of fierce but well-proportioned tusks curving forward on his snout. Then, as every Sentient Being did in Death, he'd joined The One. Because Animals-Did-Have-Doors. Philip doubted

145

her, but Blind Holes pockmarked Philip's brain, and he was an Older Model, so she could ignore him.

"Look at those sores. Wow. By the growth pattern, Id' guess those blades grew in place of whiskers." Jemin murmured, as if he might disturb a sleeper.

Brandt ran a finger along a jutting rib. "And it was starving."

So hungry, but how could it eat with those horns jutting into its mouth, teeth Sharp and Askew, every chew an Agony?

The Leader, shoving aside revulsion and dread, hunkered down, and inspected the carcass. "Caused by mutations or a virus, most likely. The pain must've driven it crazy and spurred the attack." But her thoughts unspooled another story: NeuroCorp's signal machine tap-tapping in an empty room, a similar Large Animal squealing with rage, a moment passing in a breath, a man trampled in a hail of bloody hoof prints.

"Here we go." Brandt reached into the tangle of tusks, grasped his big stick, and shook it loose. He squatted beside the Leader. "You seen one of these before?" he asked, though he already knew she'd seen a Similar Creature, having detected a Clue in her face.

Questions swam inside the Leader's head. Should she Avoid the question or answer? Could she put horror and Grief into words without her emotions running rampant and showing. Was she honest and brave or just a chicken-shit basket-case? She steeled herself.

"Unfortunately, yes. Last mission, we were checking out a cult's shrine, and a huge mutant thing that looked similar to this took us by surprise. Result wasn't pretty. What is this thing anyway?"

Brandt said, "I'd call it a boar or a feral hog. Lots of these bad boys down South, but not so ugly."

"A boar's sort of like a pig, isn't it? What a stupid waste. Didn't even get the chance to put ours down. It slammed through a wall and ran off. Right now, it's probably wandering the badlands southeast of the city."

The Leader frowned then glanced away. Apology and related Issues shifted back and forth: the perils of showing Weakness, a tendency toward excessive honesty, the merits of various styles of Brave, then she spoke.

"Sorry I froze on you. I haven't shaken off that last attack."

Brandt said, "No harm done. You came around quick, considering."

Jemin said, "Folk can surprise you in a crisis. Philip and Orl's bravery certainly surprised me."

The Team digested Jemin's comment, judged it hilarious or clumsy for reasons that eluded Orl, but kept their Laughter to themselves. Older People kept much to themselves, but their Rules eluded her. For instance, sharing weakness, then hiding laughter seemed backwards. Her approach was more sensible; keep to oneself to be Unknown and to make others nervous or confused.

Philip coughed to extinguish his laugh completely, then said, "Orl was spectacular"—desire to deflect attention from himself—"wasn't exactly bravery on my end, more a reflex. I can't quite remember why I ended up on that rock"—*not quite true, but why admit to chivalry*—"but I'm just happy to be alive."

The staff at NeuroCorp usually complimented her chips, their own technology, or her chips' abilities, like detecting the tap-tapping signal from Rasp's precious machine. They never complimented Her Own Self, leaving her feeling like an Adequate Container. So these new compliments, "spectacular" and "brave", felt Special. But the compliments didn't make her a Good Person.

Jemin and Philip collected the rope, the Leader cleaned the teams' scrapes and gashes, then dotted on a Healing Cream, and they set out on the Path. The Song returned, having fled during the Conflict. It rang between Orl's ears, the notes connected to one and other, same as the forest, the toad stools Dancing in rings, the arguing Squirrels, the Water splashing and babbling as it raced down a Creek, and the great Antlered One serenely observing them file by while rhythmically chewing. Then she spotted the Wolf, large and gray with flat tan eyes, a predator calculating Risk and Reward. A thrill chased down her spine, and her excitement leaked into Philip's thoughts, bringing the Wolf to his attention. He voiced Concern to the others.

"Nah, that's a wild dog." Brandt's comment opened a passionate debate, contrasting thoughts bouncing to and fro like table tennis balls, these chatterers, unaware their Connection to the Wolf outweighed the Wolf's name. Their thoughts, no matter how inane, distracted her from a series of switchbacks winding up the slope of a scrub-covered hillside, exposed under the fearless Sky, each step requiring Effort and Intent. Forested ridges spread to the Horizon, and above, a lone

Eagle searched. She praised the clouds each time they hid the sun's bright Eye. Finally, they arrived at the Destination.

"Hey, those are some rocks"—*excellent rocks*, said Brandt.

"Was hoping for a meadow"—*not detailed on the map as a major geologic feature, thanks Central for your support*, said the Leader as she gazed at layered charcoal-gray stone dabbled blue and green with lichen and Moss, the slabs askew, as if giant children had been called in for lunch while playing at Blocks.

"Could be a labyrinth inside this formation"—*we'll get lost and starve, ribs jutting like that horrible dämonenschwein*, said Jemin.

"The path curves right here. Maybe we can skirt around"—*use your eyes, people*. Philip made an arcing motion with his hand.

They followed the path to a gap in the rocks. A few steps in somber walls slick with rain towered above them, the stone thrumming with Age and Stillness.

Brandt squatted at a crack in the ground, his flashlight shining into the abyss. "A straight drop, and my flashlight doesn't reach the bottom. Step carefully, and I hope nobody sleepwalks, if we camp here."

Orl shuffled up to the chasm and dropped to her knees. The Song boomed and echoed from below. She caught a whiff of rotten eggs. Shadow rimmed her field of view; a picture of glowing embers filled her mind's eye. Did this fissure lead to the hell Jemin so greatly feared?

"Smells as if something farted down there." Brandt wrinkled his nose.

"Something burning maybe?" Philip's question was a response to her Vision of Fire which had slipped unnoticed into his head. The Pills must've helped her contain her thoughts; she'd need to develop better control.

"What would burn underground?" asked Brandt.

Philip shrugged. "Don't know. Just asking."

Just then, the chasm exhaled a puff of smoke which uncurled, resembling a ghostly fern frond that stank like a spoiled egg.

Jemin coughed, waved away the fumes, and stepped back. "No significant volcanic activity in these hills, as far as I know. But I'd be happy to perform a search."—*useful, be useful, be praised*.

"So, not a great campsite from several angles." The Leader checked her Map. "The path led us here, so let's hope it leads through this maze. Hopefully, we'll find a non-stinky campsite on the other side before the forest thickens up. Brandt, mark the trail in case we need to back out."

Brant shook his marking spray canister—*so satisfying, the thunk of the mixing ball*—and they moved forward. Trees clung to the rock's sheer faces, their roots resembling tentacles, tangling and glistening with damp. Lichen coated crevasses branched off to the sides. At a three-way intersection, they paused.

"Both look passable," said Leader.

Jemin shined his flashlight down the right-hand passage, illuminating a centipede as it looped through a cobbled, dew-beaded prairie of moss. "Looks narrow and wet, and I can't see beyond that turn."

Brandt called from the left-hand passage. "Got some rubble here, but plenty of room. I'll check it out."

I'll check this one.

Philip waved to the right. "Orl volunteers to investigate this direction."

The Leader frowned and looked her in the eye. Usually, People didn't bother finding her eyes while this person made an Effort. "You sure?"

I am the smallest and unafraid.

Philip raised a hand in a "why not" gesture. "Makes sense. She's the smallest and can keep in contact with me. And it takes a lot to spook a Perceiver." He grinned at Orl but felt wary.

Be safe.

Armed with her flashlight, she slipped inside the crevasse. The air smelled of Clean and Cold. Beyond the turn, the team's mind-chatter muted all at once, as if they'd been Swallowed, the quiet a relief. Distracting Noise from Others had intensified, now that the Pills were out of her system. She'd need to fiddle with her chips and dampen it down.

The passage quickly narrowed, forcing her to scoot sideways toward a dim glow and the sound of splashing water. Clearly, the team couldn't travel through a space this narrow, but she was curious. Something Interesting but Subtle lay ahead. She craned her neck. The chasm ended in a small, serene chamber. A thin waterfall trickled from above, and sunbeams played amongst the droplets. A presence occupied this lovely and singular Tomb.

She waited, Expecting.

Then Whispering began, a hissing sound, reminding her of leaves blown down an alley, a rolling tide of syllables, Words either running together or very long words.

Orl! You alright?

Ah, yes. Philip, his concern clouded by annoyance as usual, and the pressure of Others Expecting her return.

Yes, I'm here Listening.

Terrific, but listen to me. The team's getting worried and time's short.

I've found a Spirit-thing that doesn't know how to Whisper. Why are the Words Wrong?

He paused while working her comment like a puzzle. So frustrating when other Perceivers couldn't comprehend her message because they couldn't See enough. She relayed a Long Word as a sound picture, he browsed his store of Knowledge, then decided his Answer. *Probably an extinct language. The whisperer must be ancient.*

But an ancient Remnant would have already Attenuated.

Do you have a visual?

No. The tunnel is too bright. This fissure must open to the Sky.

Well. If you must, guide the remnant to a Door. But be quick. And Orl...

What?

You can't help everybody.

I know.

She concentrated on Needing-to-Move-On, and a bright point formed above and to the left. Not the usual Spot, but the beginnings of a Door. The point detected the remnant and spread like a pupil, creating a splotch of rich indigo, the color of a clear November sky just after sunset. The final shape was Round, a strange door suited to a Being who must be Different.

Go through. She sent her message, even though the Remnant remained elusive.

More Whispers, then a vague impression, as evanescent as a puff of scent, conveyed no ill intent. It wasn't hiding on Purpose; a complexity related to the Difference prevented her Touch. Perhaps the remnant was an Animal, a small mind scuttling beneath her reach. What image would entice this Different Mind through the door? How could she convey "Home" or "Rest" or "Peace"? Home would be easiest.

150

Both people and animals liked the idea of home. But whose home and where? She'd show her own home as an example: her Earth, this continent, the city, her building, her room. Only a reasonably Modern Person would understand that sequence. So any answer would also serve as an indicator of both Age and Type.

Her message flew forth, and the passages chilly walls faded into nothingness. She floated, stretched out like a Starfish, in an empty, frigid, and pitch black Nothing, silent but for the sounds of her Breath, in and out. A dazzling pinpoint winked on, then more and more, faster, until a star-spangled expanse engulfed her. A splendid blue planet ringed in green appeared beside her, the rings so close she could make out frozen particles sparkling with reflected light.

Then the Door opened and released the radiant light of The One, the source of all consciousness, waiting for her Return. She should pass through; she was so cold, drifting in the Universe alone, and the Beyond looked so warm and inviting.

The One spoke. *Not yet.*

But I'm Ready. I've always been Ready.

Not yet. A gift has been waiting for you.

A ringing sound, something hard bouncing on stone, then the universe dissolved, returning her to the grotto's floor, her rear end wedged between stone walls. Her ears popped with the change in atmospheric pressure as The Whisperer passed through.

A glint of light caught her eye, an Object lying on the floor. This Glint must be her gift and should be Accepted. It winked at her as dappled sunrays fell from above, an irregularly shaped circle or knob, cheery but not as magnificent as the ringed Planet. Still, an Artifact to be collected. Jemin would be pleased.

But her chill-stiffened limbs wouldn't bend, and the passageway held her tight, so she withdrew to a wider space, rubbed the numb from her joints, pulled off her pack, and searched for a Long Object. Here was a tent support; unfolded it would reach. She fumbled the support straight, squeezed closer to the Artifact and stretched forward. From this angle, it resembled a knot, or pretzel with Holes. The pole's tip fit into the largest hole, allowing her to drag it closer. Slowly. Carefully.

Orl?

She startled. Her wrist flicked. The pole whipped right. The artifact clanked against the wall. Slightly behind a boulder, but visible. Still in reach.

Yes?

Now everyone is terribly worried.

I'm almost done. I'm retrieving an Artifact.

But that's extraneous.

No. It's a Present.

Pause. Amusement at a Joke she didn't understand. *A present from whom?*

The Lingerer who is Gone. I won't be long if you Don't Disturb me, Philip-Who-is-Wrong-About-Animals.

Fine. But hurry.

She wriggled and leaned, trying to spot the Artifact's perforations. Imagining herself as narrow as a blade of Grass, as thin as a cat's whisker, she tilted her head and slipped it between a slightly wider gap. Now a Hole was in view. She teetered while resetting the pole into the artifact, steadied herself, then dragged it closer. The walls grated her cheek as she withdrew, then her hip bone jammed and stuck. Wedged in that mossy vice, a Tiredness overcame her. She could stay, Rest, crumble into pieces, and Wait, holding the Artifact for somebody else, somebody warmer with more energy.

Clouds billowed, the Earth spun, Stars wheeled, and the hands of an ancient clock ticked toward Noon. She was One with All, and Ready to Leave.

But no Door appeared. The One wasn't ready for her. And the Others would hack through the stone to free her, making far too much Noise. She didn't like noise, so she wriggled her hips free, backed into the Wider Space, and used the pole to draw the Artifact close enough to grasp. Safe in her fingers, it felt heavy for its size and New-To-Her but also very Old.

It's My Present

Orl emerged from the crevice, moving slowly and deliberately, as if wading through molasses. Philip took her by the arm and guided her to a flat rock bathed in dappled sun. She stretched out, clinging to the warm surface, her lips blue and trembling, her pupils slightly dilated despite the light. Her vibe felt transitional, poised between one level and the next, as if she'd flirted with death. He opened his pack to search for the thermal blanket.

Agnet hauled the radiation monitor and a patch-up kit from her pack and scanned the girl for clicks. No radiation, but she'd collected several abrasions.

Here was the blanket. He tugged it to activate the thermal-threads and slung it over Orl's shoulders. Agnet began cleaning the scrape on her cheek, and Brandt hunkered down. "Hey there, explorer. You've gone blue again. Meet any zombies down that tunnel?"

Orl gazed at Brandt as if he was a miracle. Maybe she'd taken a blow to the head.

No?

"No zombies, just a ghost," Philip conveyed to the team.

"What happened?" he asked Orl.

The ghost showed me its home, and the universe is cold.

Seems she wasn't thinking straight. "The exchange either required excessive power or the ghost purposely siphoned off energy. Some learn that trick and use it to persist beyond their expiration date."

"Fantastic," said Brandt.

"Not if you freeze to death in the process."

It wasn't trying to hurt me.

"She doesn't think it tried to hurt her." *You can never be sure. Besides, it doesn't really matter if an accidental drain or a purposeful leeching dropped your temperature. Fact is, you almost bit the dust. Confidence is a positive attribute, but don't overdo it. You're still learning.* "Be more careful next time," he added, for the benefit of the verbal-only team members.

Agnet looked up from patching up the girl's hip. "And remember to stay on task, though I'll be curious to see the artifact Philip told us you found."

My gift.

Orl reached into her pack's exterior pouch and pulled out a small yellow-brown, more or less octagonal object and handed it to Jemin. He'd been standing to one side, peering at her as if she were a formalin-bottled oddity, probably working to remember how to express sympathy or concern. Philip flinched; his aversion to the man was strong enough to kindle snarky, petty, and woefully immature thoughts. How irritating this inconsequential bore could bring out the worst in him.

Jemin turned the thing over and inspected the outer and inner rims. "Unique and made of metal. Brass, I suspect, so quite valuable. Could be an archaic mechanical element, a gear, perhaps." He turned the object over. "Or maybe an unusual key, given these pegs." His face rearranged into schoolmarm mode. "Long ago, doors were simple mechanical devices. They'd insert a key into a metal cylinder which ran through the door's thickness. The notches on the key pushed pins inside the cylinder, allowing the cylinder to rotate, unlocking the door. Course, if this is a key, it works differently." He flicked his thumb and a small lever or handle flipped up, standing ninety degrees from the octagon. "Hmm. Maybe it's a tool, similar to a socket wrench."

Thanks for the digression, Jemin.

Orl pointed to the elaborate fretwork decorating rim. *Why the holes?*

"Why the holes?" Philip repeated instantly in a sneeze-like reflex, Orl funneling through him, as if he was a puppet.

Jemin shrugged. "Perhaps it fits into a very specific pattern, the lock, so to speak. Could be decorative elements, a method to save on metal, or just a handy feature for hanging it on a hook. Looks nice at any rate."

"Who gave you this?" asked Agnet.

The cave's Other Person.

Philip translated. "The ghost."

Orl fixed her eyes on his—*a wintery, star-spangled night, silent and still, dank stone pressed against his hips. A presence wavered in the grotto ahead, a clink, a glint, the glittering key breaking the spell.* He gasped.

"You all right, buddy?" Brandt was holding his elbow while Agnet peered into his face.

Was he alright? Orl had compressed her experience, then directly shared with him. Pretty amazing, and what an experience!

He shivered and rubbed the gooseflesh from his arms. "Yeah. Thanks, I'm fine. She showed me the details. First, she had a vision of stars, then the entity tethered to the cave off-loaded the artifact. Very unusual, a manipulation that must've required significant energy, possibly explaining her temperature drop." The story sounded ridiculous out loud, though he knew it to be the truth.

Agnet raised an eyebrow. "You believe her? Because remember, she's off her meds." She glanced at Orl. "No offense."

"Or she got a snoot-full of vent gas and hallucinated," said Brandt.

"No. I believe her. The...telling...was incredibly vivid." Or was the "vivid telling" related to Orl being off her meds?

"What did you mean by—," Jemin flicked him a look then bent two fingers of each hand into air quotes, "—'entity.'"

Jemin was mocking him, somehow, but he couldn't imagine the reason. Philip fought back an exasperated sigh. "Human ghosts communicate with perceivers through their chips using the messaging module as if speaking. This 'entity' sent a weak message Orl interpreted as mumbling, but she couldn't understand it. She shared a sample with me. If what she heard was language, it wasn't any language extant in the relevant time frame. This ghost's most profound communication was visual, which would've traveled on a completely distinct channel, highly unusual for a human ghost. That's why I used the term, entity. I'm not sure Orl encountered the ghost of a human."

"What did it look like?" asked Agnet, a skeptical line between her brows.

"She couldn't see it. Too much light."

"In a cave?"

Light from above.

"It opens to the surface."

Agnet's inter-eyebrow "load of bull dung" line deepened.

"Can you try to approximate the 'auditory signal'"—more air quotes—"in writing?" Jemin practically shook with excitement.

"And what about the stars?" asked Brandt. equally enthused.

"Glow worms, probably." Jemin sounded so sure of himself, despite being epically wrong.

"What are glow—"

Agnet waved Brandt off. "Look. This is all intriguing, but we need to make tracks. I'm not keen on bunking down on a haunted geothermal vent. Plus, this maze is a great place for a monster ambush."

Orl, still wrapped tight in the blanket, frowned. Her lips had pinked up, and her eyes were bright.

You okay to move on?

Yes. But I want my key back. She held out her hand.

Jemin's hand warped around the key. "Shouldn't I hold on to this? It's an archaeological artifact, after all."

Orl stretched out her hand further. *It's my present.*

See what picking up shiny objects in caves gets you? Would she get the reference this time? She stared at him, as if trying to pinpoint a defect. Apparently not.

Brandt folded his muscular arms. "Finders keepers."

Agnet held up her palms, signing "halt". "Like I said earlier, we divide all bounty. But no reason Orl shouldn't carry her find."

Words formed in Philip's mouth and spilled like pebbles tumbling in a creek. "She must hold the key to preserve continuity. The object itself, like all objects, may be duplicated or destroyed and is of no inherent value."

Everyone gawked at him. Honestly, where had that come from? Orl didn't sound like that, either on or off meds. He cleared his throat, and, hoping to sound less outré, said, "Give it over, Jemin. We can scan it when we get back to the farm, scrape off a sample of the metal, and you can document the thing to your heart's content."

OVER THE RIDGE AND THROUGH THE SCREE

Brandt, once again demonstrating his value to the team, hoisted Orl's pack over his own. Prejudice, based on his work history and his look, had blinkered Agnet when she'd pigeon-holed him as all muscle, no brain. She took a moment to chew on her failings. Her concerns about the security man's smarts had evaporated when he'd quickly homed in on her post-traumatic stress—another mutant animal, of all things. But everybody has their strong suits, and Brandt's included strength, speed, a genuine niceness, enthusiasm, and exceptional people sense, a combination of traits that might've confused his military command. Not a surprise that career derailed early.

The trail through the dry crevasse sloped gently uphill, easy-going but for patches blocked by rubble or brush. She and Brandt hacked through one particularly tenacious thorny bramble then stumbled out of the rock formation into a sparse thicket of scraggly pines. Wind carrying dust and pine straw whistled through the branches, a desolate spot, but with fine visibility, and any open space was preferable to a claustrophobic warren of stone.

They camped in a sheltered nook below the top of the ridge. The wind whipped the campfire too low for cooking, so they settled into a cold meal. She swallowed half her canteen to force a dust-flavored protein bar down her esophagus. Orl gobbled down a high-protein pudding cup, then curled into a pill bug-style ball and conked out. Philip and Jemin volunteered for the watch, so she set up her tent and crawled inside.

An instant and forever later, she opened her eyes to the dark and murmured conversation. After a few stretches to kick gravity out of her aching limbs, she pulled herself together and poked her head out of the tent flap. The wind had quieted, but a scent reminiscent of dead dog in a wet alley perfumed the air. Two shadows huddled by the embers, Brandt and Philip by voice.

"You smell that?" Philip asked.

"Yeah, a cross between moldy bread and fish tank. Our buddies." Brandt aimed his flashlight in the foul smell's general direction, lighting up a mud-zombie who lumbered to a standstill.

"Didn't pick up on it," said Philip. "Brother, I'm useless at detecting these things."

"Don't sweat it, that's why we're a team." Brandt tapped his nose. "Some of us got extra-sensory brains, others have extra-sensory noses." He flicked the beam from side to side. About ten mud-things fanned the camp, vaguely child-shaped forms in tattered clothes, standing still as fence posts. "I'm ready to go." He raised his cudgel. "But I'll bet this bunch stands and waves, same as last night's crew."

Philip said, "Here we go. I'm perceiving something watching us."

Brandt shrugged. "Well, yeah. Those things *are* staring, so..."

"No. Something else is staring through them."

"What?"

"Whatever created them, I'm guessing."

"Whatever's creating them is doing a crap job. First off." The ember's glow silhouetted Brandt holding a finger aloft. "They're slow. Second." He raised another finger. "They're not that hard to kill...or...whatever. I'd say those are the worst monsters I've come across. So far."

"You encountered many monsters?" asked Philip.

"Sure. But only the human type. How 'bout you?"

"Same. Despite their humanoid appearance, these things don't read as human. And though they turn my stomach, I don't think those monsters are designed to hurt anybody. Orl agrees."

"She's awake? How's she doing?"

"Yes, she's awake and feeling fine, despite having her energy siphoned down to fumes. I get that everybody her age thinks they're invincible, but I wish she'd be more cautious."

Movement caught Agnet's eye. At about two-seventy, a zombie wearing a short red cape swung a basket back and forth. Suddenly, the basket hit the ground and toppled over because—well—the arm had broken off at the elbow, and the hand still grasped the handle.

Seriously disgusting.

She coughed to get the guys' attention so they wouldn't startle and hurried toward the fire.

"It's just me," she said as she joined them. "I've been listening in, and as Brandt says, these zombies clearly aren't weapons. I don't think they're trying to scare us, staggering up and just standing there, instead of jumping out from behind bushes. So what's going on? Is the creepy waving an attempt to make friends?"

"Beats me," said Brandt.

Most of the assembled zombies were waving now. Philip took a confer-with-Orl moment, then replied. "We think something patched these creatures together to observe us or get our attention. I'm guessing whatever's responsible isn't human and doesn't have the slightest idea of how to communicate, or be safe, or frightening, or appealing."

"That's a leap, but so is cave-ghosts." Wouldn't it be nice if about now her old team jumped out of the bushes and cried "gotcha!". "I wonder if the monster-maker is ole Canaan's 'singer'"

"Wouldn't be surprised," said Philip. "Notice we're encountering more monsters as we close in on the Singer."

158

Brandt grunted. "The other night, I knocked the heads off three zombies who were just standing and waving. Whoever's watching probably thinks I'm a psycho. Feels kinda embarrassing. So tonight, if they don't move on us, I vote we wave back and let them be."

"Sounds reasonable," Agnet said, "but remember, the monster that attacked Warden Honing's room wasn't so peaceable."

Philip nodded. "Yep. Larger and much more aggressive."

"Maybe their maker is learning some manners," said Brandt.

"Or maybe that one was different somehow."

Their circle of "new friends" wandered off with the dawn, leaving a whiff of sewer, a few discarded appendages, and a few splotches of mildly radioactive ooze. The team packed up, moved about fifteen meters past the residual smell and ate a stash of apples and crispy pastries that Philip had set aside. He was a genius, as was the farm's baker. Water was scarce and her hair was getting oily, so she toweled in some dry shampoo and wrapped a kerchief around her hairline.

Philip and Orl synced up and oriented toward the Singer. Then they headed along the ridgeline. The trail had petered out, but the thin forest made walking easy. Mist clung to the valleys and haze blurred the ridge tops and the horizon. Large gray-brown rodents dashed for cover behind lichen coated boulders and twisted trees. This country possessed a certain beauty but struck her as blighted—by the elevation, poor soil or radiation—or maybe this land was just old, worn out, and lonely. She pulled the counter from her bag and tested a tree, the soil, a patch of lichen. Clean as a whistle.

Philip called out. "Downslope, about halfway. We're aiming for that rock face. See?"

Agnet left off her monitoring and joined the team. The ridge's western slope dropped steeply toward a dark, tree-choked ravine. The smooth, dark surface of Philip's rock face stood out in the otherwise gray and green landscape, but what was that smudge? She flipped on her binoculars. Beyond the rock, coils of blue-black smoke intermittently belched from the ravine. "Got ourselves a fire, down there!" She focused here and there: the billowing smoke, a section of charred forest, a swath of spindly young trees. The forest had burned then regenerated on numerous occasions. "An area that burns periodically, as if the source of the fire is constant." She turned to Jemin. "You're sure this territory isn't volcanically active?"

He had his binoculars up too, his bulbous wet eyes swimming like fish in a bowl. "My chip focuses on human history, not natural history, though I dabble using conventional sources. Wouldn't mind an upgrade, but regardless, according to the *mission brief*, continental collision, not subduction, formed this range."

Oh. Of course. "Good to know. Radioactive ash fall would be disastrous for the farm. We need to file a report pronto."

Jemin frowned. "Sure, *however* the radiation seems to have disappeared."

"Maybe it never existed," said Philip.

"Not according to the survey map I *pro-actively downloaded* for this mission."

"Could the map be mistaken?" Agnet asked.

Jemin folded his arms. "Failing to document the disappearance of a twenty-five-hundred square kilometer high-risk exclusion zone is one heck of a mistake. No. The survey was routine with rigid parameters, performed by Land Management, a reasonably apolitical, independent, by-the-book department. The maps and introductory materials were highly informative." He shrugged, looking sincerely baffled. "I can't imagine a motive to hide a transformation so...miraculous. Someone should've noticed by now and migrated this sector from hazard containment to resource development. Sure, the land's not highly valuable, but there's water, timber, arable soil in the valleys. AgroCorp should already be here."

"Doing something stupid," said Philip.

"Well. Yes. But doing something."

"What did the survey say about right here where we're standing?" she asked.

"The wind was north-westerly the day of the meltdown, so this ridge lay directly in the fallout's path. Adiabatic cooling promoted radioactive rain fall at high elevation, so these ridges should be hot as a griddle."

He paused, possibly expecting some debate. Naturally, nobody else had an opinion on "adiabatic cooling," and the lecture continued. "Valleys received less rainfall and were relatively protected with some variation, depending on their water source."

"You mean the river?" A sarcastic edge sharpened Philip's voice. She gave him a stern expression; he needed to lay off, or Jemin might feel reluctant to share information.

"Go on. We're interested," she said.

Jemin flushed. "Actually, it's not just the one river. The area's water sources are numerous and localized. If a particular valley's water source wasn't heavily contaminated: underground springs, river sources outside the area of fallout, etcetera, the valley stayed clean, explaining the significant variation in radioactivity over a relatively small area."

"Well, radiation decays," said Brandt. "How old was the survey?"

"Sixty years."

Agnet said, "Is sixty years enough time to make a difference."

"Could swear the file on Riverbend gave a twenty-five-thousand-year estimate for complete recovery. Should I double check my sources? It'd take a few minutes."

"Sure. Anything you need?"

"No. I'll just sit here." He found a flat rock and hunkered down, staring blankly at his knees. Orl brushed a troupe of ants away from his rear. The rest of them found a comfortable seat to wait. A few minutes later, his eyes refocused; the guy was a long-talker but a quick-study. "I double checked the estimated time between melt down and fit-to-occupy; it's twenty-five to thirty-thousand-years. And on the survey map, this elevation is colored red, meaning heavy fallout. Downslope is a patchwork of red, orange, and yellow, highly contaminated areas alternating with protected areas. I have no explanation for the missing radiation."

"Won't complain, but—" But what the flip was going on? Her jacket's hood rustled in a stiff breeze which came from behind, east to west. The fire lay West, and the trees were sparse. They should be safe, but for how long? "Let's file the radiation mystery in the for-later bin and move on. Keep an eye on the smoke and proceed with caution."

Trees gave way to dense brush. Brandt bashed through the worst areas using a king-of-the-jungle knife until they broke through into desolate scree. Ratty shrubs dotted the debris. A lone pine stood crooked like an arthritic crone bending over to sweep the rubble.

"What's with the moonscape?" asked Brandt.

Agnet checked her map, finding no indication of the change. Another major geographic feature absent from an otherwise detailed topographic map. *Thanks again Central. Thanks for having our backs.*

Brandt knelt and scooped through the debris. "Used to work construction when I was a kid, and this stuff reminds me of fill. Look for broken bricks or other junk."

"Couldn't be fill," Jemin said. "Prior usage was State Forest, recreational with occasional low impact economic use: logging, hunting, watershed, and so on. Before that...mine tailings, maybe? But I'd expect evidence of a mine and more re-vegetation—the era of active mining was ages ago. Just doesn't make sense." He kicked a melon-sized boulder downhill.

"See the change from brush to rock?" Brandt drew an arc with his hand. "It's sudden, almost looks man-made." He was right; the demarcation between shrubs and blighted zone ran as if a razor had cut it in both directions.

Philip shook his head. "Celestial-made. Remember? Canaan said something fell from the sky immediately before the singing," finger-quotes, "started."

"Let's add landslide and impact crater to the list of possibilities." She slipped on sunshades against the glare. "We can theorize all day, but bottom line, this ankle-twisting patch stretches for kilometers in either direction. We can't skirt it, so down we go. On the plus side, we're safe from the fire, since rock doesn't burn."

An hour of steep descent later, her quads throbbed, fine dust coated her throat and tongue, and constantly focusing on her footing had drained her brain. Her next step birthed a small avalanche—*whoosh, rattle, thunk*. She crashed into Brandt's solid back. They slid together, gravity laying them out, side by side. When they ground to a halt, he grinned, his expression a bit too friendly.

"Kind of fun, wasn't it?"

Warmth spread across her cheeks. "Sorry! Lost my footing. This rubble barely hangs together!"

Orl scuttled past them, crawling diagonally and backward, resembling a seaweed festooned crab.

"There's a technique." Brandt's gaze followed the girl as she scooted down the hill. "She's got speed, but that position's got to be hard on the knees."

"She's young, her knees don't care, and she's eager," said Philip, who'd caught up with them. "The Singer is just ahead, somewhere in that rock pile."

Agnet followed the direction of his index finger to a thin crescent of rich, purply blue low arcing above a jumble of massive rocks mixed with pines. Not far now. Her aching thighs rejoiced. "What kind of stone is blue?"

Jemin shrugged.

Brandt said, "Only way to know is a closer look. Come on, Orl is going to beat us."

Below, Orl, alone and vulnerable, was rapidly approaching their target. The kid had no impulse control, racing toward who knows what all by herself.

Agnet called, "Orl! Wait up." Why was she bothering to yell at a perceiver? "Philip, tell her to wait up."

Alternating her steps wide then narrow to avoid the micro-landslides she created, Agnet careened down the hillside behind Brandt who walk-slid as if he'd been practicing since birth and owned the mountain. Orl, of course, *not waiting* as commanded, vanished between a couple of boulders. Great. Brandt might instinctively bolt after Orl and get lost himself.

"Brandt. Don't follow her. Wait for Philip. He'll know exactly where she's gone."

Brandt raised his hands in a "are you serious" gesture and pointed uphill. She turned. Philip was picking his way downhill, not unlike a senior citizen navigating a walker down a sand dune, while Jemin inched along on his rear. No point in rushing. So, she shook the lactic acid out of her thighs and eased down the remaining slope to Brandt. By the time she'd patched the abrasions she'd acquired and sealed a tear in Brandt's pants, Philip and Jemin had completed their descents.

"Can you lead us to Orl?"

Philip swallowed the mouth full he'd sucked from his water bottle. "Sure. She's fine. I told her, 'Don't touch the...uh...rock or try to communicate with the Singer. Just stand back and wait for us.' I hope she minds me. Let's get moving. She's half feral, her implants are overpowered, and restraint isn't her strong suit."

They trudged between looming boulders and through a grove of young pines until they saw Orl.

And the thing that wasn't a rock.

163

On the Rocks

The team stood stunned into silence, each person probably weighing their significance against an enormous, smooth, blue lozenge with a glossy finish that protruded from the rocky ground at about a sixty-degree angle. Was she seeing straight? Agnet retrieved a rag, wiped the dust from her sunshades, and set them back on her nose.

Yep. Still there. Still huge.

Estimating size had never been her strong suit; she'd leave that to Jemin, and it didn't matter; numbers couldn't do the thing justice. The thing was of a scale that pressed air from lungs and weakened the knees.

Brandt pointed to a sheet of blue material poking through the rubble. "Look. A fin or wing. This here's an aircraft."

"But from where?"

"Or when?" added Jemin.

Brandt shrugged. "Like the old geezer said, it crashed here forty to fifty years ago."

Incredulity fleeted across Jemin's face. "Can't have. A craft this massive would've required a tremendous volume of fuel, and fuel's been in short supply for at least two centuries. No extant community has access to that amount of fuel. Not now, not forty years ago. So many questions. I wonder what material—" He took a step closer to the thing.

"Stop, wait. Philip said not to touch it. Philip?" Where'd he go? She glanced around—Oh! There he was, wandering in a circle and muttering. His eyes roved every which way. Good gravy, he looked crazy. Not good. Not acceptable. She needed this guy sane.

Jemin shoved himself into her space. "What? Is this another discovery I can't examine?"

"Yes, no!" Agnet shouted past Jemin. "Philip! Snap out of it!"

At the sound of his name, he jolted and shook his head, reminding her of a wet dog. He gazed around, his eyes blank, until he noticed her. A moment passed, as if he was struggling to recall her face. Finally, he smiled. "Oh, hello. Sorry, I'm still dazed. All this...interference. Did you call me?"

"Yes. Jemin wants to inspect the hull, but you warned Orl not to touch it. Why?"

"Well." Philip's eyes drifted to the massive curve glinting in the sun. "Um...lovely, isn't it?"

Jemin, Brandt, and Agnet exchanged worried looks.

She tried again. "Philip! Again! Snap out of it! Can Jemin inspect the hull?"

He slapped his own cheeks and walked over to them. "Sorry. The signal is intense; I'm having trouble concentrating. But listen. Something inside is sentient and might defend itself. Before we get too close, we should make contact."

Stubborn dropped like a curtain over Jemin's pudgy face. "So go ahead, make contact. That's your job, isn't it? Meanwhile, I'll just stand here and *not touch* anything."

A lost look crossed Philip's face. "I...I don't know where to start. It's so...much."

"Maybe she can help." Brandt thumbed to his left where Orl stood, her hands held shoulder height, palms forward, her expression blissful, as if she were touching the eternal.

Oh, boy, there's another gone to the loons.

Agnet nudged Philip. "You should check in on her."

FAR-FETCHED, IN MY OPINION

The Melody enveloped Orl, a billion brilliantly colored tendrils connecting her to everything and everyone.

She Belonged.

She was Safe.

And, as she'd suspected, Many things that concerned people, really Didn't Matter, such as the message niggling at the edge of her attention, somebody connected with her chip expressing concern about something that almost Certainly Didn't Matter.

Orl? You alright?

Ah. Her conduit to the Others. He existed, his presence a small dot far away. She perceived the Others—jabbering, spinning inane theories, and arguing. Could she communicate with Philip while being inside the Song? For that matter, could she eat and drink? Such a nuisance, having to balance reality and the Song.

"...a distracting interference or energy coming off that airship."

The music swirled and swelled, a burst of glitter. An airy melody floated beyond the clouds.

166

"...less interference now. I'll try again." *Orl! Are you listening?*

These objects suspended in front of her face were her Hands. She flexed her fingers. Her body had returned from wherever it had been Hiding. She could See, or pay attention to what she saw, details such as Philip's face, his worried frown, the Others crowding behind, all stunned and thrilled by the Ship's beauty and mystery.

Hello.

Took ages to get through to you. You alright?

Yes. I've been following the Melody.

Does it have a message for us?

We will always belong. We will always be safe.

Philip, embarrassed by the Song's intense tenderness, cast an anxious glance at the Leader. *I experienced something similar and felt a presence, but I can't make contact. Could you try to make contact or look for a message? Most likely, we're looking for a distress symbol, something short and repetitive.*

I'll Try.

She'd already Noticed the mind behind the Song, but its thinking was Wrong: no flow, no internal voice or moving-pictures—no image, color, or luminosity of memory and mood. Instead, the Singer's like-thoughts clicked past, every second filled with flick, flick, flick, pins and Needles at high-speed. Perceiving this style of thought felt uncomfortable. She toggled to a visual representation. Line after line of glowing symbols rolled past. The Singer displayed script, as did the occasional literate human. But this script she didn't recognize. Sad to think that the Gulf between their minds might be too wide. She might never meet the distinctive "I am" inside the Great Blue Shell and exchange Ideas. The clicks surged—a sense of urgency, as if Something Was Wrong. Orl retreated to the Song and Philip.

The Singer thinks but Differently.

"Orl says it's sentient but wired differently," relayed Philip.

"Could be damaged. I'd be damaged, after smashing into a hillside at high speed. Hope we can be of service." Brandt's desires to rescue and save competed with fantasies of chaos and drama. He'd become so Apparent, a little-boy's-fascination-with-vehicles front and center.

A shower of jagged flickers hit her chip. Was the Singer trying to get her attention? Orl fixed a sample of the transmission in her mind's eye and shared it with Philip.

The word *Code* appeared in Philip's mind. "Interesting. Most biologics generate an analog-type signal with a language-like flow. Orl tells me this entity communicates via partitioned or isolated energy states, a phenomenon completely outside my experience. So it's an advanced but unusual."

The Leader said, "What about a computer, some component of the ship? Makes sense, given that anything flesh and blood must've died on impact."

Philip said, "Computers don't generate consciousness fields."

Jemin's eyes widened. "Maybe it's an artificial intelligence."

Dread wafted off everybody, except Jemin who continued to ramble.

"Unlikely, of course, since nobody's produced an AI in centuries. Not possible, even if someone ignored the ban. Where would they scrounge the rare earths? Every stockpile was used up in the previous century. And any amazing, unprecedented, and incredibly secret research in neuro-mimetics or implants conducted forty years ago should've born publicly accessible fruit by now."

Orl sent Philip a question. *What is he talking about?*

Artificial intelligence, AI—basically sentient computers. AIs were involved in a series of colossal disasters, so they're illegal planet wide. Didn't you learn about the Singularity Wars in school?

No. Rasp said training would serve her better than School. And he'd been correct. She might not know about War, but she knew the Singer meant no harm. And she had skills, thanks to all that training. She'd try again to perceive a message. Orl lifted her palms and closed her eyes. The Code rolled past. So many symbols, pretty but meaningless and possibly trivial, the Singer's equivalent of Breathing and Digesting. How could she tease out a Message? The signals rolled up and down in prickly little waves. Nausea inducing waves. She pulled back, allowing the Code to cascade as thought with no visual.

She linked Philip to her chip. *Can you look at this? It makes me sick?*

I'll try.

She brought forth the Visual. A few minutes passed, and Philip's stomach lurched. He unlinked abruptly, and in the process, disrupted her connection to the Singer. A reality of Song and Code was replaced with drab rock and Philip folding at the waist and spewing. He flailed an arm to warn others away.

"Back up. Might throw up again, and I don't want to splash anybody."

The Leader didn't retreat. Instead, she poured a cup of water. "Here. At least rinse the acid from your mouth."

"Right." Philip drank and spat, splashed his face and wiped himself dry. After a deep breath, he said, "I counted ten to twelve symbols in that longer sample."

"Could be an alphabet, a coding script, or non-binary code," said Jemin.

"Not an alphabet. Per Orl, the symbols are discrete," said Philip.

"How would she know?" asked Jemin.

"She feels it," said Philip. "Like pin pricks."

"One of the Asian languages, perhaps?" asked the Leader.

"No. Character scripts require thousands of symbols." Jemin leaped on the opportunity to share his knowledge, like a drowning man grabs for wreckage floating on the waters. "I favor non-binary code. Historically, we've stuck with binary because we can detect electrical 'on' and 'off' reliably. But non-binary code would be theoretically possible, if a reliable method existed to detect a gradient of electronic states."

Jemin speaks too many unknown Words, Orl told Philip.

Philip's thoughts said, *Jemin speaks too much bullshit; he doesn't know diddly-poop about computers, just like the rest of us.* But his message was nicer. *Jemin thinks the code is technology we don't use. Pretty far-fetched, in my opinion.*

Not far-fetched. Not after witnessing the Magnitude of reality, the stars, the ringed planet, the vast Abyss of space and time, a universe undoubtedly crowded with Creatures possessing distinct Minds, Bodies, and Tools. As a reminder of Difference, she sent him a slice of the galaxy.

And he responded to the image with what he assumed was his own idea: a spaceship! Of course. "If Earth couldn't produce this ship or its on-board computer, maybe aliens made it." Philip waited while the team absorbed his Statement, though he'd given voice to an opinion Brandt had already formed.

"Then it's simple," said Brandt, relieved Philip had set his thought Free. "We figure out if it's a friendly alien or an unfriendly alien. Then we decide what to do."

The Leader lifted an eyebrow. "Simple?"

"Sure. As a test, Jemin could go touch the hull."

The Leader snorted a laugh. Jemin interrupted a negotiation with his God to glare at Brandt.

"Just kidding, bro."

Orl laughed, too, making a sound that sadly discomfited the rest.

"Shall we be serious?" Jemin said. "If 'spaceship' is correct, we could be dealing with alien neurology. So that 'code' you're hearing might not mean AI."

"Or maybe we've got ourselves an alien AI," said Philip.

"Excellent," said Brandt. "Two for one."

"I'd rather watch the human race wrestle with the concept of aliens than go to war over an earth-made AI." The Leader made a woeful expression and shook her head. "I can already hear the accusations flying. How about we stick with alien and forget about AI, as in agree we never considered the concept?"

Jemin tucked in his chin and gave his head a quick shake. "What do you mean? I'm here to consider all concepts. That's my job. Considering the resources InfoCorp invested in my training, how can I not do my job? That'd be treason!"

At the concept of treason, the team launched themselves forward in time, Philip to a surgical consent form. The Leader imagined a firing squad, feeling surprisingly relieved. Sweat rolled down Jemin's cheeks while he lied to his ancient, gnome-like supervisor, while Brandt escaped by flying the spaceship through a multihued nebula.

Apparently, once People-In-Charge heard of the Singer, they would do something stupid and not good. A likely outcome, since People-In-Charge were, by and large, Stupid as well as Not Good.

"Don't sweat it. I learned on the border that concepts like treason have some wiggle room." Brandt wriggled his hand to demonstrate.

"And you can forget about impressing InfoCorp," said Philip. "Once Central hears this story; they'll bury faster than they'd bury a week-old corpse. It's all too weird and too valuable."

Jemin breathed in sharply, then said, "Oh."

Philip turned to her, still believing his silly Mouth needed to face her direction during conversation. "Let's do an experiment. Can you show zeros and ones, one after the other, in a line or list? If it can recognize simple code, we may be able to communicate."

I'll try.

170

"Please try, but don't overdo it, unless you want to spill your breakfast."

How to show a picture of numbers when Zero was too abstract to See. But she could send a string of flashing signals. Orl reopened her Mind to the AI and Blinked: light, dark, light, dark, light, dark. She lost count. Stop and restart: light, dark, light, dark, light, dark. Her zeros and ones became uneven as she lost the Beat. Stop and restart: light, dark, light, dark, light, dark. *Zeros and ones, on and off. Understand. Please.*

The remorseless Infinity of characters scrolling in ribbons and sheets gradually slowed. Many lines sloughed away, until two characters remained. These would do for zero and one, but she felt awful. Her head spun. Her belly roiled. And—

More Hidden Sources

Once Orl's vomiting tapered off, they left the crash site, hoping some distance would give the perceivers a rest from the alien's overbearing signal. They chose to camp on a reasonably flat though bleak patch of ground, gathered dried brush, and lit a fire.

Jemin cracked a Redi-meal tab, pried off the lid, and added the prescribed amount of hot water, mediocre fare after the farm's bounty, but adequate calories. *Thank you, Lord.* The other's chatter, exuberant given the day's events, melded with the song of a lone, late season cricket.

A better person would find humor in the day's irony, wait for guidance from the Lord, and persevere. *But why, oh, Heavenly Father, why test me so cruelly?*

A short stint in academia, utterly bereft of impressive finds, and today, the discovery of a lifetime dropped in his lap. But he lived amongst the Common Folk in a society rife with fear, greed, and idiotic political complications, so his best shot at renown would be classified top secret and relegated to a dusty locked archive. Governmental corporations would descend on the ship, destroy what they deemed dangerous, strip away resources and tech, and never publish their findings. They'd leverage any discoveries as they saw fit without revealing the source of innovation, a crime verging on sacrilege from a historian's perspective.

His hands would never touch otherworldly artifacts. He'd never sift through alien records, his career wouldn't advance one iota, and NeuroCorp would likely strip their recollections. Orl might be spared, if she learned to communicate with the alien. Though her efforts had come at a price. He peered at the girl. She lay on her side curled in on herself, one eye, black as a deep pit, staring straight at him. He shivered. The corporations had warped them both beyond redemption. The pitiable girl would never find a husband, and the lacuna would degrade his chip connection, ruin his recall, and his talent would wither. Worse, he'd never be able to hold forth on this miraculous event. That rapt audience would never materialize.

Why seek the approval of strangers?

Good question. How fortunate the chip hadn't dampened his introspective nature. Did he crave public acclaim? Well, perhaps a bit. He tested the Redi-meal's temperature—cool enough to handle—and stirred the thick brown bottom layer into the watery surface. When had those fantasies begun? Had he hoped to impress the Common Folk with his intelligence? Ridiculous; he'd have known they'd pigeonhole him as another obsessed, pedantic chip-head. So why had he joined InfoCorp? Nobody chooses neurosurgery on a whim, but the decision seemed remote, the details fuzzy, yet scant time had passed. Knowing himself, he must've been following a plan or chasing a goal.

An interest in Truth, perhaps?

"Don't you think that's mixed enough already?" someone asked.

The question shot through him like a lightning bolt. He stared at his smoothly blended pudding, about as appetizing as grasshopper protein could ever be. Had the "mixed" query been directed at him? Evading a potentially embarrassing response, he smiled at the faces around the fire then spooned Redi-meal into his mouth while trying to recall the lead up to his surgery. He'd been researching something in particular—something important—that was it. Lingering questions had driven him to apply for an implant. Why'd he forgotten?

Damage from the surgery or the Chip?

Possibly. Though his mind still felt sharp. Maybe he should work out the puzzle before him: how could alien life exist in a Universe centered firmly around Earth, Eden, his people directly descended from the Ancients of the Book, and himself, one of the few chosen who survived a genocide? A fascinating line of investigation.

May be better to focus on being Helpful.

Well, he did lack the relevant religious texts, and nothing in his chip did his beliefs justice. Every file on The Fold was stuffed with anti-faith lies and propaganda, portraying the Lord God as a pathetic fairytale, theorizing that humans were primates who never mature, never stop seeking the comfort of a parent, creating gods in lieu to soothe the terror of death's long night. Maybe the chip's entire data set was riddled with lies, a possibility he'd never considered. *Please, Lord, may some of its data be useful and true, so my bargain with heretics is not in vain.*

Jemin loosened his collar, having thoroughly upset himself, and set the RediMeal on the log. He'd lost his appetite, and the pudding was slightly bitter; this crop of grasshoppers must've been raised on milkmaid's cress. He should stick with being helpful, much less stressful and more practical. He enjoyed being helpful, although being helpful interlaced with approval seeking, a burgeoning weakness. But who should he assist, the Government, his people—

The Team?

Ah, the team. In truth, he'd envisioned this mission as a showcase for his talents, since being part of a team felt impossible, given his nonconformist background and—admittedly—his insistence on accuracy and comprehensiveness set him apart from others. But why not focus on the team's relatively simple issues?

Like a Simple Code?

Simple, exactly! Computer code was unnecessarily complex, and he knew nothing about it—what use were computers for people like him? A simple code would do. He performed a quick search, and the chip offered several options. But how would they teach the alien code without a Rosetta stone. They'd need to demonstrate using concrete examples. But how did it see? Examples required eyes and a visual cortex, and they didn't even know if the alien was animal or machine. He nudged Philip sitting beside him. "Did the alien show you or Orl any pictures?"

"No. Orl projected an image of the information she received, strings of symbols, not images."

"But why? What are the odds a random group of indigenes would understand a space-traveler's code?"

"It might not have been communicating. Orl might've jumped into random house-keeping processes mid-stream."

"But it noticed her blinking, a visual signal. Maybe Orl can show it pictures."

"Maybe. She's shown me memories and ideas."

"Could she show the alien mental images then name them using a simple code?"

"Probably. But flashing binary for every word might prove cumbersome, and she might not last."

"How about Morse code?"

The perceiver's eyebrows lifted. "What's that?"

"An old system for spelling out words with a series of dots and dashes. Also tiresome, but less so than binary. Could Orl learn—"

Philip interrupted with a chuckle. "She can."

Curious that Philip, theoretically Orl's supervisor, appeared unphased by the youngster's superior skills, and annoying an otherwise lacking specimen such as Philip could display such maturity. Jemin drew out his notebook and began listing Morse dots and dashes, employing his personal superpower: incredible recall, enhanced by the implant and considerable practice. This time, his toil and dedication might bear fruit. He might facilitate communication with an alien.

The sun sank below the western ridge. The fire crackled. Philip studied the list of Morse code.

"Will be slow going, but worth a shot. Look. Here come our buddies." A trio of monsters bumbled over the rocks, moving randomly like drunken decaying homing pigeons. "We think the alien uses those things to get our attention." The creatures parked at the edge of the camp and stood swaying gently, side to side.

"Let's test that hypothesis. See if we can connect through them." Now the team would laugh or shout him down. Heat traveled up his neck to his cheeks.

"Go ahead," said Chief Krause.

He angled his face toward the wind, sucked in a lungful of fresh air, faced the monsters, bent at the waist, then straightened, a straight-forward, two-part motion.

The middle one echoed his bow and maintained its position for a moment or two, the grouping reminiscent of a decomposing bench. The bent monster righted itself, then the one on the right bowed. Both stood straight. The left-hand one bowed, losing a clump of moss-green tissue in the process. Absolutely revolting. The pattern repeated.

"Well, cook a duck," said Brandt. "That's code!"

"Quick, pick up. Orl must've primed the alien with her blinking method," said Philip.

"I agree," But how irksome Philip had beaten him to giving Orl her due.

Chief Krause stood and dusted off her backside. "Good beans! We signal right back at them. Orl, give us some light. Brandt, over here. Philip on the other side. We'll copy what they do."

After four sessions of copying the creature's movements, Jemin said, "Let's send Morse code for an object. See what happens." The rock-strewn wasteland offered little choice. This apple sized rock would suffice. "Move together in sync, a bow for dash, standing for dot." He lifted the rock, exhibiting it like a fruit vendor showing her wares, and moved it side to side. Three mangy heads, ghoulishly up-lit by Orl's flashlight, tracked his hand, suggesting these things could see with those empty eyes; the horror of it all. Pity the alien hadn't employed higher quality helpers. He led the Chief, Brandt, and Philip through the correct sequence of motions. They performed the pattern, then Jemin displayed a stick, and they successfully duplicated the process. What else to try? The campfire caught his eye. Flames, of course, a primal element. The alien's civilization must've conquered fire well before they conquered space. He thrust the stick into the embers, waited for it to catch, held it aloft, and called out the code.

The zombies observed the sequence for "fire", then replayed it back. Vigorously. Too vigorously. The ear fell off the left-hand monster and splotted onto the gravel. Jemin's stomach heaved. Philip gulped loudly, the thick swallow of somebody holding back vomit. The scalp sloughed from another with a slurping sound.

"Gross." Brandt's voice sounded far away. That these things disgusted a man who'd faced combat, excused Jemin's spinning head. As the middle monster bent, its face dropped to the ground before its feet. The odor of rags moldering in an abandoned basement filled his nose. The world spiraled and went dark.

A Valid Excuse

Dawn rose as hard as the pebbles boring into Agnet's side. She creaked into a seated position and swiped her tongue through the cotton wool stuffing her mouth. A bath would be nice after watching those zombies decompose, even a dip in a stream as cold as a NeuroCorp handshake. She burrowed through her pack for a clean shirt, dressed, then flapped out of the tent into the early morning chill.

The three monsters had degenerated into heaps of moss, mud, and bone. Thankfully, the bits had stopped twitching. She wanded the mess which emitted the expected few clicks above background.

The others clustered around the campfire. Jemin stared into the blaze, seeming miserable, doubtlessly embarrassed about blacking out last night. She didn't blame him a whit. Orl swirled a Redi-meal with one finger. Philip sipped a steaming beverage, and Brandt whittled a stick while whistling low, almost under his breath. He shot her a cheery smile.

"Pleasant dreams?"

"Not with those piles of bone jittering away. Sounded like mice in the walls."

"Those three must've been past their best-by date."

"Either that or the alien is running out of juice," said Philip.

Agnet seated herself and pulled an apple from her jacket's pocket. "Or running out of radiation."

Brandt puffed shavings from his handy work. "You think the monsters are nuclear powered?"

"Just a hypothesis based on mildly radioactive, distinctly unnatural creatures."

Jemin said, "Incredible display of technology, if you're correct. But who'd create a messenger that revolting?"

Philip reconnoitered with Orl, then said, "An alien mind marooned in the middle of nowhere with limited resources sends an SOS into an unknown world. Nobody responds to its distress call for fifty years. So it gets desperate and tries Plan B, constructing—um—emissaries from local materials. From its point of view, those things may seem close enough." He grinned at Agnet. "Just a hypothesis."

Brandt said, "Why not send a radio signal? Powder must've missed a few antennae."

"If you can send messages mind to mind, why develop radio? Bad luck that most humans can't receive its transmissions, and out here, the few civilian sensitives who can pick up the signal are people the authorities would ignore, prisoners and ferals."

Jemin frowned, appearing unconvinced. "Hard to believe an enormous spaceship sat here for decades unnoticed."

Philip made a "who knows" gesture. "So many unknowns. The last survey was sixty years ago, but we guessed the spaceship crashed forty to fifty years ago. Maybe we over or underestimated Canaan's age, and the surveyors overlooked the crash site. Are we the first perceivers to visit the area, or have others noticed the signal? Did the alien sense our arrival and consider us candidates for communication? Maybe Orl and I did attract zombies to the farm."

Agnet laughed. "Let's not suggest that hypothesis to Warden Honing."

Philip laughed. "Lovely that we *can* tell Honing the monsters don't mean any harm, and he'll be able to harvest those apples, after all."

She gestured with her apple core. "I hope so. But don't forget that first monster, the bulky goober that trashed the Warden's room. It seemed pretty aggravated."

"But we'll never communicate with the alien if its...representatives disintegrate after a few words." Jemin sat slumped, his lips curving downward, looking terribly disappointed.

"Never say never and be proud. We reached out to an extraterrestrial last night, a groundbreaking achievement. Now, we'll hone our method—it won't be hard to improve on those zombies—and before you know it, we'll be talking to that monster." Maybe not this team, but humankind, at least. "So, keep open to new ideas."

"We should at least figure out if it's sane before we introduce it to the world. I'm still wondering; who builds monsters out of dead kids and dresses them in costume?" asked Brandt.

Jemin perked up. "The children must've been buried in those peculiar clothes. Who knows what happened: an epidemic inspiring peculiar burial practices, ritual sacrifice, a mass grave dug in the wake of a tragic event, a costume party buried by an avalanche? Amazing preservation of the clothes, at any rate."

Lovely. Some grisly incident had generated dead kids in costume, and like it or not, she'd learn the gory details, either from her overly fascinated historian or her pair of already traumatized perceivers. She popped a crick out of her neck.

Jemin searched faces, as if noticing the stunned silence. "I could be wrong." He flushed shell pink.

Brandt launched his whittling into the fire, spear-chucking style. "Space guy has bad taste, whatever the excuse."

"Orl has an idea," said Philip.

The youthful perceiver moved near Philip, her eyes glittering and lively for a change, making her easier to address directly.

"All right, Orl. What's your idea?"

In a moment, chagrin in combination with hopelessness crossed Philip's face. "A translator. But—"

"A translator? Way out here in the boonies?" Brandt exclaimed.

Philip's eyebrows met above his nose, as if the little hairs were gathering to discuss his despair. "Just listen, no matter how strange this sounds. Strange and unlawful. So I'll deny having said anything vaguely resembling—"

"Out with it, Philip. This mission's not getting any stranger."

He cleared his throat. "Our potential translator is on the other side, but we occasionally glimpse it when we help a ghost move on."

"The other side of what?" asked Brandt.

Jemin leaped to his feet, his eyes bugging like a poached frog. "Of eternity? You're going to ask God to translate, aren't you? Then what? Take notes and file a transcript at Central and expect them to believe you?"

Brandt winked at Orl. "You best buds with a god? Pretty high-shelf buddies, girl."

"All we know is that ghosts pass through the door into the light. That's our reality. Sure, people have theories, but I'm no philosopher. I don't know the truth, and our community rarely discusses the matter." A wheezy laugh escaped Philip; he must be nervous.

Agnet shrugged, hoping nonchalance would put him at ease. Would be nice if she were at ease, but she'd already foreseen the worst—*for aiding and abetting an underground perceiver cult, Agnet Krause is permanently assigned to the Arctic Circle.* "We'll need a quick primer on the—um—thing you glimpse."

"So entirely off the record and theoretically—"

She glared at him.

He heaved a monumental sigh. "Fine. When an earthbound consciousness is primed to cross over, a portal opens. Perceivers see the portal as a door. The light behind the door is brilliant. Some perceivers believe this light is a universal consciousness, waiting to collect a returning...er...fragment. Some believe the door and the light are a shared hallucination to expedite dispersion of energy into the cosmos, a reminder that boundaries are illusory."

"Alright." She hoped she sounded nonplused. But wow! Who'd've thought the urbane sophisticate, Philip Spool, harbored mystical inclinations?

"What color?" Brandt's question landed on her ears like a belly flop.

"What color is what?"

"The door. What color is the door?"

Philip shrugged. "It depends on the candidate, the person ready to pass through."

Brandt nodded. "In that case, I'd like walnut with a nice stain that lets you see through to the grain."

A pained expression flooded Jemin's face, like he'd stubbed his brain on Brandt's color choice. "If God's behind the door, and everything you've been taught about the universe is a lie, why would you possibly care about the door's color?" Odd, Jemin leaping to "gods" of all concepts. He probably spent hours perusing arcane files and ought to knock it off, or he'd land in a mental hospital.

Philip nearly sliced Jemin's head off with a narrow-eyed stare. "NeuroCorp bans this topic because the conversation gravitates toward illegal topics, including deism, etcetera. Thanks for illustrating their concerns, and keep your theories to yourself, unless you want to run afoul of the irrational thought ordinances."

She patted the air, a reflex to soothe powerful emotions, hers as well as the others. "Obviously, we're not talking about supernatural beings, because, by strictly enforced decree, if nothing else, they don't exist, and everything has a rational explanation. So cool it peanut gallery. Go on, Philip. How can light translate human speech into extraterrestrial code? The brief version. We've got choices to make."

He squirmed. "Fine. Right. We call this light The One for epistemological purposes only—"

"Philip!"

He pressed his palms to his cheeks for a moment, then continued. "Yesterday, Orl couldn't understand the cave spirit. When the door opened to accept the spirit, The One passed along a message instructing Orl to take that artifact. So, Orl thinks The One might facilitate a conversation with the alien. Must admit, I foresee a few complications. For starters, we'll need an open door, and doors only appear after someone's dead."

Brandt raised his hand. "Almost curious enough to volunteer, but too young to die."

Philip chuckled. "Volunteering isn't an option. Orl was cold enough in that cave to consider passing through b—"

"What!" Brandt grabbed Orl and bear hugged her. "You can't talk like that, honey. You're just a kid. You've got your whole life in front of you."

Orl's eyes bulged and roved. Philip fluttered his hands. "No. No. Hug appreciated Brandt. But she doesn't enjoy being touched."

Brandt let the girl loose, and she shook out her rags like a crow in a birdbath. He bent his knees so he could look right in her eyes. An excellent tactic with kids. The big guy continued to surprise her. "Sorry there, Orl. But you just hang in there. Teen years are hard for everyone. Life gets better. I promise."

Orl's lips wriggled and—blessed heavens—was that a smile? Cockeyed and misshapen, but yes. That'd been a smile. Philip and Agnet smiled in response, while Jemin pinked-up again.

Brandt asked, "So if we're not using anyone as door-bait, what'll we do?"

Philip said, "A ghost. When we clear out ghosts, we convince them to pass through the door. Sometimes, the convincing takes time, time we could use to reach the alien."

Brandt cried with delight in his voice. "Fantastic."

"We could head back to the village. Maybe Meister Canaan or another villager hung on after death," said Jemin.

"Or the haunted town or the iron works!" Brandt looked a bit overly eager.

"Good ideas, but time may be a critical issue. Let's rustle up a haunting close by. Somebody must've died badly in this forsaken waste," said Philip.

"If the alien's reanimating local bones, there must be a graveyard nearby." Agnet pulled her map from her pack, much help as it'd been. Using the rock formation, the closest peak, and the ridgeline as landmarks, she estimated their location and scanned for anything other than forest. Nothing. She folded the useless map and used her eyes. The slope descended into a V-shaped valley densely packed with trees. The next ridge west shot up at a sixty-degree angle. "None of this terrain calls out 'glorious spot for a town'."

"Don't forget the fire." Jemin pointed to the smoke, just a trickle today. "Some fires begin as tragic accidents."

Philip said, "And accidental deaths not infrequently produce ghosts."

Agnet glanced down the slope. Another downhill hike didn't appeal, and they should hightail it back to the farm and report. Someone higher up the food chain would appreciate juicy tidbits such as disappearing radioactivity and telepathic aliens, but...

Reporting didn't feel like the best course. Not just yet. Not because she was outrageously curious; who wouldn't be? Not because the spaceship had been stuck in the hillside for roughly half a century, so what was the rush? Not because her flight or fight instinct clanged loud as a fire-alarm each time Central crossed her mind. And not because, instead of adhering to protocol, she followed her instincts, being that egotistical, blinkered, or impulsive, a habit that invited tragedy and mediocre career progression.

No. Not because of all that.

Because the alien was a prize mystery that Central and NeuroCorp didn't deserve and would squander. And, if they were headed toward lacuna surgery, why not lay in outrageous memories and forget something extraordinary?

Also, a valid excuse to stall had been dropped in her lap.

"That fire looks like it's been burning on and off for years. Pretty peculiar. We should do a risk appraisal, alien or not. Let's take a look."

White smoke belched from a hole in the mountainside, billowed through scrawny pines, and puffed into the sky like smoke from a giant's pipe. Every so often, orange flames would wrap around the cave's upper rim as if a dragon was licking its lip. What a fire!

This adventure had it all, despite the worry in the Chief's eyes. Too bad she'd recognized the signs of trouble. And too bad finding incredible stuff meant scrutiny, paperwork, more scrutiny, lectures about forgetting what you'd seen, and if you were unlucky, surgery, a lesson he'd learned on the border.

He'd learned about orphans on the border too. Wasn't no coincidence that most of the bomb squad was orphans, and none of them could swear worth a damn either, a clear sign of being raised under the Home's "no harsh speech" policy. It'd taken six months of military service before he could comfortably spit out a semi-passable string of curse words, a talent he was losing surrounded by this team of careful-talking orphans. But yeah, nobody would miss an orphan, clean mouthed or not.

So, if this mission was to be his last, Brandt Collins, security specialist, would enjoy the "heck" out of every last minute.

He shouted over his shoulder. "Hey! The fire's spewing live flame right out of the ground!"

"Get back from there, pronto!" hollered the Chief. She stood on the ridge, arms folded, babysitting Philip and Orl while they hunted ghosts.

"Over here!" cried Jemin, also up-slope. "I found a road!"

Brandt slid down the slag heap and hiked to the terrace where the librarian stood all flushed and sweaty—the guy was seriously out of condition. Chief Krause and the ghost-hunters joined them in short order.

Jemin gestured at the ground and surrounding scrub. "Look! A settlement. See? That's a foundation. And over there's a fireplace and chimney. I can make out at least four structures. Probably a fifth to the right of that dead fir."

Brandt took in the sights. Yep. This thrashed pavement, chunks tilted or heaved as if a mega-mole had tunneled beneath, was a street that'd been slashed into the hillside long ago. Time had taken its toll.

"That's the remains of a train car. There's a stone wall, and that rusted husk was an automobile!"

Wow! An automobile. He'd heard automobiles could cruise at one hundred kilometers an hour—imagine that! Somebody must've prospered in this little town, doubtless only a select few as was the way of the world.

"Jackpot." Phil pointed down the fissured street. "Orl's detected spectral activity in that direction." Jemin's lips pressed into a tight line, as if he was disappointed. But they'd been searching for ghosts, so what was his problem?

With Orl in the lead, they headed toward a grove of maples. Poor kid. This morning, she'd rimmed her eyes with black paint, same as the vamp kids on the border, all trying to be different while looking the same. He'd been glad those homely kids had a friend-group, but Orl wasn't homely. She'd be real cute if she washed her face and ditched the half-plucked crow outfit.

All at once, she spun and glared at him, her look so intense he could swear it pierced his brain. Maybe she *had* pierced his brain and had caught him making fun of her clothes, which admittedly weren't his business. Still, he had a right to his opinion, his *private* opinion. He returned her stare, playing chicken. She narrowed her eyes and stuck out her tongue. He stuck his tongue out back at her. She croaked her funny little laugh, turned, and jumped over a meter wide crevice.

"Hey watch it, Orl!" The Chief turned to Philip. "What was *that* about?"

He took a moment to reply. "She won't say, even kind of...growled at me."

"Don't mind us. It was just part of a joke from earlier," said Brandt, so the girl wouldn't get in trouble. After all, he'd started it by insulting her clothes. But where'd she go? Brandt leaped over several deep gashes in the asphalt, then pulled up at a corroded iron fence. He couldn't see Orl, but the carved stone slabs tilting like rotten teeth amongst the weeds meant one thing: graveyard, and graveyards meant ghosts. She must've ducked inside to find a new friend.

Orl should've been easy to spot since the burial ground was small, shoehorned between the street and the slope. Maybe she'd decided to spoof him and hide. He meant to swing the gate open, but instead it fell cockeyed into the grass then collapsed in a poof of reddish dust, a victim of powder-fall and time. He wiped his fingers on his pants and stepped inside.

Long dry grass smothered the alleys between the graves, and some headstones lay flat or had broken into pieces. Lonesome places, graveyards, and no point to them. A generation or two passes, and nobody's left to remember. Then the graves become ratty and sad. He wouldn't end up a downer. Maybe he'd go Viking style and launch out to sea in a burning canoe.

A lopsided headstone caught his eye:

Melvin McGregor, 1900-1939
Beloved husband, father, son

Guess that sums up a life, don't it? Though the guy had been robbed, dying so young. Seventy would be more like it, taken out quick by a sudden heart attack during a roll in the sack.

Melvin's stone felt warm, warmer than expected, given the hour. He fingered a crack running through the top half of the stone and a semicircular chunk calved free. Crap on a pan. Breaking a guy's headstone had to be some serious form of disrespect. He tried to refit the chunk, only to break off another piece which fell into the grass. Now the thing was proper broke. Disappointed, he tossed the stone aside. It landed with a thunk and— Sank. Straight down, then—crack and clatter— The rock vanished!

He leaned over and stared down at a pitch-black hole. A handful of pebbles poured from the rim into nothingness with a tinkling sound. Funny, this little avalanche out of nowhere. Then McGregor's tombstone listed sideways.

He backed off, spun on his heel, and managed a few long strides before a thunderous roar filled his ears, giants mid domestic dispute, all the dishes flying. He sprang toward the downed gate, then lost his footing, and slid backwards into a crater.

No, no, no!

He scrambled like a crab up a dune, eyes glued forward and up, because in a few minutes, he'd be clinging to the rim. No way was he falling into a pit. Not that Philip's door to the beyond sounded scary, but dying broken and alone in the dark was a bullshit exit strategy.

A coffin pitched out of the soil, splintered, and spilled its contents. The owner's skull bounced off his left hip before it disappeared into the abyss. Next a tombstone flopped over and skated toward him on a stream of pebbles.

As he shouldered it away, he lost traction and slid. Now his feet dangled in air, as if below his knees, the crater had transformed into a chute straight down.

Crapsticks. Maybe today he *would* die. But he'd fight for every remaining second.

Swack. Something had slapped into his side. A rope! Jemin's rope, dangling half a meter away. *Thank the stars*. He tucked knees to belly, launched himself inch-worm-style, and snatched it. The rope—substantial, though somewhat slick in his hands— felt like life. He pulled himself up, hand over hand, then rested his knees on a rock...no. The corners were too square for a rock; must be another coffin. No matter, any place to firm his grip would do. Because he wasn't dying today. No way. He'd die old as the hills and under the sun. Maybe he'd opt for a sky burial— bones clean by birds, then wrapped up tidy and chucked in the ocean. No dirt involved.

As if insulted, the soil pressing against his belly disappeared in a violent cascade, taking his coffin knee rest along for the ride. He plummeted, his stomach hurtling into his throat, then he swung, desperately clutching his lifeline. Another downward plunge, and the rope snapped taught. He bobbed, helpless as a puppet on a string, hands strangling the rope's tail end, no maneuvering room, no play.

Cold truth was that the people at the other end of this rope were nice people, each competent in his or her own way, but they weren't especially strong. No sir. And the muscle he carried made him heavy. Now, basic math had him dying. And he didn't want to die today, or worse, pull them down with him.

"Don't be fooling around up there," he shouted.

"We got you," the Chief yelled. "Hold tight."

No flippin' kidding. He'd hold tight as a sergeant's sphincter, since this section of sinkhole lacked a single decent foothold. And double curses, a spoiled egg stink was wafting subtle from below, barely noticeable over the thick reek of earth and rot. Didn't need a Jemin science lecture to know that smell was toxic fumes, but he refused to pass out. Passing out was for delicate ladies in corsets and lace caps and did not befit security personnel.

A sharp jolt yanked him up a few feet. A miracle, a chance. Ahead, a hefty bone jutted about three inches out of the muck. He tested it with the tip of his boot. Felt stable—good and wedged in—so he shifted his weight onto the bone and shot one arm further up the rope. *Thank you, Universal Consciousness, or whoever*. With better purchase, he could climb.

And he climbed like a monkey with its tail on fire, finding a root, then a boulder, a coffin lid, all the while ignoring the gravel pouring on his head, the yawning pit, and his burning arms.

The distance to outside shrank. Here was the tricky part, hauling himself over the sinkhole's lip. He planted his feet and catapulted his body into daylight, elbowed away from the edge, and—for the love of all that was wholesome, pure, or pretty—he planted a fat, wet kiss on terra firma.

No. His kiss had landed on a grave marker which read:

Bessie O'Brien, 1890-1942
May the Angels Call You Home

"Nice to meet you, Bessie."

I Can Attend

Once the team had put a good distance between themselves and the cave-in, Philip pressed his wrist against the cool of his water bottle, hoping to soothe the raw and oozing stripe of rope burn that stung like a beehive. *Thanks, Jemin. Thanks for dropping the rope.* He shot the quivering jellyroll a sour look.

Jemin mopped his brow with his light blue handkerchief and glared back. "It's not my fault the rope slid; my hands are always slightly damp."

"I'm not complaining." said Brandt. "Heck of a ride, but thanks to you all, I survived." The big man looked hale and hearty and probably wouldn't be sore come morning, whereas every muscle in Philip's body would ache for days, dull and persistent, like low tide slapping the base of a sea wall.

Hurry Up!

Philip gritted his teeth and messaged Orl back. *I'm coming. Just taking a moment after a near-death experience which wouldn't've happened if you hadn't run off.*

Agnet turned three-sixty. "Afraid to ask, but where's Orl?"

He pointed down the ravaged street. "Over there near that pile of stone and one of the candidate specters. I can't see her from this angle but she's messaging me from that spot."

"Good. I feared we'd lost her in the graveyard...or, um, former graveyard."

"Nope. She's alive, well, and itching to make contact, so I should catch up. You could follow, staying back at least ten meters to reduce interference. But if you'd rather clear out of this insanely dangerous place, we'll understand." He glanced at Jemin hoping he'd implied cowardice.

On cue, smoke belched from a fissure in the road, and Jemin recoiled. But Brandt guffawed and slammed his fist into Philip's shoulder.

"Even if we were chicken, and we're not, we're staying. Somebody's got to have your back, bro."

Philip regained his balance, thanked them, and hurried toward Orl while brushing the dirty imprint of Brandt's knuckles from his sleeve. But he didn't get far because a semicircular chunk of the road was missing. He inched toward the sheer drop off, stopped a conservative meter from the edge, and poked his nose forward, acutely aware he'd lost faith in the ground. Ground should be firm and constant, not a sudden yawning abyss nor a steep cliff sweeping down to a jumble of debris on a valley floor. Through his field glass, some of the rubble resolved into headstones and bones—cemetery contents, a convenient source of materials for their zombie-building alien.

I'm over here. Hurry up.

He tore his eyes from the vertiginous incline to Orl. She stood amongst tawny weeds, her dress fluttering in the breeze like a flock of tattered starlings. He clambered up-slope, giving the giant divot wide berth, jumped a steaming and malodorous fissure in the pavement, and joined her.

Then she sent him an image of the place they stood. Nothing remarkable, only weeds, the valley, and the ridge. Just as he was wondering why she'd bothered with an energy intensive duplicate of reality, the blacktop zipped together, the crazed sidewalks smoothed, and houses sprouted on either side of the street, as if they'd been dramatically shifted into the town's past. He caught his breath.

Are you showing me a specter's time bubble?

Yes.

Impressive! Chip technology must've exploded in the last ten years.

Her expression was complicated; he would've given anything to know her mood, but reading other perceiver's energy signal was offensive, and Orl would easily catch him in the act.

She messaged back. *This bubble is strong since it's shared by Many. You can see and send it too.*

Nice of you to think so, but no. Not me with my puny chip. Shall we choose a candidate from the Many?

She gestured him forward, and they walked along a block of similar, two-story wooden houses built right up to the sidewalk, practical buildings that must've housed average, working-class folk.

Then he noticed a child slumped to the sidewalk, her small fingers clutching a brown paper bag, a blond curl peeping from beneath her little red cape. She looked as if she could be sleeping, unable to stay awake, having missed her nap. But he knew she wasn't sleeping.

Next, they found twin girls, four or five years old, with gossamer wings attached to their backs. They'd settled into each other, as if cuddling, so adorable, so excruciatingly tragic.

Philip's throat constricted. Witnessing tragedy was part of the job, but tragedy involving children was the worst. NeuroCorp recommended staying aloof, unbothered, apart. "Fake it 'till you make it", as the saying went. He'd been in the field for nearly a decade and was proficient at faking it. So why hadn't he ever made it? Why hadn't experience hardened him?

This happened long ago.

I know. But it's still upsetting me.

Being upset by catastrophe isn't a weakness. It means you have Compassion. And compassion is a path to Wisdom.

She had a point, a surprisingly mature point. And why fight his nature? He'd never been and never would be impervious.

Here, a woman lay flat on her belly, her face squashed into the bricks, her arms spread alongside her torso, as if she'd made no attempt to break her fall. So strange, all these people collapsing, even though their bodies and the surrounding buildings showed no overt damage.

He churned through possible causes: mass poisoning, certain types of atomic or sonic weaponry, impossibly virulent disease. Then gasping sobs turned their heads toward a faded-blue clapboard house. In front of the house stood the remnant generating the time bubble, a seven- or eight-years old boy dressed as a soldier or pirate. A makeshift sword dangled from his belt, probably shiny paper wrapped over wood or cardboard. For several reasons, it was a pity the specter was a child. He'd need to inform Orl of the most practical reason.

Little kids pass quickly. Just say "mother waits behind the door" and off they go. Usually that's a positive, but we'll need several minutes with an open Door if we want to contact the alien. So try to stall.

Orl gave him a look that conveyed "you have the insight of a sea slug."

Ma! Where are you? Everybody's fallen down. Ma! Poor kid, calling for his mother today, as he had for centuries.

A Door manifested above the child's head, a royal blue Door with a brass knob. Brandt would enjoy this detail. Orl approached the boy while Philip lagged; adult specters could be vengeful, angry, petulant, or freaking lazy, but kids were always just lonely and lost. He didn't relish getting close to lonely.

The ghost raised his head and dragged his sleeve across his nose. He dashed his eyes up and down Orl. *Are you supposed to be a witch?*

No. I just like Black. What happened? Why did these people fall?

There was a 'boom', a rotten smell, and the ground shook. Then everyone fell. And I can't find my Ma. Why can't I find my Ma?

Because she's not home. She's gone through that Door.

Orl pointed, and the Door opened a crack. A warm glow seeped out, and Philip felt the pull of the One. NeuroCorp could naysay all they wished, but concrete knowledge that relief waited at journey's end had been the highlight of his career. And boy, could he ever use some relief— Listen to himself! Honestly, if he wanted to make forty, he really should swear off ghosts.

The specter gasped. *Ma?*

Beyond the Door, you won't be alone... For crying out loud! What had he done! They were trying to stall. The transmission must've slipped out of his chip as if by reflex. He sent Orl a mental nudge, hoping she wasn't also wrapped up in the transmigration.

Remember why we're here! Can you tap into the Singer?

He felt her chips open wide, an oddly intimate, rarely transmitted sensation. The undulating signal she used to call the song abruptly flooded his mind, followed by a visual of flowing code, the glowing symbols so near he reached out, but they floated through his fingers.

Ma!

At the sound, reality jackknifed from the alien's code to the spectral town in which the ghost-boy was bolting up a flight of steps toward his Door.

Wait!

But the kid didn't wait. He ran. Philip threw himself forward, another pathetic attempt to tackle a ghost. The kid's shade dissolved in a blast of light, the Door slammed shut and pinged from existence, and Philip fell through the fading steps and slammed, forearms-first, into weed-crazed asphalt chunks.

He rolled onto his back, groaned, and massaged his elbows. Orl didn't bend down to help or message him. She just stood there, looking at him like you'd look at an unusual toadstool. So, he brushed himself off, stood, and thought up plan B. They'd find a second candidate, and fast before the entire town sunk into the earth, someone who wouldn't pass without being convinced. In short, a thick-skulled adult. He glanced up the road.

A specter wearing a gray-brown narrow-brimmed hat and matching suit paced on the porch of a storefront, watch chain dangling at his waist and kerchief poking from his front pocket. Quite the dandy. A cord dangled through the open store door, tethering the man to the entrance. Orl's face remained impassive, so he took her by the hand and guided her to the ghost, in case proximity mattered. A Door, weathered boards matching the suit, popped into existence in the usual location.

Why does a small. Fire. Hang. From he/his flesh-image?

Philip chuckled. Orl was attempting poetry or had gone entirely peculiar.

That's a cigarette, a tobacco leaf stuffed inside a paper cylinder. He's lit one end on fire and is sucking smoke into his lungs through the opposite end.

Wait. Hadn't one of those farmyard ghosts smoked? Yes. Squire Tubby. Orl hadn't asked about smoking at the time, but that specter had smoked a pipe.

And the. String?

Back in his day, older students passed down the ghost lore, including descriptions of specter paraphernalia. Maybe NeuroCorp had clamped down. He could be patient and explain, but they didn't have all day.

Don't worry about the details now. But later, bone up on the last five-hundred years of material culture. Trust me. It'll come in handy.

I/we am/are paying attention. Now.

Another garbled, intermittent transmission. Philip paused, waiting for the connection to settle down, then messaged.

He's trying to contact somebody, often an ambulance, police, or spouse, using a communication device called a telephone.

What was this specter shouting? He tuned in and homed in on the word "compensation." Oh brother, this fellow must've been a real peach. But a peach of the optimal variety, the type loath to abandon valuable property.

Does he/she. Suffer?

Yes, but we'll release him after we contact the alien.

Weirdly, the word "suffer" arrived with imagery of melodramatic scenes and gruesome injury. Of course, the guy suffered. All specters suffered, a fact she knew well, no need to illustrate. And what was wrong with her pronouns? Her head was moving slowly from right to left, the motion oddly smooth. Scanning. A chill lifted the hair on his arm, and he dropped her hand. He wasn't conversing with Orl; he was conversing with something else. Something non-Orl, but also non-ghostly; possessing spirits were never so...calm. He stepped up his chip's anti-intrusion module and braced himself.

Excuse me, but who/what am I speaking to?

I/me/we am/are.

Faces: human, humanoid, animal, some impossible to categorize, flashed past at heart pounding speed.

So...not Orl. Are you inherent to Orl's chip or from elsewhere?

Else, place. Through Orl, not Orl

From the spaceship?

Space of ship. Oval.

I mean, the large blue object stuck in the rocks?

Harg. Yes.

Harg? Had the thing just...laughed or had the laughter been Orl? Then an image of the ship flashed by. So presumably, yes. This entity was their alien.

Is that Door helping you communicate?

Explain. Door.

The rectangular apparition to the left and above the "flesh-image".

Orl turned and pointed to the Door above the specter's head. It had opened a crack and the brilliant light of the One poured through.

With fuel-relay, I can attend. I notice you/these ones. Reset circuitry to make known me/I. This one. Orl's arm jerked up and down, hand flapping at her side as if displaying herself. He shuddered.

Orl! Are you alright?

Her mouth arranged itself into a parody of a smile.

For. Now.

Do we have much time?

No. She/we/I are tired.

Philip wiped his palms on his pants, his brain a gaping void. What did he need to know? Why'd they come here? Oh, yes, the mission.

A couple quick questions, if you don't mind. Are you building creatures out of bone?

An image flew by: monsters waving where a field met the woods. He recognized the setting from the night they'd camped at the edge of the farm. Then an image of churning bone and earth filled his mind, poorly formed joints twitching until one bone wagged at him.

Notice me. Out of what is. In the thickness of this world. Help.

A mental bias might be in play, but the alien's rambling could fit his hypothesis; it'd reanimated corpses to attract attention. What should he ask next? Ah. The mission.

We've noticed you. More creatures won't help, so please stop making them. They frighten people. There, he'd done his duty. Both Agnet and Berg would be pleased.

Visions of monsters crumbling to ash and people pointing and screaming in terror flicked past—were these visions the alien's or Orl's? Moments ticked by, and he worried he'd blown his chance. Maybe it hadn't understood 'frighten'. What should he have said?

Apologies. I/we will. Stop.

Point for Philip!

Thank you. So, how can we help you?

I/we suffer. Alone. Trapped. Heat. Fire.

We will help. How close is the heat?

Too close.

How many— Oh, brother. How was he going to express time? *–suns must go by before you burn?* In his mind's eye, the sun arced from horizon to horizon showing the passing of days.

An answer came; a sun composed of minute glittering squares in every shade of yellow imaginable rose and fell. Four times. Four days.

Soon.

As Philip formulated his next question, Orl collapsed.

⊐ust Laying Out Options

A few hard, uphill hours later, they staggered into camp. The azure rim of the spacecraft arced above the rocks, reminding Agnet of her quandary: do we race back to the farm and report, or do we attempt to extract the alien?

Her eyes caught movement up-ridge and beyond the ship. She retrieved her binoculars and focused on two people in white containment suits skittering down the rock-strewn slope. A combination of guilt and anxiety spilled out of her blood and spasmed her guts, a recently acquired reflex to contact with authority, even though Internal had found her blameless for Mac's death. And she wasn't ashamed of this team; they'd achieved the stated mission goal and were all still alive; she should feel proud. Instead, she felt uneasy. She ought to throw in the towel, buy a bakery, and hire that guy from the farm.

Brandt, still cradling Orl, said, "We got company. Any guesses?"

Philip moved his spyglass to his eye. "Look at those two struggling. I'm amazed they made it this far in those suits."

"I thought the same. Not sure I'd've bothered with this trek, if the contamination had been as advertised. Those two must be motivated. Let's hope they've got some imagination." Imagination would exclude Tomlin and Piscolt. Too much imagination would be Fong. Please, don't be Fong. Agnet glanced at her worn and filthy team, trepidation writ on their faces. At least these new players didn't look like anybody's good news, a relief since she couldn't stand a snitch. "Let's lay Orl down, then get our ducks in a row, and quick."

Philip shifted some larger stones and arranged a pad for Orl, then Brandt gently stretched her out. She looked peaceful, as if sleeping, but her breathing was shallow, almost imperceptible, and her pulse felt thready and faint.

Agnet sat back on her heels and pawed through her medical kit. "This epiPen and phenylephrine might raise her blood pressure, if that's the problem."

"Might, but I'm leery about experimenting," said Philip. "Her chip is broadcasting vitals, so I can keep tabs. If her heart rate plummets, we can rethink the epiPen." He turned to Jemin. "Maybe you could do a medical science search?"

"Sure?" Jemin's shifting eyes suggested he was less than sure. "My contemporary medical files will be scanty, but I'll check the recent past."

She handed the medi-bag to Philip. "Sounds like a plan. Those two will expect a report, so let's cobble one together. Before we lose you to your chip, Jemin, how'd you summarize our situation? Mission critical details only."

Jemin flushed and squirmed, as if fighting the strain of brevity. "We've located a spacecraft containing a consciousness that communicates through Orl." Philip cleared his throat, and Jemin shot him a grudging glance. "With Philip's help."

"Philip?"

"The alien created monsters to grab our attention but has agreed to stop." Philip smirked, adding a quiet "thanks to me" that he aimed at Jemin.

"Brandt? Anything to add?"

The big man stared up the slope. "An underground fire is headed for the spaceship which doesn't have an emergency exit. Or at least no exit above ground. Pretty lame design, if you ask me."

"Terrific points. That about sums us up, if we ignore a couple of very loose threads and the fact our story sounds mega-crazy."

"Good thing the enormous spaceship backs up our story," said Brandt.

"Another good point. So, given the situation, what do we do next?"

Jemin raised his hand. "I'm torn. That alien could be dangerous, the worst sort of abomination. It raises the *dead*, for heaven's sake. Is it only me, or does that bother anybody else?" He glanced about, shoulders shrugged, forehead a thicket of furrows. "I'll admit to being curious—think of all we could learn. But should we, a group of inconsequential nobodies, meddle with an entity that powerful? Should anybody? Speaking off the record, if we turn it over to Central or NeuroCorp, the government, in its colossal arrogance, could get us all killed. And by all, I mean our entire species."

Philip said, "My thoughts are similar with a few twists. Orl might be more consequential than the rest of us. As I've mentioned, she's unusually powerful, more than the sum of her chips, and might be the key to understanding this alien. Given she's unconscious, I feel both obliged and reluctant to relay her impressions. She doesn't think the alien's evil but believes other organizations, whose names I won't mention, are evil. Evil as a concept has always seemed simplistic, though lately... Let's just say, recent events have disturbed me."

She nodded, grateful for Philip's and Jemin's frankness. "Here's my immediate issue. On paper, we've fulfilled the mission, to which extraterrestrials are...extraneous. We could simply return to the farm, report, and head home."

"But if we don't free the alien, as I promised," said Philip with a cringe. "It could panic, and produce more monsters, hoping to flag us down or worse. Honing won't be happy if monsters chase us back there."

"A point I hadn't considered," she said. "However, and I hate to say this but, if Orl's interstellar friend burns to a crisp in a few days, problem solved, and a boon if the alien is dangerous or if the alien's technology is dangerous in our government's hands."

Silence fell as they digested this unpleasant insight, then Brandt's brow slowly creased until he resembled an aggrieved bear. "Phil said it laughed, *and* it's Orl's friend. So, in my book, it's a person, a friend, and a *guest*. Leaving it to burn violates several lines of my personal code. We should save it and forget about the paperwork or NeuroCorp or those pencil-necks at Central. And aren't you curious? Because wake up, it's an alien! How many times in life do you meet an alien?"

Jemin added, speaking rapidly, his cheeks a pair of overripe apples, his nose a cherry. "Also consider we, our species and several others, are in dire straits. Who are we to turn our nose up at extraterrestrial technology? Especially if that technology includes a process that speeds the decay of radioactive isotopes."

Agnet made a peacemaking gesture with her hands. "I'm just laying out options. Keep in mind, if we dust off our hands and hike back, we've sacrificed the valuable alien. If we rescue the alien, we've exceeded our scope of service and endangered humankind. No matter which way we jump, our actions could be used against us. We might not be able to win, here. Understand?"

They nodded, their solemn expressions mirroring her emotional state. After all, Central could already know about both the vanished radiation and the alien. Having selected *her* as team leader, they may have expected a rescue attempt, because they knew she'd overextend her authority; Given that she *always* overextended her authority.

"Then, knowing we may be making the absolutely wrong decision, who wants to save the alien?"

Brandt's arm shot up like a hungry gator exploding from the water. Philip and Jemin exchanged glances; she hoped they wouldn't vote opposite each other, out of spite.

Philip, wearing his hiding-anxiety-by-feigning-boredom expression, flicked his hand upward from the wrist. "Screw it. Life is about interesting experiences, and this experience promises to be interesting, though possibly too interesting."

Jemin extended one finger then slowly unfolded the rest. "I've invariably been too curious for my own good."

"I'm assuming Orl's a 'yes'?"

Philip nodded.

Decision made, she sighed and allowed her muscles to relax. It was all the same to her, from a political perspective, and did she still care about politics, or had she grown tired of dancing around assholes? Her discomfort with the hierarchy, combined with Orl's backstory, and Jemin and Philip's observations, had pruned her desire for Central's approval. Besides, her career had effectively derailed this summer. So, she'd overreach, as expected, and find the alien, also probably as expected. And then, contingent on events, select her next best course of action.

"I'm in. Let's rescue ourselves an alien. I'll meet those two up-slope," not that her hamstrings and rear would appreciate the stroll, "get a feel for them, and decide what to share. Until we're all on the same page, tell them we're hunting monsters and inspecting the fire. If either corners you, keep them talking about themselves. Ask after their comfort and about their mission. Use a bit of misdirection, but only if absolutely necessary

The faces behind the visors, a woman in her early thirties, and a man in his forties or early fifties, weren't familiar. The woman's badge read "Elaine Pruett, Team Leader". Must be an eager beaver to be in charge so young. Pruett set her fists on her hips.

"Chief Krause. You and your team are unprotected. Containment suits are required in an exclusion zone."

Righteous indignation was a clumsy way to start a conversation. Best to smooth past it.

"Appreciate your concern, but the area's clean."

"Nonsense. I've monitored regularly." Pruett snatched an object dangling at her side—a meter wand—pointed it at the ground, and a hissing, cicadas in high summer, filled her ears.

Agnet tugged out her own meter and tested the same rock. Nothing. Not a click beyond background. Reaching a lamentable conclusion, she aimed the wand at Pruett's meter. The clicks grew louder and more frequent the closer she came to the detection window, then blurred into static.

Pruett gasped, yanked the base unit from her pocket, and hurled the yellow gadget skyward. It arced high, wand fluttering behind like a silver tail, and landed with a clatter some distance away.

"Nice throw," said her companion, his badge obscured by a rust-colored stain.

"Thanks." The young woman bent over, resting palms on knees, her shoulders shaking. "I've been carrying that unit for days. Days."

The fellow knelt beside her. "These suits provide excellent protection. You'll be fine. Probably got no more exposure than a visit to the dentist."

He helped her up, and she held out her gloves.

"Any contamination?"

Agnet scanned her head to toe, including the insides of her pockets. "You're clean. The contamination didn't spread."

The man asked, "So, you haven't detected any radiation at all?"

"Only a bit and that was on the monsters."

"Good to know. Don't see any monsters around here, and I'm suffocating in this suit. When you're ready, don't hesitate to explain about the monsters." He flipped up his visor.

Pruett unfastened her helmet and ripped it off with obvious relief. Despite being stuffed in a sweaty helmet for hours, the woman's bobbed hair lay perfectly flat, not a strand out of place.

Regardless of the perfect hair, Agnet commiserated with this lady, truly commiserated, given she'd dodged the same radioactive bullet. But her personal feelings about Property would stay personal, for now. Because one contaminated meter suggested ineptitude, while two suggested intentional contamination. It'd take time to process that information, and sharing too much too early, whether to keep everyone informed or to put others at ease, consistently got her kicked in the teeth. Instead, she properly introduced herself.

The interloper molded her face into business mode. "And I'm Elaine Pruett, CMD." She raised a glove by way of greeting. "Let me introduce Cull, Medical and Geoscience. Thought we'd find you at Ridgelands, but Warden Honing told us about your excursion and expressed concern, so here we are."

Had she said Medical and Geoscience? "Anything untoward happen at the farm while we were following our lead?"

"Dancing monsters, according to the warden." Pruett grimaced, clearly suppressing a smile.

Agnet couldn't resist laughing. "Believe it or not, dancing monsters is a real possibility. How long ago?"

"Two nights."

"Thanks to our perceiver's hard work today, the monsters should quiet down, and mission accomplished. Sorry to say, you may have hiked out for no reason. What's your assignment?"

"Report status, support, or extraction, depending on circumstances."

Central didn't extract this early and without cause, and the timeline didn't make a lick of sense. "I'm surprised, as it's only been a few days since we left Central. But nice to know somebody cares."

Worry lines flickered across Pruett's forehead. "So short a time. Really? The backup request cited lack of contact."

"Not much to say until today. Must say, you got out here fast. They send you by catapult?"

Pruett's lips pruned, not much of a sense of humor, apparently. But Cull smiled and hiked a thumb westward over his shoulder. "We were down the road in New Delphi when the call came. Caught a ride to the farm and after a quick check in with Warden Honing, we followed you over the ridge. Thanks for marking the trail."

"Hope you sampled the farm's cuisine."

Cull grinned ear to ear. "Understandably, they didn't allow us on site but served us a fine meal."

"It's that bad in New Delphi?"

Cull and Pruett exchanged grim looks.

"Well beyond bad," said Cull. "But don't worry. This protective gear is fresh, and they thoroughly disinfected us at the perimeter."

Pruett quickly added. "However, the mission was a containment success, the best one could expect, considering. Speaking of bad, what happened to you?" She looked Agnet up and down and quirked a lip. Alright, she must be filthy. Not an unusual happenstance and the reason she never packed a mirror.

"We've been investigating a burn risk."

"And your oddly dressed man down, I'm assuming they're a perceiver?" She waved a hand in Orl's direction.

Despite her many disapproving opinions regarding Orl's fashion sense, Agnet prickled at the woman's vaguely insulting tone. Hopefully, she was being oversensitive.

"Yes. A junior perceiver. She overused her chip today. Tremendous luck, a medic turning up. We surely could use your help. Come down to camp, and we'll run your badges, then I'd deeply appreciate you examining Orl." She shot Cull a hopeful look.

"Glad to be of service and happy for you to run my badge. Can't say as I blame you, not knowing who to trust. Not after that shit-show in New Delphi." Cull balanced his pack.

Pruett wrinkled her pert little nose at Cull, as if he'd mis-spoke. "We're happy to confirm full documentation. Then I'll want the *entire* story.

"No rush. Orl will need to recover before our next move." Not that she knew her next move. Yet.

She folded her arms. "And that move would be?"

"Still deciding."

"So happens Central has placed me in command. From here on out, I'll be making the decisions, so I'll require every detail."

Command?

Agnet pulled her eyebrows off her hairline. "Welp. My perceiver's health is our first priority. And we're exhausted; it's been quite a day. I'll bet you could use a break too. Let's parlay when everybody's revived."

Pruett pressed her mouth into a firm line, probably wondering if Agnet's suggestion violated her command.

"Fine." But she spat out that "fine" same way a person spits out a moldy apple seed.

A Private Mission

Agnet, looking rattled or distracted, returned with the interlopers in tow, a tall, gangly, older fellow, and a woman who emanated disapproval like a toxic gas. She explained that Central, concerned for their safety, had deployed the pair as backup, and now, their chief was this unknown woman. The new chief puffed her chest out, looking like a sparrow defending a pile of cake crumbs.

The universe had a cruel sense of humor.

But thankfully, the older fellow was a medic, a fabulous happenstance, as Philip Spool was no nurse, and Orl's condition hadn't improved. He took charge of Orl's care and seemed competent, despite a crotchety bedside manner. The group hovered a few steps back, giving the doctor space to work. Agnet shot Philip, Brandt, and Jemin weighty glances, then whispered to Brandt and Jemin. Brandt sat by the doctor and Orl, as if he'd been asked to keep an eye on Orl. The historian went red in the face, plucked a notebook from his pack, and strolled toward Pruett.

Agnet beckoned Philip closer.

He leaned in. "Watch. Jemin's trying to act casual. What a scream. Did you sic him on that woman, trying to bore her into submission?"

"Without a shred of remorse or pity," said Agnet, a lopsided grin on her face and a twinkle in her eye. "Jemin should keep her occupied for a while. Meanwhile, let's gather some firewood."

Philip grabbed a burlap carryall, and they strolled to an out-of-earshot cluster of scraggly shrubs. He spread open the carryall and tossed in some kindling. Hoping they appeared innocently busy, he asked, "I sense that woman's nettlesome and green. Is she really in command? And if so, why?"

Agnet hunkered down and snapped a dead branch off a bush. "She's the least of our problems." Then she launched into a story about Pruett's radiation meter.

"Same as yours! Coincidence or conspiracy?"

"Good question. I've been having a think. Maybe Property's decon procedure is outrageously defective, but maybe somebody didn't want us to notice this land is uncontaminated. According to the Warden, several teams traipsed through this summer; I have a hard time believing nobody noticed the discrepancy between 'exclusion zone' and 'zero clicks,' raising several questions. What happened to the radiation? Who's keeping the good news secret, and why?"

She broke the branch into pieces and loaded them into the carryall. "I'd theorized Central *hoped* we'd find the ship. But now, I'm not so sure. Would we have hiked this far if this zone was aglow with gamma rays? Imagine struggling down that slope in full protective gear."

Philip snorted. "The climb down was tough, suit or no suit." Then he thought a moment while using a twig to clean under his nails—he'd kill for a bath. "What if someone wanted to discourage us from leaving the farm?"

"Why?"

He shrugged. "So we'd concentrate on the monsters?"

Agnet shook her head. "From what the Warden said, Central doesn't give a fig about those monsters. Why else?"

"So we wouldn't find the spaceship or alien?"

Her face brightened. "That's an intriguing angle. But we traveled out here only because you and Orl heard that alien singing. And if those earlier teams had a perceiver on board, NeuroCorp knows perceivers hear that signal from a distance."

Her comments rang a bell, as if he'd had a similar conversation or... The almost-memory had a smell, earthy and rich, like rain falling on parched soil. He snapped the stick and turned to toss it in the carryall, but his vision blurred, as if a shimmering fog had blown in.

Crap on a stick. This was a prodrome.

He shoved his fingers into his pocket, cursed his tight pants, and closed his eyes against a nauseating visual distortion. A jumble of sights played on the backs of his lids, the images hyper-real and over-saturated. The Song clanged in his ears, so close, too loud, and—

A woman stared down at him, a vertical frown line between her eyebrows. She'd better watch it, or that line would become permanent.

"You alright?"

"I think so. Where am I?"

201

"Lying under a shrub. You jerked your head to one side, then toppled over. Caught me off guard, but luckily, the shrub broke your fall."

"Can they see me from camp?"

"Not from this angle."

Philip took a deep breath, happy only one person had witnessed his fall. Losing control was so embarrassing, and he couldn't be clumsy, ill, or otherwise defective; the team depended on him, and he needed his job. He sat, dusted dried leaves from his shirt, and smoothed his hair, tidier now but still exhausted. The sun's position suggested late afternoon, but he felt midnight tired. "I'm good. Sorry. What were we doing?"

She squatted beside him. "Collecting firewood and talking."

"Ah. Right." Agnet, the firewood, this idiotic and highly unlikely mission... Last thing he recalled, Agnet was asking questions. Maybe he could jump back into the conversation, acting natural, as if nothing had happened. "What was your question?"

"Does NeuroCorp... Wait. If I repeat the question, are you going to pass out again?"

Pass out? He wasn't a fainter. Why would he have... He pressed his fist into his forehead—sometimes he could be so slow. "I didn't pass out. I seized. Not a big deal, just a post-lacuna complication. Your question may or may not have triggered the seizure, either way, don't sweat it. Most seizures are random."

The lies tumbled out of his mouth, a reflex to soothe and deflect scrutiny or stigma. Nothing worse than making people feel uncomfortable—next thing you knew, they'd resent and avoid you. He wriggled a vial of MemStop out of his pants pocket, tipped his head, and snorted the acrid liquid. "I must not have gotten to my meds quick enough, but this dose should cover me. Ask your question."

The frown line reappeared, her concern reminding him of his fragility and general uselessness. He should be at home, his recovery spurred by Gervais's continual barrage of insults. He'd take those insults over pity any day.

"I'm fine. Ask away. Oh, and I'd appreciate a recap."

He watched her shove her anxieties aside. Perhaps he'd reassured her, or his seizure had interrupted critical business, and she needed him back on track.

"Seeing as you're sitting down, here it goes. Have other perceivers been out this way?"

"Not that I know."

"Any chance NeuroCorp knows you and Orl can perceive the alien?"

"Don't know."

"Alright. Next, and warn me if you feel a seizure coming on, Pruett claims Central expected updates. Were you supposed to file updates?"

"Who would want to hear from me? And honestly? A request to report would've stunned me, since I assumed the mission was trivial: mass hysteria, debunking, and some counseling, or such like. The only message I foresaw was you sending a bird for our ride home."

"What about Orl? Was she supposed to contact Central?"

"She would have needed my help to interact with the prison staff, so no, but—" The rumor mill had NeuroCorp experimenting with long range communication; maybe Orl's chips were part of that project. Some evidence supported that theory; her connection with the alien was stronger than his, and she'd pinpointed the alien's location from a fair distance. So perhaps Orl's chips *could* broadcast long distance messages. Had she already reported? Had she failed to report? If so, why? The answer to that last question came to him at once: because she'd stopped taking her pills.

"I should speak with Orl. Let me see if she's awake."

He maxed his chip and scanned. There she was, quieter than usual, but fully perceivable. He asked after her health.

"She's lying over there, pretending to be asleep so she can ignore the medic and his fearless leader."

Agnet chuckled. "Easy to forget she's just a kid. Go ahead and ask your questions. Tell her we need the truth, given the situation. Nobody will be angry at her."

Philip asked his questions, and found he'd guessed correctly.

"She's a kid, alright. A medicated kid who's finally answering my questions. Must remember to thank the doctor. Orl had private mission: perceive a voice, home in on its location, and report back. But she detests her handlers—"

Agnet interjected. "The NeuroCorp rep at the launch meeting? What was his name?"

"Rasp. The fabled Dr. William Rasp. I was terrified of him during my training and spent a lot of energy flying under his radar." A sheepish smile stretched his lips. "Frankly, I nearly had a heart attack when he showed up at the pre-mission briefing."

"Can't fault your judgment; that man resembled a suited-up snake."

"Snake sounds about right. Orl also didn't like the pills Rasp fed her, so the moment she was out of his sight, she quit them. But she thinks it'll be obvious she's off her meds if she reports."

"So essentially, she's gone rogue."

"Yep."

"Blithering heck. Did she tell you what the pills were for?"

"In her personal lingo, the pills kept her from being 'more'."

"Begging the question, more what?"

"She can't or won't explain, but most NeuroCorp meds either enhance abilities or dampen them."

"So why the rest of us? What're we doing here? NeuroCorp could've sent Orl and a handler, or its own team."

Philip passed the question to Orl and forwarded the answer. "We don't know."

Agnet sighed. "Here's a guess—NeuroCorp wants the location of that alien but has reason to keep its distance. So, they convinced Central to organize our monster hunt and disguised Orl as a trainee. We supposed to babysit Orl and obscure the mission's true purpose."

More reasons to loathe his employer. "Could be. Maybe Pruett and Cull showed up because Orl didn't follow her script."

"Exactly. Those two may be straight shooters, sent here because they were close by and without family." She winked at him, more gallows humor. "Or, one or both may have a hidden agenda. What do you read off them?"

Philip tossed a few sticks in the carryall, continuing with the ruse, even though everybody back at camp must be fully aware they were having a private chat. Even Brandt, who'd just said as much to Orl.

"Not much. Pruett's game face is nearly impenetrable. Cull's flat, because he's suffering empathy exhaustion, though according to Orl, he's a 'one-self' person, meaning 'what you see is what you get,' a common configuration for data heavy chip-heads."

"Lot of advantages to 'one-self' people. What makes people hard to read?" she asked.

"A bunch of factors. Empathy for one. High empathy types tend to express more on their faces, sending a ton of info while searching for social and emotional cues in others. I can practically see the mirror neurons flashing. Social skills make a difference; highly skilled people can maintain a game face. So highly socialized, low empathy people are flat as a pancake, like our new pal Elaine Pruett."

"A classic corporate puppet. Not my favorite type."

"Me neither. But they have their uses. In brutal situations, like infection containment, low empathy types won't let other's suffering cloud their judgment. Our team is a mixed bag suited for a low-key psychological mission but not much else. So much so that I figured this mission was intended as a recovery mission, for you and me, and a training mission for everybody else."

"Something easy so we could dip our toes in the water."

"Exactly. But now I have no idea why they threw this team together."

Agnet grimaced. "I have a theory on that, but I'll keep it to myself. I doubt Central sent Pruett, thinking we needed help making hard calls. I've made plenty, though each has taken a toll. And though I concede that putting myself in other people's shoes has clouded my judgment from time to time, I haven't regretted my decisions in those instances, even when roundly criticized later." She stood and shook out her legs. "All this theorizing. I wish we had something solid to work from, and I'm getting stiff, sitting so long. Come on. Let's collect a few more sticks, so we look legit, then get back to camp. And when we're back, have Doc Cull check you over."

She held out her hand. Philip grasped it and pulled himself up. His arms still ached from hauling Brandt out of that pit, but he didn't feel woozy. Just a shade distant, as if a subtle filter obscured reality.

"And then what?" he asked.

She stared upslope in the spaceship's direction. "I have no idea."

A Sense of Dissonance

Brandt greeted Agnet with a cheery wave when she walked into camp. Orl, on the other hand, hid behind her mane of unkempt black hair. The girl had reason to fear Agnet's reaction to the truth about the pills; her refusal to follow NeuroCorp's orders had endangered the team. But given Orl's backstory, Agnet couldn't find it in her heart to be angry. She and Philip tossed the kindling into the fire pit, stacked a few logs, and joined Jemin, Elaine, and Cull. They appeared deep in conversation, or mid-lecture—Jemin was doing the talking.

"An accidental explosion ignited rail cars loaded with coal. Then a freak temperature inversion trapped the toxic smoke between two ridges, smothering the valley floor. Over two-hundred people inhaled carbon monoxide and sulfur dioxide, among other gases, and died. The accident coincided with an outdoor festival, involving costumed children collecting treats. Took days to contain the fire, and the company paid the survivors a pittance, calling the event an Act of God."

Children gassed to death during a celebration; how heart-shrivelingly dreadful. She chewed on Jemin's remarks for a time, as did the others. He glanced at her, looking uneasy, not an uncommon expression for the historian. Maybe he feared they'd conflate the horrible message with the messenger. Truth be told, sometimes she did exactly that. But more often, it was Jemin's deadpan delivery that irked her; him rattling off horrors as if they didn't affect him. At least, seemed he'd kept the focus on monsters and fire as instructed. He was trying to help. She gave him a smile and a reassuring nod.

"How long ago was this accident?" asked Philip.

"About two centuries before the big tide." His eyes searched the air in front of his face. "Oh? Was that it? Yes. The town's name was Pitting's Gap."

Everybody else seemed to miss the slight divergence from normal behavior, and Jemin continued talking.

"Two-hundred years ago would correlate with the—uh—artifacts we saw," said Philip.

Jemin nodded, his expression eager. "I can't prove my theory, as the town hasn't appeared on a map for centuries but given our oddly clad child-sized monsters, I felt you'd appreciate the information."

He searched their faces, as if seeking approval. Or seeking tips on how to feel. Poor slob. She splintered the silence. "Welp. Very helpful and interesting but bone screw awful. I'll slam the door on my imagination for a while, and Jemin, stay off your chip, least for a couple of days."

"Yes, ma'am."

Elaine turned to her and folded her arms. "Did you and Mr. Spool enjoy your chat?"

"Absolutely! I always appreciate Philip's insights, but he needs a checkup. Doc Cull? Our lead perceiver had a seizure. Could you give him a once over?"

Philip waved her off, but Cull rounded on him, chatted a moment, took him by the elbow, then strolled him toward Orl and the medical bag. The rest of the group broke into a terse conversation about Philip and his condition, both Jemin and Elaine showing or feigning concern.

But Agnet paid little attention.

She had decisions to make. Elaine Pruett read as a pain in the rear, a rule follower, probably reliant on approval from the higher ups. But the New Delphi incident must've exhausted and disheartened her some, and the contaminated meter might've shaken her confidence in Central. Maybe she'd be open to new ideas.

Agnet's instincts said, "person at a crossroads" while her galaxy-level paranoia shrieked, "chuck the woman and her perfect hair into the nearest sink hole." Sadly, she wasn't a murderous type—life would be so much simpler. She'd just need to trust her questionable instincts and offer Elaine Pruett a window into this outlandish mess.

But only after a fair warning.

Elaine broke her reverie. "Jemin's been very helpful. And his story aligns with the Warden's, but I'm still unclear why you hiked so far from the farm."

The woman tucked a silky strand of hair behind a delicate ear, challenging Agnet's resolve. But she ignored the petty and shallow tendencies of her worst self and plowed forward.

"I'll show you the last part of the puzzle. Afterward, our story will make sense. However, I must warn you, this mission is a loser. An epic, full-stop, barn-busting, career-ending loser. Knowing our story might mark you as an outcast, or worse. Your best bet may be to walk away, say you never found us, and return to your lives."

Jemin gulped, the sound reminiscent of a rainy season frog pond.

Elaine blanched, then pursed her lips. "I've never abandoned a mission and don't intend to abandon your team. My orders were quite clear: aid and assist, extract, if necessary, no matter the circumstances. What do you want to show me?"

Agnet turned to Jemin. "Did their IDs checkout?"

He nodded.

She pointed up-slope. The spaceship's rim, just visible over the treetops, glittered in the late afternoon sun.

Elaine's jaw dropped, but only for a flash, then she tucked in her chin. "My word! I...I hadn't noticed...that!"

DISPOSABLE

Elaine Pruett's ears felt impossibly hot. The only eye-catching object in a bleak landscape, and she'd missed it! How? The contaminated meter had been quite enough humiliation for one day, thank you. She hid her shock and dismay by scrutinizing the gleaming sickle suspended above the pines, vast enough to be a climate shield or containment pod. Aware of Krause's expectant gaze—couldn't ignore the woman forever—she strangled out a response.

"Isn't that intriguing? I'd love to have a look." Right after she spoke, worrisome thoughts flashed through her head. She'd be following potentially hostile strangers to a secluded area where they might slash her throat and leave her in a ditch, not an unreasonable course of action, given the circumstances. She'd been overconfident. She shouldn't've mentioned the change in command so soon or stowed her side arm while changing out of the containment suit. And Central should've assigned her more people. Curse it. She hadn't expected to meet up with Krause in the middle of nowhere. At the farm, the Warden would've backed her up. Sure, he seemed to admire Krause and her team, but he would've caved to chain of command.

"Cull won't want to miss out," she said, not that Cull would be much protection, but he was of value, given their medical needs. They wouldn't want to lose him.

"I'll see if he's available," said the historian. Without a "by your leave" he trotted off toward the others, taking with him her chance to retrieve her gun without ruffling feathers.

She and Krause stood in awkward silence for some minutes. A stiff breeze rattled the fabric of her jacket, whipped the dust from gray boulders, and harried a sorry twisted little tree. This desolation must be getting to her—she could almost hear whispers in the wind. Elaine smoothed her hair and applied a brittle-feeling neutral expression to her face.

In truth, she was tired. She'd rather opt out of Krause's foolishness, lie down, and sleep for a week or two. But a professional didn't show weakness. A professional plowed forward despite the odds. A professional got by on no sleep, burning muscles, and little food, thriving on adversity. If getting a decent report required trudging uphill, she'd just have to trudge.

She mulled through excuses for not noticing that gigantic structure. In truth, she'd been fixated on the people downslope, wondering about the girl's condition and anticipating Krause's reaction to demotion. Then that peculiar little man had begun babbling. Krause had probably put him up to it. But he was a convenient excuse.

"Can't believe I didn't notice that big blue dome. On the way down, I was watching my step. And then, the historian..." She applied a conspiratorial smile to her lips. "Well, he just went on and on."

A loopy grin played over Krause's face. "Jemin sure can jaw. And that ship is easier to miss than you'd expect. We thought it was a rock when we spotted it from up-slope."

Good to know, but also sort of sad, Krause admitting incompetence. She'd heard such impressive stories about the woman. But in person, her expression often appeared vaguely apologetic. And she spoke to her subordinates so casually, asking, instead of commanding. *Kind not Weak.* Perhaps, but the two walked hand in hand.

Elaine waved her hand toward the pod. "So who built that, and why?"

Krause opened her mouth, but Cull, Jemin, and Krause's security guard converged on them, a study in contrasts bringing to mind an ill-conceived carnival act: the scarecrow, the toad, and the strong man. Speaking of strength, Collins could crush her windpipe with a single finger. Isolated, outnumbered, and outmuscled, well done, Elaine. Sweat prickled her hairline. If she commanded Krause's people to stay put, would they obey her or would they laugh?

Jemin told Krause, "I offered Doc Cull the same opt out you offered Chief Pruett, but he's game."

Elaine clenched her jaw. How dare a junior nobody offer her subordinate anything! She glared at Jemin until he shrank behind Krause.

Cull eyed the distance to the pod and frowned at her. "I'm no youngster, and the last thing I need today is a hike uphill. You mind telling us what's up there? These fellas are being coy."

A moment of panic—her not yet knowing the answer to Cull's question, him jumping rank and boldly asking questions. The medic's conduct had deteriorated in New Delphi, no surprise, given the horrible conditions. Now, tainted by Krause's out-of-control crew, would he become even mouthier?

She snapped at Cull, "It's obviously an abandoned pod, probably workspace or storage for some defunct environmental project."

Collins shook his head. "No. It's way more awesome. Can't wait for your reactions when you see it up close." Her lips tightened at the man's unprofessional demeanor. A rebuke formed on her tongue, but the slow-witted oaf was doubtlessly loyal to Agnet. *Big and Bad. He'll hurt you.* The wind hissed and blew dust in her eye. She blinked the grit away and dabbed at a tear. What'd she been thinking? Oh, yes. About Collins. The man was enormous; she'd better tread carefully.

Yoder was saying, "—artifact of the greatest importance, and fascinating from a materials science perspective. We cut our last visit short, so I'm dying for another look."

Elaine rested her fists on her hips. "Get to the point. What's up there!"

Krause chuckled. "I think they're hoping to surprise you, but I don't fault your impatience; it's been a long day. Here's the bottom line. Behind that rise, an enormous spaceship is planted nose-first into the ridge. See that curved line above the trees? That's the spaceship's hull."

Spaceship? A giggle, more nerves than anything, escaped her, though Krause's weathered face displayed no humor, not even a hint of a smile. Elaine resisted glancing at the overly earnest historian, fearful acknowledging him would prompt another torrent of rambling verbiage. Instead, she met eyes with Cull.

The grumpy old medic raised a skeptical eyebrow. "You joking? Because I'm tired and the day truly has been long."

"Even with the surprise *ruined*," Collins threw Krause a disappointed look, "you're going to love it. And there's geology up there. Rocks all over the place. Plus, the ship's hull is *blue metal*."

The historian's bulbous head bobbed with enthusiasm. "I tapped it, and it rang like a bell."

"Never come across blue metal before. Maybe you can tell us what it's made of," Krause added, as if hoping to motivate the burned-out has-been by tapping into his professional pride.

"They must be joking," she said to Cull. Here was her chance to end this farce and command them back to camp, but those murmurs on the wind—*go and see, beautiful, Magnificent, Important*—raised all sorts of doubts.

The lines on Cull's forehead deepened. He scratched his cheek and looked from her to Krause, as if waiting for Krause's lead—the nerve. "Heck of a drift from mass hysteria at a prison farm to spaceship. You want to explain?"

Krause started up hill and beckoned them to follow. "I'll tell you on the way. But I warn you, this report will sound beyond far-fetched."

She shrugged. "Not unexpected, given the makeup of your team."

One eyebrow lifted high on Krause's forehead. Elaine's cheeks warmed again; that hadn't come out right. She cleared her throat.

"I was referring to perceivers," though the dossiers suggested oddballs all the way down. "Usually, perceivers mean the mission is...has an interesting twist. I mean, monsters, after all."

Amusement fluttered Krause's lips. "Welp. You're correct. This mission is nothing but interesting twists."

They trekked up-slope, Elaine's thighs aching with every step, but seeing whatever these people believed was a spaceship would be worth the pain. Krause commenced her report, but minutes into a story about another contaminated radiation meter, blood began pounding in her ears. Krause's lips moved while Elaine's mind filled with images of her meter's wand thwacking against her thigh as she hiked through the forest. That meter was supposed to protect them, not blast her DNA with high energy particles.

And two contaminated meters? A bizarre coincidence, surely

not intentional. Maybe someone like Krause—aging out of team leader, too difficult for a desk job—was expendable, but Elaine Pruett was young, in peak condition, and her record was spotless. *Doesn't matter.* She'd done nothing to deserve radiation exposure. She was destined for success. *Replaceable.* Her lips trembled. Why did she keep badmouthing herself? She needed to rein in her negativity. After all, her career depended on maintaining control, keeping up appearances, and keeping her eye on the prize. *Nobody cares.*

The wind, her suspicions, and her aching muscles took a toll, and by the time they reached a pile of enormous boulders, she couldn't quite remember the point of this excursion, having only caught snippets of Krause's story: a spaceship, a cave-in, and the perceivers sensing something inside the ship. The story's threads didn't string together.

"So that sums us up," said Krause.

Cull pulled back one cheek, the lop-sided scowl he used when unimpressed. "Story's a whopper; I'll give you that, but I know my physics and nuclear fallout doesn't just disappear. Sure, by now, the cesium and iodine isotopes should've decayed, but uranium two-thirty-five and plutonium two-thirty-nine have half-lives of about seven-hundred million years and twenty-five-thousand years, respectively. Should've taken fifteen to thirty thousand years for this area to be habitable."

Thirty thousand years was a long time.

"I looked at it from every possible historic angle," said Jemin, then he and Cull launched into a sea of blather.

Krause said to her, "If I'd been carrying that hot counter, I'd've badged-out during our first excursion, and we'd be cooling our heels at the farm."

"That's where I was told you'd be." *Lies.* "And if you'd stayed put, I wouldn't've been as heavily exposed." She cringed at the irritable and bitter sound of her words. But she was bitter. Some ass in Property had screwed up and put her in harm's way—she'd hunt the responsible tech down and make them pay—and this assignment should've been easy, but it was rapidly going sideways.

Elaine forced herself to follow the others through a gap in the rocks. A flash of brilliant light blinded her as their path came to a crest. She instinctively sought cover, waited for her vision to clear, shielded her eyes, then surveyed the terrain.

Oh.

Wow!

An arc of ultramarine blue hung over the boulders and trees ahead, highlighted in scarlet by the late afternoon sun. No. Suddenly, the view made sense. The trees under the arc were a reflection. She was looking at an immense blue oblong with a highly reflective surface. Its majesty struck her chest like a stray mortar shell. Cull gasped in a rare display of powerful emotion.

She shut her slack jaw, swallowed, and said, "Well."

"Yes. Well. Exactly," echoed Cull.

They spent the next forty-five minutes touring the object's periphery, Cull and Jemin recording, then debating every detail, rattling on about alloys, fuels, and impact craters, every few minutes proclaiming the ship's incalculable value and impossibility.

It wasn't impossible; it was just stupid. "Why hasn't this thing been spotted from the air? It's enormous!"

"Good point." Cull jotted a note. "The area's remote, and I doubt many aircraft fly by these days. Even so, it probably would've been missed from above, since the reflectivity and color mimic water."

Of course. Water. She glanced at their reflections, wavering like shadows upon the surface of a deep pool. So obvious. She was off her game and should keep her mouth shut.

Krause sauntered beside her, hands in pockets. "We've accomplished our core objective: no more monsters, but we're left with a spaceship and alien in peril. So now what?"

Alien? Had Krause mentioned an alien? As in foreigner or extraterrestrial? Must've missed that tidbit, thanks to exhaustion and that high-pitched wind. But if she asked for clarification, she'd stick her foot in it again. And why bother? The absurd report must be a fabrication meant to distract her or corrode her trust in Central.

All true.

Had she thought it sounded true? Now she was truly confused. And tired. The wind whistled—*Secrets and Lies*. Gooseflesh rose on her arms. This blighted moonscape gave her the creeps. *Marooned. Alone.*

Krause was searching her face. She had to focus.

"We've been discussing our next move."

Discussing? Did Krause still believe she was in control? And if so, why was she discussing? A true leader doesn't discuss; she decides. She might collect data from team members but wouldn't *confer* with them. Subordinates respected commands. Commands were efficient. Krause must've really slipped.

Others know Other Things.

Who cares? Decisiveness was her strong suit, and she knew exactly what to do.

"Our next moves are return to the farm, report, and leave the 'spaceship' in the hands of specialized technicians. Unless one of your squad is a 'spaceship' expert."

Krause chuckled. "No spacecraft pilots or engineers on our team, far as I know. I wish we had the time and expertise to study that ship. It's truly a marvel. However, the clock is ticking. In a matter of days, the alien and its ship will be consumed by fire.

Elaine remembered the fire; the historian had pointed it out, down in the valley below while he'd droned on about ancient history. "Seems unlikely. That fire's aways off, the ship's metal, and it's surrounded by rocks and a few skanky pines. What's to burn?"

"Not sure why, but the alien believes the fire will reach it in a few days. If we had months or years, we could return to Central and call for reinforcements and experts: linguists, airship technicians, what have you. But if we only have a few days, we should spring that alien, pronto."

"Can't it just...open a hatch?"

"No hatch visible, and we don't understand the creature's biology. For all we know, it's swimming in an aquarium."

Alright. Krause meant alien as in extraterrestrial. Please. The woman needed to give the bullshit a rest, but why not play along? "Then it might die when exposed to our atmosphere."

"Maybe it's choosing asphyxiation over incineration. Wouldn't blame it, myself. But you've raised some good points. Perhaps the perceivers should take another crack at interviewing the creature before we retreat."

Good idea. But Philip had said the first interview was responsible for the girl's injuries, and Elaine's mission was clear: deliver the young, female perceiv̲e̲r̲ intact to NeuroCorp or euthanize her. And they'd been serious. NeuroCorp was always serious. They'd supplied her with the appropriate drugs and lodged internal lethal force permissions. Or so they'd claimed. *Murderer. Liars.*

No not a murderer, not Elaine Pruett. But she couldn't say "no" to NeuroCorp, no matter how much she'd wanted to, even if they were lying through their teeth. Some nerve, them using her as an assassin, ordering her to eliminate a child, no less. And they'd put her in a terrible position, placed in command with disregard to rank or experience, isolated and outnumbered.

On top of everything, Command had saddled her with a physician. If she was forced to kill the girl, Cull could call her out, and Krause's people would take revenge. Nobody would remember her bravery and hard work.

She shivered, a pox on this wind and that bizarre girl. Might be easiest to allow Krause a second interview-*good idea*-and let the "alien" snuff out Orl. Her hands would be clean. She could claim mission accomplished, lay any blame on Krause, and avoid being type cast as a hitman. Ugh. Talk about a dead end. Sticking to the shadows, feared and despised, cold-blooded killers never ascended beyond a middling rank.

"Doesn't sound like a bad idea. I could use proof of this alien and more information might bolster your claims."

A flicker of surprise crossed Krause's face. "Ah. Glad you concur. Of course, we'll need to wait until both perceivers are up to the task."

"Then at the earliest possible opportunity."

Hopefully not too soon. Maybe NeuroCorp expected a quick resolution, but she wanted to hole up in her tent out of this disconcerting wind and collect her thoughts. If the girl didn't die, she'd need a plan to force these nitwits back to the farm.

Breath Condensing in Wispy Plumes

Evening fell, crisp and still at ground level, but high above, thin sheep-clouds scudded past, partially obscuring the star-studded sky. Bare branches reached like gnarled fingers, while the stones glowed silver in the moonlight and cast deep shadows.

Agnet sat with Philip, Jemin, and Brandt, the chill air biting at her cheeks and nose, despite the campfire. After returning from the spaceship and making noises about sharing the watch, Elaine and Cull had sacked out, their nap stretching through dinner. Nobody was of a mind to wake them. Orl also slept, hopefully recovering her bandwidth. And Agnet's fireside companions looked as tired as she felt, but she needed to bring them up to speed. So they conversed in soft voices, their breaths condensing in wispy plumes.

She finished her radiation meter spiel with "She hiked with the meter's head dangling from her pocket. Lucky habit."

"Or she's a talented actress," said Jemin. "We should check her pocket for a lead lining."

"A lead-lined pocket would pull the suit to one side, a sloppy asymmetric look Elaine would never tolerate," said Philip with a wink.

Agnet smothered a laugh. "Checked the pocket. No lead, no radiation. What did the ID scan tell you?"

Jemin replied with some demographics, then added, "Both are recent transfers from up North. They're legit, but they haven't earned my trust, and I don't care for Chief Pruett's tone. Don't relish being under her command, but what am I supposed to do, mutiny?"

Agnet found herself scratching her head. "When we first met, Elaine seemed strait-laced, stiff-necked, and by-the-book. Thought I'd typed her. Even tailored my report to suit, leaving out the ghosts, the visit to the feral village, and our AI hypothesis, thinking her judgments on...um...offbeat issues might create unnecessary conflict." She glanced at each man to confirm they were paying attention. "And I'd appreciate you all respecting those omissions. But up by the spaceship, she went wonky on me. Almost became a different person: preoccupied, even confused. The by-the-book persona did bleed through, now and again. In fact, she demanded we return to the farm and report, but I managed to convince her to delay so we could interview the alien again. Almost felt bad, as if I was tricking a toddler out of her candy."

"Proves you're still in command, which is fine by me, because switching officers when the mission's under control and just about to get phenomenal, makes no sense. And it's not fair—" Brandt threw a thumb toward Elaine's tent. "—since she doesn't outrank or outclass you. But I'm not chasing a court martial. So, I hope you can talk her into rescuing the alien."

"Well, thanks," said Agnet. "I'll try. The issue of command doesn't upset me per se. I'm more worried about outcomes and want to see the right thing happen here."

Philip said, "Agreed. Bickering over control will waste time." A moment passed, then he added, "Orl has some interesting thoughts on Pruett."

"Do tell."

"Apologies. I'll be paraphrasing." "Orl's terminology can be—" He threw her a wry smile. "—idiosyncratic. She claims the new commander is working hard to be her chosen self, though being that self has become difficult lately."

"She certainly seemed distracted by something, and internal battles will do that to a person."

Jemin frowned. "How would Orl know anything about Chief Pruett? The woman spoke briefly to her, making the sort of pro forma supportive comments you'd expect from a superior wishing for a swift recovery. She certainly didn't confide any personal details."

"Some people are good at theory of mind, but..." Worry lines bracketed Philip's mouth. "Forming a solid theory takes time, so I wondered myself how Orl had formed those impressions, but she wouldn't elaborate."

"Welp. Orl's a queer duck, but I hope her theory's right. If Elaine's at a crossroads, she might be amenable to changing plans."

Somebody came crunching through the rocks from the direction of the tents, Cull, by the sound of the stride. She was proved correct, and they exchanged greetings. The lanky doctor took a seat at the fire and popped open a RediMeal.

The flickering firelight aged him; hard shadows pooled beneath his prominent cheekbones, and a receding hairline left him all forehead and temples, as if his skull was poised to surface. But according to Jemin, the man was only five years her senior. Her mouth felt uncomfortably dry.

Cull gave his rations a grim once-over and said, "Several notches down from the farm's chow." After a taste, he sighed, then waved his spoon at Agnet. "Have to apologize to you folks, showing up like we did. Seems to me you have the situation under control."

"It's alright. I'm sure Central had their reasons." She made pleasant conversation while he suffered through his supper, avoiding the topic of New Delphi and thanking him again for making the strenuous hike from the farm and treating Orl.

Jemin asked, "Was curious about your combination of chips, if I heard correctly. Medical and geology?"

"That's right. Was plain geology for many years. Then recently, Central strung together excuses: a disaster at the border, loss of personnel, and so on. Offered me a handsome bonus and chipped me up. I've been short sighted before, but brother...what a mistake." He rubbed an eye. "New Delphi was a nightmare and proved I'm no medic. Wish I could get home and put up my feet, but fear I'll find notice of my next assignment pinned to my door."

"So, you prefer geology?" asked Jemin.

Beyond obtuse. Agnet's belly shriveled with embarrassment, but Cull just raised an eyebrow and replied in an even tone. "Significantly prefer."

Jemin appeared thrilled. "Your observations at the crash site fascinated me. I was wondering..." He described the sinking graveyard, the stinking fissures, and the gaping mouth of fire they'd encountered in the morning.

Cull, his weary face a mask of patience, said, "Sounds like a coal seam fire. These ridges are riddled with coal seams, many exposed to the ground by mining or erosion. Anything can set them off: lightning, explosives, even arson, and they can burn for millennia."

"Millennia?" asked Brandt.

"Thousands of years."

"I know what 'millennia' means. I'm just saying, 'wow'."

"Dangerous bastards, coal fires. They heat gases and water trapped in the ground. The gases suddenly expand, or the water evaporates, creating cavities which can collapse at any time, the likely explanation for your sinking graveyard."

"Thought so." Jemin appeared pleased with himself. "But I appreciate the confirmation. The 'whys' are so much more interesting than the 'whats', if you understand my meaning."

"I believe I do," said Cull.

A red-hot log crackled, sending a flurry of sparks into the sky. She watched the embers fly; fire could be an entertainment, a comfort, and a tool, but when it wasn't on your side, it was a ravenous beast. "Could a coal seam fire spread upslope?"

Cull nodded. "Yep. So, the fire in the valley could be the same fire that's threatening the spacecraft and the creature inside. Four days, you said. That's not much time."

Jemin hopped in his seat. "Perhaps you can answer a question that's been troubling me. I've read about reentry: spaceships hurtling through the atmosphere, subject to incredible heat. Wouldn't a spaceship be impervious to fire?"

Cull shrugged, as if considering space flight was an everyday occurrence. "Depending on speed, the hull would heat to, say, fifteen hundred degrees on entering the atmosphere, temperatures any spacecraft would be designed to withstand for a short period. But coal fires burn up to two-thousand degrees, hot enough to melt tungsten, and they can burn for years."

"Space invader fricassee," murmured Brandt.

"Or human fricassee." Cull gestured round the fire with his spoon. "You've witnessed high velocity subsidence near a coal fire and understand the dangers. A ball of flammable or toxic gas could be expanding underneath us this minute. We'd best pack in the morning and get gone."

"Don't nobody fart," said Brandt. "Or you'll cause a stampede."

"Recommendation noted, Collins," said Agnet with a grin. She continued, directing her comment to Cull. "But we counted on one more chat with that extraterrestrial after Orl recovers."

"Hope she recovers fast, then." Cull's face grew grim. "Almost afraid to ask, but you think your mission was really about monsters?"

She shook her head. "No."

He rested his arms on his knees and stared into her eyes. "I'm getting unpleasant vibes from this business. In Delphi, Chief Pruett played the stickler though I could tell she basically meant well. But ever since we headed to the farm, she's been one glum puss and won't say what she's not liking about this mission. You think it's survivable?"

"Depends on how we play it."

Cull inspected his boots for a time, then met her gaze again. "I hope you know what you're doing, 'cause if you're playing for survival, I'll play along. May seem old to some of you, but I've still got things I want to do."

Singular Worlds Apart

Orl quietly recovered once they'd stopped Bothering her. The Blue chip flourished and grew wider, deeper, and Strong. The green and yellow chips' processing efficiency flew off the charts as they absorbed her Friend's modifications. The alien's code would no longer overwhelm her, and she would be More—if she could shut out all this Extra Noise.

She missed the Quiet of inhabiting just one head and even longed for her pills. But her chips were Open to All—the Song and these jabbering minds. While she rested or pretended to sleep, the other's thoughts floated into her mind unbidden and at the most unlikely of times. So disconcerting to be picking at a hangnail while someone else is desperately searching for a lost tin of mints. Mints mixed with hangnails—a minty hangnail, a hanging mint, then a memory of Jemin's sister popped up out of the blue. He'd lost her long ago but had been Reminded of her by a flat Oval rock, a perfect skipping stone. And now Orl had been infected with his sadness along with the anxiety surrounding the missing mints.

She noticed that visiting a single mind drowned out The Others, so she parked herself in Philip, but he was uncomfortable, due to being Outside where things—like dust, cold, and wind—were beyond his control. Sometimes he imagined going home and buying something new, a Self-Present, pretty things, some useful, some not. Her favorite was a peach-colored scarf—he should buy that later. But his Craving of Objects bored her after a time. So, she investigated his greatest mystery, the annoying Fat Black Spot in his memory. At its edge, she found a phrase of the alien's song, as if he'd met Her Friend some time ago. She disliked that notion—the alien was her special friend—and listening close to the Spot made Philip queasy, so she didn't probe the matter too deeply.

She left him for The New Woman who tracked each conversation for shame and blame, respect and scorn, her reality constructed from the opinions of others. Pride battled fear, fear battled pride. A rich substrate over which to sow Confusion and Doubt and thwart the woman's horrible mission.

Meanwhile, the True Leader calculated risk and advantage, taking into consideration All of Them, their stores of food, and the personal safety of Orl's Own Body and Mind, as if these things mattered more than Orl the Useful Tool. The Leader had had similar thoughts before, but they still made her face crumple and her eyes wet, though she couldn't imagine why.

Feeling Too Much was tiring, so she pried into Cull and Jemin's data hoards, finding a soprano's clear voice rising above the Trumpets, adrenal glands dispensing Fright and Flight, dust circling a Moon in equilibrium with gravity, trees being pulped for Paper, and poems by Wordsworth, Shikibu, and Angelou. The Poets made little sense, but she liked the Song of their Words. And she liked the fact that using these chips, she could Educate herself and rise above NeuroCorp's neglect—a savory nibble of Revenge.

Jemin and Cull's chips felt similar, but their minds did Not. Jemin thought about Ideas while Jemin's religion, almost a second self, continually discharged Judgment.

Cull tolerated the camp's chatter while reliving the horror of New Delphi, the inadequacy of his ministrations, his muted emotional reaction, and the government's inadequate response. He wanted to go home and Tinker with Bits of Wood in private.

She watched the slice of World which entered Brandt's mind through his eyes, ears, and nose, and listened to his fantasies about women and their body parts and his thoughts about Mechanical Things like the spaceship, bombs, and his tent poles. He enjoyed the New Words she offered him from Jemin's store and understood more than the others realized.

Each mind was terrible and beautiful, a Singular World Apart. But the mints and the tent poles began to swirl on a dance floor. The mints trotted close, and as they asked her for a dance, the world fell away.

In the morning, she greeted the Song, cleaned her teeth, and rubbed powder into her hair, which became greasier each day. The team fluttered around her, worried and harried, concerned and eager. But she Was Fine and had no desire to dally, as Cull's mind was constantly reminding her of the bubbling fire under their feet.

So, they packed and hiked to the Spaceship. The Leader hushed Jemin and Cull who were "going on a bit much," but she couldn't hush the four noisy crows arguing in the trees; South must wait while a score was settled.

When they arrived at the ship, Philip spoke to her. His words were unimportant and quickly forgotten because he was Not Needed. Still, she would Include him in the conversation because, if the New Woman poisoned her, Philip would have to speak to Her Friend for the team. So, he better know how.

Wave after wave of the Song blotted out the team. Memories scattered like petals in the wind: a gull defending a trash can, ants swarming over a drop of honey, the Big Leafed Tree thrashing against her window during a Storm. She sent picture after picture, not sure if Her Friend knew Nature. Maybe It took comfort in the mechanical world, hard things with Edges, but she'd never paid much attention to machines. If necessary, she could Steal memories of machines from another mind. After some moments had passed, she sent Philip a Message.

Same as before, I've shown It images to get its attention.

Oh?

She sent him some details to tell the Others, so they could pretend they were involved. He looked at the Leader, then the New Woman, feeling awkward about whom to address, then chose a point in between.

These people and their stupid games Wasted her Time.

"We're ready," Philip told them. "We'll use the same technique as last time, images blended with words. Orl says the process will go smoother now because the alien adjusted the connection."

The Leader's thoughts exploded with questions and worry at the word "adjusted". She opened her mouth to complain, but explaining would cause further delay, so Orl flicked Distracting Ideas of Urgency until the Leader settled down.

The New Woman, noticing an opportunity to be Important, said, "Proceed as we've discussed and break off at the first sign of trouble."

Brilliant plan, lady, thanks, thought Philip.

Seemed the time wasting was over, Orl began to Perceive, leaning into her training, Blue's full strength, and her More. She would Spread and Seep and Flow into everything, and with the changes to her chips, she could withstand the wildest torrent of information. She was Not Afraid.

A patch of air just ahead distorted, and a form materialized, a person, a woman with straight black hair and almond eyes— no—not a lady. An Older man with a close trimmed, graying beard. He faded away and morphed into a Teen Boy wearing colorful Shoes. The people continued to evolve, one into another. So many different skin colors, outfits, and hair styles— a wide assortment of people, but only Human People. Their lips moved as if they were Talking, but she received no message.

A stream of code prickled at the edge of Orl's consciousness. On, unter-on, elba-off, acta-off, and so on. Eventually, she would Name all the symbols, each an exquisite silver sparkle. Her thoughts stuttered in time with the scrolling, and the flickering people vanished.

Suddenly, she stood on an endless beach under a clear blue sky. A sea eagle hovered above the ocean, a bird that consumed every Grain of her attention. She could make out each of its rust-colored feathers, its golden Eye, and the black tip of its hooked beak.

It's drawing your attention away from the code. Don't focus on the code; it'll sicken you and cut the Interview short.

Philip! She'd forgotten him. His presence blazed, a Floodlight of Real.

It's easier This Time, even without the Door.

Yes. And the alien's images are so crisp! Who do you think all those people were?

Maybe It was showing us It's known many People and will Understand.

I hope so. Let's ask our question before something goes wrong.

Their question was "*How do we rescue you?*" An obvious question but packed with Abstract Notions difficult to picture. To Ask they visualized images they'd agreed upon this morning: a kitten being rescued from a Tree, a Panicked Man being pulled from the sea, a child being carried from a Burning house, every image might require more Knowledge of Humanity than the Singer possessed.

Her Friend imaged a round portal set in a gleaming surface—*a porthole in the hull*—a Spot of light skittering over rotted timbers and rubble heaped against a stony wall—*somebody shining a flashlight underground*—a dark tree-covered ridge steeply angling Skyward, a massive door into the mountain—

We've seen that door. At the ironworks. The door Brandt wanted to blow up. Remember?

Of course she remembered. Orl conjured up their journey, Philip adding his perspective. The big door. The ruined ironworks, "a bad place," the Lone Man had said. Then at the stream, she/I/we knelt, water running through narrow fingers slender as Reeds, translucent as glass...

A hail of anxiety like Pins and Needles spewed from Philip as he grappled with the Peculiar Image. *Where'd that come from? Whose fingers are those?*

The stream-side image collapsed, and a woman appeared. She clasped her hands, holding Grief like a dead sparrow, then turned and waved as a thin figure walked into the distance.

A Walker. Had she met that walker? Orl pulled the Artifact from her pocket, broadcasted its shape, then envisioned the cave—the splintered rock, dripping water falling on Moss, ice crystals ringing a planet—and sent the images spiraling towards Her Friend.

A new image formed: a patch of light playing on rock, those same slender fingers setting the artifact into a matching cutout space and rotating it. The artifact slid away, and they were bathed in light.

A portal or door... That metal thing you found really is a key!

Code buzzed between Orl's ears, the Singer's avatar flickered, then the scene resolved into a Lady, her eyes the color of lichen in the rain.

This thing wears many faces, though it seems to favor this one. We've seen it two or three times—Philip's thoughts stuttered—*as if a symbiosis, a collection, or a hive.*

Orl considered his words. Symbiosis, like the cattle egrets in Jemin's hoard of private knowledge, different creatures relying on each other. Hive meant bees or ants, hard workers who stung or bit and served a Queen. Collection—carefully selected, fancy old teacups or a particular group of paintings in a museum. Collection meant each individual was a valued member of the Whole. She liked the idea. Her friend was a Collection.

The Lady faded and vanished.

A Door to the Dark

A Higher-Level Heathen

About an hour after Philip and Orl finished with the alien, the rumination began. The distracting thoughts brought Jemin shame, since a historian and active investigator should consider relevant matters, like the shift in mission parameters, the historic significance of first contact, or why the perceivers had only managed to ask a single question. Sure, the location of the spaceship's door was crucial information, but so many conundrums remained unsolved, the alien's intent for starters.

Regardless, the entire headstrong team seemed raring to charge ahead on a smidgen of data and a shovelful of enthusiasm. He would've counseled restraint, if he'd felt comfortable swimming against the tide. But he held his tongue and got busy with his own concerns—all Jemin Yoder wanted to know was *where did the alien stand in the eyes of God*. The question held him in its thrall, even though the Good Book didn't mention aliens, his folk didn't stray from the Book, and therefore, contemplating the alien would further distance him from his faith.

However, he had no choice but to stray, since his actions henceforth should theoretically pivot on the answer to this question because, if brave enough to be true to their faith, the righteous didn't rescue a heretic; the righteous allowed the heretics to burn. A dry lump formed in his throat, and he swallowed, imagining a harsh conversation with Philip and Chief Krause. Intrusive thoughts of conflict and fiery death dogged him during pack-up and as they picked their way through the crash zone and into the forest.

They took a breather at the top of the ridge. Low clouds covered the sky, and the air was crisp, as if snow was a possibility. He removed the wax paper from a snack bar, and in a few bites, his emotions settled, and he felt ready to return to the question about the alien. The chip, apostasy enough for one lifetime, was useless in this circumstance because files on The Word portrayed his faith as a pathetic fairytale, theorizing that humans were primates who never mature and thus never stop seeking the comfort of a parent, creating gods in lieu, to soothe the terror of death's long night. The realization his chip was riddled with lies had pained him deeply, and he'd pleaded with the Lord; *may some of my chip's data be useful and true, so my bargain with these unbelievers will not have been in vain.*

He buried those painful memories, ready to puzzle out the quandary by himself, relying on what he knew of the creature and his prowess in philosophical deduction.

First, the thing was sentient, according to Orl and Philip, and sentient entities, whether biologic or electronic, contained a soul, or so doctrine avowed. So, it must be a child, or if he could be so bold, a grandchild of the Creator.

But God had handed the Law to a man, and the Redeemer was of this Earth, born human to ensure the salvation of the chosen people, a human people. So, not only had the alien never encountered the Word, but the Word was not meant for the alien.

Hence, unlike the usual misguided human apostate, such as Philip, or a child raised by animals in the jungle beyond the reach of God's gifts, this creature's putative soul lay *outside* the structure of human-based religion. It was a higher-level heathen, a heathen unbound by the Twelve Commandments inscribed on the Holy Placard and possibly beyond salvation, both deeply pitiable and incredibly dangerous.

But consider...

Jemin startled and darted his eyes left and right, trying to identify the speaker. Leaves crunched beneath his feet. Philip's backpack swayed just ahead, a crisp, pine-scent filled the air, and Brandt hummed quietly behind him. Clearly, nobody had spoken.

...the historical record shows the original Chosen People lived on the Indian subcontinent, while your ancestors roamed Europe, wearing bearskins, and sacrificing herbivores to a pantheon of nature deities. Only later did the teachings Spread to Your ancestors. So, like the alien, Your People were once Not Chosen.

A valid point, and well-made but—

And if all sentient Beings are children of your God, then they are Equal. If we classify aliens as Not Equal, we may Fear them. And Fear is the seedbed of Hate. Or we may treat them badly, and they may come to Fear us. Either way, from Fear will come Hate. Your God won't like the Hate.

Every hair on his body stood at attention. He sneaked a look behind him.

Brandt waved a hand. "Don't worry, smart man. I've got your back."

Jemin managed a grin, then turned back to the trail. How strange! The voice must be internal, but it sounded too coherent for a hallucination. Must be his chip, though his chip shouldn't be switching on at random, analyzing his thoughts, and offering opinions.

He deeply appreciated its measured discussion of philosophy, the type of discussion he'd hoped the chip would contain, but as files he could access, not as a voice. But why would it spontaneously launch a debate? Had it adapted to his mental environment, now interpreting his thoughts as queries? And its discourse was surprisingly polite, given the virulent anti-faith propaganda it contained. He made a mental note to take the chip's interpretations with a grain of salt, but perhaps the chip was accessing files containing general philosophical principles and applying them to the question at hand.

Or perhaps he was losing his mind.

Regardless, the chip was correct. Salvation *had* spread around the globe, well beyond the original Chosen People. And he didn't *want* to hate the alien. Hate was such an ugly word. Outlanders and apostates were pitied, and...well...expunged by various methods from The Fold. Some of those methods were harsh, true, but the victims weren't hated.

He should stay positive. After all, who was he to close the door to salvation? Maybe the alien's redemption was an initial step to the universal spread of the Word! Maybe he'd play a role in that spread: his hands grasping a lectern, the aliens staring up at him with rapt attention.

Is not seeking the adoration of Strangers considered immodest by The Fold?

Jemin's cheeks flared. He stumbled, foot caught on a branch, and tipped forward, unable to twist, thanks to his stiff pack. The ground rocketed toward his face. Then a force jerked him back, and he hovered a few centimeters above the dirt.

"Easy there, big fella." The voice was Brandt's. The big man hauled him upright.

"Sorry." Jemin firmed his trembling lips. "Not paying attention."

"No problem. But I might've missed you go down. Got my eye on the woods, most time—remember that boar? So, you'd best keep your eyes on the trail, and leave the looking around to me. You seem kinda distracted."

Oh, he was distracted, all right.

"Yeah. It's just the idea of the alien, and what the alien means; you know, the big picture." Jemin waved his hand in an arc, trying to indicate his existential crisis. Lord above, would a man like Brandt even understand the term existential?

Brandt chin wagged acknowledgment, and gratitude washed through Jemin like a tidal wave, someone listening, taking an interest. "I can see how this situation could lead to an existential crisis, but I gotta tell you. Now is not the time. We got monsters. We got an alien. And coming up, we're going to have Central *and* NeuroCorp breathing down our necks. So, sneak an angsty moment now and again; maybe when we break for lunch, but otherwise, keep your crisis under wraps, so as you don't get yourself killed."

Brandt punctuated his remarks with a manly shoulder punch and ushered him down the trail.

Jemin rubbed his shoulder. "Will do. And...thanks."

Philip called to them from a few meters ahead. "Everything alright?"

Brandt replied, "Just used the word 'existential'. Picked it out of nowhere and laid it on Jemin Mr. Superbrain. So, yeah. Everything's fantastic."

Jemin settled his pack and trudged ahead, his eyes fixed on the negligible trail and a bit stunned by Brandt's cold bucket of reality. A shadow darted between lichen coated boulders just to the right. He stifled a shriek and picked up the pace, keeping his eyes fixed to the winding path, trying to keep his mind on the here and now. Although, the chip *had* made a valid point; he gravitated toward fantasies in which he lectured, either about academics or religion, as if an audience inhabited his mind. "Observe this curve in the trail. Let me tell you it's significance" would be an apt parody of a Jemin Yoder daydream. Sort of ironic, considering how terrified he'd been of the bombastic Pastor Yaemond.

The chip piped up. *The psychiatric module mentions seeking Social Prominence as a symptom of an Insecure attachment bond.*

Holy Triad, defend him! How dare a sliver of gadgetry psychoanalyze him? *DO YOU MIND?*

Sorry, just responding to your Query. I have a Question of my own, if you don't mind.

I... This is absurd! Here's how it's supposed to work. I have a question; I access the database and query. Queries flow in one direction, me to you. Data flows in one direction, from you to me. I store new information that comes my way in my memory. I might digitize that data and pass it along for storage in the next chip generation, but you shouldn't be gathering information from me, asking questions, generating ideas, or jumping into my thoughts. Why did you start talking? Are you malfunctioning?

The chip didn't reply, a mixed blessing, as now he was back to being alone. He'd spoken too harshly, so he threw out a gentle and complementary question.

Besides you're the one with the resources. Why ask me?

He waited for a reply, but none came. For heaven's sake. Here he was, trying to revive a conversation with his chip. He really must be losing his mind: a brain tumor, a rare version of post-implantation syndrome, acute post-traumatic psychosis...

No. You're perfectly healthy. I just couldn't access information on the alien's soul and found the topic interesting. I thought your wet-ware might hold the Answer, but it's tedious to search through its random and idiosyncratic file structure.

Lord preserve him, it could read his mind! At some point, he'd sought to lodge a chip in his head, a sort of alien presence. What had he been thinking?

Why did you want me, anyway?

I wanted information. What else! But oddly, he couldn't remember exactly why he'd wanted a chip. Had he been studying something specific?

Your memory isn't corrupted, but the access pathways are overwritten. Mind if I take a Look?

Thanks for asking permission to snoop. Could it detect sarcasm?

I am not programmed for Sarcasm.

Just go ahead. Have a look.

A moment later, it said, *you wanted to know what became of Your People, but I disappointed you, in that regard. Also, you wanted to impress others with your Knowledge.*

He chuckled. Imagine, thinking he'd impress the Common Folk with their own technology. *Sounds about right. I was misguided, so don't take my failures personally. What was your question?*

Could an Extraterrestrial Savior have appeared on the Alien's world?

A remarkable hypothesis, but who was the chip kidding? The alien wasn't saved or here for salvation. It was probably a harbinger of the end times. Either aliens would attack, or Central would leverage some alien technology and trigger a global apocalypse.

Or the Alien might be an Angel.

What do you know of angels?

The religion module covers Angels in Great Detail. And you consider them from time to time.

Again, the data's supposed to flow one way!

You think I could live In Here with Nothing Else To Do and not learn from You?

I'm reporting you as broken, first thing when we get back home!

Smack. Pain flooded his nose. He pushed away with his hands, feeling a rough surface beneath his fingers. Bark. A tree. He'd walked into a tree. Jemin stepped back and cradled his smarting nose in his hands. Something felt wet. He looked down.

Blood.

The world grew dim.

Foam on the Torrent

A loud yelp interrupted the first spate of clear-thinking Elaine had managed that day. She must've lost several hours as they were already over the ridge, her thoughts fleeting past like ghosts. The others had noticed her mental lapse. Spool had generously blamed the alien's energy field, though they probably thought she was nuts. She'd show them.

"Guess we should see about that ruckus," said Krause.

They backtracked and found Yoder laid out on the forest floor.

"He walked into a tree." Collins raised an eyebrow but managed not to laugh.

Krause said, "Classic absent-minded professor."

Scholarship was a sorry excuse for inattention.

Cull tended to Yoder's nose. Spool wiped, replaced, and straightened the flustered historian's glasses and spoke quiet reassurances. Collins stood guard while relating a story about a close encounter with a telephone pole. The mad little perceiver gal hung a few paces back from the others, twisting a lock of hair, her head hanging low.

Some team, not a spine to be had.

Normally, Elaine would've issued a stern warning and insisted Yoder man up. But when running with mice, best to squeak, then pounce when least expected. She asked after Yoder's welfare in a stern tone and with a serious expression that could be interpreted as either disapproval or concern.

As she spoke, the weak link struggled to keep his eyes headed in the same direction. With vision that poor, no wonder he was uncoordinated. Spool even needed to help Yoder to his feet. Such a contrast, the pale puffy faced historian and the tall, dark, and handsome perceiver. Central should raise the bar and park this toadstool in a basement file room.

Weak link. That was it!

Yoder was clearly unfit for duty, so she'd command him back to the farm. He couldn't go alone, obviously. He'd need an escort, a role best suited to Krause who'd become superfluous since she had taken command. With Krause out of the way, the rest would follow her downslope, as if they were headed for the ironworks. But when they hit that perfectly straight trail, the one that ran directly to the prison, she'd have her bearings and be able to order everybody back. Without Krause to oppose her, they'd have no choice but to follow her lead. Then she'd turn the frowzy perceiver trainee over to NeuroCorp.

Back at the farm, Krause would be obligated to report. Her story would sound ridiculous but worthy of investigation, Central would send reinforcements, including a psych squad who'd strap Krause into a strait jacket. Didn't matter if froggy backed Krause's story; nobody would pay attention to his sniveling opinion. The troubled and strange were routinely ignored. Later, Chief Elaine Pruett would file her own version of events.

Mission done and dusted.

The wind started up, moaning low in concert with a high-pitched whine. How she hated that wind, a vague wrongness that left her thoughts...

Scattered like Foam on the torrent.

Yes, but "foam on the torrent"? The phrase sounded poetic, and she wasn't fond of poetry. Something was amiss, but she needed to fake normalcy, so she joined the other's conversation: Yoder making excuses for his accident, Krause insisting he ease up on his chip, Cull listing symptoms of chip-overuse syndrome using his voice of doom, Philip, arms crossed, as if silently tut-tutting the witless chip-head, the girl-perceiver staring at her intently with a single black-ringed eye.

But the wind drowned them out. Funny, she could hear it but not feel it. In the canopy above, a slight breeze rustled the stubborn leaves still clinging to near-bare branches, movement too gentle to explain that whispering. Wouldn't it be nice to leave this forest and never, ever return.

She fell in behind Spool, haunted by the idea she'd decided something important. Someone needed to go somewhere, tell someone something or do something, or send somebody... But who, what, where?

To free the Alien.

That was it. She'd extended the mission parameters. Central expected proactive bravery from her, and as usual, she'd delivered. Sure, she felt odd, but so what? After they freed the alien, she'd get a checkup, jiggering the truth so the corporate medic wouldn't report her for making decisions while compromised.

Strolling through an endless forest with *nice* people... *to free an alien, good, brave.* Free. Free from the forest. Where would it go? Why?

She'd report this nonsense later. Then get a checkup.

What'd she been trying to remember?

OFF THE RAILS

Brandt glanced from Jemin, still jabbering excuses, his nose concealed behind a bloody bandage, to Pruett, taking in the glazed look in the woman's eyes. He leaned close to Chief Krause.

"My imagination, or have those two run aground?"

The Chief pulled a SnacPak from her trouser pocket, popped the lid, and pulled out (*extracted*) a cracker. "Not just aground but stowed in dry dock."

At a whiff of oil and salt, the juices in his mouth started to run. "Hope they straighten up before we meet the alien."

She dipped the cracker in nut butter and handed it to him. "Me too. Let me know if either of them gets weirder."

"Will do, Chief."

He silently thanked Orl for "extracted". Stellar that the girl had developed an interest in words, but her heavy eyes and drooping head shouted "exhausted". She better lay off the vocabulary lessons.

Chewed by a Dog

Coming down-slope, they veered onto a path which promised to bypass the granite maze and take them directly to the steel works. It wove through gray trunks rising from a carpet of yellow leaves, a haze of twigs grasping at the overcast sky like starved fingers. A grim scene, and no quaint little inn around the corner, no bath, and no hot meal. Plus, the chill had seeped through Philip's gloves. But the moment he tucked them into his pockets, losing options to break a fall or keep his balance, he'd pull a Jemin, slip and land flat on his face. Best to flex his fingers and keep walking.

The atmosphere didn't lend itself to chatter. When Jemin tripped over a root, his surprised cries, and the response of the team seemed muffled, remote. Brandt projected only muted satisfaction after gracefully sliding down a carpet of leaves. And as the day wore on, Orl lagged. She'd occasionally drift off-trail, as if sleepwalking. Finally, she curled up against the trunk of a fallen tree. He wriggled her out of her pack, then Brandt hoisted her over his shoulder.

They trudged into a clearing. Wind-piled leaflitter sloped against a concrete block structure that leaned a few degrees off vertical. Stones filled gaps where the walls had collapsed, and concrete rubble and logs blinded the windows. A make-shift door of boards, branches, and rope hung from the lintel. It rocked in the breeze.

"That's pretty weird," said Pruett, who'd snapped out of her daydreams but still seemed subdued.

Cull stepped up to inspect. "The rope is new. See, it's hardly worn. But the boards are old, possibly water salvaged." With the side of his foot, he swiped an arc of ground clean and revealed a jigsaw of asphalt glued together by weeds. He muttered, "Asphalt requires heavy maintenance in this climate with all the freezing and thawing." He glanced at Pruett. "Nothing weird, here. I reckon a rough sleeper has repurposed an abandoned structure."

"The style of the original building and proximity to paving suggests industrial, storage or a pump house," said Jemin, not to be overshadowed.

Brandt, who'd set Orl by his pack, waved the nattering chip-heads aside, unholstered his weapon, and provided cover for Agnet who rapped on the door.

"Hey! Anybody home?"

A moment passed in which the breeze rustled the branches, loosing a spiraling cavalcade of dried leaves, and the trees creaked and groaned. A handful of brown fingers grasped the door and pushed it aside, opening a crack the width of an eye.

Silence dangled like a sickle, then a crackled voice said, "Oh. You people again."

A man staggered out, leaning heavily on a crutch fashioned from a Y-shaped branch, the remains of his left leg dangling well above the ground. A greasy sweetness wafted from the shelter.

Pruett whispered, "Who is this person?"

Agnet shrugged. "Can't place him."

But those dreads looked familiar to Philip. "We met on the rail-trail when returning from the village. Face paint, a spear—remember?"

Her eyes widened in recognition. "Hello there, Sir. Seems you haven't fared well, as of late."

He grunted. "You neither. Lost your fine suits, I see."

"No radiation out here. Not a trace. So we ditched them."

"Radiation gone, huh? Helpful for the nature, I suppose. But no matter to me." He glanced down at the remnants of his leg. "Blood poisoning gonna get me before cancer has a chance."

The scent of meaty rot permeated the air. Elaine wrestled down an expression of disgust and stiffened her spine. "Nonsense. Cull here is a trained medic, and we're close to a governmental facility complete with nursing staff and a surgeon."

"Cull? Unfortunate name for a medic." The wounded man raised one corner of his mouth. Impressive that he still had a sense of humor.

"Been mentioned," replied Cull.

The hermit's good knee bent, and he slowly sank to the ground.

Brandt filled a fold-it cup with water and handed it down. "Speaking of names, I'm Brandt Collins."

Bleary, bloodshot eyes roamed Brandt's big mug and must've detected the raw nice that powered their unlikely security officer. "Clayton Treadway. Pleased to meet you." He threw Brandt a curt salute and sucked down the water.

Cull unpacked his medical kit, and after a brief discussion, Jemin and Brandt headed off to collect timber for a stretcher.

Clayton waved his hand. "Patch me up best you can and get gone. I'm not going to that prison, just couldn't manage it."

A disapproving look settled over Elaine's features. "Why not? The staff will feed you, provide up-to-date medical care. I'm sure they're inspected regularly."

He chuckled. "The farm didn't get inspected but once, my entire term. But I don't mind. It's Honing, lookin' at me disappointed. Now that, I couldn't take." Clayton covered his eyes with his free hand, his body shaking. Whether from sobs or fever, Philip couldn't tell.

Cull masked up and unwrapped the stump which ended below the knee, bulbous and raw, like a ham hock chewed by a dog. Greenish white crust sloughed onto the stained wrapper. Philip's stomach rolled.

"Gonna need some painkillers and antibiotics on board before I work on this wound. You allergic to anything?"

Clayton shook his head, already looking woozy. "Nah. I'll take anything you got, Doc."

Cull paused and spoke under his breath to Elaine, then fished around in his pack and pulled out wrapped packs of various sizes. He refilled Clayton's cup, supervised while the guy swallowed pills, then laid him out, rolled up his sleeve, and began searching for a likely vein.

Pruett signaled them aside. "Cull tells me the poor fellow has less than a fifty-fifty chance."

She's trained herself to insert a Kindness.

I'm aware. What's the intent?

A recognition of an Absence. A desire to hide her Deficit.

Well. Not everybody is naturally empathetic. At least she's coherent. She sharpened up about the time you conked out. I figured she picked up interference from that ship and needed distance. Wouldn't've pegged her for a latent perceiver, but you never know.

Orl didn't reply.

"Philip's our expert interviewer," Agnet said to Pruett, generously tossing the ball to the younger woman.

"Go do your thing. He'll stay lucid until the meds kick in, so you won't have much time for questions. Use the opportunity wisely."

How he disliked the officious tilt of Pruett's chin, but he kicked himself into professional mode and knelt beside the patient opposite Cull who was setting up a rustic treatment field. Treadway's pupils had dialed down to pinholes, and he wore a faraway smile evoking the wonders of childhood. Must be some solid drugs, though stoned people were hard to read. Philip dredged up a pleasant expression and started easy. "Wouldn't worry too much about Honing. He seems like a nice guy."

Clayton grinned, looking crafty as a fox. "Bet he liked you; you're just his type."

Annoying how everybody jumped to the same conclusions about Philip Spool. He skated under the man's teasing and maintained a steady, neutral expression.

"The warden was welcoming, and he seemed genuinely concerned about the farm and the trainees."

"Trainees, my ass. We was prisoners. But I'm not speaking ill of the man; he has good reason to shame me. Don't I know you from somewhere?"

Philip wiped sweat from Treadway's clammy forehead. "Nah. Just have one of those faces. You have a reason to feel guilty?"

He looked aside, his lips twisted with grief. "My time is short, no reason not to tell my sorry story. It was my idea to take up the offer. And I encouraged the others that passed the test. Honing had a bad feeling, despite them promising pardons and reintegration expenses. He tried to set us straight, and now, they're all dead, or worse."

"Did the people making the offer threaten you?"

"Once we was in, they made it clear that changing our minds would be deeply unwise, if you know what I mean. Then one fellow disappeared, and Honing went real quiet. Right after, they carted us to the lab and experimented on us."

"Who?"

"Government folk. You all about the same to me, though you definitely familiar up close."

Philip messaged Orl. *Anything more here?*

No. The project managers weren't wearing insignia. But he remembers a face that looks like You.

Like him? And how was she accessing Clayton's cache of faces?

"But see here." Clayton motioned toward his stump. "Here's all I have to show. What Palmer's become done tore off my leg. Would've finished me if I hadn't squeezed into a hole in the rocks."

Cull wiped down a spot on the man's arm. "Just a prick here. Hold steady for me, Clayton."

"Palmer turned into a monster?"

"Yes, brother. One horrible monster."

"We've been told the monsters are finished."

"Maybe some. I've seen the little ones crumble up, but my boys are made of tougher stuff. They're still on the prowl. This stump is proof. You be careful."

"Where are these 'boys'?"

"Back at the lab or roaming the forest."

"The lab?"

"I slipped away and should've never gone back. But my conscience yapped at me. Stupid move, 'cause nobody survived, bodies scattered every which way, bits and pieces. Thought I saw Palmer. But when I came close." Clayton looked sideways and grimaced. "He was...wrong, and...thicker, and wouldn't answer. Stared like a dead man and came at me, dragging what I thought was a log. Well, I thought he was dragging it, but when he came close, I could tell it was stuck to his arm. And it weren't no log. It was a leg, a human leg." His hands trembled. Cull nudged Philip and shook his head, sharp and stern.

"Take a breather." Philip grasped Clayton's warm, wet hand. "It's past. We're with you now."

Clayton took a deep breath and closed his eyes. "I'll be all right. None of it matters, no more. But I'll tell you, seeing Palmer all messed up like that was more than enough. I ran. Locked the door behind me, figuring I'd trapped him inside. But he must've got out, so be careful. He's one vicious son of a bitch."

"Trapped inside where?"

"In the mountain behind the old factory. You stay far from that place; its bad news."

"And the test you took, the offer, the experiments: what was it all about?"

238

Clayton hoisted himself up on his elbow, the whites exposed all the way around his iris. "They said it was about language and computers, but they wanted our *brains*. I figured it out and escaped, but my brain ain't working so great now; I keep hearing voices."

"I'll bet you do." The guy was juiced to the gills.

"Honing warned me. Told me you can't trust them corporate types." Clayton thrashed and struggled to sit.

"Whoa there, mister." Cull laid a hand on his shoulder. "Down you go. Barely a drop of pressure in your veins. I've hooked you up to antibiotics and fluids, so lie still and let the medicine do its job. Hang this bag, Spool, but leave slack in the line." He held up a plastic bag filled with clear fluid that dripped into the tube attached to Clayton's arm.

A length of rusted rebar conveniently protruded from the shelter's wall, perfect for hanging the IV bag which looked small, travel sized, and probably insufficient, given the gray tone of their patient's skin. Clayton's mouth hung slack, now. His heavy eyelids drooped low, a sliver of his whites fringed by thick lashes. Philip watched his chest for movement. There, a slight up and down. He was out cold, but still alive.

LIKE PUPPETS ON A STRING

Philip joined the three women who'd strategically seated themselves upwind of Cull's surgical theater. Pruett sat ramrod-straight with her hands neatly folded in her lap. Agnet slouched forward, elbow on knees, idly untwisting a length of frayed rope, and Orl had withdrawn into her hood; the intermittent signal from her chip suggested she was nodding in and out of sleep. He recounted Treadway's testimony, best he could.

"Forced experimentation on human subjects?" Agnet's eyes hardened, her lips drew into a straight, thin line.

Pruett tucked her chin, in the manner of a schoolteacher ready to reprimand her class for cutting up. "Decidedly illegal. No matter how high in the government you've climbed."

Gee. What a surprise. They worked for ruthless sociopaths. Who knew?

She turned to Agnet. "A report is well overdue. The sooner we notify Central, the sooner somebody will pay for their crimes."

Agnet tugged a few fibers from the rope, not meeting Elaine's eyes. "Were the test subjects those men who escaped the farm in summer?"

"I suspect so. Hang on, let me confirm." He opened his pack and found the list of summer's escapees carefully nestled in the waterproof side pouch designed for documents.

Jerobe Palmer and Clayton Treadway. The names slapped his eye. "Six names total, two matches, Palmer and Treadway. Leaving, if what Clayton said is true, four "original" zombies: one savage monster roaming the forest, three whereabouts unknown. Of those three, one may have been the monster that thrashed the Warden's room. The other two may still be under the mountain, exactly where we're headed."

"At least we'll be prepared." Agnet tied her rope into a slip knot. "Clayton said he locked the mountain door when he tried to trap Palmer, implying he used a key. Remember the doors Brandt wanted to blow up: a large door for machinery, a smaller door for people? We tried the small door. It was locked."

Pruett said, "But Palmer escaped. Either he also has a key, or there's another exit."

Philip said, "There'd have to be air vents and drainage. So even if we can't find the key, we can gain access."

I can find the Key.

Orl sounded fully awake. *You can?*

She nodded and pointed to Clayton's hut.

"Excuse us. We're going to search for the key. Orl has a line on it."

"Welp. The girl sure has a way with keys. Have at it," said Agnet.

Philip nodded to the two chiefs, wondering if Pruett expected him to ask permission, then realized he didn't care because he'd crossed a threshold of some kind. Later, he'd have to examine the size and shape of that threshold and figure out where it led.

Giving Cull and his patient a wide berth, Philip and Orl approached the hut. The improvised door swung open easily. Then the stench hit his nose: a combination of overripe fruit, feces, and decay. He leaped back, his stomach heaving into his throat. But Orl doubled over and flat out vomited, then pressed up against the hut's concrete wall, pale and gasping. Poor kid.

He fanned the air in front of his face and collected himself.

You alright?

Barely.

Stay put. I'll hunt through his belongings. Though the reek in that hut would stalk him to his grave.

Relief washed over Orl's face, and she smiled. An actual smile that suddenly transformed her into a regular young woman. Then, out of nowhere, an image filled his mind, the experience akin to a hyper-real waking dream.

Too bad the dream's subject was cloth heaped in a dark and dirty corner. She must be sending him the key's exact hiding place. How on Earth did she know? He turned into the breeze, sucked in a lung-full of fresh air, pushed the door open, and ducked inside the cave-like space. His eyes adjusted to the gloom, then he scanned the room for a visual match. There. A pile of rags or clothing on its way to rags.

A front Pocket.

Kneeling, he sorted through the debris and discovered a pair of overalls with a prominent front pocket. And inside the pocket? Yes! A smooth oval bearing several buttons: the key. A shallow breath forced itself on him, his guts spasmed in response to the smell, and he dashed out the door.

Once he'd put a healthy distance between himself and the cabin, he breathed deep. But Clayton's stench had clung to the lining of his nose, a rude testament to the fact that one unfortunate event could turn a person into an animated petri dish. Orl's knowing the location of that key might be testament to other facts, deeply disturbing other facts.

Philip buried his suspicions, showed Orl the key, and thanked her. In response, she glowered, retracted into her hood, and stomped off, a tempestuous Gothic tortoise. She might've sensed his suspicions. He could chase after her, but Agnet was now sitting alone, snacking on crackers, giving each a longing look before popping it in her mouth. Now was his chance to speak to her without being supervised by that tiresome little martinet.

He joined Agnet and quietly said, "Where's Pruett?"

Agnet swallowed and sipped from her hydration pack. "We were discussing our next move. I pointed out that the parties responsible for failed human experiments would go to great lengths to cover their tracks. That those great lengths might include silencing us. Permanently."

"You really think our situation is so dire?"

"I do, but Pruett didn't agree. She spent a few minutes defending the system. I reminded her of the contaminated meters, likely meant to keep us at the farm, so we wouldn't encounter spaceships or evidence of human experiments. Elaine didn't care for my take on matters, fussed, got bossy, and then just after you came out of Clayton's hut," Agnet's eyes locked onto his, "she went drifty, like she's been most of the day. She wandered off and plonked down like a lump of clay. See her just staring?" She hiked a thumb over her shoulder. "What's going, Mr. Perceiver?"

What was going on? Philip darted a look at Pruett. She was perched on a log, her face a blank slate, her mouth slack. Then he sighted Orl, standing on a flat rock about five meters away, her back toward them. He had his suspicions. Both Jemin and Pruett had been acting funny, and Orl knew more than she ought. He rummaged through memories of the last few days and pulled up a few unnatural thoughts, mostly about being nicer to Jemin and less judgmental, manipulative and sanctimonious maybe, if those thoughts had come from Orl, but not dangerous. And they'd been so very stealthily inserted. He couldn't detect the girl in his head right this minute; she was probably laying low. But could he be sure?

He froze, feeling exposed, spied upon, any sense of privacy slashed and lying in tatters on the ground—his collar was too tight; he couldn't breathe. Panic flashed through him like balls on fire. What a mess. The idea perceivers "read minds" terrified normal people, and NeuroCorp worked hard to deny mind reading was possible. But maybe their newfangled chips had new properties, highly intrusive properties, not only mind reading, but also mind control. If he, a perceiver, was freaking out, everybody was going to freak out, and Orl was probably afraid.

She should be afraid.

Before he upset the entire team, he needed proof. Maybe he could trick her into slipping up again. After settling his thoughts, he clicked on his chip.

Was curious how you knew where to find that key.

Just a lucky guess.

He silenced his chip, and thought, 'Bullshit. Nobody's guesses are that lucky.'

Yes, they are! Sometimes.

Ha! Caught you! I didn't send that last comment. You plucked it from my head, same as you plucked the key's location from Clayton's head, didn't you?

242

She whipped around and glared at him. *Your chip is on! You're so Stupid you can't even tell.*

She was wrong. Philip Spool wasn't a noisy fool, unconsciously flipping on his chip and thoughtlessly spewing mind chatter. Not him. Sure, he'd merged with his chip to some degree, but he was still in control. Just to be sure, he checked his chip's settings. It was off. He *absolutely positively had not* sent Orl that last sentence.

My chip is off and admit it; you listened in on Clayton's thoughts and learned about that key. Thought you didn't like lies, but who's the liar now?

I don't care about Dying Man; he stinks. And you stink, too! Orl stomped into the woods, as if terribly insulted.

"Your expressions keep changing like someone drawing a fresh hand of cards every minute. You talking to Orl?" asked Agnet.

Philip described the conversation and the trap he'd laid. "Remember me telling you that those NeuroCorp pills made her feel 'less'?"

She extracted another cracker from her tin. "So lately, we've been experiencing 'more'?"

"You too?"

"Yep. You want a cracker? They flake nicely. Almost remind me of the farm's pastry, if I pretend hard enough." She held out her tin.

"No, thanks." He didn't want to intrude on her happy place. Besides, that brand of cracker tasted like dust.

Agnet nibbled a corner, then said, "Thinking back, I'm pretty sure she's influenced some of my decisions and has fed me information. Not with a crowbar, but with a nudge. Felt something was off—my intuition is pretty good, but not so...verbal. I'm not arguing against her, um, suggestions; things worked out for the best, and she sure helped with that monster-boar. But still. Feels as if she played me like a puppet on a string. And I've been thinking about Elaine, the way she toggles back and forth between militant and dazed, as if some outside force had its hand on the switch. Handy, having that woman hushed up, but mind control's not a tactic I can condone."

"Some of my recent introspection hasn't sounded authentically me, either. We've also had Jemin waltzing with a tree, and I think Brandt said something about words dropping into his skull out of nowhere. Where are they by the way?"

"Yonder, just beyond the cabin. I asked them to stay within earshot. Brandt's setting snares and collecting firewood. Jemin's 'helping.' She wolfed another cracker and chewed for a while. "Nothing Orl's done to date is unforgivable, as far as I'm concerned, though Elaine might not agree. And while I'd appreciate Orl's input, I don't want her in my brain, influencing my choices on the sly. Or eavesdropping on me, especially since some of my thoughts are uncharitable. Can she cool it? Would she, if we asked?"

"I'm not sure. She's off her meds, and the alien altered her chips. I wonder if NeuroCorp knows what they created; mind reading is an immense leap forward."

She shook the crumbs from her pants. "A problematic leap, in my book."

"It would come in handy during an interview."

"But imagine the potential for abuse. Imagine NeuroCorp leveraging mind control. Wait, we don't have to imagine; just look at Elaine. Orl's nearly driven her insane. The girl's gone beyond spooky, Philip. She's basically a weapon."

Pruett was still staring into the trees, chin tipped to one side. He'd never cared for hard-core corporate types: dedicated, sincere, always on the lookout for imperfection in this imperfect world. Rather nice that Orl had parked her in dreamland. "Maybe Orl should continue to—"

"No. No, she shouldn't. Look. I don't like Elaine any more than you do. She may charge into Central, get us all killed, then get herself sectioned, transported, or executed. But I'd rather try talking sense to her than let Orl fry her brain." She upended the empty tin and tapped it on her knee. Some crumbs sprinkled to the ground; some landed on her pants leg.

"When Elaine learns what Orl has done, she'll never trust any of us."

"I sure hope not. But speak, or whatever, to Orl. Make her stop."

In Trouble

Philip would have loved to make Orl stop her mind games. But she'd disappeared and gone dark, hopefully ignoring his messages and not fallen off a cliff. He couldn't make out an obvious trail where she'd stormed into the woods moving south-west. If he tried to follow blindly, he'd probably get lost, never make it back to camp, or stagger back hours later exhausted and covered in ticks.

He needed to recruit somebody forest-worthy. And that somebody would be Brandt, who was busy trimming side-branches from a long, straight, very dead tree while Jemin was doing his best, as in struggling, to assist in some highly ineffective manner, possibly trying to steady the trunk. Philip strolled over, hoping neither would ask him to help; he wasn't a fan of unfinished wood.

He nodded to Jemin, who shot him a sour look, then addressed Brandt. "Could you help me find Orl? She ran off into the woods."

Brandt looked up from his pruning, puzzlement writ on his face. "She eager to be monster chow?"

"No. She's afraid she's in trouble."

The big man straightened up. "Is Chief Pruett mad about a word?"

A puzzling question. Pruett seemed mad, as in the sense of crazy, but not as in angry. "Sorry, but you'll have to explain."

"You know. New words, like 'existential'."

Existential? Oh, yes. That'd been the word that'd "dropped into" Brandt's head from nowhere. But... Had he made an association between the new words and Orl?

Brandt frowned. "You alright? Your face looks like you're watching pregnant ladies mud wrestle."

"I... You think Orl gave you the word 'existential'?"

"Don't be ridiculous, Orl can't speak," said Jemin.

"But she learns *intriguing* words," he winked, "and shares them with me, direct. Either *obtaining*," another wink "them from the alien or from a chip, I suppose. Was wondering if she'd been feeding Chief Pruett too many."

Had Brandt just calmly said...*that*? Did he have any idea—

"What do you mean 'direct'? What do you mean 'from chips'?" Jemin's eyes bobbled like jelli-shots on a drunken server's tray.

Good grief. The conversation had skidded out of his control. Jemin didn't need to know about Orl's mind-surfing, but Brandt, who knew the truth and was *entirely unphased*, wouldn't back him if he tried to shove this genie back in its bottle.

Brandt shrugged. "She pops into my head, now and again, and drops a word. No big deal, it's probably just some perceiver thing."

Philip groped for plausible damage control. "No. Not a *usual* perceiver thing. She's probably just accidentally drifting because her chips are the latest version, and the alien adjusted them. I'm sure she doesn't mean any harm."

A soft, nervous laugh escaped Jemin. "I thought my chip was speaking to me, but..."

A talking chip? Someday, he'd entertain friends with that story, but in the moment, he needed to deescalate. Philip forced a reassuring smile.

"Probably just a chip misfire, something minor."

Brandt clapped Jemin's back, nearly ending the historian's life, from the look on his face. "No. Must've been Orl. Which is good news! It means you're not losing your marbles, after all."

Jemin glanced left, then right, as if planning to bolt. "But...but...if she knows my business, I'm doomed."

"Nobody's business is that bad, brother. We're all human. And if it's about the religion, none of us gives a dog's dingus." He gently punched Jemin's shoulder. "You go on believing as you please." A mischievous grin stole over his lips. "Can't live your whole life in an existential crisis."

Religion? Jemin fawning over the old feral, his stern disapproval at the term "feral", his secret source, a group of feral boys: episodes from the recent past clacked by like beads on an abacus, calculating the explanation for a hefty slice of the plump little historian's weirdness. For the love of the stars and beyond! How had Philip Spool, senior perceiver, missed something so blindingly obvious?

Because you were busy being Mean.

Orl!

He blew open his chip and searched, cursing her name and hoping she heard every word. But he couldn't detect her. In his proximal reality, the conversation had stalled. Jemin's mouth hung in an O, until he swallowed and stammered. "How could you tell?"

Brandt's eyebrows lifted, a surprised expression. "I worked border security; I know my ferals. You got your various turbans and robes, and the holy rollers with pale skin and thick glasses. The captain figured it was the inbreeding." A sheepish look flooded his face. "No offense. But I'm surprised InfoCorp would chip a feral."

Philip winced, but as usual Brandt's obliviousness, his social trump card, canceled out his offensiveness, and Jemin replied with equanimity.

"Usually, us kids from the Fold are educated separately and funneled into service jobs or the trades. But every student in advanced classes brings in extra funding. So, when my test scores came back high, my intake documents disappeared, and suddenly, I became a general-population orphan. Please, whatever you do, don't report me to InfoCorp or that awful woman. She's the type of hardliner who would file a complaint. And regarding Orl—" Jemin's eyes misted. "We just discussed philosophy. She must've been curious and kept me company while I hashed out various theories. I didn't mind. Well. Until I crashed into that tree, but no permanent harm was done." He touched the dressing on his nose.

"Unfortunately, she's gone a bit far, and she knows it. So, she ran into the woods," said Philip, pulling them back to the matter at hand.

"By 'too far' you mean Chief Pruett?" Brandt circled a finger near an ear. "What did Orl do? A psychic lobotomy?"

"Sort of." Honestly, what did the big lunk *not* know? "Anytime you want to share your insights with me or the Chief, please don't hesitate. Might save us all time."

"Sorry." Brandt scanned the toes of his boots. "When things get kind of obvious, I figure everybody knows. And I'm happy to help hunt her down. No kid should be out in these woods alone."

Jemin bobbed his head, and appearing entirely sincere, said, "I'll help, too."

They lost a few minutes collecting supplies and notifying Agnet of their plans. She decided to stay put and keep watch over Pruett, Treadway, and Cull, while they headed into the woods.

Brandt quickly spotted the line of broken bracken that marked Orl's trail. Poor kid, running off like a scared rabbit. And for what? So she read his thoughts from time to time; he didn't mind. He was doing her a favor. Those NeuroCorp weirdos had messed her up, raising her in a test tube, or whatever, and she had to learn about normal people somehow. His mind was as good a place to start as any. Sure, some of his memories were X-rated, but he'd done nothing shameful, just sexy good times all around. And maybe his service record wasn't stellar, but he stood by his decisions. Command could claim 'dereliction of duty', but sometimes a man needed to do what was right. He had nothing to hide.

The others would come around. Well, everybody but Pruett.

Dry fern crunched beneath his boots as they marched through a thick swath of bracken. Too much bracken meant too many deer or a thin canopy, and this forest was decidedly sparse. He blocked out the sound of footsteps and listened to the woods. Sparse and too quiet, and the quiet wasn't about radiation. Hardly a click so far on the meter Jemin had borrowed from Chief Krause. Sure, most birds would've flown South by now, and Deer were skittish, but the weather was still too warm for squirrels to have holed up for the winter. And squirrels were fearless, always scolding and flicking their tails at much larger animals.

No prey could mean predators. Brandt fingered his pistol's grip—a lightweight piece of junk was better than nothing.

"Best stick together," said Phil, as if he could read the worry in Brandt's mind. And heck, maybe he could.

They walked through an ancient graveyard, monuments leaning at random angles, Orl's trail pressed into the grass between the stones, then they came across a flat-topped stone pyramid.

Jemin looked it up and down, then declared, "A pig iron smelter. I think it predates the cemetery by some time."

Seemed Jemin had thrown a wide one. The thing would be useless as a pig shelter, and it wasn't made of iron. But a pig sized door opened into each wall. In fact, a hefty pig—hopefully a normal pig—could be hiding inside right now. Roast pork would make a fine dinner; he could tell the Chief the meat was chicken so as not to set off her post-traumatic boar-stress.

He found his flashlight, hunkered down—leaving room to maneuver, in case a pig charged out—and shined the light into the pyramid's heart.

All he could see was shadows and empty corners.

"Well, nuts on the half-shell. No pigs inside, and this next patch of ground is stony. May take me awhile to pick up Orl's trail."

Phil and Jemin exchanged a look, the type that usually meant Brandt had missed something, but no matter. These guys were decent men and wouldn't rag on him about it.

Phil said, "I won't mind the wait. I need a moment. That building's not exactly empty." He knelt by one of the openings and waved them away.

Brandt set out to hunt for Orl's trail, Jemin close behind. The little guy looked nervous, so he asked, "What does your religion say about talking to the dead?"

"Nothing positive. 'Perceiving', as they call it, would be labeled witchcraft."

"Wouldn't see it that way myself, but I ran into folk on the border who'd've thought the same. What would your people think about that thing behind the door that helped them talk to the alien?"

Jemin wrung his hands, a look of despair on his face. "I couldn't decide if they were rudely intruding on the Almighty Creator and asking petty favors or cavorting with a demon. Nowadays, they'd be excommunicated and shunned, but in ancient times, the Church would've burned both Orl and Philip at the stake for that episode. Philip twice over."

"Dang. Pretty harsh. Why Phil twice?"

"Because of his...er...preferences."

"You mean those tight pants? Them being impractical isn't a bother to anyone else other than ole Phil."

Jemin stammered, then choked out, "No. I mean...well...his...um...dating preferences."

Took Brandt a moment. "Oh. That's not proper. Only people should care about that are him and his sweethearts. And given that guy's face, those folks'll be more than plenty. Way more than will sleep with both of us over several lifetimes."

Jemin went pink as a piglet. "Well. The Book disagrees, and The Fold follows the Book."

"How about you? Do you agree?"

"I don't know. On the one hand, it's hard to shake the ideas I grew up with, and he—it's Philip by the way; he cringes every time you call him Phil—makes me uncomfortable. On the other hand, I really don't care about people's personal situation; the less known the better. But if it makes any difference, the Elders would've staked me up beside the perceivers on the pyre." He tapped his left temple. "The Book doesn't mention technological enhancements, so they're seriously frowned upon."

Brandt's thoughts drifted down South to grim times, corpses staked up outside a feral encampment, a strip of charred gingham flapping in the breeze. Some of what he'd seen made more sense now, given Jemin's comments. Not that the insight helped—no sense in dwelling on all the ways people could hate. He shelved the memory before it could get to him. "Swim forward like a shark or drown in the dark," was his motto. 'Course sharks went terminally extinct a couple years ago, but he clung to the motto, regardless. It had a nice ring.

Phil—or Philip, according to Jemin, strolled over, hands in pockets, his eyes empty and staring into space, as if returning from the library instead of a haunted pig shelter.

"What's the news, bro?" asked Brandt, hoping to snap him out of it.

He blinked a few times, then replied, his voice kinda slow and spacy. "The ghost was recent, reasonably coherent, but in epic denial. Believes she's lost and her team will find her any minute, then she's eager to report an incredible discovery."

"Whoa, excellent. What'd she find?"

"The containment zone is almost free of radioactivity."

"Ah, rats. Something we already know. So, how'd she die?"

"Bullet to the back of her head." He grimaced. "She had a nasty exit wound in her hairline."

"So how do you know without seeing a body? And where is the body anyway?"

Phil sighed. "Who knows. They could've carted it off, or they left her lying where she dropped, and animals dispersed the remains. Either way, ghost images are almost always a projection of the person in their last moments."

"That's offensive and unnecessary," said Jemin. "Why torment a lost soul with the gory details of their demise?"

250

"One theory says evidence of death, like serious wounds, helps people accept their situation and move through the Door." Phil shrugged. "But who really knows?"

Jemin spluttered, red in the face and working himself up to a lather. "And how can you discuss execution style murder so calmly? It's horrible. How do you know we're not next?" He glanced behind himself, as if expecting a tactical unit to jump from the trees.

"I'm not calm," said Phil. "I'm stunned and trying to process. For all I know, we might actually *be* next. I thought Agnet sounded a bit paranoid, but now..."

Brandt Collins had already processed, having read this script before. And more than once. His memory flicked back to Zendick, the newbie private so eager to report the ampho lab they'd discovered in the pines, unaware that Lieutenant Bud had a piece of most labs in the region. They'd warned him, but he didn't believe them. At least the end had come quick for the poor bastard.

"Paranoid? About what?" asked Jemin.

Phil acted like he hadn't heard the question. "Anyway. She and Orl conversed earlier, then Orl went that way." He pointed toward a dense thicket.

"Did you at least help her soul move on?" asked Jemin, his arms folded hard across his chest.

"No," said Phil, sounding worn down and cross. "I couldn't come up with an angle. The simple solution would be promising the specter we'd file a report on her behalf. Likely, she'd flit if she felt her obligation would be fulfilled. However, now I doubt we'll be filing a report. So, saying I'd report would be a lie, and lies upset Orl, even though she's lied to me plenty." He drew a ragged breath then exhaled slowly. "If either of you can think of a strategy that doesn't involve a lie, don't hesitate to share." He flashed Brandt a pointed look.

Jemin said, "Well. Good of you to *tip toe* around Orl, but aren't you the lead perceiver and in charge?"

A half smile lifted one of Phil's cheeks. "Think about it. Orl can alter people's thoughts, so who's in charge? And she's run off, presumably angry or afraid or both. Upsetting her further would be foolish."

"Her powers don't bother you? Even though she's only a girl, many would go rabid with professional jealousy." Jemin sounded polite, though Brandt sensed the gloves had come off professor-style. But the little man had probably lost this round since "many" probably meant Jemin.

People always gave themselves away when they guessed at what made other people tick.

Phil sighed, a deeply patient sigh, akin to the patience Brandt'd inspired in librarians, schoolteachers, and commanding officers. The woes of the world hung heavy, this patience declared, mostly because everybody else was as dumb as a box of rocks. "She's paid dearly for her skills. I hardly envy her, and I'm not in competition with her or anybody else."

Brandt gave Jemin a nudge. "And hey, nobody's 'only a girl', definitely not Orl. Got to watch thinking like that, or some only-a-girl's gonna bite you on the ass when you least expect." The guy needed to be set straight, because a man with Jemin's gut, chin, and glasses shouldn't consider any girl, not even those hard prison ladies, an 'only-a-girl' lest he wish to remain a lifelong virgin. Beggars couldn't be choosers, given the inbreeding. Phil, on the other hand, had style, passing credit to a teenager, no skin off his lips, no bruise on his ego. But seemed the world had rolled Phil flat, and he didn't feel good enough about himself. Had to be a happy medium somewhere.

Philip will be fine when we fix the Hole in his Mind.

"Orl?" The guys looked at him expectantly. Brandt scanned the area. "She talked to me. She's close."

"What did she say?" asked Phil.

"Something about fixing a hole." He left it at that. Because a mind-hole was a private matter, something high-level best left to Orl and the alien. Plus, he'd always sensed friction between Jemin and Phil. No need to give Jemin extra ammo.

They headed in the direction the ghost recommended, but he knew exactly where she was, as if she'd set off some kind of beacon. Orl might be weapons grade, but she was still a good kid.

After ten minutes of threading through the trees, they stepped into a tawny meadow. The sun warmed his raw cheeks while his eyes adjusted. Ahead, Orl sat cross-legged on the trunk of a great big (*substantial*) fallen tree; her hands folded in her lap, her tattered dress fluttering in the breeze. To her right, a hefty crow strutted on the log; it checked them out with a beady eye, then cawed like a grumpy old man. Seated before her, their backs towards the team were three large animals.

The middle animal swiveled its head.

Toasted balls on a stick, here came more of this crap. Brandt drew.

The beast roared.

Too Much Drama

Philip's heart caught in his throat. The boar was simultaneously magnificent and hideous: a rust-colored coat marred by gray patches, eyes subtly asymmetric, an extra miniature ear jutting from the point where its jaw met its neck, and threads of glistening saliva dangling from its long, sharp teeth. What nightmare had concocted this freakish horror? A second boar, even larger than the first, slowly turned its head, eyes brimming with blood lust and hate. The third loosed a mournful howl through a mouth cluttered with spear-like teeth. What was the deal with this forest and boars?

Familiarity with the Door may have eradicated his fear of death, but dying as fangs ripped him to shreds held no appeal. Surely, something would intervene. Or someone, such as Orl, who sat on a big log behind the animals. The sky behind her roiled with color, as if a sunset and the aurora borealis had combined forces, and three images undulated in the crazy light, a path winding into the forest, a tunnel through the rocks, and a bower of wild roses. Either she'd gone paranormal on him, or he'd stepped into a vivid hallucination. Philip ducked behind a shrub and the others followed. Jemin plopped to the ground like a sack of wet oats, dropped his face into his lap, folded his arms over his head, and folded over—the turtle approach.

"Am I the only one seeing the psychedelic sky?" Philip asked.

"I see savage monsters." Jemin moaned and trembled. "Monsters, everywhere. I shouldn't be here. I'm of no use against monsters. And I can't die. I'm far too busy to die."

"I'm pretty sure none of us wants to die," Philip said, forcing patience.

"But in my case, death equals eternal damnation, though..." Jemin shot him a complex look that probably meant "you, deviant reprobate, are just as damned as me."

With the thrust of one fang a monster boar could extinguish Jemin forever, and Philip Spool would never hear of his spiteful religion again. Here, piggy, piggy, piggy.

Brandt drew his pistol. "Kid's really in trouble this time. I knew she shouldn't've been wandering around all by herself! My bullets will only make 'em angrier, so I'll go around through the woods, come up behind her, snatch her, then run for the forest. It'll take those boars a minute or two to realize she's gone, and by then, we'll be up a tree. You two best make for your own trees, right now."

No! Stay put or you might get Hurt!

Orl's message hit with an electric crackle. A bolus of feeling flooded Philip's mind: pain and fever, hunger and thirst, confusion and grief—a cavalcade of brute feelings passed to him through Orl from the boars, who must be suffering horribly. He shuddered, took a moment to collect himself, then told the others, "Those beasts are in pain. She's not afraid; she's helping them, but they're still incredibly dangerous."

Brandt said, "Whoa. Yeah. I heard her, too. Kid must have a soft spot for animals, but I'm not dropping this peashooter until they're gone."

But I'm not going Back!

Philip peered around the bush. The three bucolic images hanging above Orl shimmered, then faded. Orl narrowed her eyes.

I won't release Them until you Go Away.

Release them? Had those images been Doors? Could Orl control doors, and had she been right? Did animals really pass through? He swallowed his questions—he'd pry the philosophic details from the girl later.

None of us are mad at you. The Chief's not mad either, though I can't speak for Elaine.

I'm not going with That Woman. I won't Go Back.

You mean back to Central? You sure? You could probably still go home and make excuses, maybe get away with a lacuna and reprogramming. I'm sure they wouldn't hurt you because you're so unique.

A Valuable Specimen. They only want my What, not my Who.

Alright... But if you run, NeuroCorp will hunt you. And if they catch you, you'll be erased.

I DON'T care. I'd rather Exit than go back.

Did he feel the same? He thought of the murdered prisoner, Treadway hiding out in the woods, battling the ruins of his former friend, that sad, lost ghost on the trail still hoping to file a report, and the worry in Agnet's face. He swallowed hard. They'd uncovered evidence of raw and unfettered evil.

And unlike Orl, he wasn't valuable or unique. If he returned home, NeuroCorp would treat him to their latest interrogation techniques then discard him like used cooking oil. He had but one path forward.

I'm not going back either.

That said, he flashed on his apartment, his favorite chair, its especially soft and lovely decorative throw, Gervais selling that same throw to his drug dealer.

They're not Friends, if they steal from you, and you dislike them.

I like some of them! Regardless, I'm going feral, despite the lack of bathing facilities and decent meals. *Because returning to Central is tantamount to suicide. I'll probably die from exposure anyway, but at least I'll die on my own terms. And if you want, I'll help you find the alien. You shouldn't try alone.*

Orl glowered. The sky darkened. Schools of stars fell, leaving dazzling trails that burned afterimages on his retina, even though that sky couldn't be real.

They said, return her or poison her. So, I fixed her, but The Leader and YOU want me to stop.

Who her? Who was she talking about? His thoughts darted like minnows dispersed by a stone, none of the eddies comforting.

Who sent who?

Rasp sent that New Woman, and I Don't Like her.

The thick sky flashed, and thunder rumbled. Honestly, too much drama. The new woman must be Elaine. He'd encountered several "Elaines" in his career, all tradition and hierarchy, following procedures and rules like blind lemmings, terrified by change, and resentful of innovation, always on the lookout for slackers, and often interpreting his protective shell of emotional distance as lack of commitment. But people like Elaine had passion and a strong sense of right and wrong, a combination that usually prevented them from committing murder. Well, at least cold-blooded murder. No wonder Elaine had wanted to head back to the farm. No wonder she was so uptight.

I don't like her much either. But I doubt she wanted to kill you. And honestly, you could've asked for help. If you'd told me about Elaine, we wouldn't be here in this stupidly dangerous situation, separated from the rest of the team and threatened by pain-crazed megafauna.

Orl hid behind her bangs. A boar roared, the sound a distillation of agony, she winced, then sent a quiet message, like a hiss on the wind. *If I told, Nobody would like me anymore, knowing what I Did, knowing what I Am. They'll be Afraid of me.*

Ah.

"What's going on now?" asked Brandt.

"Orl thinks we'll reject her because she stifled Pruett and listened in on our minds."

"Nah. She's welcome. Don't store much in my mind anyway, if I can help it. As for Pruett, she should head to the farm. We already have a Chief."

Jemin peeked out from under his arm. "Stifled is fine, since Chief Pruett strikes me as false. And, assuming I survive this episode, Orl's welcome to drop in for a chat and rifle through my chip anytime." He side-eyed Brandt. "I've given up on privacy around you people."

Philip, however, had limits and serious reservations. *Some of us are very private people, so you need to announce yourself. No sneaking around, no messing with people's thoughts, just talk to us.*

But...sometimes I slip.

That's alright. Everybody makes mistakes.

What if I find out someone plans to Act Bad?

Tell us. And we'll talk it over.

"What if You're going to act bad?"

Philip sighed. *Up 'till now, I haven't been very bad.* Not that he was especially good, life was just easier under the radar— which sounded incredibly cowardly. No wonder Jemin's sniveling irked him so badly. *But if I decide to act badly, and you happen to notice, let everyone know. Important stuff only please, not little fibs or petty thefts. Alright?*

Fine...Should I tell You if you're going to act bad?

I'd probably already know, but sure. Good grief. She must expect him to lose his marbles, a real possibility, given this mission's twists and turns.

The monster boar-on-steroids began tearing the grass with its hooves, squealing piteously. It listed to one side; the animal's hindquarters must be malformed. Jemin lifted his head, his glasses askew, a bead of sweat on the tip of his nose.

"Can't she control those beasts?"

We're not taking you back to Central, so why not send those poor creatures through their Doors?

Orl almost imperceptibly nodded. The turbulent, oil-slick sky dissolved, leaving a pale autumnal blue dotted with clouds. The three Doors re-solidified and pure white light streaked across the meadow. The multiplied Door-pull felt intense, but impersonal, as if now wasn't Philip Spool's moment. He had a mission to accomplish, and for the first time, the mission would be of his choosing.

Three packets of savage energy leaped for the Doors, and the creatures' physical forms collapsed; the absence of their pain washed past like a gentle swell.

Orl stood, folded her arms and glowered at him. *I was right. Animals do pass through the door.*

Yes, yes. You were right. And I'm glad. I've known a few worthy animals. He smiled, thinking of a cat he'd befriended and old Ruby Worthington's dog.

"Glad that's over. Way too much drama for me," said Brandt.

"What would you expect from a teen?" asked Jemin.

"You don't know the half of it," said Philip.

Jemin was still on the ground, floundering under the weight of his pack, so Philip held out a hand. Brandt grabbed the top of Jemin's pack, taking some of the weight, and between them, they righted the historian, and started across the field toward Orl.

What Else Did She Have?

Golden sunlight slanted through the autumnal woods, the shadows continually shifting as branches stirred in the breeze. A gentle breeze and a significant improvement over that hissing wind. She could remain lost in these trees forever, but... Where was she? And the time... Elaine checked her badge: sixteen hundred, late afternoon. Funny. Hadn't she just been speaking with someone, but hadn't that conversation been closer to midday?

No. Not again. She'd lost more time. Again! This nonsense had to stop. Her fingers felt icy and stiff despite her gloves. And, oh, the creaks in her joints! She must've been sitting for hours.

To get her blood flowing, she shook her hands and rubbed her knees, then stood. A blanket slipped off her shoulders and fell to the ground. It didn't look familiar. She drank deep from her water bottle and glanced around. Leaves pinwheeled across the clearing; the trees swayed like a crowd of drunkards. Where had everybody gone? Hadn't she been arguing with Krause or Philip about...something. Had she driven them off?

Had they ditched her?

To her great relief, she spotted Krause and Cull seated by the injured man. His name escaped her, but he wasn't infectious. He'd been injured; she remembered his rotten leg and the amputation. Apparently, the guy still clung to life, though survival meant a bleak future. A future she'd share, if her brain kept cutting out. A lump formed in her throat.

They must've noticed her...absence. Of course, they'd noticed; somebody had wrapped her in that blanket and left the water bottle. Thinking back on hazy conversations and changes of scene, at least a day had passed in a fugue state broken by occasional lucid moments. People must've been making pointed comments, giving each other meaningful looks, asking each other, "What's wrong with Chief Pruett?" But if she admitted weakness or asked for help, her problem became real and public, and her career was over. And what else did she have?

Nothing.

She didn't have family. Every relationship had floundered on the shoals of her over-packed travel schedule and her high standards, each man gradually revealing their lazy inadequacy. And she'd never started a side-gig or a hobby. Without her career, Elaine Pruett was nobody.

But maybe this blackout had been her last. Maybe she could get back on track. Maybe she could salvage this mission. She should march over and demand an update, but the idea turned her stomach. What if they asked for her input and discovered her only information about the mission was a sense of unease and imminent failure?

Elaine took a long slow breath, pushing down panic. If she played it cool, acted as if everything was fine and listened for clues, she could reconstruct the missing pieces, and regain control. She unclenched her fists, fixed her face in a neutral expression, and strolled toward Cull and Krause.

Would Be Handy, Being a Sociopath

After Philip and his mismatched comrades charged into the forest, Agnet took a seat that kept Elaine, Cull, and Treadway in her sights. Then she mulled over her choices and worried. Splitting up was almost always a mistake, but she hadn't seen a viable alternative. Somebody had to watch the camp, and somebody had to find the socially inept, super-powered teen.

Time passed like molasses spreading across a table, more opportunity to fret over the away-team and consider the future. Then her last apple called to her from her pack. She held strong against the apple; no sense in stress-eating something so precious, and focused on the future, which was marginally more important than the apple and much more important than worrying.

For starters, she tossed around the question of Treadway. If he lived, someone would have to escort him to the farm. A quick, authoritative person strong enough to carry one end of a stretcher, deliver the poor man, and leave without answering questions or being drawn into conversation. It'd mean missing a fine meal, but she fit the description, as did Brandt.

But the perceivers, the historian, and the crazy lady would need Brandt's muscle to fight monsters and find an alien. Could Cull accompany her? Nah. He was too old to be a litter bearer, and the prison staff might draw him into a long medical conversation. Of course, that conversation might be vital to Clayton's survival; she shouldn't be so selfish. Perhaps the perceiver team could wait until she and Brandt returned, which would waste half a day at least. The coal fire clock was ticking, and heck, NeuroCorp, or more likely a proxy, may have already arrived at the farm.

Her granite seat grew chilly. What'd happened to the guys? The woods that'd swallowed them betrayed nothing and innocently swayed in the wind. Imagining sprained ankles and other more dire scenarios, she repeatedly shuffled the team like a deck of cards but kept dealing a wild card: Elaine.

What should be done with Elaine?

A sociopath would quietly eliminate both Elaine and Treadway and proceed with business. But sadly, or happily, depending on perspective, Agnet Krause wasn't ruthlessly practical, and this mission would remain a sticky and ineffectual mess, thanks to her inescapable sense of right and wrong. She sighed and dropped her forehead into her hands.

Something moving too fast on far too many legs wriggled across the toe of her boot! A sharp flick sent the critter flying. It hit the ground and undulated into the leaf litter. See there. She was even too soft to swat a creepy crawler. She even applauded its daring escape. Cold-blooded murder was clearly off the table.

Hello.

"Hello?" Agnet surveyed three-sixty and found nobody. Cull looked up, a question mark on his face. She shrugged and called to him.

"Thought I heard a voice. I'll look around."

Nobody lurked behind the nearby tree trunks or a series of hulking moss-encrusted boulders. She peered into the branches, finding them empty, no pixies or haints, not even a squirrel or bird. A flurry of leaves spiraled into the sky. That "hello" must've been a trick of the wind.

The insect was Busy. It had no quarrel with you.

She jumped, heart thudding. The voice sounded so close, but when she spun on her heel, no one stood behind her.

"Uh. Glad I'm on good terms with the bug, but who is this? Where are you?"

It's Me, Orl, sending a message Directly from Far Away.

What? Orl's traipsing into her brain had disturbed her as a theory, but as a reality...a shudder ran down her spine, and she resisted an urge to shake out the intracerebral intruder.

Sorry if it's weird, Philip made me. I didn't want to, but he said to apologize.

Forced apologies were about as appealing as a burned cookie.

I'm more than Burned-Cookie sorry, but only sorry about Half.

"The half where you got caught?"

No. The half where I Bothered you when I meant to help.

Fair enough. "I'll accept that apology. And thanks for saying hello and letting me know you're visiting. Makes your visit more like talking to a second person in my head. Your other visits, when you were pretending to be my thoughts, felt more like hearing voices, as if I was losing my marbles."

I figured you'd be less bothered, if I acted like a thought.

"Well. Turns out I'd rather chat just like this."

Alright. Philip doesn't want me to be thoughts either, and I have to treat everybody The Same. Even the Not Nice Woman. So, she will wake up and be Angry. I'm supposed to say sorry to her too, but I Won't.

"Why not?"

They sent her to Bring Me Back or Poison Me. I'm NOT Going Back.

"Oh. Can't blame you for reacting poorly to the idea of being poisoned. But you should've told us. We'd've helped you."

I wanted to keep it Secret.

"Keep what secret?"

Listening to Minds and Impersonating Thoughts because it makes people afraid.

Agnet could understand Orl's perspective, despite the strange phrasing and cadence of the girl's communications. But she always saw everybody's perspective and probably threw people undue slack. She could even imagine Elaine's situation, a junior officer exhausted by a nightmare mission, then dealt a lousy hand she was too green to play.

That's what Philip thinks too.

"What?"

About Her. He thinks she may not be a Monster, Human-type. Sure, she doesn't want to Kill me—she'd rather take me Back. But I Don't Care.

(As things stand, Orl doesn't trust Elaine and fears her reaction to the brain games. Fears in a social sense only; Orl wouldn't let Elaine harm her. She refuses to return to camp but is dead set on finding the alien. I can't change her mind. We could hike to the Iron Works from here and meet up with you once Elaine has cooled off.)

So...that all was distinctly different—must be Philip.

He doesn't want to Go Back either.

(Yes, sorry. Philip, here...I met someone who posthumously confirms that we've seen too much. Tell Elaine that, somewhat ironically, knowledge of the missing radiation, not to mention the human experiments and the alien, will be almost certainly lethal. A report riddled with lies might hold them off, but NeuroCorp would extract the truth eventually—and not very pleasantly.)

Agnet shivered at the thought of a NeuroCorp debriefing. "This distance-talking sure comes in handy. I'll try to set Elaine straight. Hope she hears me this time. Regardless, some fraction of us will meet you at the Iron Works tomorrow, depending on Treadway's condition. I was wondering if—"

Bye.

"But I still have questions!"

Tired. Bye.

"Wait!"

She paused her thoughts, hoping to sense a presence, hoping the signal had just gone weak. But Orl was gone.

An Opportune Time to Scoot

Cull stared at Agnet over his patient, his forehead a tangle of furrows. "Please tell me you're not going loony too."

With Elaine still zonked out, this moment was her opportunity to confer with the good doctor in private. Agnet raised her palms. "I'm perfectly sane, but you'll have to suffer through another far-fetched tale. I'll be right over." Agnet first searched Elaine's pack, relieving the woman of a few troublesome items, then joined Cull. She knelt next to Treadway, his breath even and shallow. Fortunately, the man's stink had abated, him having lost that foul leg.

"So... Turns out, Orl's not the usual perceiver," Agnet began. "She just spoke to me from a distance directly into my brain. Swear on a pile of fried chicken."

Overly bushy gray eyebrows merged above Cull's bony nose. "Hang on, let me check my facts." His eyes closed, and his balding pate subtly bobbed. Minutes passed, then he abruptly came to. "According to the medical literature, telepathy isn't possible; though it'd sure be useful, now that all the wire's oxidized or in orbit." He shrugged. "Of course, the info on my medchip is heavily curated. Field docs rarely need to know the latest in chip technology."

"Turns out, secret and highly experimental NeuroCorp chips make telepathy possible. And wow, telepathy is amazing. I can stop envying the folks who lived during the age of all that whiz-bang gear 'cause I've had the experience of instant contact with somebody miles away. I understood Orl clear as day...more or less; she is a bit odd."

"Is she medicated?"

"Medicated?" Agnet calculated with Orl's welfare in mind. The fewer people that knew of her treasonous pill-ditching, the better. "Wouldn't be surprised. Why do you ask?"

"While digging for Clayton's antibiotics, I found a pile of psych meds: MindEase and NeuroStop, several other newfangled derivatives, strong stuff." Cull frowned. "They peeve me, those idiots chasing mind control and the side effects of their own tinkering when research should focus on antivirals and vaccines." He paused, gazing into his lap, probably riding a wave of post-traumatic stress, then continued. "Anyway, I'm sure those meds weren't in my kit when I arrived in New Delphi. Been wondering if someone slipped me the meds in New Delphi, expecting I'd need to treat Philip or Orl."

"Huh. I'm sure they're each carrying their own meds, and they've been alright, considering... Philip believes Orl was supposed to report telepathically, a test of her abilities perhaps. We don't know her range, but the nearest population center is New Delphi. You run into any perceivers in Delphi?"

Cull folded his arms and thought a minute. "Late in the game, a pair of goons rushed me to the bedside of a young fellow of about Orl's vintage. His handler wasn't wearing insignia but struck me as a senior project manager. They leaned into me about saving the kid, but I was too late; he was already comatose, and his boss was in the early stages. Neither survived. Anyway, the bedside table was loaded with chip-specific psych meds. But I didn't ask if the boy was a perceiver, as I decidedly did *not* wish to know those people's business."

"This kid died how many days back?"

"My memory's hazy on New Delphi, which is a good thing." He counted on his fingers. "I'd estimate four to six days ago."

Add a day for a death notice to reach NeuroCorp headquarters—they should know by now, unless nobody survived to send a bird. So, from NeuroCorp's perspective, Orl's failure to report could be due to her contact's death. But how strange, deploying personnel to a quarantine town. "When did you first hear about the Delphi outbreak?"

"Several weeks ago, just before we headed out."

"Hmm. I only heard about it a few days ago."

"Not surprising. Central keeps lockdowns quiet to avoid a general panic."

"So, NeuroCorp could've sent that perceiver to Delphi not realizing the town was mid-epidemic."

Cull shook his head. "Documented or not, he would've been turned away at a checkpoint. More likely, that pair had been stationed at Delphi for a while."

Her head swam with possibilities, but in the end, too many unknowns prevented her from guessing NeuroCorp's next maneuver. "Hard to decide a course of action in these circumstances."

"Easy for me. I stay with this man until he pulls through or dies. Should be fine, on my own." He waved in the direction the guys had taken. "This might be an opportune time for you to scoot."

"Scoot where?" someone asked in a reproachful tone.

Agnet glanced up, and there stood Elaine, her mouth set in a grim line.

A Seditious Tirade

Elaine approached Cull and Krause quietly, listening to their conversation about New Delphi. Unfortunately, unlike Cull, she vividly remembered that cesspool of a town.

Cull said, "I'd estimate four to six days ago."

After a moment, Krause sighed. "Hard to decide a course of action in these circumstances."

"Easy for me. I'll stay with Clayton until he pulls through or dies. Don't worry about me; I should be fine on my own. Might be an opportune time for *you* to scoot."

Scoot? And where exactly did Krause think she was going? And why did Krause think she had the right to decide anything? She put her hands on her hips. "Scoot where?"

Krause turned and looked up. "Oh, hello. How're you feeling?"

"Just fine."

Cull shot her a skeptical look. "You're not fine. You've been staring into space since noon."

The stricken man moaned and goggled at them, his eyes glassy and crazed. He swore profusely and began to thrash, then the IV line pulled loose. Cull grabbed his patient's wrist, probably meaning to check a pulse or stanch the flow of blood from the IV site, but the man writhed like an eel, bodily fluids flying every which way, so Elaine lunged for his shoulders and bore down. Krause straddled his hips. Cull fumbled with the IV. Then all at once, the man went limp, his face ash-gray, his empty eyes staring into eternity.

New Delphi all over again. Elaine sat back on her heels and wiped the man's sweat from her hands. A terrible end, but not unexpected because...because why? Who'd he been, exactly? Surely not one of the team, given his filthy hair and ragged clothing.

Cull pressed two fingers against the dead man's neck to prove the obvious. Looking disgusted, he tossed a rag aside. "Lost another one, and I'd held onto a sliver of hope. Really should stop with the hope."

"Rough way to exit." Krause glanced around the clearing then frowned. "The ground's too firm to dig, given the cold and the paving. Maybe we could bury him inside his hut and pile stones against the door, sort of a rustic mausoleum."

Cull shrugged. "Quick jump to practicalities, but not a bad idea."

"I don't mean to be uncaring. It's just that he could attract animals, and these woods are home to some fearsome critters."

"Then I'll lay him out as respectful as I can."

"Thank you." Krause stood and brushed off her pants. "I'll round up some stones before we lose the light."

"I'll help." The choice between gathering stones and mortuary assistant was a straightforward decision.

About forty paces away, the weathering of a tower with multiple archways had calved rough-edged concrete slabs, perfect for building a wall.

Elaine gestured to the dilapidated structure. "What do you think that was?"

"Don't know. Maybe a temple? Look, someone decorated those walls." Agnet pointed to flakes of blue, yellow, and red paint. "Pretty garish for a temple. We could ask Jemin."

Ah, yes. The pasty-faced historian. Tedious little man. "He does love an excuse for a lecture."

Krause laughed. "That he does." She spread a tarp over the forest floor, and they covered it with stones large enough to stack but light enough to handle.

Elaine was glad for the work, a simple active task, to warm her muscles and take her mind off her predicament. Pressing her heels into the dirt, she rose, moving slowly not only because this stone was heavy, but because she felt strong, aware, and alive. Her competence would return eventually; she was probably just recovering from a subtle flu. Cull was a doctor. Maybe he knew of viruses that caused amnesia. But when she imagined asking for his advice, she remembered he was a subordinate, and Krause was competition; she couldn't confide in either. She staggered to the pile and dumped the rock with a *clack* that echoed off the tower and tree trunks.

As they dragged the first load across the leaf-strewn remnants of pavement, Krause shot her a glance. "Was planning to escort Treadway back to the farm."

Treadway? Must be the dead man. Vague urgency tugged the edge of her awareness. "The farm" meant something, but she couldn't put her finger on it. Hadn't a farm been her destination? "Back to the farm sounds like a reasonable plan, Treadway or not."

Krause paused and reset her grip on the blanket. "It's an option, since your mission's accomplished."

"Central will appreciate an upbeat report, I'm sure. News hasn't been good lately." Unwanted images from New Delphi flitted past her inner eye.

Krause gazed at her thoughtfully. "They might. In the morning, you and Cull could suit up and hike back. I'll stick around and wait for the others."

"I've been wondering where they've gone."

"They're off hunting."

"Well, I hope they bag something worth the wait."

The conversation had revealed little, but her bland responses had gone unremarked. She'd need to continue carefully fishing for details.

At the threshold of Treadway's hut, they laid a foundation for the barricade. Cull joined their stone collection detail, and they finished the task before dark. When the last slab was placed, Krause delivered a pathetic eulogy.

"Well, Clayton. Didn't much know you, but I'll bet you had your good points. Sorry you didn't make it." She carefully placed a line of seven pebbles on top of their impromptu wall and saluted.

Elaine had gleaned from the conversation that this Clayton, presumably Clayton Treadway, was a convict who'd gone feral, so he probably hadn't been a good guy, but at least now, he wasn't shrieking with pain, and they wouldn't need to cart him to the farm.

266

She returned to her pack, stowed her gloves, rinsed her hands with disinfectant, dug out a Redi-meal, and made herself comfortable. Krause and Cull continued chatting near Clayton's hut. The conversation must've been intense, given Agnet's hand waving and Cull's folded arms and head shaking.

The tab popped with a satisfying *crack*. But was she ever sick of slimy and almost flavorless Redi-meal. A hunk of grilled meat would hit the spot. Too bad she'd miss the hunter's return.

Her spoon froze in midair. Hunters? Somehow "hunters" clashed with her memories of this team: Krause, Cull, the useless historian, Philip, the mad little perceiver gal, and a big fellow—a security officer. What was his name? Philip, on the other hand, was memorable, an elegant man with a handsome face. Too bad he was a perceiver, likely to be chronically depressed if not full-on mentally ill. Wait one moment... Philip was no hunter; neither was the pudgy historian. And weren't they in a containment zone? Who'd hunt contaminated animals? Come to think of it, why wasn't she wearing her suit? Dislocation flooded her, a lost feeling reminiscent of her early days in the Home.

It wasn't fair. She was too young for dementia, and she couldn't have lost her mind, not Elaine Pruett. Somebody had done something to her: drugs, poison, a head injury, or a lacuna. She shook with rage.

"Given your expression, I'd say you're remembering."

Elaine almost jumped out of her skin at the sound of Cull's gravelly voice. He and Krause loomed over her, looking down. She'd let them sneak up on her, but she was younger and stronger than both these has-beens. She tensed, poised to explode from her seat and run.

Then Cull, wearing a neutral expression, crouched near his pack and opened it. "Are you? Remembering, that is."

She stared into her Redi-meal, giving him nothing, not even the courtesy of a reply.

Krause plonked down on a weathered concrete block. "I'm glad; remembering means you're recovering, though you'd've been better off permanently forgetting this mission. A blank-slate could trek to the farm, report, and skate through interrogations, but now—returning you to Central would be like sending a mouse into a chicken coop."

They both looked open, ready to hear her, but how could she trust either of them when anything she said could get her killed? And that aggravating high pitched whine wasn't helping;

must be the wind again, but at a distance, as if whistling through the rocks up-slope.

She bluffed. "What are you talking about? Central's waiting for my report, as usual. Nobody's waiting to pounce."

"Do you remember enough to report?"

No, she didn't, so she'd go on the offense. "Where are the others? And don't tell me that they're hunting. Hunting, my ass. What's going on here?" She slipped her fingers into her pack's side-pouch, felt for her gun, and wrapped her fingers around the grip, her hand trembling like the paw of a cornered gerbil.

Krause said, "While you were spacing out, I nabbed the bullets from your clip and stole your spares. Sorry for the theft, but no point in people getting hurt."

She froze, her thoughts reeling. How had Krause seen her hand move? Should've been impossible from this angle. "Wh... I— Nobody's gone hunting! Where are we, and why aren't we wearing containment suits?" The wind shrieked.

Elaine cupped her ears. Krause and Cull faded into the distance. Then everything went dark.

A radiation meter smashing into the rocks.

Dark pines reflected in a mirror as blue as the sea.

A girl with ratty black hair—Orl. Return her to the farm or...

The recent past sloshed in her head like vomit in a bucket. The howling wind died down. Cull's worried face filled her vision: he looked in one eye, then the next, presumably checking her pupils. She brushed him aside and hid her face in her hands.

"I found the lethal injection kit, too," said Krause, "and disposed of it. We realize you didn't want to kill Orl. We understand you're trying to be decent and do your job."

Her cheeks burned like a house on fire. They knew everything. Now, exposed, loathed, and unarmed, she'd die in this remote backwater, without honor or acclaim. "Of course, I didn't want to— I kept trying to herd you to the farm. But you kept chasing fairy tales and wandering off. Then what did you do, poison me or something?" She clutched at her sleeves, frustrated, trapped. "And why? Why would you thwart a valid mission when it's obvious something's wrong with the girl. I don't—I wasn't given the details, but she's dangerous."

Krause flipped a hand, a nothing-can-be-done gesture. "She *is* dangerous, *but* she's on our side, whereas the people we're working for *are not* on our side. Those people are much more dangerous to you than Orl."

Cull swallowed a bite of apple, his craw bobbling like a yoyo, then said, "Consider the situation. Someone in Delphi loaded me up with NeuroCorp meds. And the experiments Clayton talked about sound like NeuroCorp to me. So maybe *NeuroCorp* maneuvered us out of Delphi. Maybe Central's in the dark; they may even think we've deserted and might not believe your report. Might even assume you're angling for a section or dodging responsibility. Or maybe Central made a dirty deal with NeuroCorp. If so, then the pox on 'em. But one way or the other, we've stepped in a quagmire."

"You can spin conspiracy theories all night, but neither of you really *know* anything. *All I know* is that time keeps leaping by. Next thing, we're somewhere else, someone's suddenly talking at me, or the sun's gone down. I don't understand, but something's wrong. Something's been wrong for days. I need a checkup." Her voice sounded shaky and shrill, but she wouldn't cry. She wouldn't.

Krause leaned forward, her expression intense. "Nothing's broken. You're not going crazy. Now, I'm going to tell you something disturbing, but you need to know—Orl can read minds."

"She...ah...I..."

"Yes. She knew about your private mission, about your stash of lethal drugs, and a minute ago she tipped me off when you reached for your gun."

Pruett glanced from Krause to Cull. "How is that possible! That can't be true!"

Cull shrugged. "Apparently, the chips in Orl's brain are special. Pretty neat trick: I'd love to understand the science behind it."

"No wonder NeuroCorp wants her back!"

Krause said, "Except she hates them and has no intention of returning home. So, to prevent you from completing your mission, she kept you...distracted."

Cull snorted. "Distracted? More like insensible."

Krause raised an eyebrow at him.

Elaine's heart slammed beneath her ribs as if she'd been chased by a bear. "Am I the only one? Has she been prying between your ears, too?"

"Yep."

"What about you, Cull?"

"Not sure. Last couple of days, I notice my thoughts aren't sticking in Delphi as much. That's a plus, in my book. So, if that's Orl, I thank her."

Spoken as if stealing private thoughts was a favor! "Doesn't that offend or anger either of you? What's wrong with you people?"

Krause said, "I won't lie to you. The idea of mind control, especially by someone so young profoundly bothers me. So Orl and I struck a deal. She'll converse with me, but not creep into my mind and interfere. But do I have concerns? Do I worry she might build on her skills and learn to outmaneuver me? Of course. Still. I'm siding with Orl over NeuroCorp because Orl appears to have a moral compass."

"Some compass. She destroyed my future, stole chunks from my life, and tried to drive me insane. I could've jumped off a cliff or shot myself!" And she still might, if this nightmare didn't end.

"I remind you; she acted in self-defense. But she won't cloud your thoughts, again. We've insisted." Krause held her in a nail-gun stare.

"And don't forget the bigger picture," added Cull. "Even if we could, should we hand somebody like Orl over to NeuroCorp? I say no."

Strange how the utterly unappealing mutant teen had two seasoned professionals wriggling under her thumb. "So, we don't return and report, then what? What's your brilliant plan?"

"We head to the old ironworks, enter the mountain, and find the alien."

The alien. Oh, for land's sake. She'd forgotten about Krause's "alien". She buried her face in her hand for a moment, then gave Krause her most poisonous look. "Why waste time chasing pipe dreams? If you're determined to desert, put as much distance between yourselves and your last documented location as quickly as possible. Each day you don't report is a day you could draw Central's attention. The clock is ticking."

"I agree. But before we go, we've decided to search that mine for evidence of those experiments, evidence we might be able to leverage, and find the alien. Its clock is ticking too."

"So kind, your concern for the alien, but I personally don't want to die for no good reason."

"Keeping that alien and its tech out of NeuroCorp's hands is reason enough for me." Cull yawned into his fist. "And since we're walking dead, there's no risk."

"But if we find anything, an alien, new technology, evidence of an evil scheme, what's the point? We can't send a report up the ladder. We can't *do* anything with the information ourselves. We'll be completely cut off." Elaine folded her arms tight across her chest, trying to hold down a sob. She wanted no part of this stupid and selfish plan.

Krause rested her elbows on her knees and smiled knowingly, though she didn't know a damn thing about Elaine Pruett. "Granted, it's not much of a plan, and we don't know where it'll lead us. But given the circumstances, we're all prepared to wing it."

"And I suppose I have no choice but to join you."

Cull shrugged, looking apologetic. "Seems so. But you'll be alright, Elaine, because we have a significant advantage. Orl, *who's on our side*, can sneak into people's heads and change their thoughts. I almost pity the fools who track us."

Elaine lifted her eyes. Early evening stars had begun to dot the indigo sky. She'd just been doing her job, a job she'd treasured, and like these stars, she'd held a place in the big picture. But now, she'd failed, or run afoul of governmental politics, if Krause and Cull could be believed. Either way, she'd been disconnected from everything that mattered, and here she was, surrounded by lunatics.

She was trapped.

Supported by the Angles, I Rose

Brandt and the squad crouched behind the crumbling husk of a sizable pipe. Through a hole in the corroded metal, he had an excellent view of the ironworks and the thing that wasn't quite a giant spider. He knew his arachnids, and this thing wobbled on four thin multi-jointed legs, not eight, like a real spider. But spider or not, it stood between them and the door into the mountain.

"So, what is it?" Jemin asked.

"I would've guessed it's one of the monsters that spawned from the dead prisoners, but Orl says it's not a zombie, not empty or cold," said Phil...Philip—he had to get it right, even though the name "Philip" sounded fancy or foreign or something.

He tapped his palm with his cudgel, reminding himself of its weight. "Those legs look unstable. Should be quick work."

"Oh, Lord. More violence." Jemin mopped his brow. "Can't Orl get inside its head and make it go away?"

Philip slipped off his pack and opened it, then glanced toward Orl; she hunkered about three meters away, behind the ruins of a brick wall with Cull and the two other women. "I asked her not to try. Remember the monster at the farm? It nearly killed her when she probed it too deep."

Jemin twisted his yellowed handkerchief. "Ever notice how God crushed man's plans for spaceflight by running us out of materials just when the technology matured? Clearly, we're not meant to travel through space or fraternize with aliens. And fully cognizant of the ramifications of my actions, I'm aiding and abetting contact with an alien and exploration of a spacecraft, serious trespasses against the will of God. I really shouldn't be here." He made a fist and pressed it to his lips.

Philip pulled a long, flat box from his pack. "You're just afraid of that monster, admit it."

Jemin went on. "I keep reminding myself the alien is a sentient needing help, so maybe the Lord will forgive some of my trespasses. But the experience of dying still holds no appeal."

The look of murder crossed Phil's face. Brandt had caught only every fourth word of Jemin's excuse, but it sounded like whining. So, he made up another story.

"Yeah but, if Central finds the spaceship, they'll fly it to the stars and spread bad juju across the galaxy. If you let that happen, your god's going to be seriously pissed off."

Jemin opened his mouth, but Philip interrupted him with a snort, then said, "I've hit my limit, you two. Keep your voices down." He opened the box and removed a spyglass and a carefully folded moleskin which he used to clean the lens, his movements tidy and precise, despite him being annoyed. The man really had style.

Brandt side-eyed Jemin, who looked like he'd taken a bayonet to his gut. He had mixed feelings about supernatural beliefs, having witnessed the Exclusion Decree's sad aftermath on the border. But he hadn't cared for the "it don't matter, 'cause paradise is around the corner" attitude of the religious ferals. Plenty mattered, as far as he was concerned; things don't get better on their own, like sickness and poisoned land, no matter how hard you pray. He'd take medicine over prayer every day and had wished those ferals thought the same, at least for their own kids. A death cult, the captain had called it, and he wasn't half wrong.

But in the here and now, a mousy little historian looked ready to cry, and it was hard to bear him any ill will. He gently elbowed the guy.

"If it makes you feel better, I don't want to die either."

"Me neither," Philip snapped. "So pull yourself together." He raised the spyglass to an eye, then inhaled sharply. "Who have we here?" He handed the glass to Jemin, who peered through it and gasped.

"The face! That's Elder Canaan's face, but he should be dead!"

"Well, he ain't. Come on. He's someone we know, and we don't want to be rude." Brandt stood and gave the Canaan-creature a wave.

Canaan's rear legs folded into a squat, and he waved back using an arm like stockings on a clothesline. Dang. A person never knew what was coming in life, did they?

"Are you insane?" asked Philip.

Chief Krause skidded to the ground beside him, her speed surprising considering the dark circles beneath her eyes. She looked wrecked, as did Pruett and Cull. Treadway's death must've been hard, and according to Phil, the three had been fighting. Chief Krause had won that fight, as far as Brandt could tell, and was back in control. Pruett was "recovering from her spell and under observation," a nice way of saying she couldn't be trusted, a fact which'd been obvious to him for some time.

"Are you waving at that...monstrosity?" the Chief asked.

Jemin stammered, "It's Elder Canaan...sort of."

Philip passed his spyglass to the Chief. She had a look, then drew back, her face plastered by the stiff look of somebody holding back disgust.

"Welp. That's highly unfortunate."

"He seems friendly enough," said Brant.

She shrugged. "Suppose then we should trot over and say hello. Just everyone, stay away from those...appendages."

Closer up, the new Grandpa Canaan made a little more sense. Some lumpy stuff had glommed onto his arms and legs, making them longer. But the job had been poorly done. The joints were randomly spaced, clods dropped off every so often, and nothing was regular or symmetric. No wonder the oldster moved with a ripple, not a stride.

The others were huddling behind him and the Chief, and the Chief looked kinda stunned, so he took the lead. "Hey! Mister

Canaan. Good to see you again! What happened? Thought you planned to off yourself, but here you are."

A smile nearly split the old man's wrinkled cheeks, and his eyes sparkled like a kid's. "Ah! My friend, the soldier. Good to see you, too. You're a straight-talking man for an outlander, coming right to the heart of the matter like a charging bull. Well, I felt the Lord calling me home and planned to end my days. But I couldn't fool myself into taking those pills by accident! Remembered my trick every time and had to stay my hand, as taking my own life would blacken my soul."

"Sorry to hear your plan fell through. Would've worked if you'd been as senile as we'd thought, but oh well. How'd you change into a spider?"

Canaan laughed, swaying side to side on his wobbly limbs. "I tested the pills ye gave me. One, maybe more. Yes, more. And the medicine opened my mind to the Lord and blessed Blue Lady. And lo, they spoke to me. Told me to rise for one last mission. And so, supported by the angels, I rose."

A clump from an "angel" plopped onto the cracked threshold. Up close, the limb extensions were obviously clods of moss and dirt wrapped around bone. Monster material, all right, with that same moldy polenta smell. Brandt snuck a glance at Jemin; the poor guy looked totally traumatized. And no wonder; Canaan's funky new mods (*appurtenances*—good one, Orl) weren't the work of Jemin's god. The alien—somebody that Jemin's god wanted to blackball—must've fixed him up to help them. Brandt held his tongue; no need to contradict the old guy's tall tale or further upset Jemin.

Chief Krause whispered, "God, alien. Not much difference, in my opinion. So, let's not mention—"

Nice to know she was on the same page. "I hear you, Chief."

A thunk followed by a squelch sounded to his left. He spun, weapon drawn. And double dump in a post hole! A nightmare trailing slime lumbered toward them, its mouth agape, razor-sharp teeth glittering. And it was huge, the size of a mess tent with arms as thick as his chest. He let a few useless bullets fly, just so he could lay claim to firing on a monster.

"The apostate! Run for the door, my friends. I will defend ye." Canaan screeched as he stood to full height, four meters at least. He tossed his gangly arms and clacked crab-like claws.

Grandpa Spider against the Blob. This. Would. Be. Awesome.

"You heard the man," shouted the Chief. "Run!"

274

He was dying to watch the fight, maybe even land a few of his own blows, but she was right. Now was their chance, and Canaan deserved an epic last stand. He bolted fast as a rabbit on fire, aware of someone grunting and puffing behind him, probably Jemin; the guy really needed to hit the gym.

"The key! Who has the key?" Chief Pruett's eyes were wide as dinner plates.

Phil, working his hand in his front pocket, shoved forward. He fumbled out a key, hand shaking as if palsied, and held it against the release-plate.

Hello open door!

A horrible scream shook the air. Brandt couldn't resist a glimpse back. Canaan had speared the great round monster with a writhing arm-tentacle and was burrowing a massive divot in the creature's belly. Someone grabbed him by the shirt and tugged him into the dark.

The door slammed shut.

Monsters and Mines

Abandoned in a Hurry

Brandt froze in the inky blackness, hoping the others had had the sense to freeze, too. A light popped on—Agnet's flashlight. But it didn't shine far into the gloom, and every foot-shuffle and cough echoed back at them from afar, evidence they were standing in an enormous cavern carved into a mountain. A ton of rock and dirt hung between puny little him and the trees growing on top of the ridge. Might as well be standing in a giant's fist. He swallowed, suddenly aware his heart was slamming in his chest like a caged chimpanzee.

A small hand slipped into his. It was Orl's. The sudden dark must've scared her, poor kid. He gave her hand a squeeze, the giving of comfort comforting him in return. Then the Chief waved the team forward. They kept close to a curved wall, and shortly, came upon a panel of switches.

Cull flipped the levers. A couple of lights flickered high above, and several people gasped, probably impressed by the cavern's size. "A solar cell must feed these lights; nothing else would last without tending."

Well, kudos to the solar cell, 'cause nothing ever looked finer than those few puny bulbs. And now he could see the honeycomb of struts supporting the ceiling's gigantic dome, which made him feel a bit more secure. Like he'd said before, the place was big enough to be an airship hanger. And to prove his point, an airship-size tractor with conveyor belt-style wheels took up a fair share of the floor. But pieces of the machine were missing as if it'd been scavenged for parts or raw materials.

"She's a hydrogen robotic excavator, relatively recent and contemporary with this dome," said Cull. "Whoever was storing this baby lucked out; everything inside this mine would've been protected from powder-fall."

The Chief asked, "But Jemin, didn't the mining hereabouts stop hundreds of years ago?"

He nodded. "Regional coal deposits were depleted by the mid-twentieth century."

"'Cept that excavator tells me someone found a rich deposit of something about seventy years ago," Cull said. "I'm guessing uranium."

"Huh." The Chief tugged on her chin. "Jemin, did you come across any records of this operation?"

"No. Seems it was kept quiet," said the historian. "Not surprising because by that point, resources were dwindling, competition was fierce, theft and looting were real threats, and corporations were evading environmental protections, hoping to maximize profits before everything went down the tubes. Good reasons to lay low."

"Perceivers, can you hear the alien's signal?"

"Yep," said Phil.

"Good. Let us know when we're getting warm. Collins and Pruett, stay to the outside, listen for trouble and be ready. Everyone else, stick to the wall and keep chatter to a minimum."

They fell in, the Chief's flashlight playing on the curve of the wall. The place smelled of rain-washed gravel roads, and here and there, junk littered the floor: crates, papers, clipboards. Cull and Jemin stopped to pick through a pile of equipment, but the Chief ushered them on. In about thirty paces, the beam bounced back, reflected by a series of windows.

Brandt cupped his hand against the glass and peered inside while the Chief shined her flashlight over computer terminals, desks, the backs of chairs—a typical old-school office. "Reminds me of *PoliceCorp,* you know, the old times cop series with Syra Elts?" Chief Krause shot him a blank look. She must not be a fan, though she reminded him of Syra's character in that show, tough but level-headed. And hot.

She tried the door. It was locked.

Flimsy office doors were child's play. "Be happy to kick it in."

Pruett gave him an irritated look. "Breaking a window would make less noise."

"Allow me." Cull stepped up and screeched an arc into the glass with a tool. Then he gently tapped with a miniature hammer and jiggled until a generous pie wedge of window fell into his gloved hands. He eased the glass to the ground, then put away his cutting tool and hammer.

"You always carry a glass cutter?" asked Philip.

"It's a chisel. Never know when you'll find an interesting sample."

"Excellent," said Chief Krause. "Now, who has the longest arms?"

Phil bent his long, slender self around the sill, and *clack,* the door swung open with a gust of stale, plastic perfumed air. They filed inside, except Pruett, who stayed at the door, saying she'd act as a lookout.

Fine with him if she stayed out here unsupervised. The odds of her bolting alone into the dark were tiny. And if she did, it'd be her loss.

The overheads didn't work, but Philip found a desk lamp, and between the lamp and their flashlights, they could see well enough for a search.

Chief Krause righted a chair and pushed it under a desk. "Looks like the place was abandoned in a hurry."

Yep. Junk littered the floor: a broken mug handle, shattered tap screens, and...wow...an unopened roll of Tropical Zingers. Nobody in their right mind would jettison an entire roll of Zingers. He squeezed a candy through the wrapper and popped it in his mouth. Tasty, if slightly stale, but not seventy years stale.

"Yep. Left quick, after one heck of a brawl, and more recently than seventy years ago." Brandt held up the Zingers. "Found these unopened and only a bit stale." He pointed at the pool of bluish green light. "And the desk lamp is algae-powered, new tech when I was a kid."

The Chief grinned and gave him a thumbs up. A happy pride stood him a bit straighter. "Good call. Zingers came out when I was in my twenties."

"Here." He handed her a candy. "In this light I can't tell the flavor."

She popped it in her mouth. "Think that's supposed to be tangerine. Thanks."

After passing 'round the candy, he headed toward a file cabinet leaning cockeyed against a desk. But a large, dark thing piled in a corner behind the desk caught his eye. He stilled himself, watching for movement, but it just lay there, like a thing, not a creature. A pile of clothes, maybe? A body? He nudged it with his toe, and *thunk*. It toppled forward onto his foot, and dang, that smarted. He yanked the bruised foot from beneath—was that a head? But a head, even a fat person's head, shouldn't be so heavy. He dragged the thing into the open. It resembled a corpse, but the proportions were off. These could be arms, but— "Hey Chief, what've we got here?"

She was behind him in a second, shining her light. "It's a robot."

It was built thick-set and ugly with a bulldog jaw and no fine detail, such as pores or eyebrows. A row of blank eyes ringed its head, and tools and treads served as hands and feet. Shoddy effort, if they'd been trying for humanoid.

Cull pushed forward and gave the thing a once over. "It's a mining robot from the tractor's era. The timing would coincide with the last stages of the space race. No surprise they left it intact—EarthCorp is still fantasizing about mines in space."

She squatted next to Brandt and ran her Geiger counter over the robot and the cabinet. "None of this gear is radioactive, at any rate."

"These robots would've been powered by electromagnetism, not nuclear." Cull peered underneath a half-splintered desk, squatted, and pulled out an old computer. He removed the cracked and yellowed case and studied the machine's guts. "A hefty portion of these components have deteriorated, so this computer has been out of commission for ages." He glanced at Jemin. "Shame we won't be able to access data on those people. But seems they left robots, equipment, and computers, as if expecting to use them later, but never returned."

Jemin, who'd been fooling with the computer case, pursed his lips. "Disappointing. But the brand and model number confirm the computer and the robot date to the same period."

A quick search drummed up three more robots. They dragged them all to the middle of the office and lined them up on the floor.

"I wonder how strong these things are." Jemin's voice climbed high at the end of his question, as if nerves had sent his pitch flying.

But Brandt had to admit the robots spooked him out, too. And so did this trashed, deserted room. He doubted anything good had come out of this place. Best if it secrets stayed buried underground.

"Anybody know much about robots?" The Chief glanced at the ring of worried faces.

Cull raised his hand, looking unsure. "I've got some experience, mostly book learning."

"Same here," said Jemin.

The Chief let the two professors, both afire with curiosity, loose on the bots. Brandt, not a tech guy, moved to the door where Pruett stood, stiff as a board and on high alert. "Anything out there?"

She shook her head. "Just a lot of black. But I don't like the way that black is staring back at me."

He looked upward; the dim lights were no replacement for stars. "I hear you. I'm realizing that being underground doesn't agree with me."

"Me neither," she replied, a slight shake to her voice. Good to know he wasn't the only team member quietly freaking out. Come to think of it, both Philip and Orl had gone beyond quiet to silent, not a good sign.

He'd need to keep an eye on everyone.

An Extra Layer of Horror

The dusty control room thrummed with energy from the dead, at least seven, who'd died under highly unfavorable circumstances. And the ghosts' eyes kept following him, so strange since specters rarely paid attention to anything beyond their own bubble of reality. Yet, a ghostly woman seated at a desk was turning her head in his direction. He ducked his chin before she could make eye contact, overwhelmed by a hunch that acknowledging her would annihilate him.

He cowered, eyes fixed on the ground, his heart pounding in his ears, and...another sensation...a constant grinding agony, its pitch so disruptive Philip could barely sense Orl or the alien. A bead of sweat trickled down his neck. Why this sudden phobia? He'd been ignoring ghosts for decades no matter their condition be they headless, bloated and pale, or stunningly beautiful. Clayton was right; this place was bad, sour old bad layered over sweet-spoiled new bad. No, not bad. Evil. He couldn't quite breathe, as if evil had stolen all the oxygen. And damn, his boots were tight. He loosened the straps and stretched his ankles. Something gripped his arm. Orl. She stood close, too close, her expression too intense.

I'm listening to you but telling you I'm Here, so You Can't be angry. Don't focus on the Unremembered. Breathe.

Good grief. He'd been caught mid-panic by a kid, how insufferably embarrassing. Philip sucked in a lungful of air, hoping to pull himself together.

I just caught a case of the creeps, that's all. Doesn't feel like a seizure prodrome, but thanks for reminding me.

He wriggled a vial of MemStop out of his pack and shoved it into his pants' pocket for easy access. His jangled nerves must mean a seizure was coming on; that was it. No big deal.

Agnet, Jemin, and Cull were standing over a robot, the two chip-heads babbling technical jargon. Tech bored him but focusing on the trio put the dead out of view. Unfortunately, he found the robots, with their glossy exterior, oversized limbs, and crude hands, almost as disturbing as the ghosts. Fortunately, the vile custom-made torture chambers lay inert on the floor. If they moved, he would almost certainly scream.

"Torture chambers?" Jemin's glasses slid down his nose as he stared at Philip. "These things look more like a brutish street gang to me."

Had he spoken out loud? And how'd he dream up 'torture chambers'?

"This one's been modified recently," said Cull. "Shell plastic was replaced by a modern polymer; the old material must've degraded."

"Will they understand simple commands?" Agnet asked.

Cull replied, "Base programming should usually include follow, stop, shutdown, that sort of thing."

She shrugged. "We could switch one on and bring it along. Might come in handy for crushing rocks. Or monsters."

Philip's stomach dropped, as if a black pit had opened in his guts. Instinct was sending a powerful message: turning on a robot would add an extra layer of horror, and he was already maxed out on horror. On top of everything, his feet were killing him. A curse on these boots.

"A diagram of a similar model indicates controls on the dorsal surface." Jemin adjusted his glasses, rolled the thing over with a grunt, and snapped open a fabric covering. "Ah, ha." He set his thumb into a recess, popped off a lid, and tossed it aside.

The lid drew Philip's eye and held it. CoffeeQwik-colored plastic with a dull sheen, each robot a slightly different shade because—a shiver moved down his spine—because they'd tried to match each subject, make the new bodies homey and familiar. Why did he know that? A wave of déjà vu and nausea nearly knocked him off his feet. Lights sparkled at the edges of his vision, then a sharp pain bit into his shin. Orl's glowering face—she'd kicked him!

You were here! You saw what happened!

He ignored her; she was mistaken, and he was busy. Somebody had asked him to do something, but he couldn't recall the task. Maybe he was late. Too late. He should run, but the chip-heads had laid the robots in a row between him and the door. He'd have to leap over them. Best to kick off his boots first; they'd slow him down.

Cull said, "Right here. The on-switch is in this recess."

Philip's knees grew weak. "Don't turn them on, they'll scream."

They're already Screaming. You can hear it!

Jemin looked up. "Who cares about screaming? Look at the state of this office! These robots could be violent. We'd be crazy to activate them."

Agnet drew near, her eyes full of concern. "Orl says something's wrong with you. Are you feeling all right? And what do you mean by 'scream'?"

"Time's passing, people." Pruett whipped her comment over her shoulder, radiating fear, her fear magnifying his own. Brandt, standing beside Pruett, gave him a thoughtful look, and Philip spun away, overcome with an urge to hide his anxiety.

Orl shook his elbow.

The Unremembered is close to the surface. Can you touch it? Were the robots part of the experiment? Are they empty or full?

How would I know?

He hadn't been party to this atrocity. This what? Had not been. No. Never. Someone had given him an important job, but he couldn't follow through. He backed away. *I have to get out of here. I can't take the screaming.* What screaming? What was he saying? *I'm not supposed to be here. Something's gone haywire, and I'm supposed to—*

A flashlight's harsh beams snuffed out, darkness fell, then a soft, yellow light gradually surrounded him. Beyond the light, he could just barely discern his companions, their indistinct forms standing stock-still, as if frozen in time.

"Well, hello, Philip."

The ghost lady left her desk and came up behind him. He grappled for a name and stumbled upon Marilese, sharp as a tack with a tongue to match. Formerly, she'd been a handsome woman, but now a caved-in skull and distorted features, as if a giant had stomped on her head, significantly detracted from her look. They'd worked together, several times, the last at an old mine. Disjointed memories ricocheted past, and—oh, no, no. The truth doubled him over, and he groaned. He *had been* involved. He should've suffered the consequences. He should be among the dead.

When he looked up, Marilese gestured around the room. "You were right. We were wrong. And about everything. The project was a disaster from start to finish. Satisfied?"

"I don't know. Don't remember. I've forgotten so much. I…"

A wry grin flashed across the remains of her lips. "Lacuna?"

He nodded. "Amazing I remember you at all."

She snorted, letting fly a wet-looking blob of tissue. "Lacunae aren't an exact science, despite what the doctors tell you. Neither is consciousness transfer, as our experiments vividly demonstrated. Let me fill you in on what you missed when they strapped you down and bundled you off, Mr. Psychological Breakdown. Every transferee vehemently rejected their new home. Apparently, biologic-analog-style consciousness performs horribly in a digital environment. Just as you predicted, right before you flipped out. Several others, including Gantry and Singh, agreed with you, and following your lead, they put in for medical leave." She smirked. "Fat chance of that ploy working. All the dissenters disappeared. And must say, I'm quite surprised you survived. Did you return to say I told you so?"

Philip shook his head. "I'm on an unrelated mission tracking a signal."

"The same signal you reported to me?"

He shrugged. "Don't know. The mission's been nothing but secrets and hidden agendas from the start." This conversation was dragging on and something urgent—some task—something was preying on his mind. "Say, I ought to leave. Somehow, I've messed up. I made a promise but can't remember what I promised or to whom. And whatever I agreed to do, I don't want to do it. But—"

She grimaced, an expression that did her mangled face no favors. "Listen to that blithering. Sounds like NeuroCorp left you a present in that lacunae. Wouldn't be surprised if it's a self-destruct sequence, maybe a sequence I designed. How ironic."

As he stared at her in horror, she faded, her image smeared by a banded zigzag pattern.

When she reconsolidated, she tilted her head and blinked several times, then said, "We see. A defect. Wake up, undress, and ask the soldier to bind you."

Her voice had changed, the words now clipped and subtly mispronounced, as if the wrong syllables were being emphasized.

Baffled, he asked, "What?"

"Hidden in yourself or belongings. Search Phil Lip. This one—" Marilese pointed to herself. "—saved her story. Top drawer. Reach. Right now, you Need to. Wake up. Now."

Marilese juddered for a moment, the movement unnatural, even in these nightmarish circumstances.

"Wait! Don't go."

She threw him one of her imperious frowns. "Why would I be going anywhere? I've work to do, important thoughts to think." She tapped her temple or tried to. With a shudder, she yanked her hand away. "What's this?" She picked an object off her finger, stared as it hung flaccid, then flicked it aside, disgust and horror flooding her face. "Why are you standing there? Can't you see I need a doctor?"

Rage filled her mutilated face which became so hideous he stepped back and covered his eyes. "You didn't survive, Marilese. I'm sorry. If you can't leave on your own, I'll help you pass on. I promise."

"She/I would appreciate. Leaving. But helping her is the least of your. Worries. Wake up."

"Philip! Wake up."

This Won't Be Pleasant

Philip opened an eye. The debris laden floor stretched out before him, its intersection with the wall forming a limited horizon. Something hard poked into his cheek, and a chill was seeping from the floor into his skin, so he tried to sit, but his arms were tangled in something. So were his legs.

Orl's tilted head filled his field of view, her face so close he noticed her dove gray irises were ringed in black.

We tied you up, like you Asked.

I asked?

Yes.

Cull's voice floated across the room. "I could sever the connections to its limbs. Not sure about this pair of wires."

Hopefully, Cull wasn't talking about him.

What are they doing?

Collecting the Right Parts.

She moved her head out of the way and gestured toward Jemin and Cull. Both still crouched beside a robot, as if little time had passed without Philip Spool's participation.

Right parts to...?

Throw through the Door.

What? Why would... Philip answered his own question. The Door wouldn't accept machines but might accept human consciousnesses trapped inside machines. Trapped... The past came rushing back: the dank mine, the terrified prisoners, the nervous and unhappy staff, and at the helm, colder than an undertaker's side-action, Dr. William Rasp. Speaking of cold, Philip was freezing, bare flesh pressed against the icy floor, though, thankfully, somebody had covered him with a blanket. What'd happened to his clothes?

Brandt stripped you.

Ah, yes. The self-destruct protocol inserted during his lacuna surgery. Had his life bottomed out at "buck-naked human bomb"?

Did he find an explosive?

Not yet.

Check my boots. I couldn't stop thinking about them, and I never think about them. Clunky work boots weren't worthy of one iota of his attention.

I've told Brandt about the boots. He'll dissect them.

So much for those boots, and he didn't have a spare pair.

I hope he's being careful. And Orl, I just had the strangest experience. During the seizure, I was speaking with the ghost seated at the desk behind me. Part of the time, she sounded like herself, but then she faded out. When she rematerialized, she spoke about my present-moment situation. Asked me to search her desk, told me about the explosive, and said "wake up" over and over. No ghost has ever shown an interest in me or the present moment. Is she still there?

Yes. But it was me telling you to wake up.

Could you ask Brandt to pull out the drawer and feel for something taped to the desktop's underside? Don't do it yourself; the ghost will drag you into a conversation, and she's not very nice.

Orl nodded. As she stood, Agnet knelt beside him. "Glad to hear you talking. We thought you were a goner when Cull said your pulsed dropped like a pinecone down a laundry chute."

Pinecone? Honestly, he liked this lady and her eccentricities, and he respected her. Must be a story behind that pinecone reference, but... His throat constricted into a cement-hard lump. She'd probably loathe him after he confessed to his role in that experiment. Still, he had no choice. "I was here, involved in the experiments."

There. He'd said it. But spitting out the words didn't come as a relief. He balled himself into a fetal position and sobbed.

Agnet laid a hand on his shoulder. "I know, because Orl knew. You've been giving her hints, in some under-the-table subconscious manner. You confirmed her suspicions when you woke up, just before you asked us to tie you up. What a scene. Just let it all out."

When the worst had passed, he wiped his face across the blanket. "The lacunae buried most of those memories. A ghost reminded me during that seizure, one of my former workmates. Apparently, I had a nervous breakdown and left the mission early. Otherwise, I'd be haunting this room too."

"Orl believes people are stuck inside those machines, and they're miserable."

"She's right. NeuroCorp was attempting consciousness transfer, man to machine."

"To what end?" She held up a palm, stop-sign style. "On second thought, I don't want to know. Orl wants to boot them up, open a door and help them through. But listen, we've already asked Cull and Elaine to digest a heaping pile of weirdness in a brief time; I doubt they could swallow more. They don't need to know about that supernatural door, so Jemin and Orl are quietly looking for the robot's...uh...brain. Cull thinks we're just trying to safely turn the thing on."

Jemin calls it a Soul.

He was forming a snide reply, when Agnet said, "Yeah, sure. If that's his word for it." Philip startled, and Agnet grinned at his surprise. "Yep. I heard that too. I'm on her wavelength now; see what I mean about enough weirdness? Anywho, Orl's offered to open a door. If the—uh—souls can't escape those machines, she'll chuck the consciousness storage gadgets through the door-to-forever and hope for the best."

So, they planned to turn the robots on. Their suffering would sink through his skin and pain him down to his marrow. Would he survive that agony, or would this be his last dance? And, oh—stars up high—Orl would feel it too, and she was only a kid.

"Don't be surprised if Orl and I keel over. Turns out biologic and digital systems don't mesh, the result is excruciating, and we may not be able to block out the pain."

Brandt sat down next to Agnet and held out Philip's boot. "Look here." He peeled back the boot's sole, revealing a cavity containing a wire-wrapped cylinder.

Sweat prickled Philip's neck and armpits, unappreciated, as he was already a few days overripe. "I've been walking on that?"

"Yep. But your weight couldn't've detonated it. You'd've needed to activate a trigger. Do you know where the trigger is?"

Philip stared at him, realized he'd dropped his jaw, and snapped it shut. "I...you didn't find it in my clothes?"

"Nah. Worst-case scenario, the trigger is biologic. You fart in the wrong key, and we're all confetti."

Agnet said, "Please tell me you deactivated that pop-and-splatter!"

Brandt's eyes went wide with surprise. "Course I did! Wouldn't've brought it inside otherwise. See this wire? And this?"

He pointed out some imperceptible features of the bomb's innards that proved he'd disarmed it. But Philip's heart still hammered like rain on a plastic roof. One hiccup or sneeze, and he could've blown the team to smithereens.

Unsure he wanted the answer, he asked, "How does a biologic trigger work?"

"There're heaps of different types. Usually a pattern of movements, something small like fingers or eyelids. For an unwilling or clueless bomber, like yourself, a cough or even a mood could do the trick."

"Well smack me with a wet noodle, what'll people come up with next? Is it safe to untie him?"

"Should be," said Brandt. "But I'll keep an eye on him and try to spot the trigger, though the urge-to-activate may pass once we've cleared out of this dump. I'm guessing this place is the trigger for the trigger, if you take my meaning."

Agnet began loosening the tie around his hands. "Does seem NeuroCorp wants this room gone, and I bet I know why." She lowered her voice.

"Philip says this room's teaming with the ghosts of disgruntled NeuroCorp employees. NeuroCorp knows about ghosts and the alien's signal. They may know perceivers and that alien are like moths to a nightlight, and that any perceiver who follows the signal to this room is likely to chat with a ghost. Worried the cat might leap out of the bag and sink its fangs into their corporate neck, they layered in backup plans to destroy evidence of their wicked doings. Sure, they weren't expecting us to ignore my contaminated radiation meter, and wander out this far, but still. I don't appreciate being categorized as acceptable collateral damage."

"Pretty slimy, setting up a suicide bomber in any circumstance." Brandt nudged Philip. "Hey, that trigger could also be in your pack. We can search together later; you may be blind to it."

"Why bother, now that the bomb's deactivated?" He'd prefer to forget NeuroCorp's latest egregious violation as quickly as possible and patch up what remained of his dignity.

"If we learn the trigger, we can blow this baby." Brandt displayed the noxious little device like a carnival prize. "Might come in handy. Like they say, 'reuse, recycle'."

"In handy," his ass. At least he was free now. Agnet wound up the ties and tucked them into her pocket, while he brushed debris off his skin. Philip stood, clutching the blanket to his body. "What about my boot? I'm not roaming around this mine with one foot bare."

"What's the holdup?" asked a voice behind him, Pruett's and sounding snappish.

"We need a few minutes. These robots and some other..." Philip vaguely gestured, avoiding eye contact with the mangled specters. He wiped his sweaty hands on the blanket. "...details of the room are incredibly...loud and blocking the alien's signal. Would be much easier to track the alien if they were...terminated." And then everybody could leave. Everybody. Nobody wanted to be here...definitely not the poor slobs stuck in those robots.

Pruett glanced at him, unease mixed with pity. Then she asked Agnet, "Is whatever he's talking about necessary?"

"Yes. Mission critical."

Brandt tapped the boot. "Meanwhile, I'll fix this baby up. As luck will have it, I packed a tube of shoe glue."

Pruett stared at Brandt and Philip as if they were variants of the same disease, shook her head, and returned to her post.

"Oh." Brand held up a small translucent rectangle with a series of golden prongs extending from one side. "Found this gizmo taped under the desk."

Philip plucked it from the security man's meaty fingers. "This is a memory chip. Incredibly valuable in its own right, but if I'm interpreting that ghost correctly, it may be Marilese's data backup. Our evidence." He handed it to Agnet. "Store this somewhere safe."

She took the chip, glancing at it with wonder in her eye. "I'll pop it into an empty mint box and zip it into my dry pouch. Why don't you get dressed and help Orl find those...parts. Please be quick about it. And keep the noise down. I don't like the looks of that cavern." She strode toward Pruett and the vast darkness outside.

Philip pulled on his clothes. He felt coherent, and some of the fear had dissipated, but his throat went dry at the thought of those robots. Across the room, Orl sat with the tech boys around a prone bot. She was just a kid, a brave kid, trying to do the right thing. But she didn't realize how bad this would be. If he pulled himself together, he could be there for her. He willed himself across the room and knelt by Orl.

Jemin peered up at him, trepidation sluicing behind his lenses. "Thought you were out cold."

"Seizing, not unconscious. Go easy. He's in a postictal state," said Cull without looking up from the bot.

"Did you treat me?" Philip asked.

"As best I could."

"Thank you."

Cull heaved a sigh; the man looked exhausted. "Lucky for you I was carrying the appropriate meds, a circumstance I doubt NeuroCorp foresaw. Happy to use their goods to help a man while tossing a wrench in their plans."

Jemin and Cull, working faster than Philip would've thought possible, gutted the robot. Jemin paused, faced Orl, then indicated the various boards and boxes he'd laid out over the robot's back.

Uncertainty or fear flashed across her face. She suddenly appeared very young.

Philip met her eyes. *This won't be pleasant. Protect yourself.*

I know. We feel the Screaming already.

Orl turned to a specter, Adam Burquel, a former robotics expert out of EarthCorp, and began conversing, the first step toward generating a Door. The ghost stopped searching his desk long enough for Orl to point out his rather substantial injuries: an arm ripped away at the shoulder, a dripping gouge in his flank, both incompatible with life. A Door materialized, pronto.

"Switch the robot on," Philip whispered.

Click. An indicator light flashed. A quiet whirring filled his ears. Then—

AEI Ah Ah IIIEI.

A grinding wail issued from the robot's bulky jaw, the sound a storm of angry gulls. It echoed in the cavern beyond.

Sharp. It hurts. I can't...be. I ca... LET ME OUT.

Orl pressed her hands over her ears and crumpled. He caught her by the waist, then pain, like a red-hot rake dragged through his skull and dropped him to his knees.

"Shit," shrieked Cull. "Must've missed a wire." He snatched a pair of snippers, started clipping, and the robot fell silent. But the pain didn't stop.

A *thud* sounded in the distance.

The team gasped in unison.

"We got company," said Pruett.

"What's wrong with Orl?" cried Brandt.

She was limp, white as a sheet, and covered by a sheen of cold sweat. Brandt carefully rolled her to the floor.

"The robot's—flooding us. I can't—" Every very. Broken or punctured, and the pain... He must. Try. Fight. He grabbed the robot's components.

"Let's hope he's in those contraptions," said Agnet.

Philip turned, vomited, then wiped his mouth on his sleeve.

"Good grief. You've gone gray as gravel. Let's get this done, and fast. Where's your door?" asked Agnet, her voice a low hiss.

"Near. Orl, above—" He wadded up the robot's suffering and shoved it aside, shuddering with the effort. "—her left shoulder."

She and Brandt hauled the robot up by a pair of its armpits. "Move the damn door as low as you can, and we'll dump the whole thing through if we have to." They rolled the robot past Orl's inert body, and Cull, who was already tending to her.

Lower the Door? How could he lower a Door? Doors were nonmaterial. And they were never low, they were always above. Escape was always above, as if souls were trapped birds seeking safety in the trees.

Marilese stood beside her desk, observing him with her one eye. She wasn't far from Burquel's Door.

His head filled with broken glass. *How. Can't. I—* No, that wasn't him. That was the robot trying to have a coherent thought. He could manage a simple message, couldn't he? *Could you lower the Door, please?*

She squinted, as if peering through fog, waved, and gave him a half-smile. *Hi, Philip. Come to tell me you were right, all along?*

She'd gone back to the beginning of her loop, as they all did, so tedious. He clung to the moment when she'd warned him about the bomb. In that moment, she'd been aware of the present. Maybe she was special. Maybe she would help.

Please. Lower the door. Please, help. This pain. It's too much. Nobody deserves this kind of pain.

Marilese's image flickered. *Help. As you. Help me. So, I help.*

She wrapped her transparent fingers around the Door jamb, a gleaming rose gold, and miraculously, drew the Door down to about knee height. Philip leaped forward and gesticulated wildly. "There, to the right. About thirty centimeters off the floor."

The Door cracked open and released a line of brilliant light. The consciousness of his former workmate, an egregiously mis-assigned guy who'd drunk his way through the mission, shredded, then siphoned in wisps through the gap.

Orl and Marilese wailed, *Hurry!*

Brandt huffed and grunted. "Easy for you to say. This thing is heavy."

The door opened wider; Burquel was almost gone. Philip threw the electrical components through the Door; they sailed through and slapped onto the cement on the other side, remaining solidly in this dimension. Agnet and Brandt strained to lift the robot, but then! A blue fog rose from the robot's chest-equivalent and began fingering its way to the Door.

He called to Agnet and Brandt. "Stop! You don't have to toss it through. Get back!" They dropped the robot's arms and backed away. "Jemin! It's working. Switch on the other robots."

In response to Burquel's passing, more Doors materialized, some overlapping, some solitary, a painter's palette of colors. Trish Spenser dematerialized with a loud pop. Then a bilious green Door opened for Marilese, the sickly color fitting, since she'd been a horrible supervisor, one snide comment after the other, and stingy with office supplies to boot.

But he was also horrible, an integral part of this mess. He shouldn't have survived whatever had happened to Marilese and the others. Should he leave too? Death might be a better option than the grief, guilt, and self-loathing which would surely haunt his nights. And the light was so beautiful. It would cleanse him. He'd be free. Relief washed through him, as if a boulder had been lifted off his chest.

He would follow.

He was ready.

He tried to take a step, but his leg was stuck. Pulling free from the Door's brilliant glow, he managed to look down. Orl. She'd grabbed his ankle with both hands.

Wait for your Own Door. We need you.

Her strange, pale eyes held him fast, and he realized his awful headache had dissipated. Those men were free. And Orl was correct. He had no business dying; he had work to do.

In a blink, the Door's hold on him disappeared, but here came Pruett, head cocked as if listening, hands held out toward the glow of a Door.

Philip shouted, "Elaine! You're too close. Return to your post. Someone stop her. She's in danger!"

A dreamy smile decorated her doll-like face. She took another step, and Cull tackled her to the ground.

Wispy plumes of green, rose, and yellow vanished into the light.

Snap.

The Doors disappeared.

A Monster is Coming

Orl basked in the Quiet. No more Screaming. No more Pain. All the people trapped in this room were Gone, but Philip had Stayed; he hadn't left her alone. And in the Quiet, she could hear the Alien singing its magnificent song, a soothing river of Thought, Sound, and Light. She held Philip and the Alien in her mind and understood. They'd both witnessed NeuroCorp's ruthless experiments and had reacted as best they Could. Of course, reactions had Unintended Consequences, as happened in this universe.

All the time.

The Not Nice Woman and Cull untangled themselves, both appearing deeply embarrassed. Cull pondered the Utterly Inexplicable behavior he'd just witnessed, including his own, and thought *we're completely off our rockers, every one of us.* The Woman held her face in her hands and wept, devastated that the Doctor had foiled her escape from the Nightmare to which she was so Loyal. She'd grown Thin, damaged by Too-Near-The-Door combined with Not-Enough-Reasons-to-Stay. She'd thought herself strong but was Not Strong without a purpose, and her purpose had been ruined. If another Door opened soon, Not Nice would bolt like a spooked rabbit, and nobody would be sad, a fact which Was Sad as an idea by itself.

Brandt and the Leader tossed on their packs, planning to Go Soon. Jemin conversed urgently with his God. And Philip held her. Close. Too close. She wriggled free.

Then she felt Something Cold.

Philip messaged; *A monster's coming.*

I know. She jumped to her feet. *A Passage leads through the mountain to the nose of the Ship. I can follow the Song to double doors up ahead. We need to Run.*

Philip spread her thoughts as sounds, in case the others had missed her Message. Jemin ordered the three Undamaged, now Just Regular Robots to follow, the Doctor helped Not Nice off the floor, and the Leader flipped on her flashlight.

The double doors shone behind Orl's eyes like a Beacon. When they ran, she would reach out with her Mind, and haul the team forward Faster. Even Jemin, who was not the Best Specimen—his heart already raced like a panicked deer—would have to run. But if they couldn't run fast enough, and the monster caught them, she could hide behind Brandt, because he Would Be Sad if she died, he was Large, and he believed in Her.

Ear Noise intruded into her Perceptions—worried people bleating like sheep. So irritating, these interruptions from the Real and Now.

Slurping and Sponging

Agnet stood with Brandt by the exit, staring out into the dark. Under the pale glow of the dome lights, a small hill approached, accompanied by creaks and thuds, and redolent of spoiled meat, mold, and swamp gas.

Closer now, she could make out at least eight sturdy legs, haphazardly constructed from machine parts. But the legs struggled to support the creature's bloated body, and its belly dragged on the ground. On the bulb that passed for a head, an array of antennae waved above empty black eyes. Oh, yuck. The "antennae" were grotesquely re-purposed rifles, a step ladder, and a human leg, only recognizable because of the boot. The thing was hideous, a gestural well-fed tick, and it labored toward them, groaning and squealing like a rusty door hinge.

"Seven butt holes on a skewer. Look at that bad boy," cried Brant.

"Guess we know who stripped that digger," said Cull.

"Might also explain what happened to the bodies," said Philip.

Agnet shouted, "We ready to go, team?"

"G-g-g-good to go. Now. Right now." A pitiable shriek escaped Jemin when he caught sight of the monster, in contrast to the non-reaction of the implacable and silent, no longer haunted trio of robots rolling behind him.

"Aw. That goober is useless." Incredibly, Brandt sounded disappointed. "It's gotten over-large. Jemin, hand over your rope and pick a robot."

The extremely out-of-his-comfort-zone librarian, his cheeks trembling, his eyes wide, garbled a syllable or two, and struggled with his pack like a three-year-old child heading out for their first day of preschool. Brandt took charge and wrestled the pack off the flailing historian's back, found the rope, and tied one end to the base of an office chair. "I'll take out a leg."

"Do it, you crazy son of a loon," said Cull. "I'll handle the bot. Just tell me what you want it to do."

"And I'll cover you, in case that blooper shoots out a tentacle or whatnot." Agnet inserted a cartridge into her pistol.

"I'll be needing that rope back." Jemin called after them, his voice strangled by fear.

They sprinted toward the shambling monstrosity, Brandt swinging the chair-base overhead like the cowboys of ancient lore. Agnet positioned herself equidistant from the monster's knobby head-like-thing and Brandt. A good view, though how much help would her plastic shooter be if this adventure went sour?

The creature roared. Brandt let fly. The chair-base flew in a graceful arc then spiraled around a sorry attempt at a leg. Rope firmly clutched in both hands, he yanked. The chair-base caught with a clank and held firm. He ran the rope end back to the robot and tied it to the thing's waist. Cull sent it rolling, and with a hideous slurp, the leg came free and fell with a clatter. Black liquid whooshed from the wound, and the creature slumped with a *SPLOT*, then lay at a tilt, legs twirling helplessly in the air.

"Genius, Collins," said Cull.

"Aren't you afraid of anything?" she asked.

He flashed her a grin. "Afraid of plenty, but not sloppy monsters."

They returned to the team. Jemin had had the presence of mind to halt the robot and free it from the rope. Brandt untangled the rope from the monster's leg, untied it from the chair-base, coiled it, and handed it to the still quaking historian.

"Thanks for the loan, partner. That was a close call. Thought the thing might wee on me, lifting that leg and all." He winked at her.

"Superbly done. You're one powerful man," said Philip sounding significantly saner than he had in the control room.

A squelching sound turned her in the monster's direction. And yuck. It was dragging itself toward them. "Honestly, this thing doesn't know when to quit. Let's skedaddle."

"Follow Orl," said Philip.

Elaine backed into the control room, a lost expression on her face, as if she'd woken from that dream where you're living in an unfamiliar house and have a sneaking feeling you haven't paid the rent. "But I was so close. Maybe if I wait, I'll get another chance. You all go on."

Brandt, moving quicker than expected for such a large man, grabbed her by the waist and hoisted her over his shoulder. "Nope. We're all going."

Orl scurried along the wall deeper into the mine. They followed as if being dragged by a net—except Elaine. The crazy lady kicked and shrieked like a cat in a bag as Brandt thundered along beside her.

"Settle down," he hollered. "Or you'll be part of—*absorbed*—by that bloated cesspool."

Faster. Before it heals.

"Faster," cried Philip.

"Faster, faster!" shrieked Jemin, the poster-boy for terror.

The noises behind them suggested a giant sponge was slurping itself across the floor. Then she heard one *thunk*, then another. It was back on its feet!

Her light bounced off a pair of plasti-crete doors, but they hung askew, as if something had ripped them from their hinges.

"Plow through," she shouted. "The monster's too big for the opening."

Agnet followed Orl over the threshold. Dank air carried a mix of smells: rock dust, rotting wood, and dirt. She slowed then leaned to catch her breath against the tunnel's cool, rough wall. The others gathered around panting. Jemin, bent over, hands on knees, sounded especially winded. The robots circled the group several times, gradually reducing their speed, as if they hadn't been designed for rapid deceleration.

A greasy wave of stench and a thundering groan announced the monster's arrival at the tunnel's mouth. Lumpy, gray flesh bulged through the opening as it tried to ooze its way through.

"See what I mean," said Brant. "Those things are useless. Would be kinda cool to..."

"No. No it would not, considering the megaton of rock above us," replied Cull.

Brandt expelled an "oof" and bent over.

"Don't take it so hard, big guy. Just imagine the stink if you blew that thing up," said Philip.

"He's responding to my knee in his flank. Put me down, oaf, or I'll do worse." Elaine sounded snippy but fully awake. Brandt promptly set her feet on the floor. She briskly dusted herself off, and squinched her nose. "That stench is absolutely disgusting. Let's move out."

"Feeling better?" asked Philip.

She pursed her lips. "I'll be better with distance between me and that horror show."

If not feeling better, then feeling more like herself. More's the pity.

Forward was their only option, but to be gracious, Agnet asked, "Which way, kiddo?"

Orl pointed down the semicircular tunnel.

WE'LL SURVIVE THIS TOO

Philip sidled through the calf-deep, cold black puddle, his shoe's sole flapping like clown lips and dragging in the water, his back firmly pressed against one wall of this long, lonely tomb. A bout of claustrophobia squeezed the air from his chest. He shouldn't have dredged up the word "tomb".

The alien's signal was his only comfort, a rhythmic hum, loud now, and almost musical. He sent a message into the dark; *please protect me, and if you created these horrible creatures, please call them off.*

Elaine sloshed alongside him. "Isn't this fun. Sometimes I wonder why we bother staying alive."

It was the Door talking, not the woman. "That feeling will pass."

Jemin chimed in. "Miners wanted to live, so they kept canaries in coal mines. The birds were susceptible to minute traces of methane and carbon monoxide and would asphyxiate well before a human. If the canary croaked, it was time to run."

Elaine huffed. "Well. *We* don't have a canary."

Philip sent another message, this time to fate, the universe, anything that might be listening and that might have some leverage; *please, may neither of these people ever, ever have my back.*

"Hold up. Robots, halt. Anybody else hear that?" asked Agnet in a low voice.

The robot's mechanical whir hushed, and the human contingent stood as still as fence posts, straining their ears.

Water sloshed around his ankles and plinked in the distance.

Somebody sniffled.

Then, *scrape.* The soft sound came from behind them, something dragging across the tunnel floor.

Brandt reflexively gripped his cudgel. "Sounds small or far away."

"Doesn't mean it's harmless." Agnet flicked her light down the cleanly bored mine. "I can't see anything moving. Let's pick up the pace. Maybe we can keep it well behind us. Philip, with that bum shoe, how about you ride a robot?"

A flush of shame rose up his neck. He didn't want to be anywhere near the robots, much less be carried by one. But his lingering fear of the machines was stupid, and he didn't wish to air his neurosis. "No. I'm fine, but thanks."

"Fine, as in, you want to slow us down and get us all killed?" Elaine folded her arms and curled a lip.

"Don't worry, we'll fix up your shoe first chance we get. Sorry my first try failed you. The glue needed more time to set," said Brandt. "But for now, there's no shame in catching a ride when your shoe's falling apart."

Agnet nodded. "No shame at all. In fact, we'll all ride as far as the robots can take us.

"Let's load Orl and Philip onto this fine specimen." Cull slapped the arm of the nearest robot. "Robot, prepare to carry."

The bot raised two of its arms and formed a shelf.

Cull grinned like a ten-year-old kid. "Dang. Hit the mark with that command! Guess you've got to be lucky once in a while."

Orl jumped aboard a robot arm then glowered at Philip. *Come on. Don't be scared. It's just plastic and wires.*

Apparently, he was riding a robot, like it or not. But he didn't want to be a burden or a problem, so he'd just have to suck it up and ride. Should be alright. After all, the bots were just bots now—just as long as he didn't look at them. He pushed himself up onto the robot's plank-like appendage and sat opposite the fearless teen, his gaze anywhere but in the direction of the robot.

Agnet said, "Jemin and Cull, Elaine and Brandt, why don't you share rides? I'll jog along, then take a turn when I wear down."

Brandt gave Agnet a reproachful look. "I'm security. I need to keep a lookout and have my hands free. I'll be the one jogging."

Elaine said, "Think of me as backup. I'm in excellent physical condition and slept well last night." Then she smirked.

Agnet took a deep, slow breath, a look of long suffering on her face. "Thanks, both of you. I could use a rest."

Jemin and Cull gave the team a primer on instructing robots, at least what they'd learned so far.

Cull added, "Not sure how they'll respond if you fall off. They might keep moving, in which case, you'll be crushed under their tracks. So...don't fall off."

How comforting.

The bot motored up. Philip clutched its upper arm and squeezed his eyes shut. Then the arm shifted position, and he slid into the robot's chest. After a moment of anticipating a fall and a gruesome death, he hazarded a look. Seemed the arm had more than one elbow, and he'd been locked into position. On the one hand, he wouldn't fall. On the other hand, he was being cradled by a machine. He must've won today's humiliation lottery.

They zipped along the smooth passageway, their speed somewhat unnerving. Brandt kept pace, his flashlight's beam bouncing on the floor ahead in rhythm with the big man's steady jog. But robot riders had been instructed to keep their flashlights off, unless an emergency arose, to conserve batteries. So, Philip took comfort in the dull red glow of the robot's visual array, not much illumination, but a reprieve from the mine's interminable shadows.

He pulled off his ruined boot and rubbed the bruises and nicks he'd acquired running like a demented fool from the blob-monster, barefoot on one side, his newly glued boot clutched to

299

his chest. Honestly, his dignity was never coming back, but how wonderful to be off his feet. The robot's horrifying past and its hideousness were best forgotten.

Pretty neat, traveling by robot, huh?

Orl frowned and wrapped her arms around her tightly tucked knees, somehow reminding him of that owl. Owls probably didn't engage in friendly chit chat. He'd try a change of subject.

Do you think Elaine can shake off the Door?

She cocked her head, as if listening to a faint sound, then replied. *She has lost her Purpose.*

Do you think she's a danger to others?

Only if she decides we are Dangerous, and she hasn't Decided.

So, Elaine was a greater risk to herself than to the team but was worth watching. And how much of a risk was he? Philip drifted back to that previous mission, the one that'd driven him over the edge. He'd made a fuss over those consciousness transfer experiments, a project supervised by the terrifying William Rasp. Unusual for a responsible operative, like him. He wasn't a liability. He never made a fuss; he laid low, hiding behind a protective shell of ennui, and playing his cards tight to his chest. Didn't he? And he preferred to stay well under the radar of NeuroCorp bigwigs like Rasp. But the plight of those prisoners, their suffering, the lies, the callous disregard for other's sensibilities and rights must've gotten to him. He'd cared enough to fall apart. And he seemed to care about his current team and this hopeless mission. Why then did he see himself as cool, collected, and above the fray? Had NeuroCorp erased memories of him caring? Was his true personality completely different to the version he'd embraced?

Probably, considering all those Holes in your mind.

Orl! How many holes—no, don't tell me. I don't want to know. Now toss off.

I can't help myself! You're sitting right There, and I'm bored!

I tried pleasant chit chat.

Talking about the Obvious is the most boring!

Some people are happy passing the time being pleasant. If it doesn't work for you, just take a nap. We may not have another opportunity.

The robots hummed, rattled, and crunched for what felt like hours, the only excitement a clatter of falling rocks and the brown tinge to the flashlight's bouncing dot of illumination.

Brandt slowed and came abreast. "We close?" His flashlight's beam flickered, and he gave the light a shake, probably hoping to revitalize the algae.

Yes. Up a tunnel to the right. Orl pointed.

"That way," said Philip, still reflexively translating for Orl and duplicating her gesture, although Brandt had already trotted off.

He came to a stop in a few meters, then cried, "Robots, halt,"

Philip lurched as the robot came to a sudden stop, eased his foot into his shoe, and dismounted. Brandt shined the light up a narrow, upward-sloping passage. Thick wooden poles supported hefty ceiling beams. A sickly yellow mold or leeched minerals coated the rock walls, and boulders, chunks of wood, and rubble cluttered the floor.

Cull hopped down and ran his fingers over the tunnel's stone walls. "Timber supports over rough cut walls. This section's much older."

Brandt shined his light across the roof. "That beam looks like a tree trunk."

"It is a tree trunk," said Cull. "The robots could clear this tunnel, but that'll waste time. We best walk from here."

Scrape.

Somebody inhaled sharply.

Brandt handed the flashlight to Agnet, quickly opened his pack, and pulled out a sturdy camp lamp. "I'm going to aim the way we came. Everyone stand behind me so you don't look directly at the lamp; it's blinding."

They waited, silent except for the occasional fabric rustle of standard issue polypreen.

Scrape.

Brilliant white light flooded the tunnel, and fast as a whip, something at the edge of visibility retracted into the dark.

Brandt flicked off the camp light, and Agnet switched on her flashlight, but in the moment of utter darkness, Philip understood what he'd experience if buried alive.

"Moved like someone electrocuted an octopus tentacle," said Brandt "Whatever that is, it's not human. It's bad news, and it's closer."

And it had that unmistakable aura of cold decay. "It's a monster."

Orl nodded in agreement.

"Oh, just terrific," snapped Elaine. "Is being trapped in a cave with a monster part of your clever plan?"

Agnet pinched the skin between her eyebrows, as if suppressing an urge to slap the officious witch. So difficult, these people who express fear as anger, then spew blame.

"From what Clayton said, I'd expected three monsters, and here's number three." Agnet glanced at Cull. "Glad I took that nap."

"Same," he replied.

"In our favor, seems this monster doesn't enjoy light. Let's conserve power. Mine's dwindling, so everybody keep yours at the ready."

Philip patted his jacket's interior pocket, feeling a charge pack and his flashlight. Touching the items flooded him with both a sense of security and a sense of the ludicrous—here he was, at the mercy of unicellular organisms. The light had been sitting unused in his pack for weeks, so he gave it a jiggle to disperse the algae.

Cull said, "Sorry, but my flashlight disappeared in New Delphi, the day the people we were trying to save rifled through my pack and pilfered most of my gear."

"A horrible experience. Can't believe that we survived," said Elaine, making her first negative comment about the New Delphi mission. Philip was glad to hear it. He'd had enough of her false boosterisms, undoubtably meant to cheer the underlings and impress Central. Maybe she'd started to think for herself.

"We'll survive this too," said Agnet, her fingers absently running over her holster. Here was a stubborn woman translating fear into action and hope. "Orl, keep that spaceship socket or whatever accessible. Did the alien give you instructions?"

I know what to Do.

"Good," she replied, leaving Philip nostalgic for his old job translating for Orl; he wasn't good for much else. "Let's hope our luck with doors holds. Cull or Jemin, ask the robots to push through this wreckage and follow behind us. They might come in handy."

They tramped forward, avoiding the worst of the rubble by sticking to the center. Somewhere ahead, water splashed, but thankfully, the tunnel was relatively dry. The alien's signal grew louder with each step, and Orl, her expression conveying focus and intent, scampered ahead.

The alien had a strong hold on that girl, and not for the first time, Philip wondered if their relationship was healthy; a kid that isolated could be sucked in by anybody. Brandt paused every so often to flood the passage behind them with light, both to discourage their follower and check on the robots doodling behind them.

After ten minutes of slow going, the beam from Agnet's flashlight hit a rocky wall.

A dead end.

They were trapped.

Observed by Multifaceted Eyes

The tunnel ended in a jumble of timber and stones, a disappointment to the Others who'd expected a door or the ship's gleaming hull. Orl pressed against the rubble and listened. The Alien was So Close. The wall's stones were large and wedged tight, but she would find a way through—she'd Promised.

The others were old but might know what to do in cases of Blocked Tunnel. So, she sat and waited to Ask once they'd finished yammering about the Obvious.

But her waiting was interrupted by rain—inexplicable rain, considering they were Deep Underground. The heavy, warm droplets splashed like tears on her cheeks, sunlight spangled the drops with a rainbow of color, and dragonflies the size of her Palm dashed to and fro.

Dragonflies don't live in caves. You're dreaming, remarked the part of her Mind that sat apart and observed, and the Observer was correct, none of what she saw made any sense. But she was awake, so these images must be Visions, memories, or picture songs, not dreams. These certainly weren't *her* memories. No. These images came from Outside Elsewhere— the Alien. Orl pressed her ear against the rocky wall and listened to the Alien sing in Dreams.

A dragonfly landed inches from her nose and studied her with multifaceted eyes. Then it zipped left, skirted around a large stone, and disappeared.

Orl pursued it around the stone and into the tunnel's left corner where a crevice split the rock. She made herself Thin and sidled through into a large, echoey space. Cool mist settled on her skin, and before her, the dim light from the tunnel was reflected by the Spaceship's sapphire hull.

Something fluttered near her ear; she cringed and almost slapped it away then remembered the Dragonfly. It said, *The portal is nearby. Feel for it with your hands.*

She laid her fingers on the water-slick hull, and slid her hands in wide circles, around and around, hunting for any irregularity, while moving slowly away from the tunnel and her Friends. Which might be a Bad Idea. But each time the Darkness overwhelmed her, she leaned against the hull and listened for the alien's song which infused her with a sense of Home and Not Alone.

The sound of splashing water grew louder, and she felt first a Seam, then a shape like a star or flower—the Keyhole. She worked the Artifact out of her pocket and using both hands guided it home.

Click.

With faint whir of machinery, the door retracted inward, and a pale glow encircled the door's rim. The motion stopped, then the door moved right, the light growing from a crescent to a round, like the waxing moon. Warm but stale air, smelling of Spare Room, struck her face. But inside looked clean, with creamy white walls, a tan floor, orange and yellow railings; no signs of a Fight, no Garbage-can Monster smells, and No People. Just the alien's Song, a spiral encompassing the Universe, a call she must answer. Philip also heard this call and would answer, bringing the others along.

No need to Wait.

Orl stepped inside.

Clack, Clack

"We going to be able to move these rocks?" asked Agnet as she stared at the discouraging jumble of rock and broken beams.

"That'd take some time and might loosen up unstable rock above," said Cull.

Clack. Clack, clack, clack.

The team turned as one toward the weird sound echoing up the tunnel.

"What? For heaven's sake, what now?" shrieked Jemin.

"Oh, shut your mouth," snapped Elaine.

Brandt flipped on his lamp and shined it over the ceiling and walls. Something looked different, but the changes were hard to process. She'd need to take it in piece by piece. First, only one robot was visible; the ruddy one she'd tentatively named Clive. It was trundling up the passage while clearing the floor with a shovel-like appendage. Behind the robot, a radial array of short white lines ringed the mine, and the wooden beams behind the line had disappeared. What'd happened to the other robots and the beams? And what were those lines?

"Can anyone explain what I'm seeing?"

Clack, clack, clack, clack. The lines advanced one by one. A puff of cold moist air, smelling of neglected vegetable bin and open grave, hit her face.

"Suffering, sucking hash," said Brandt, echoing her sentiments. He angled his lamp, this way and that, provoking no response from the...whatever. Then he focused the light on one, then another writhing lump pressed up against the wall.

For the love of peas. "I believe you've found the other two robots."

He grimaced. "If its strong enough to trap two robots against a wall, it's serious bad news."

Thanks for the update, Brandt.

"Orl! Where's the spaceship?"

No reply, either auditory or intracranial.

She spun around. Not many hiding places, here at the end of a tunnel, but nevertheless, the girl had vanished.

"It's a gullet." Elaine's voice, icy and exacting, struck Agnet's ears like a pickax of exactitude.

Philip asked, "Still wondering why we bother to stay alive?"

Elaine glared at him. "No. Not if dying means being swallowed by that monstrosity."

"Believe you're right, Chief Pruett." Brandt shined his light deep into the greasy black recesses of the thing's throat, highlighting a spiral of gray bumps. "See those teeth? I bet those are rocks." He shook his head, looking unimpressed. "Be embarrassed to die by the mouth of a creature so poorly made."

A cave-width maw with rock for teeth? Seriously? They needed to leave, and now. Agnet internally screamed; *ORL. WHERE ARE YOU?*

Philip glanced about, looking confused and said to nobody in particular, "I can't hear her either," as if their minds were sluicing together, same as puddles in a heavy rain.

She caught his eye. "Then search the walls, side to side, ceiling to floor. She must be somewhere."

"I could toss a squib. The finest nano-lite pyroclast. Sweet little thing, but—"

"But we'd die, either from the blast or the resultant cave in," said Cull, his tone dry as broom straw.

Brandt's chest rose and fell in an enormous sigh. "Yeah. Ain't it a shame."

Clack, clack, clack—the monster advanced another meter.

"I wonder how long it'll take that thing to eat a person," Brandt said, as if remarking on the weather.

"Not interested in finding out," she replied.

Jemin whimpered, his glasses askew. "Oh, the horror. Being ground between those filthy teeth, and then what? Eternal damnation, that's what."

Elaine scowled at the overwrought little man, her face thundercloud dark, and dismissed him with a snort. "Isn't this a pretty and *entirely unnecessary* pickle."

Philip called out. "Found a gap in the wall, and here's Orl's pack. She must've dumped it to squeeze through."

Jemin pressed his palms together. "Hallelujah. Let's go."

Cull side-eyed Jemin then heaved a shoulder in the shrug of the world weary. "Just as soon be inside, as I doubt that thing can swallow a spaceship."

They joined Philip at the back left corner. No wonder she'd missed the gap on first glance; a ledge of rock jutted out and hid it from view.

She leaned against the cool stone and angled her flashlight inside the dark space until the beam disappeared into blackness, then...there. A reflective, brilliantly blue surface: the spaceship's hull.

"Hello, spaceship!"

Then she took another look at the crevasse and realized who would and wouldn't fit through the jagged space.

"Looks like I've logged too many hours at the gym." Brandt's expression was grim.

"Looks like we're going to have to split up folks," said Agnet.

Of Bottles and Ships

Madness and Negativity

Jemin did his best to flatten his belly and squeezed through the passage, desperate to escape the abomination oozing up the tunnel. A jagged stone caught his shirt, tugged at the placket, and *ping* went a button. It bounced on the floor then flew behind him, a permanent loss since he could neither turn nor bend. In the best-case scenario, if monsters or the alien didn't kill him, he'd be fleeing through the wilderness, minus a button, undoubtedly the first of many small but eventually lethal insults. Lord, preserve him.

A last effort propelled him into a dim, mist-filled space. Pruett stood with one hand on a hip, her sharp elbow too close for comfort, her other hand slinging the beam from her flashlight up and down the cavern.

"Where is that reckless girl?" she asked, her question a whip-crack.

Philip startled and looked their way, as if recalling the very existences of Jemin Yoder and Elaine Pruett. Their existences must've been a disappointment, because he shook his head and called, "Orl?" He waited a moment, nose in the air, posed like an ancient, heathen statue, then frowned. "I don't perceive her; I hope she's inside the ship and the hull's blocking her signal." He continued in a softer tone, almost talking to himself. "But, on the other hand, the alien's signal is loud as if every molecule in this cave is shouting. It's probably drowning Orl out." His eyes twitched to the side, and he drifted off.

Pruett's face contorted into an expression of unbridled disgust. "Perceivers. So utterly useless."

May the Lord have mercy on this interminable woman and her harsh comments, he prayed, though the prayer was a falsehood, devil take the snappish termagant. Jemin had accepted Chief Krause's leadership, despite his initial reservations—women, after all, weren't meant to command. But she'd won his respect with her even handedness, bravery, and calm responses when under pressure. Whereas this vituperative upstart rankled him beyond redemption. He steeled himself, ignored the scorching flush traveling up his neck, and delivered his harshest reprimand...taking into consideration her rank, athletic build, and combat experience. "Your negativity isn't helping matters."

She sneered, drew herself up, and loomed over him as best she could, considering their similar heights. Having faced many bullies and having always come away worse for the wear, he cringed.

"Neither is your pathetic and illegal zealotry. So, if you'll excuse me, I'll use *my flashlight*, an actual object not woo-woo brain energy or a supernatural creature and find that blasted girl." She stomped off a short distance away, her flashlight playing over the hull and the cave's floor.

"She complains about lack of discipline, then wanders off leaving us in the dark." Jemin flicked on his flashlight. "We're supposed to stick together, and now we're draining two precious batteries, thanks to her hypocrisy."

Pruett shined her light into his face, blinding him. "So why don't you do your job, instead of standing there grousing?"

Philip leaned down, his lips close to Jemin's ear, uncomfortably close, considering the perceiver's orientation. He whispered, "She wants us to follow. See how slowly she's moving, flashlight fixed on the ground, each step hesitant? I sense she's terrified. And unfortunately, her terror translates to mean and bossy."

Jemin whispered back. "For the record, I'm terrified too."

"So am I. Why wouldn't I be? It's dark and wet in here, and the three members of this team who can pass as competent adults are in the tunnel battling a monster."

Jemin turned this simultaneously validating and insulting comment around in his head, then found an opening. "Why don't you consider yourself competent?"

"I can barely think, thanks to the alien. But listen, you have the right idea—we should stick together. And Elaine may be a pill, but she also has the right idea—we should find Orl. So, let's ignore her hostility and follow."

They caught up with Chief Pruett, though Philip dragged, his fingers trailing on the hull, his expression that of a sleepwalker, eyes soft, roving, and unearthly. Could the madness that'd possessed him in the control room be returning? A shiver passed up Jemin's spine, and he offered a truer prayer to the Almighty. *Please, dear Lord. Open your heart to the least of your creations and curb the insanity devouring the pitiable soul of the faithless sinner Philip.*

A few minutes later, a gust of warm air brushed Jemin's face, and light flooded the cavern. His vision adjusted. Now he could make out a warm glowing circle, as if an enormous beast had opened an eye. A quavering shriek filled the air.

"Silence, coward," hissed Pruett.

Merciful heavens. Had that shriek come out of his mouth?

She turned to Philip. "The porthole was wide open. Light must be on a sensor. Can you hear Orl?"

"Not above all this noise," he replied while looking every which way, as if tracking the movements of a cloud of invisible grasshoppers.

What was the man looking at? And what did he mean by noise? There wasn't any noise. Lord preserve him. Instead of protecting Jemin from Chief Pruett or leading them to Orl, Philip had gone crazy again.

Against his better judgment, he followed his team-mates through the porthole onto a steeply sloped floor. The material wasn't especially slick, but moving around would present a challenge. He could haul himself along using this railing affixed to the wall. It was set a bit high, spinning his thoughts toward giants. At least they might be able to converse with giants.

"Where's the alien? It could at least welcome us and offer a simple 'thank you.'" Chief Pruett's voice rasped across his ears.

"Not sure we're dealing with something...corporeal." Philip's eyes roved randomly around the room, a foyer of sorts, well-lit but spare and functional.

Pruett glowered. "Pull yourself together. We don't need another episode out of you, jabbering to invisible people, and injuring yourself. And by the way, I will require a full explanation for that fiasco in the mine's office when we've finished with this idiocy."

Philip shot Jemin a despairing look. "Yes, fine. Give me a minute to search for Orl."

Pruett opened her mouth, but he held up a finger. "Honestly. A few minutes. Just...be quiet." Then he shut his eyes.

Each minute stretched Jemin's heart like a rubber band. The wait didn't look comfortable for Pruett, either. She tapped her foot and her eyes flicked about, her agitation palpable. He couldn't stand to look at her, so he studied the corridors, the ceiling, and the panels of buttons set in the wall, Pity they were in danger because this ship was an intellectual prize. He and Cull could spend years unraveling its secrets. Of course, they wouldn't be able to share their knowledge with the masses. But he no longer cared—sharing with the few interested individuals on the team would be enough.

Pruett's whisper sliced through his thoughts. "If you go anywhere, mark a trail." She patted down her pockets, pulled out a chalk stick, and tested it on several surfaces. The walls must've been too smooth, but the chalk adhered to the rail's slightly grainy surface. She handed it to Jemin. "I'll check on Krause, Collins, and Cull. They've been too long."

He must've appeared as stricken as he felt, because she added, "I'm sure they're all fine. Otherwise, Cull and Krause would have joined us by now. Well, Cull, at least. Krause might overplay her hand trying to save Collins."

He choked out an "oh" at her horrible thought; how could she be so cold? Hopefully she was wrong. Chief Krause was brave, but not foolhardy; she'd survive. But losing Brandt, a true righteous heathen, broad-minded and kind, with his firsthand knowledge of the border and backwoods skills, would be a disaster. And had she forgotten *they had been asked to stay together*?

He should say something, but she glared at him, and he nearly choked on his tongue. He swallowed and managed to say, "Be careful and hurry back. We need your help." Or at least, he needed her. Two companions would allow him to walk in the middle, shielded from attacks in both directions.

Pruett gave him a look of abject pity, stared past him, her cheeks slack, her lips down-turned, as if lost in morose contemplation. She met his gaze and shrugged. "I'll see. Hard to make plans when you have nothing to lose."

Then she slipped through the portal and was gone.

DOESN'T LOOK PROMISING

Philip couldn't detect Orl, not the slightest trace; either the material of the ship or the AI's signal was scrambling his transmissions. But she must be here; she must've unlocked the portal; she couldn't be dead or unconscious.

Jemin and Elaine were yakking, but he couldn't hear them, and didn't really want to. Their conversation was inaudible over the omnipresent alien signal which now sounded like singing in his mind, just as Orl had always described it, glorious, complex and compelling, thousands of waving lines of color, pictures, melodies, or poems. His blurred senses were inadequate to describe the experience, and he lost himself if he tried to focus on individual threads of the signal, some mundane and domestic, some outlandish—wheeling galaxies, an unlikely mountain vista, and an inexplicable social event. Were these artworks, dreams, or memories? He did and didn't want that question answered.

"Are you getting anything?"

The comment jolted through him like an electric current. Ah. Jemin, interrupting at exactly the wrong time as usual and asking for results. But as Elaine had so tactfully mentioned, he was useless, and hadn't found Orl. Might as well confess his ineptitude.

"No, I haven't pinpointed her yet."

"She almost certainly headed for the alien. Why not give up on searching for Orl and locate the alien instead. Should be easy, since it's so noisy."

Oh. Of course. The obvious solution, and why hadn't he thought of it? "Absolutely. Thanks. Sorry, I'm not thinking straight. I'll figure out where the signal is coming from."

Truth was, the signal came from everywhere, so— Wait. Maybe it tugged a bit stronger in this direction. He turned until the pull was at its strongest, then he saw it! The signal had coalesced, line wrapping around line, forming a single rope that rose and fell in gentle undulations.

Philip reached into his pocket for his flashlight. "I have a direction. That corridor directly ahead. Let's go."

Jemin's eyes darted from side to side, his expression telegraphing fear tinged with shame. "Urm. We were supposed to wait, and Elaine is checking on the others, so..."

"Is she?" He glanced about. The woman was gone. He wouldn't miss her, but Agnet had asked him to keep an eye on her. She'd said Pruett was unstable and traumatized. Well, he was unstable and traumatized too, maybe that was why he was struggling to care that she'd gone missing.

"We could wait for them," Jemin offered, his voice quavering.

Yes, they'd had orders. Yes, they should wait. But the signal's pull overwhelmed those considerations; they didn't have much time; he needed to meet with this creature at its source; everything would be explained. Jemin, being all about information, should understand the appeal of this last consideration.

"Shame about Elaine, but—"

"I couldn't have stopped her if I'd—"

"I know. Don't blame yourself for her decision." He glanced at the alien's signal streaming into the dark passage ahead. Might be safer to explore with a companion, even if that companion was less than ideal, but he had to give Jemin an out.

Philip sat and slipped off his useless boot. Now that they were inside, the risk of tripping on the partially detached sole was higher than cutting his foot on debris; hopefully the rest of the ship would be as tidy as this room. He tossed the useless thing aside. "You're welcome to wait here, but I'm worried about Orl, and we need some explanations. I've got to follow that signal."

Jemin squared his shoulders, looking like a boy playing soldier. "We aren't supposed to split up. I'll come with you."

"I'll appreciate the company." The signal emitted a tantalizing refrain, whooshing away a moment of doubt, and Philip clambered into a tall and narrow hall. He managed the hall's tilt by setting one foot on the floor, one on a wall, placing a hand on the other wall, and shuffling like an octogenarian. Jemin's grunting and huffing, and the occasional *scritch* of the chalk, were reluctantly reassuring.

The passage led to a circular tunnel. When they stepped inside, rings of light clicked on in sequence, closest first, then off into the distance. A silvery glow reflected off smooth white tiles and canisters of glass, or some other clear substance, which lined the walls.

He eased into the cockeyed tunnel, using the same technique he'd used in the hall, but the sides were festooned with cables, panels, and recessed nooks in addition to the canisters, making solid footing difficult to find. The noises behind him suggested Jemin was struggling, too. Inside the canisters, milky white mist twisted, turned, dissipated, and condensed. A tendril unraveled from the signal, extended to a canister then flowed inside, releasing at contact a radiant shower of sparks. A thin, wavering song filled the air.

"Beautiful," whispered Jemin. "What do you think it is?"

Philip's powerful sense was that the containers held individuals, each singing a unique song, entities, or in Jemin's parlance, souls. The alien might be more a "them" than an "it." But to avoid a sticky metaphysical conversation, he answered, "I don't know."

At the tunnel's end, a circular door opened into blackness. He flicked his flashlight over metal grating—a suspended walkway—and peered into the gloom, hoping to trigger another series of automatic lights. No such luck, so he slowly advanced, his hand clenching the nearest rail, one foot on the canted walkway, and one foot supported by a slender beam. A bead of sweat trickled down his flank.

The space was immense and circumferentially covered in racks of those same glass containers, each penetrated by a thread of the signal, and twinkling as if lit by fireflies. They gasped simultaneously. Philip's head swam, and he checked his footing. A mistake because those same glittering lights spread out beneath him, and the metal grating was barely perceptible in the dim light. He could easily be in outer space, and the faint glimmering lights could be the stars. An entire universe of souls surrounded him. Suddenly aware Jemin had grabbed his sleeve, Philip steadied himself and waited until he trusted his balance.

"You alright?" Jemin asked.

"Lost my balance. Glad I didn't leave you holding a torn sleeve."

Jemin released a sound halfway between a giggle and a wheeze. "This wasn't a good idea. I want off this precarious bridge and out from under...these." He waved a hand, indicating the canisters, but didn't look up, even subtly ducked his head.

Ahead, a single pale green thread snaked and glittered down the walkway, the only thread of the alien signal that hadn't disappeared into a canister. "I suppose the only way forward is...forward," he said, the metal grating cookie-cutting through his socks into the soles of his feet while Jemin's boots clanked behind him, the sound bouncing back off the vast walls until it resembled a fierce rainstorm. At a dead end, the signal dove into a stairwell—or a portal, more precisely, since a ladder's handholds curved over the rim.

"That doesn't look promising," said Jemin.

No. It did not look promising. It looked spine chilling, the glittering alien signal and a ladder, cockeyed thanks to the ship's list, descending into blue-black shadows.

"Agnet will have a heart attack when she sees this."

"Chief Krause? Why? She's not afraid of anything."

"Didn't you notice her face when we exited that wretched airship? She doesn't care for heights."

"No! She climbed down as if it was nothing. If she hadn't, I wouldn't have been..."

"Able to follow? She probably put on a convincing game face, so we wouldn't get spooked. I must've perceived through it, that's all. But glad the rest of you fell for her act, otherwise I might have gotten the jitters and stayed on the plane, too." Philip tossed the flashlight's lanyard around his neck. "It'll be hard to climb a ladder with this tilt. I'll have to lean into the wall and sort of slide, braking myself with the rungs."

"Wish I had my rope." Jemin twisted his hands. "I'd gladly lend it to you, but it's in my pack back in the mine. We should probably wait for—"

No. He couldn't wait. He had to follow that signal. He had so many questions, and Orl better be down there. "I wish you had your rope, too. But I'll have to make do. When I've reached the bottom. I'll holler up an 'all clear'. Then you can start down."

He grabbed the handholds, dangled a foot into the portal, and felt for the first rung. Once his footing felt solid, he lowered himself, forearms to the floor, and reached for the next foothold. And reached. The steps must be spaced far apart. Or maybe the ladder had broken on impact and rungs were missing. He leaned forward so the flashlight would shine down, and thankfully, a full set of rungs reflected the light back at him. But he'd have to slide more than he'd anticipated. With one hand clutching the ladder's rail, he let his rear drop, pressed his shoulder into the wall then felt for the next step. When the toe of his boot hit a rung, a wave of relief flooded him, but his rear continued to plummet. He grabbed the rail with both hands and held fast, maintaining an awkward crouch on the second rung, having nearly yanked his arms from their sockets. The portal's wall felt slick as ice, a profound safety hazard. Somewhere out there, an alien architect deserved to have its license revoked.

"You all right down there?"

"Fine. Don't talk to me. I need to focus."

With his next step, he slid like a noodle down the drain. His stomach yurped into his throat as he flailed a foot forward, willing contact with anything.

There! A rung. Sweat dripped down his temple.

Fear death-gripped his hands to the rail—this climb was much worse than that stupid "air landing", so very much worse. He was insane, climbing down for the sake of an unknown and possibly unknowable alien, and for Orl, who didn't even like him. And worse, she'd probably clambered down this chute like a little monkey. He should climb back up, but—his throat constricted with fear—he probably couldn't.

Several minutes filled with regret and hyperventilation passed before he was ready to move. The next step came easier, and he fell into a rhythm, except for a near-death experience when his sock-clad foot slipped off a rail. He cursed Brandt's shoe glue, the missing boot, and the sock, ripped the stupid thing from his foot and let it fall.

Finally, he dropped into a narrow hall, stumbled on the tilted floor, and collapsed against the wall. He'd kiss the floor, but the notion of alien germs stayed his lips.

While shining his light up the shaft, he called out, "Made it. But consider staying put. I'm taller than you, and it wasn't an easy climb for me."

"I gathered by the sounds you made."

"Oh. Wasn't aware. Too petrified. Stay put and wait for the others. Agnet, Brandt, even Elaine: they're all physical types; they'll know what to do. Alright?"

"Alright." Jemin's reply echoed down. "But if they don't show up, I'm coming down, so mark your trail. Here comes half the chalk."

The chalk stick tumbled down. To Philip's surprise, he plucked it out of the air with ease. The walloping dose of fear must've sharpened his reflexes.

"Be careful." Jemin's voice sounded far away and lonely as the stars.

"You too."

With Any Luck

Agnet asked Philip to keep an eye on Elaine, then asked Elaine to keep an eye on Jemin and Philip. Then they were off through the crack and into the unknown.

"Stay together," she shouted through the crevasse.

Philip replied, "Will do."

Agnet turned to Cull who was fiddling with the remaining robot, the pair uncomfortably close to the monster's...er...lip. "Come on, Cull. You're next."

"Nope. Me and the robot are working on a few commands."

"Dip out, skinny man, before you become a side of string bean," said Brandt.

Cull chortled. "Trust me, if push comes to shove. I'll bolt like a scared little puppy. Meantime, let me play with this machine."

Brandt turned to her. "Then it's your turn."

"We'll see." She had her eye on a hulking log, one of a row, each about two meters apart, all notched at the top and supporting beams which, in turn, supported ceiling timbers. Maybe they could remove one, and—

317

Clack, clack, clack—

Cull and the robot shifted closer to the crevasse as the mouth advanced, the robot wobbling over heaped debris like a drunken recruit.

"Can you work that timber free?"

Brandt's gaze followed her pointing finger. He eyed the wooden column up and down. "Yep, and in a hurry."

"Can't add much muscle, but—" Cull dug through his pack and pulled out a hammer. "Might be small but it can pry loose nails. I got a chisel too." He tossed it and Brandt plucked it from the air.

Brandt inspected the hammer's head. "Thanks. You're a good man, Cull."

Agnet cleared rubble from the log's base, then used the chisel to peel away strips of soft, stringy wood, giving Brandt room to rock the column back and forth.

Clack, clack—

Using the wall to brace herself, she fitted her feet against the post. "What are those white lines, anyway?"

Brandt grunted out the word "femurs" and pulled as she pushed.

"Robot, drill," said Cull.

She ignored the lack of drilling sounds and hazarded a peek at the monster. Turnips fricassee. He was right. Those things were human femurs. She pushed harder. Something gave. Dust and grit sprinkled down from the ceiling.

The log was now twenty centimeters off the wall. She wiped dust out of her eyes and Brandt shook out his arms.

"Robot, dig," Cull's command louder this time.

She waited for the sound of a drill. None forthcoming she said, "Wish the lazy junk pile would listen to Cull."

Brandt rolled his shoulders and stretched his flank. "Don't know much about computers, but I hear they're fussy about protocol." He gestured to the lamp he'd placed on the ground to illuminate the column. "Don't know much about monsters either but notice the light doesn't bother it anymore. I'm guessing its eyes are squished against the tunnel wall."

"Shame to lose that advantage."

"Doesn't matter. We have this massive advantage. Come this way, my wooden buddy." He wrapped his substantial arms around the log's circumference and twisted. She shoved, sweat trickling down her temples.

A chunk of wood slapped to the ground. With any luck, only that one piece of roof would fall. Brandt tilted the column forward, and it came free.

Clack, clack, clack...

He dragged the massive log, then rolled it in short arcs toward the gaping maw. She watched him, stunned. She'd known the man was strong, but this maneuver was almost ridiculous. The gullet's lining rippled and heaved, a slimy iridescent greenish-blue, and the smell—her stomach turned. Fighting the nausea, she lifted her butt off the floor and hurried to be of use.

Clack.

A ghoulish femur slapped down next to her foot. Together, they heaved the log up a few inches, thunked it right behind the glistening bone, then shoved it upright until it was wedged tight against the roof of the monster's mouth. Brandt hugged the column and joggled it hard, testing its sturdiness. They backed away. With any luck, they'd pinned the horrible gullet to the tunnel.

"Same as happens to me from time to time, when I take too big a bite of apple," she said.

Brandt nodded, his face solemn. "Me too. Suppose we should be more careful."

"Robot, activate tools." Cull sounded rather aggrieved.

Agnet thought she heard a clanking sound in response, or maybe she was desperate. "You think that trunk will stay vertical?"

Brandt shrugged. "It's thick and stuck tight. Suppose it depends on how fierce that thing can struggle."

"Robot, drill."

No sound of drilling, and maybe a creature thrown together from body parts, rocks, and mud could flow around an obstructing tree trunk. Agnet fixed her eyes on the femur at forty-five degrees; the advance always started at that bone and proceeded dextral. They waited, then *clack.*

Clack, clack.

The bone at one-eighty lay just in front of the log's base. It extended forward a titch, then *scrape*, it dragged back along the stone, as if—

"Trapped like crickets in a taco. Fist bump." Brandt offered his significantly oversized fist.

She waved him off. "Not so fast. Don't want to jinx it by celebrating too soon. And how can you be that strong?"

He glanced at his boots, looking shy in the face of praise. "Used momentum. Nothing to it."

She caught his eye. "Oh, no. That wasn't 'nothing to it'. That was legendary."

Two-seventy advanced, *clack*, but the apex bone only managed a feeble *scrape*.

"Robot, use sledgehammer."

No sound of hammering, just Cull swearing a blue streak— guess he wasn't raised in the homes. But during the next go 'round, the bones clacked down at their same position and the creature didn't advance a millimeter. After a few rounds, the clacking slowed, and the creature's sides peeled from the wall with a sick slurp.

Brandt turned his lamp toward the thing. It writhed, dilated until it'd recoated the tunnel's wall, then held itself rigid. He looked awfully pleased. "See what I mean? The eyes are on the outside and it can't stand the brightness. It's stuck between a light and a tree trunk, to coin a new phrase."

"Hope we live long enough to use that phrase." She raised her fist, and they bumped. "Job well done."

"Robot, activate drill."

Whirrr.

Fine powder and a chalky scent filled the air.

"A manual would've been handy." Cull stepped away from the cloud of dust. "But now that I've figured out the lingo for the tools, let's widen this gap and get gone."

Elaine leaned against the spaceship's hull, her knees quaking, every single decision and circumstance that'd led her to this moment replaying in her head and driving home the inescapable facts that her companions were lunatics.

The last straw was Philip calling the alien "incorporeal." Something she couldn't see or touch, what use would it be? How could she control it? And it was obviously *doing* something to Philip, probably sneaking into his brain, controlling his thoughts, and driving him crazy. She couldn't trust the alien any more than she could trust that little witch.

But what would she do instead?

She took a swig from her water bottle, then plotted and rejected several schemes: monsters blocked her escape, no safe haven awaited her, and she couldn't lie worth a damn. Sneaking off and throwing herself into a dark pit or waiting to be blown up with the ship wasn't her style. If she was going to throw away her life, she'd go out in a blaze of glory. But who would care? Who would know?

Nobody.

Absolutely, nobody.

She'd always known what to do: the right thing. And the right thing had always been obvious, to everybody, the entire chain of command. Do the right thing and reap the reward was the plan, a clean and simple plan. How did people function outside of a chain of command? She had no idea. She'd lost more than membership in a respected organization; she'd completely lost her bearings.

But people make decisions on their own all the time. Shouldn't somebody with her command experience be able to choose a path forward? It was just she wasn't herself. If she'd been herself, she would've stayed in that tunnel and battled against the monster—she'd always been brave. But...but in service to Central. Now seemed she couldn't find a reason to bother.

And the monsters were disgusting. She shuddered. In fact, everything about the last few days had been disgusting— monsters, insanity, aliens, Orl invading her brain—when all she'd wanted was a commendation for her work in New Delphi.

A high-pitched whine interrupted her thoughts, then pounding and crashing. Somebody was bashing through the wall, and she doubted it was that bag-like monster. Krause and friends must be widening that rocky gap. They'd head straight for the light streaming through the porthole. Elaine could fall in, make excuses, and play along, and then what? She needed more time to come up with a plan. She didn't want to face these people and listen to them gloat about defeating the monster. So, she withdrew into the darkness. Water trickled down the rocks behind her, and mist settled on her skin, as she huddled in the shadows and listened.

"See that glow up ahead?" asked Collins, pointing out the obvious as usual.

"Now, isn't this neat? A perfectly round door. I'm not picking up any radioactivity," said Krause.

"They must be inside. So much for waiting for us," grumbled Cull.

The sounds of their voices curdled Elaine's juices, Krause's especially. How she hated that corny homespun drawl. Some Chief. And look at her team: a dummy, a religious nut, a psychological weapon, a lunatic, and Cull—the bastard who'd betrayed her. Without a doubt, Elaine Pruett was this mission's last agent of common sense. She had to *do something*, in the best interests of, if not Central, then the planet.

The trio of humans and the robot boarded the ship. Elaine crept toward the porthole, drops of water rolling down her collar. She listened as they decided to shed their packs in the entry hall, park the robot, and collect their gear later. Next, they discussed whether to shut the door.

Her heart froze in her chest at the thought of being trapped in the dark, alone.

Then Krause said, "We can't be sure everyone is onboard, so let's leave the door open."

Relief nearly doubled her over, and she released a long exhale. All she needed to do was wait long enough for them to settle on a path, not an obvious choice since she'd erased Jemin's initial chalk marks. They'd head off in the wrong direction, then she'd enter the ship, and rifle through the packs.

Amazing what some people will leave in an unattended pack.

Agnet, who'd *specifically* told Philip to wait outside the ship until whoever survived the monster joined them, struggled to maintain her composure because the spaceship's lobby, for lack of a better term, was empty. No Philip. No anybody.

Splitting up, in her experience, was almost always a horrible mistake, often the proximal cause of a deathly blow, a trap, or a crippling injury. And the idea of *that particular* trio roaming around on their own—Elaine and Philip with their mental problems, and Jemin with his imaginary-being-based belief system—was especially troubling. She'd tried to shield them from the monster, and they'd repaid her by deserting their posts. Thanks, guys. Thanks a ton.

Cull folded his arms and gave her an apologetic look. "Expected as much out of Elaine. But Philip?"

"A strange bunch, perceivers, but I respect Philip and think he's a good guy. I just hope NeuroCorp didn't embed any other neurologic trip wires into his lacuna."

"I've studied lacuna surgery, not that I approve of the procedure, and doubt they double-dosed him. Too much tinkering upstairs, and they lose people, a problem since perceivers are valuable, certain types more so, as they're rare. I'm guessing Philip's a rare type, or he would've disappeared after the robot mission."

"Thanks for the reassurance."

Cull grimaced. "Wish I could feel reassured about Elaine."

Brandt, who'd been inspecting the halls branching from the lobby, said, "They forgot to mark a trail."

Seven shades of spoiled hash. They should've known better. "Anybody getting vibes from Orl?"

Cull and Brandt both shook their heads.

"All right. We'll just have to cope with this bolus of high-level stupid. We've coped with worse." She put her hands on her hips and eyed the exits. Philip's ruined boot was lying close to the widest hall, directly across from the portal. "Let's explore this way first."

"The one running uphill?" asked Cull, a mournful expression on his face.

"We should be able to haul ourselves along using the handrail. How 'bout we *show some courtesy* and mark our trail? Brandt, would you fish out your marker?"

They clambered up-slope and into the passage. After a few paces, debris covered the floor.

Agnet hunkered down and flashed her light across the litter. "At this point, Philip would've been missing his boot, and there's no trail through this mess. They didn't come this way."

Cull picked through the detritus. "Glass, shards of metal and maybe ceramic or a heavy plastic." He rotated an ivory fragment under her flashlight. "And bone. A metacarpal, if I'm not mistaken. Bit long for the present day, but it could be human."

Brandt leaned in. "Yep. Too spindly for bear."

"What do you mean by 'long for the present day'?" she asked.

"We're smaller now. Malnutrition and chronic disease have taken a toll."

"So, you think this bone is old? How old?" A note of awe had crept into Brandt's voice.

Cull shrugged. "Hard to say. Mister Canaan said the ship crashed fifty years ago, so theoretically, the bone is relatively recent. Perhaps this individual was privileged or engineered." He paused and side-eyed Brandt, adding to her nascent hypothesis about the burly security agent. "Though not sure why they'd aim for large; I'd think spaceflight would favor a smaller, more efficient frame." Cull placed the bone on the floor. "Anyway. Wouldn't mind exploring ahead. We won't find the team, but we might uncover pieces of this puzzle."

Agnet nodded. "Agreed, but let's be quick about it."

They shuffled forward, Agnet clearing a path with the side of her boot. In a few meters, the hall opened into a ruined chamber. Rock protruded through jagged remnants of the hull, broken pipes dangled from the ceiling, and detritus littered the gray carpet.

"The impact slashed the hull, no surprise, but what do we have here?" Cull pointed to a column of windows and consoles running up the wall. He wiped dust off a translucent surface and peered inside. "Could be a storage locker. Can't see much." He flickered his light into a ripped-open section of wall and rested the beam on a series of curved ribs.

She drew back, the remains seeming so sad and lonely. "Looks like these weren't storage lockers; these were bunks."

Brandt angled his flashlight into a one of the small windows. "Somebody's in this one, face like a prune in the desert sun."

Cull took a gander. "Wonder if the alien built any monsters out of its own crew."

"Feel pretty done with monsters," said Brandt.

"Hopefully, our alien possesses at least a shred of decorum." She metered the space. "All clean, a good sign, since radiation seems to be a key monster ingredient."

Cull cupped his hand over his chin. "This crash must've been a monumental disaster. But I've heard not a word of it. Sure, you're both thinking governmental coverup, the usual. So am I. But why wouldn't they salvage the metal or computing equipment on the sly?" He gestured around the room. "Central works geology like dogs to find traces of raw material, and sitting here is a high-quality motherload. Why?"

She sorted through her thoughts, replaying the few vague memories Philip had shared of his prior mission to the mine and his conversation with the ghost. He'd mentioned the alien's signal but not the ship. Not once.

"Here's my best guess. Our government doesn't know a thing about this ship. In fact, Central may not know much beyond 'monsters at Ridgelands Penal Farm'. All NeuroCorp may know is that Philip detected a strange signal while working in the mine. Maybe they're curious about the signal, but don't want inquisitive minds near their failed experiment. So, they sent in their long-range signal detector, Orl, with memory-purged Philip as backup, and tried to limit us to the farm by issuing me a contaminated radiation meter. It's even possible that NeuroCorp's only vaguely interested in the signal, and that their primary concern is Orl; this mission might've been her proving ground, no more."

"How do you figure?" asked Cull.

"NeuroCorp's actions are the best clue to their motivations and plans." She lifted a finger. "First, they asked Central to assemble what they thought was an exhausted and/or inexperienced team to 'hunt monsters,' probably expecting we'd uncover a prank or hoax. Most likely, the only people concerned about those monsters were the warden and his...what was the word?"

"Trainees," said Brandt. "But 'exhausted and inexperienced' isn't fair. I think we've done a bang-up job hunting monsters."

"Me, too. A fantastic job, despite the odds. They grievously underestimated us all." She raised a fist, and they bumped. "Now, continuing my list. Two. I surmise that NeuroCorp expected Orl to pinpoint a signal from the farm and report its source: no travel, no camping required. But if by some outlandish circumstance we wandered into the mine, both Brandt and Philip were supposed to detonate explosives,

325

presumably to destroy evidence. However, an explosion might've collapsed tunnels or triggered a landslide, cutting off access to the signal's source and damaging the spaceship. Hence, either they don't much care about the signal—a possibility—and the incredibly valuable ship—rather doubtful, in my opinion—or they don't know the incredibly valuable ship is here."

Agnet raised another finger. "*Then* NeuroCorp sent Elaine to retrieve or eliminate Orl, no mention of either the ship or the signal." She gestured to Cull. "They planned for trouble with perceivers by loading you up with neuro-meds, as if you might need to sedate Orl and/or Philip. If they'd planned for aliens and spaceships, I imagine they'd've sent a different crew."

She glanced at her hands; six fingers held aloft. "Given the evidence, I surmise NeuroCorp didn't expect us to leave the farm, doesn't know about the ship, and doesn't really care about finding the source of that signal. The only thing they're interested in is Orl. They want her back."

Cull pursed his lips, then gave her a thoughtful look. "And if they can't have her, they want her dead. Which means they're afraid of her. Upshot of which: she's dangerous."

. "Orl's not dangerous! She's just a kid," said Brandt.

Agnet shook her head. "Nope. She's dangerous, but, as we explained to Elaine, she's *our* dangerous, at least for now. We've got their prize poisonous peach, and we've stepped into their dirty laundry. And that's why they'll try to track us down."

"Over my dead body." Brandt crossed his massive arms.

"Probably mine too. But right now, I'd trade a year's supply of lentils for that girl's location because I'll bet, she's jawing with the alien, or whoever, at this very moment. And maybe. Just maybe, that whoever can help us."

An odor lying somewhere between a grease fire and a strikingly pungent fart defiled her nose.

"You smell that?" asked Cull.

Brandt sniffed the air like a scent-hound on the hunt. "Sort of reminds me of burning road, one of the old black roads made from that glued together rock."

Interesting that Brandt could identify the smell of burning road. Must be a story there, but for another time. She followed her nose to the gashed hull. "Yep, a burst rotten egg of a smell. It's coming from outside."

"Reckon that's our coal fire," said Cull. "We should scram. That fire will be spewing toxic gas."

Agnet took a last glance around the chamber—no—the mausoleum, and quietly paid her respects.

The trip back to the lobby was more a controlled slide than a stroll.

"Hope those folks died in their sleep," said Agnet.

Cull replied, "Least those bones stood witness to the fact we're dealing with Earth business. Maybe we can find sanctuary with whoever built this ship."

Brandt grimaced. "Kinda disappointing. I'm sick of Earth business."

She threw Brandt a wry smile. "Me too, my friend. Me too."

GADGETRY BEYOND COMPREHENSION

Philip followed the signal down another lopsided hall, through an arch, and into a blinding wall of psychedelic insanity. Images flashed by—a flock of birds erupting into flight, water gushing from a pipe, a hoard of umbrella-clutching citizens waiting in line, and pale branches against an indigo blue sky. But the images weren't simple or flat. No. They seemed to spread or bleed into each of his senses. A tree leafed out and the foliage's spring green burst into a symphonic bouquet and sparkled like fireworks, the embers of which prickled his skin. A small boat tossed in the waves of an ink-dark sea, the undulating motion of the waves becoming a tuba's melodic solo. Rain pummeled a dusty street, every drop vibrating his bones. He cringed, ducked, and guarded his face, aware it was all an illusion, but unable to control his reflexes. And in the center of the stimulus vortex, there she stood.

Orl.

She swayed, moving in rhythm with the signal's beat, images spilling from her chip or her mind; he couldn't tell the difference anymore. The chamber reeled. He reached out, hoping to break his fall, fumbled his grip on an uneven surface, and slid to the floor.

Even sitting, the torrent of input was too much. He closed his eyes and shoved a finger into each ear, but shutting down his senses didn't help. Orl's cacophony was burrowing into his consciousness through his chip and melding with the alien's signal. His only chance of escape was sleep or something like a fugue state.

So he clocked out, letting time pass like a riptide, surfacing periodically to send Orl distress calls—*stop, quiet down, too much*—but she didn't reply. But while sending a message, the answer to his predicament struck him—it was so obvious, he should've thought of it immediately; he really must be impaired. Basically, his chip was open full bore, fine for locating the alien, but overkill in this stimulus tsunami. He dropped channels until Orl's light and sound show abated to a gossamer overlay.

Reality settled into focus. He lay on a perfectly level floor, as if he'd adjusted to the ship's tilt or this room sat on a gyroscope. Faint mechanical noise hummed in the background, and a translucent canister, larger than those he'd passed by earlier, nested on a thick pedestal in the middle of the room. Its contents roiled like storm clouds.

Seats ringed the pedestal, the arrangement reminiscent of a workstation. They were high-set and over-sized, as if designed for creatures taller and broader than the average human, just like the far-spaced rungs of that accursed ladder. Consoles and gadgetry beyond his comprehension encrusted the walls, lights twinkling across some sections while others remained dark. One screen showed a blob of flickering red, another hung silent and blank, while a third displayed the barren rock and spindly trees of the impact site. Movement in the screen's corner bobbed his heart into his mouth. Had the ship been discovered? No. Just a crow, but the bird served as a reminder. They needed to move, and quick.

Orl. I turned down my chip. Can you hear me? We've got pressing business. You can't spend all day spinning fantasies.

Go away. I'm Busy.

Such an annoying kid.

Such an annoying You.

What are you doing?

Sharing.

What? With whom?

With the Alien, of course! They asked to see our world.

So where's the alien? he asked, though the answer was obvious.

All around us, as you know. Orl shot him an impatient frown. Despite her rudeness, he was glad to know she could still interact with the real world.

What is it then, mechanical, part of the ship, an AI?

Sentient Beings are the Same. If we see them as Different, we may Fear them. And Fear is the seedbed of Hate. If we mistreat them, they may come to Fear us. And their Fear may evolve into Hate.

His turn to be impatient. *Did that mean 'yes, it's an AI'?*

No! It's not artificial. It's Real. And it's not an It. It's a They. An entire civilization of Theys.

Philip rubbed his forehead. It, they, artificial or not, the alien wasn't a fleshy thing, a living organism, a biologic system. If it involved smoke, jars, and mechanical infrastructure, people would interpret it as something constructed, artificial, hence an AI. And almost everybody on the planet, including himself, equated AIs with devastation. What were they unleashing?

"Survivors."

He glanced up at the speaker's familiar voice, seeing Marilese, now whole and healthy, though slightly transparent.

"Ah. Not an exact simulation, this person-image familiar to you. But we have met. Do you not recall?"

He did recall. The alien's halting speech was distinct from Marilese's snappish condescension; he'd heard this voice twice, in the control room through Marilese's remnant and in the haunted mining town.

"One time, other. We. You and I. Do you not remember?"

No. He did not, suggesting the memory of this other meeting had been destroyed by the lacunae. During his first mission to the mine, he must've perceived the alien. "No. Sorry. I...I was damaged."

She froze momentarily, then stuttered back to the conversation.

"An insult to your memory. We understand. We met. You complained rather loudly, and we agreed. Correct interpretation: unethical study, coerced consent, lax safeguards, inadequate technology, methodologically flawed."

A minute lag between her lips and the sound of her voice raised a question. Was he hearing or perceiving?

"Inside head. Easier now. So near." The image nodded at Orl. "And with help."

Fine, any type of communication would do; so many questions remained unanswered, but he was selfishly fixated on the toxic nightmare of that experiment, the ghosts in the control room, and the screaming prisoners trapped in those robots. He'd ask his questions, get them out of his system, then turn to more pressing issues. His lips quivered with a burgeoning sob as he choked out, "Why didn't you stop the experiment and release the test subjects?"

Marilese winced and clasped her hands. "Not able, bottled up like so." She reached out as if to tap the canister, but her finger passed through the glass. "No live ones to aid us. So, we encouraged you. We heard you. You understood. You/we shared the pain and fear."

His second question was inconsequential; the past was nothing but ashes and ruins. Still, he needed to know. "What happened after I left? How did it end?"

Her head bowed, as if by grief, a peculiar reaction for a computer. "You were removed. We saw some through Jared, but he did not hear. Us. Failure was decided. Proceedings canceled. Pack to go, they said, but weapons instead. Jared died, and we saw no more."

The projection paused, her expression somber. "We lost you, our promising one. To speak." Then a broad smile stretched her lips and reached her eyes. Whatever he was conversing with understood the finer points of human interaction. "But returned! And with special friend."

Orl's eyes glowed, full of pride or adoration.

"And now. Choose."

"Choose? Choose what?"

CROUCHED AT THE EDGE

Jemin crouched at the edge of the precipitous ladder and switched off his flashlight to conserve power. No need for vision while praying; was there? And he had nothing to fear. No monsters could manage that walkway. And Philip had said the alien was 'incorporeal', as in ghost or part of the ship's computer. A being made of mist, air, or electrons couldn't rip off his face, could it? After all, physical violence generally requires a physical presence. Right?

He swallowed and wrapped his arms around his knees, making himself as small as possible—Jemin Yoder, historian just minding his own business by sitting in a fancy coffin stuck nose first into a dying planet. Imagine coming all this way for nothing but trash picking and rations. He listened into the silence for a time, then began his prayer. He asked for forgiveness and forbearance, but he prayed hardest for guidance. Then he quieted his mind and listened.

To silence.

So frustrating because right now, he could really use some help. After all, there's testing and then there's testing, and the Lord could only expect the average human to withstand so much.

But his Heavenly Father hadn't spoken to him since childhood, and ages had passed since he'd felt the Holy Presence in his heart. He thought back through the years. Schooling had overtaken his life; no wonder the Fold shielded themselves from the Government's offers of education. Then, the chip had consumed him, its endless data reducing the miraculous to the mundane. God must've abandoned him in disgust.

If the team also abandoned him, he'd need to choose a course of action, though his choices were few. Given the events of the last few days, hiking alone to the Farm no longer frightened him, but then what would he do? Play innocent, pretend he'd gotten lost and missed the entire adventure? He was an excellent actor, having hidden his origins for over a decade, but acting couldn't stop an Orl-like NeuroCorp operative from plucking information directly from his brain. Telling the truth would certainly get him nowhere. Imagine babbling about aliens, spaceships, and monsters to the Chief Historian. *The reproachful look in Master Petronus's eyes as they gently guide Jemin Yoder into a padded cell.* And a padded cell was his best-case scenario.

Merciful Heavens.

Jemin squeezed his knees closer to his chest and huddled. Rehashing his options had dumped him at the same dire conclusion—his only option was to sit in the dark and hope the team would find him.

He took solace in his chip, allowing time and information to flow unimpeded. Then, miracle of miracles, a voice rang out, bouncing off of metal and glass, a gravelly real-world voice, Cull, grousing as usual. And there! The beam of a flashlight dancing on the grated walkway. His teammates, alive and well! Praise be.

"Hello. Up ahead. It's me, Jemin."

"Jemin! What are you doing, alone in the dark?" The Chief's voice, sounding concerned, not reproachful, and immensely reassuring.

"Conserving my battery." He jiggled his light, switched it on, and illuminated his face.

"So now you say, glad you guys are all right! Thanks for killing that monster." Brandt's tone was more jokey than cross, a relief since Jemin never uttered the words others expected to hear.

"You can't expect a pat on the back for doing your job. I certainly don't."

Their laughter ricocheted off glass and metal, a pleasant rollicking sound, and he hoped they'd appreciated his humor—his parched and parsimonious delivery often meant his jokes went undetected, and they might be laughing *at* him.

But even if they were laughing at him, he was deeply glad to be amongst them.

Chief Krause said, "Speaking of jobs, weren't you-all supposed to wait for us by the door?"

Jemin cringed, glad the dark obscured his features. The Lord on High demanded that truth be spoken, hence he must—quite rightfully—throw Philip to the wolves. But he'd long been unpopular and disliked, so he knew how this scenario would play out. The team wouldn't remember Philip's recklessness and obsessive mania. No. They'd only remember Jemin betraying his more popular comrade. Regardless, the import of following the Word exceeded the allure of popularity by a significant margin.

"Philip's worrying over Orl was so intense, he couldn't wait."

"Funny," said Cull. "Spool doesn't strike me as rash or overly sentimental. Did he seem in control of his faculties?"

"Marginally? His drive to follow the alien's signal surpassed reason, in my opinion. I expressed concern and reminded him of your orders, but he couldn't be persuaded." He stopped there, afraid he might start to sound whiny.

After a short, murmured discussion, the three struggled across the walkway and joined him. Jemin explained the off-axis ladder, and Philip's perilous descent. "He told me to stay put, figuring I'd break my neck on the way down."

The Chief shined her light down the portal. "Yep. Good call. Was just thinking it couldn't get worse than that rickety walkway."

"Ta da," cried Brandt, as he pulled the rope from his pack. "Forget your fear; the rope is here. They say you should never travel without a towel, but I reckon a rope adds more value than a towel."

"I'm wondrously pleased to see that rope." In fact, Jemin's relief was so intense he almost felt giddy.

332

Brandt shot him an apologetic look. "Don't worry, I only borrowed it. The rest of your stuff is waiting for you in the entryway."

More proof his humor was too subtle for these heathens. "To clarify, I've only been ribbing folks about borrowing the rope, a life saver each time we've used it, mostly because it's been in someone else's hands."

Brandt grinned ear to ear. "Glad to know you joke around, bro. Well, watch this rope save our hineys once again." He fed it down the chute.

"Hold up." Jemin snatched the rope's end from Brandt's hand and tied it firmly to the ladder's handhold. "According to my database, a bowline knot should hold fast."

"Looks solid. I'll go first. Just copy my style, and you'll be fine." Brandt grabbed the rope, lowered himself on to the ladder, then bounced down, rung to rung, an arboreal gorilla, each move graceful and seamless.

He called up. "The hall below is clear. Come on down."

Chief Krause caught Jemin's eye and shook her head. "Forget about following Brandt's style. The man is outrageously strong. Wrap your legs around the rope and ease yourself down. Otherwise, you'll shred your hands. Rest on a rung between moves if needs be."

Sweat prickled Jemin's armpits as he contemplated his first step. "Happy to defer to your rank if you'd like to go next."

"No. I need you both downstairs to catch me when I fall."

He stared at her, horrified.

She patted his arm. "Kidding. I'm just kidding. Now get."

He inch-wormed down the ladder, his biceps screaming, his heart pounding, his moist palms slipping on the rope. Halfway down, he mis-stepped and slid like an eel down a drainpipe, the drop taking years from his life and leaving a nasty rope burn. He huddled on a step, ignoring Chief Krause and Brandt's concerned questions, and prayed. *Lord on High, preserve the fragile house of your humble servant's soul.* After an eternity, he continued his downward creep until his feet hit the slanted floor, and he fell forward, right into Brandt's massive chest.

The big man grasped Jemin's upper arms and steadied him. "Whoa there, fella. Good job." He shouted up, "All clear. Your turn Cull."

Jemin expected the older man to struggle, but he dropped through the portal in minutes.

The big man helped Cull find his footing. "Well done, doc. You fly down?"

Cull grinned, an unfortunate expression as he was uplit by Brandt's flashlight and resembled a heathen's October pumpkin. "Rappelled. Done my share of rock climbing and spelunking in the service of geology."

The Chief took only a bit longer than Cull.

"Welp. That's done and good riddance." She wiped her hands on her trousers, not even out of breath.

"Philip must've been wrong. He thought you were afraid of heights. Said the climb down would slay you," then he choked, realizing he'd betrayed Philip once again, entirely unnecessarily this time.

"He perceived right. I *am* afraid of heights. Terrified, actually. But you gotta do what you gotta do."

"'Gotta do what you gotta do' sounds like the last decade of my life," said Jemin.

"You, me, and everybody else." Brandt glanced up the chute. "Climbing out won't be as fun."

Fun? Action hero types: their prowess was confronting, but they came in handy. Then a thought dawned on Jemin, a discrepancy he should've noticed right away.

"Where's Chief Pruett?"

"Isn't she with Philip?" asked Chief Krause.

"She left us to check on your progress with the monster, or so she said. I told her we were supposed to stick together." Oh, great. He sounded like kinder tattling to their ma.

"Where'd you start to mark your trail?" asked Brandt.

"In the lobby. Pruett even gave me the chalk, so I'm sure she doesn't mean any harm. Maybe she fell or got lost or—"

Chief Krause interrupted, her voice cold. "We explored two other halls before heading this way, because the chalk marks in this direction started about three quarters down the first hall."

"That's not right," Jemin cried. "I drew a big arrow right beside the entrance to the hall we took."

"Chalk rubs off pretty easy," said Brandt.

"Right now, Elaine's a hot mess," said Cull. "But I kind of figured she was more a danger to herself than others."

Chief Krause said, "Some folks crumble in the face of uncertainty and can go pretty haywire. But at least now we're on the alert."

She flickered her light down the hall, then fixed the beam on a section of railing. "Thankfully, Philip marked a trail. Let's go."

Unintended Consequences

A few steps down the corridor, Agnet heard a voice, Philip's voice, and the insubordinate nimnut was about to make a choice! They were a team for crying out loud, and she was supposedly the leader; nobody should be making impromptu choices. She raced toward a dim glow ahead and burst into a round chamber, nearly stumbling on the flat floor—nice to have her feet planted firmly on the ground after all those cockeyed halls. One of those big glass lamps or fuses or whatever sat in the room's center, emitting pale bluish light. Orl stood staring into nothing, her pupils dilated wide as a doper's after a weekend at the pipe. Philip was sprawled out on the floor, clearly in no shape to decide anything.

She shouted. "No choosing until you tell us what's going on."

Cull made a beeline for Philip and slipped his medical bag off his shoulder, preparing to break out his gear. Brandt shouted "Orl!" He raced to her and wrapped her in his arms, and smushed her to his chest in a smothering hug that lifted her feet off the ground. The girl loosed a muffled squeal and struggled until he gently placed her down. She straightened her dress, a crow shaking off the rain, and stole glances at the team, meeting Agnet's gaze for a nanosecond, then slipped behind Brandt.

"Can't hide from me, Orl. And thanks for sneaking off."

No reply from the little skulker. Agnet surveyed the room, noting a second opening one-eighty from their point of entry. Chances were, Elaine would've followed their trail, if so inclined, but one could never predict the movements of an unstable adversary. Agnet caught Brandt's eye and motioned to the hall they'd just vacated. He nodded and went to stand guard.

"Jemin. Monitor the other entrance." He shot her a startled goldfish look. She pointed to the door, and he slunk to the far hall, probably wishing he could catalog artifacts instead of being useful. The perpetually preoccupied historian wasn't her first choice of guard, but Philip, who still lay prone, eyes closed, as if napping, might need Cull's doctoring skills. She joined Cull at Philip's side.

"No injuries beyond a few bruises," said Cull. "Seems profoundly asleep to me."

She shook Philip's shoulder. "Wake up! This is no time for a nap and don't choose a dang thing, even in your dreams."

His eyelids flew open, and he gasped, as if startled by their faces. "I'm awake. I was...I'm fine."

"Oh, yeah? Then why did you pass out like a drunken recruit?" Brandt asked without averting his eyes from the hall.

"Don't think I passed out." Philip sat and dusted off his back, although the floor was so clean it nearly sparkled. Orl approached, avoiding all eye contact, and sat cross-legged beside him. He flashed her a nervous smile. "I was... Orl and I were communicating with the—um—alien. Moments ago, she transmitted heaps of very interesting information. I'm trying to grasp it all. What a day." He leaned his head into his hand and shook it slowly, side to side, exhausted or overwhelmed maybe, but his running-off still rankled her.

She folded her arms as a bulwark against his suffering. "Very glad to see you alive, and yes, you've been through a lot, as have we all. But what are you doing here? You were supposed to wait."

He sighed. "Glad to see you alive, too. And sorry for taking off. But I couldn't resist the signal. It practically dragged me down here, despite your orders. Can't believe I climbed down that ladder wearing one boot and without a lifeline."

Jemin cupped his mouth and stage whispered. "He certainly was acting peculiarly."

Philip rolled his eyes, a return to his usual haughty self. And Orl's pupils no longer resembled twin black holes, but who knew what the alien had done to their minds?

"Watch the hall, Jemin. 'Couldn't resist' sounds like hypnosis or mind control."

He pinched the bridge of his nose, another typical Philip-ism. "No. Yes. Maybe in part. They hurried me along because time is short, and we're their only chance of survival."

"They who?" asked Agnet.

"What we've been calling the alien. The source of the signal. They're stored in canisters like that one." Philip gestured to the translucent vat of percolating clouds, its contents as turbulent as cream in a blender. "We passed thousands on the way down."

"Those? I figured those were big light bulbs, and that stuff boiling inside was glow-algae," said Brandt, his camp light blazing down the hall, his back to the team.

"Light bulbs?" Philip chuckled. "No. Those are people...or at least consciousnesses. An entire civilization loaded themselves onto this ship and fled because their home had reached endgame."

"They think this planet's an improvement?" asked Cull.

"Hard to believe, I know. But apparently, things can get much worse. They wanted a second chance and hoped to help us dodge some pitfalls, but gaps in our technology caught them off guard. For starters, they were expecting long distance communication, something based on energy waves."

Jemin piped up, always so eager to contribute. "We had similar technology pre-deluge, but lacked the materials to replicate it, given the scarcities and the collapse of supply-lines, and then, well..." He flushed, as if personally responsible for the mineral cache ringing the moon.

"Interesting, but eyes on the hall, thanks."

Philip acknowledged Jemin's contribution with a nod. "So, they couldn't hail us. When I turned up as part of NeuroCorp's vile secret mission, I inadvertently contacted them via my chip. Seems, to my surprise, I have some long-range communication abilities similar to Orl's. Their hope was renewed, but then I pitched a fit about the experiments, and NeuroCorp hauled me off. Desperate to get anybody's attention, they set loose a group of monsters."

"No accounting for taste," said Brandt.

"I'll say. But those crude creatures were the best tool available on short notice. In the aliens' defense, those things weren't purpose-designed, more an unintended consequence of an earlier attempt to make contact. Years ago, they created an avatar and released it, hoping it'd find help. But it never returned."

"The creature Orl found in that cave?" asked Agnet.

"Exactly. The process that created the cave creature, sort of a molecular automaton, went infectious, feeding off the radiation in the containment zone and organic materials. Initially, the creatures maintained a link to the ship. But the reaction went haywire, creating rogue monsters, like those in this mine and the boars, any fresh corpse significantly contaminated by radioactivity was at risk. I know the experimental subjects underwent brain scans with contrast agents, presumably radioactive. But I have no idea why boars would be more contaminated than any other animal."

"Mushrooms." Cull's incongruous comment was delivered in a voice as dry as a week-old bread crust. "They concentrate cesium 137, and pigs gobble them up."

"Can attest," said Brandt. "We were warned not to hunt hogs on the border, lest we wanted to glow."

"So a reaction out of control—where's that heading?" asked Cull. "Toward a zombie apocalypse?"

Philip waved down Cull's question. "Don't worry. It's over. Even before we asked the alien to cool it, the reaction was slowing down. Radiation fueled it, and now that the region's essentially decontaminated, no more monsters, and the initiating compound decays in the absence of a substrate."

"Seems these aliens are clever but not immune to unintended consequences," said Agnet.

"Who is?"

"Well, nobody. But I wonder if they'll improve our circumstances or make things worse."

He shrugged. "Even they don't know the answer to that question, so I seriously doubt we'll ever know if we made the correct decision today. But the uncertainty doesn't seem to trouble them; their perspective is very deep time. That said, seems our civilization has already made a series of bad moves, markedly increasing the odds of an extinction event. In other words, our situation can't get much worse."

Cull waved at a screen set into the wall. "Speaking of unintended consequences. There's your coal fire."

An intensely red circle rimmed with orange and yellow filled the screen, the occasional flame leaping high. Suddenly, a scarlet rivulet raced forward.

Cull gasped. "See that? A fissure packed with coal just ignited. That fire's really moving. The oxygen in this cavern's probably helping it along."

Philip's throat lump bobbed. "Explains the alien's sense of urgency."

"We've got to stop calling these things aliens," Agnet said. "Humans manned this ship. Normal—well—slightly large humans. We found their remains. This vessel is from Earth."

"Well. Yes, and no." Philip glanced at Orl.

Thud.

Jemin collapsed, and Elaine pounced out of the passage, wild-eyed, hair ever-so-slightly mussed, as if she'd gone feral if not insane. In one hand, she held a gun, in the other, one of Brandt's explosives.

She locked eyes with Orl. "If you spend a single second inside my skull, you crazy witch, I'll blow us to the sky."

Orl scooted behind Agnet. Philip pushed himself backwards until he was almost underneath the counter that ran along the wall. Cull stayed his ground and folded his arms.

Elaine glowered at Agnet. "Keep your hands up, and drop it, Collins, or somebody dies."

"Aw for the love of peas, Elaine." Cull's face was suffused with irritation but betrayed not a gram of fear. "Calm yourself down and let me examine Yoder. What'd you do to him, anyway?"

Her face curdled. "Shut up, you lousy traitor. You inept fool. You... You... You pack of idiots. Did it occur to any of you that this thing, this machine, this *artificial intelligence,* is lying? It's lying to you! But you're stupid enough to sic an AI on our planet! Dupes and traitors!"

"We're listening to it and entertaining options. Why wouldn't we? Our own people have betrayed us, and we desperately need help," shouted Philip.

She shifted her aim to Philip's chest. "What will *that thing* do for us, bubbling in its pickle jar? It's LYING! It wants to trick you into saving it. Maybe it'll steal our minds, like her!" Elaine's gun now pointed directly at Agnet's chest, although, Orl was presumably the intended target.

Something twitched above the massive glass canister. Working hard not to tip off Elaine, Agnet observed it as best she could with her peripheral vision. From this angle, she could see nothing more than a dot of intense light glinting on the canister's rim.

She side-eyed Philip, but he seemed unaware of the light. Possibly the counter blocked his view and given his trembling and the fury on his face, rage was keeping him busy. "What's your plan, Elaine? Turn us into NeuroCorp? You think they'll reward you? The alien knows NeuroCorp lacks scruples. If we desert them, they'll destroy the ship, the mountain, and their entire civilization to keep their secrets. You'll be ashes with nothing to show for demolishing an entity that soaks up radiation and preserves consciousness under glass. What's wrong with you?"

A flickering tendril of static extended from the canister and arced toward the crown of Elaine's head. A zap—hopefully a little zap—might distract her long enough... They had to keep her talking. Agnet cleared her throat. "A—uh—community that rejects the idea of working for NeuroCorp can't be all bad."

"My kind of alien," said Brandt, always ready to provide cheerful digressions. "Still bummed out about the broken ship, though. Was hoping to take it for a spin."

Now a miniature lightning bolt hung over Elaine. Would the alien fry this woman to cinders? While it'd be good to know if the huge jar of clouds had aggressive tendencies, she refused to follow NeuroCorp's lead and use Elaine as a test subject. She'd let Elaine know. Either this situation would morph into a standoff, or Elaine would react, giving herself and Brandt a moment to draw.

She opened her mouth to say "look up." But Orl stepped forward, stood close, and clutched a handful of Agnet's sleeve. She let fly a soft "croak."

Elaine threw her an acid stare. "What! Scared now? See how it feels to be under somebody's thumb?"

The girl massaged her throat and ground out a sound close to "sree." As if rejecting her first attempt, she shook her ragged mane, wiped away a tear, then seemed to brace herself. A very soft "saw-ree" left her lips, more a gurgle than speech, a frog's apology, but the meaning was unmistakable.

"Apologies under duress don't count. You don't count, freak."

A click sounded, the loon had flipped the safety.

Agnet yanked Orl behind herself. "Elaine! Look up!"

She laughed, though her expression remained grim. "Do you think I'd fall for that old ploy?" She swung her gun, pointed it directly at the canister, and pulled the trigger.

"Down!" Agnet screamed as she hit the floor, dragging Orl with her.

Pop.

Shring. Shring. Shring.

"Ouch!"

Crackle.

A shriek rang out.

The smell of charred meat filled the air.

Elaine stood, staring piteously at her palms, a mess of black and red, blood dripping to the ground. Agnet turned toward Brandt, who, by the sound of that "ouch", must've taken the bullet. Sure enough, he was leaning against the wall, gripping one shoulder with his opposite hand, blood slicking to the glossy flooring.

"Didn't drop fast enough," he said, looking apologetic.

"Terrific. Three injured." Cull examined Jemin, then snapped at Elaine. "Like I asked before, what'd you do to this man? His pulse is in the gutter."

She interrupted her sobbing to scream, "I'm not telling."

"Honestly, woman. You've reverted to toddlerhood."

Elaine held out her dripping hands, her face a mask of pain and fury. The gun had melted into a shapeless lump and seemed fused to her palm. "What did you do to me?"

Agnet wrinkled her nose. "Yecch. That's gotta smart, but I did nothing to you. Didn't even see a thing 'cause I hit the floor."

"The alien defended itself," said Brandt. "Hit you with a mini lightning bolt. Can't say I blame it."

Then Orl sprang up, hurtled past Elaine, shoving her hard out of the way, and darted into the corridor. Moments later, she returned holding a needle and a vial.

Cull plucked the vial from Orl's fingers. "Stolen from somebody's first aid pack." He glowered at Elaine. "Wasting painkillers and nearly killing a man in the process. Thanks. Thanks for that." He fumbled in his medical bag, retrieved a vial of clear fluid, and unwrapped a syringe. "This should do the trick." Jemin jerked in response to the needle and woke almost instantly, but his eyes roved like a visitor, absorbing the sights and sounds of an utterly unfamiliar place. Philip sat the shell-shocked historian on one of the outsized chairs then sat alongside him. Agnet assisted Cull, listening to him carp about "wasted materials," while he extracted the bullet from Brandt, patched the entry wound, then slathered Elaine's hands with antibiotics and painkillers and wrapped them in gauze.

"Thanks, doc," she said as they peeled off their disposable gloves.

Cull eyed his balled-up gloves and sighed. "Only three pairs left. But you're welcome, for what it's worth." Cull clicked his instrument case shut and tossed it into his bag. "Enough time wasted. There's a coal fire on our tail. Let's get moving."

Agnet turned to Philip. "So. Where were we? Oh, yeah. The not-alien. And, as Elaine just established, preserved something stronger than glass." She pointed to the big bottle of smoke. "Which country sent that thing, and are they accepting refugees?"

He and Orl exchanged glances. "Here's where it gets weird."

"Weird-er," said Jemin, slouched in his seat, his grin a bit too wide.

Philip's forehead twitched, a subtle frown.

341

"Just ignore him," said Agnet. "Spill the beans."

He cleared his throat. "They're from Earth but an alternate Earth on another timeline."

"An alternate Earth?"

"Yep. An Earth with plenty of metal and fossil fuels but facing terminal environmental problems."

"Such utter bull turds," hissed Elaine, as if whispering through gritted teeth.

And she had a point. Alternate Earth was a hard swallow, although— "Pretty far-fetched, I'll grant you. But so are monsters, spaceships, and evaporating radiation. And what do they want? What were you choosing when we butted in?"

He clasped his hands and squeezed his fingers together, reminding her of an agitated rodent. "They want to pack themselves into every available space and flee. So, they're proposing a time-sharing arrangement."

He couldn't mean... "In what? The robot?"

"No. The robot's inadequate. In our chips and—"

Brandt's eyebrows tried to levitate off his forehead. "Whoa. An alien's going to take over your brain?"

"Told you so," said Elaine, speaking to her bandages.

"No. Share chip space until they build a new home." He glanced at Orl. "Imagine an extra high-powered, conversational data source."

Agnet rested her fists on her hips. "Don't tell me she already—"

Philip winced. "She did. She's an impetuous pest, but she's fine. Still our delightful Orl." He faked-smiled at her, and she stuck out her tongue in response. "However, her guests are using chip capacity, so she won't be slipping into people's heads for a while. Elaine was lucky. Burned palms are nothing compared to what full capacity Orl might've done to her."

Elaine, still fixated on her bandages, muttered, "Interdimensional travelers have infiltrated your weapons-grade perceiver, Chief Krause. Was that part of your clever plan?"

A corner of Philip's lip subtly curled. "You'll notice the alien didn't kill that lunatic outright."

"I noticed. But she's making valid points. You don't share brain-space with someone just because they're *not* a murderer."

He gazed into the distance, the decision's strain dragging down at the corners of his mouth. "I have my reservations; it's a significant privacy invasion, for starters."

"Understatement of the century." Jemin giggled at his own comment.

Agnet shot the historian a worried look.

"It'll take a while for the drug to clear Yoder's system," said Cull.

Philip continued. "But they need us. We are their portal to the physical world. All their live individuals, those few colleagues who survived the environmental apocalypse, died in the crash. The song they've been singing is a requiem, for themselves, for their comrades, and their world. That's the signal Orl and I perceived." Philip hugged his waist, his face drawn, dark circles under his eyes. It'd definitely been a heckuva day.

"Great, but if every chippy agrees to host an alien, we only save four. What happens to the rest?" Agnet asked.

"Orl is hosting several, but the main storage is in the escape pod."

A stunned silence enveloped the group; the word "escape" rang in her ears.

Brandt spoke first. "Escape pod as in mini-spaceship?"

Philip shrugged, a no-interest-in-vehicles gesture. "Well, yes. A smaller airborne craft, at any rate. They also need our help to fly it. Two of the automated systems were disrupted by the crash, and now only a pair of hands can do the job."

"Fantastic. Totally worth getting shot. High-five aliens...or whoever." Brandt raised a palm.

Philip gave an uneasy little wave in return. "Granted, we can only store a few extra citizens, but regardless, they'll lose a portion of their—"

"Souls?" Jemin cracked another outsized smile.

"*Citizens*. The escape pod will only hold so many. Every extra person we carry is a treasure saved. Understand, these aren't regular people; they're old, some are downright ancient. Following a normal life, they've lived multiple virtual lives, trying to expand human perspective past the current three generation limit. They're packed with information and experience."

Elaine's laugh was devoid of all humor. "Regardless of their great wisdom," she rolled her eyes, "they ruined their planet. Now you're eager to let them have a crack at ours."

"Not enough of the population was on the same page. They watched their world die and see parallels in our situation and believe they can help, at least delay the inevitable. They've already started negotiating who stays behind." His voice cracked on the word "pod", an emotional laceration in his usual detached delivery-style. Orl stepped over and grasped his hand. He licked his lips and swallowed. "The conversation is terribly sad. Their society is highly...um...integrated."

Jemin, all smiley and seemingly oblivious to the change in Philip's tone, said, "I've shared brain space before and didn't mind the company." He winked at Orl. "Probably shouldn't march through trees while conversing, but how about a historian or a theologist? We could compare notes."

"Yoder, you fanatical donkey's behind. You're high as a kite and shouldn't make important life choices," said Elaine.

"Another valid point," said Agnet. "About the choices, I mean."

Cull said, "I'm sober as a state funeral, and, if it's temporary, wouldn't mind hosting a physicist. I'm curious about that disappearing radiation."

"Flipping chip heads. And you call me crazy?" Elaine shook her head, her expression a salute to disgust.

Jemin pursed his lips. "Crazy is as crazy does, Miss Pruett. You might consider being nicer, and if you smiled more often, you'd be much prettier."

A thundercloud of an expression overwhelmed Elaine's face. Jemin pointed and tittered in response.

"Beans afire, Cull. Do something *about that man!*" If Elaine didn't beat him to death, she might. Prettier if you smiled...for land's sake.

A distant boom interrupted Cull's response. The ship juddered. The floor rocked gently up and down. Agnet rode the waves by holding onto a chair back. "Let that serve as a reminder; our options are severely limited. Perhaps we should avail ourselves of that escape pod, right now. Is access contingent on hosting a...citizen?"

"No," said Philip. "No obligation. Every chip-holder chooses for themselves, and everyone is welcome, regardless. The alien...or whatever...needs all the help it can get."

"So do we, my friends. So do we. Make your choices, and let's jump on board. Where's the pod stowed? Cull, give Elaine a hand. Do we have time to grab our bags from the lobby?"

Brandt heaved himself up, his wounded arm cradled in a sling crafted from excess material from Orl's dress. "Your pals will teach me to fly, won't they, girl?"

She nodded, her cheeks plumped by a lovely smile.

He gave her shoulder a gentle punch. "Might hit a few trees, but, dang. This'll be excellent."

Into The Bright Blue Sky

A doe on the ridge paused her grazing, raised her head, neck fully extended, and ears lifted high. The hillside shuddered. Boulders rumbled down the slope, and the air filled with the grinding screech of metal on rock. And *boom*, a winged orb leaped into the sky, hovered for a moment, then sped away.

Applause filled the escape pod as they zipped over the forest, a hard day's journey accomplished in minutes. The others joyous conversation filled Philip's ears but before he could join in, Orl, securely strapped into the seat adjacent, caught his eye. She stared at him, her expression calm and knowing, a very non-Orl expression.

Sometimes, to go Forward, we must go Back.

Now, that message sounded like Orl, cryptic and mildly foreboding, but...

Back where?

To NeuroCorp.

The End

Afterword

Thanks for reading *Harvest of Shadows*. I hope you've enjoyed this tale. Feedback is vital to independent authors, so consider posting a rating or review of this title on Goodreads or on the website of your favorite bookstore. Every review is deeply appreciated, no matter how brief. And I've done my best, but have you found a typo? Please let me know at stella@stellajorette.com

This novel is a selection from the *Songs out of Time* fantasy/science fiction series. More books in this series, as well as reviews, and musings, can be found on my website https://stellajorette.com. While visiting the site, please consider joining my subscription to access additional stories related to this novel.

Acknowledgments

As always, thanks to my beleaguered husband for slogging through a primordial soup version of this manuscript. The readers of RoyalRoad provided encouragement and insightful commentary, including fellow author Peter Maloy, whose writings inspire me, and whose careful reading helped strengthen this novel. Many thanks to the talented but anonymous individual at 100 Covers who created the cover art for this book.

Jorette, Stella.
Harvest of Shadows
Imagine Imprints
Paperback. First edition

Cover art by 100 Covers
Section art by Stella Jorette

www.ingramcontent.com/pod-product-compliance
Lightning Source LLC
Chambersburg PA
CBHW022205010726
47493CB00002B/412